I0633804

NEON Jezebel

Za'chary Westbrook

Copyright © 2023, Za'chary Westbrook
979-8-9884364-0-9

All rights reserved. No part of this book may be used or reproduced in any manner whatsoever without written permission, except in cases covered by Fair Use copyright laws in their respective countries.

Any fan works based on this book would be really cool.

Cover art by the author
Cover model: Kristen Pimley
Cover font: Aviator; licensed from CreativeMarket
Interior fonts: Modesto Text, Chandler42, Albertan Pro; licensed from Adobe

Beta Readers: Mandi Asplund, Damian Brown
Editor: Megan Sherrin-Kim

For Lisa
tu m'as convaincu de recommencer à écrire

Contents

Prologue:
The Asclophare Job

July 31st, 1917. Upstate New York.

The sun had set and the late summer swelter still clung to the air. Della Caine rode her brand new Excelsior X into the parking lot of Asclophare Pharmaceuticals and killed the engine. As the motorcycle settled beneath her, she lifted up her goggles, letting a stream of sweat into her eyes, which she wiped away with a gloved hand. Next she took off the soft, leather helmet and let her poor, crumpled hair tumble down. The strands clung to the sweat on her neck. Off came the gloves, open came the jacket, and she fanned whatever cool air she could manage onto the exposed skin of her throat.

There were photos of women riding in skirts and suggestively long coats with their bare legs pressed against the fuel tank. Della, feeling the heat off the exposed engine through her jodhpurs, couldn't imagine driving like that for very long. Not even in summer.

The plus side of the heat was that she wouldn't need a cover story. If any of Asclophare's night security men found her out here, she could just tell them that she was taking a breather. In this heat, the only question that would raise was where she was going. Then there'd be the offer of a drink and the suggestion of a fondle and where things went from there depended entirely on how well these boys had been raised.

She took a newspaper from the motorcycle's saddle bag and fanned herself with it. She had already looked it over in daylight. The headline announced: 'James Walker & Wife Die in Tragic Accident'. Della hadn't known who that was, right away. Reading the story, nestled on the front page between a story about German trenches and another about an accident at a navy yard, she did remember something about them. The Walker Corporation was a big shipping interest, headquartered way up north in Silkhaven. Connecting that to the names 'James' and 'Lolita' brought back a vague memory about them supporting a wet presidential candidate, but she couldn't remember if that had been Wilson or Hughes.

At any rate, it wasn't a story about the war, which was nice. Della had decided that she was done with the war the day she had been evacuated from Paris, depriving her of her audition with the Opera Ballet. All shuttered now, she supposed; but it would have been nice to know if she could have gotten in.

The headlines didn't matter, now, the Asclophare parking lot was too dark to read the tiny story print. The gas lamps were lit at 6pm in the summer. They were extinguished, starting at 8pm, all year round. It took the security men an average of eighteen minutes to extinguish them all and it was after 10pm now.

The security room, located on the other side of the building, had a single electric light. There were three night watchmen who rotated shifts, so there were always two on duty, while the third took the night off. Tonight, it was Tom and Garland. Tom was a voracious Trolley Dodgers fan and Garland usually had a copy of the latest *Top-Notch* or *Detective Story Magazine*. The third man, Walter, was the stickler. Without him, Tom and Garland were happy to pass the night reading by their single electric light. Importantly, pass it on the east side of the building, where they'd be hard pressed to hear a motorcycle driving up from the west.

Still, you never knew when someone was going to get itchy feet and go for a walk. So, Della had a cover story buttoned up and her shirt buttoned down; just enough to give them the thrill of her décolletage, should they point a flashlight at her. The bossman had had the place watched for a week. He even sent another young woman, younger than Della, up here one night to have some car trouble. The reports from both spies had been Della's daily devotions since Sunday.

In the darkness, well above her head, Della heard the grating of wood on wood as a window opened. Despite the black of night, she turned instinctively to look. Her eyes made out the faint shape of the office building, pocked with fuzzy spots of deeper darkness where the windows were.

A heavy tat sound caught her attention, as something hit the ground near her. Della rose from her bike and walked carefully in the direction of the sound. It took a moment, but she found the large envelope. She picked it up, folded it into her newspaper, then stuffed said newspaper back in her saddlebag.

A well-oiled machine; this was how the bossman worked.

He gets a lawyer to request an example work order from Asclophare; telling them that somebody gave him one such work order and he needs to verify it. No alarms ring out; that's what the bossman does above the table. He's a third-party, unbiased. *You know how it is.* Then, the lawyer gets a sealed envelope from a man he's never met who says he works for the bossman (he *does* work for the bossman, but the lawyer can say the stranger said it—like maybe it wasn't true—if he's ever on a witness stand). The lawyer puts the example work order from Asclophare and the sealed envelope in another, larger envelope and then—silly goose that he is—leaves that larger envelope on a table in a cafe.

That envelope gets picked up by someone in the cafe and

the lawyer never sees it again. *What is the world coming to?* The cafe-sticky-fingers hands the envelope off to someone he knows; the sort of man who knows the sort of people who steal things in cafes. *"Unsavory" is the word.* This unsavory character opens both envelopes and takes a long look at the work order. Following instructions that were in the first envelope—the one from the mysterious stranger—he makes a forgery of the work order with the details changed drastically. *You know, just to see if he could. He's not a real forger, anymore. He's gone straight, your honor, but he likes knowing he hasn't lost his touch.* Whatever was in that first envelope—besides cash—is now kindling.

This forged work order goes in the trash. After all, he had no intentions for it. So, it's as much a shock to him as it is to the prosecutor that someone came along and took that forged work order—crisp and clean—out of the trash. *Shameful, really, how the city has declined.* Whoever the dumpster diver was, he put on a nice three-piece suit and went to visit a pair of former burglars: both reformed, *a credit to the justice system.* Well, he gives them a work order saying that Asclophare wants their security checked. It's all there. These two gone-straight thieves are being hired by the company to try to steal a fake report on some new drug Asclophare is working on. Honest work, putting their life of crime towards the public good. *Ain't it sweet?*

So, cash in pocket, these two go to work. They break in with no difficulty, find the fake report, and—following the three-piece suit's instructions—toss it out the window. *How were they supposed to know it was real? How could they possibly know what happened to it after?*

That was how the bossman worked.

Della—with the very real drug report in her saddlebag— tugged her gloves back on, tucked as much of her hair as possible into the riding cap and pulled the goggles down. She started walking the bike towards the parking lot's entrance, preferring not to start the engine until she was on the road. That is, until she heard the gunshots.

A different kind of well-oiled machine.

Feet up, engine revved, headlamp on, Della shot into the night. She would never know what had gone wrong that night. It would never occur to her to ask.

A moment after she was on a road that wound deeper into the Adirondacks, another motorcycle roared to life behind her. It was another Excelsior X, same color, same plates. The rider wore brown leathers identical to hers, only a little broader in the shoulders.

Ryan Wolfe was a good driver, a clever boy, and an accomplished liar. His main use to the company, though, was that he was almost the exact same height and build as Della. He followed her away from Asclophare, the light of his headlamp occasionally close enough to glint off her wheels.

Then, it disappeared entirely. That was in the plan, so Della did not look back.

An hour later, Della was parked at the entrance to the road up to Paradox Bay. The radium dials on her pocket watch told her that it was almost 11. She would give Ryan another five minutes, then continue without him. When he arrived, he hopped off his motorcycle almost as soon as it had stopped.

"Did we get it?" he called, misjudging the volume of his voice without the cycle's cacophony.

"Yep," Della said, tucking her pocket watch away and zipping up her jacket. "You were very nearly late."

"I was very nearly arrested," he replied. "There was a penny racer on me, but I lost them. It just took a bit longer than usual." The moon was behind him, outlining his really very nice shoulders in blue against the ink black forest that this little dirt road cut through.

"How much fuel did you use up?"

"I'm still on a half tank. Haven't used the extra, yet. Do you want me to go it alone, from here?"

"Not if you'd be gallant enough to escort me. It's not safe for a girl to go about on her own, at night."

"That's true. I've heard there's thieves on this road."

"What is the world coming to?" Della said, pulling her goggles back on.

Ryan bounded back to his bike and had it started not a second after hers. She didn't give him a signal, just took off down the road. However, she stayed at her first speed longer than she needed to, longer than Ryan did, letting him overtake her.

Men needed victories in a way women did not. For a woman, a victory—any victory—was nothing more than setting the world right; for a man, it was setting himself right. A body could go on a lot longer thinking the world was wrong than they could thinking themselves wrong.

Besides, this road was the biggest question mark in the whole plan. The bossman had given her a map and they had spent hours memorizing the twists and turns from above before it went into the fire. Della could, theoretically, drive the whole way blind, provided she stayed at 30mph. With no sign of the police following, she could keep her light on. However, not knowing the exact condition of the road, she didn't dare go above 30 for long. She was in no mood, tonight, to reach beyond the grasp of her expertise.

She sped on through the dark forest, minding the loose ground of the bends in the road that presented themselves exactly when expected. On one turn, one of Della's tires caught a groove cut by old rain water that brought her to a brief halt. It turned her in such a way that she could glance back the way they had come, and she spied a pair of headlights far behind, but gaining.

It seemed Ryan had not lost the cops, only been allowed

to think he had.

She gunned it and shifted her speeds up as quickly as the Excelsior could take it. The next turn was gradual and she leaned into it, praying there were no big rocks ready to shift out from beneath her. Once she had cleared that one, she saw the dim glow of Ryan's bike for a moment, before it turned.

As she began another anticipated bend in the road, there were a couple of bright flashes of light much too close to be Ryan. They were like little bolts of lightning floating the air, burning out almost as soon as you saw them. If she had realized a moment sooner what they were, she might have stopped or swerved or leapt from the motorcycle. But there was no ease of the throttle, no squeeze on the brakes. Della was driving at almost 40 miles per hour when a giant ball of white erupted in the air in front of her.

It was perfectly white and perfectly round. The widest point was several feet above the ground and its lower curve sank into the earth. It pierced the darkness far better than the moonlight. It burned her eyes, and yet it was not luminous. It was as plain to see as a cue ball at noon, sitting on black felt, and yet it cast no shadows.

Della felt every hair on her body rise up. A wave of the most primal fear—deep and certain—washed over her. Every ancestral voice that had passed their survival knowledge down through her blood was screaming as those genetic ghosts ran cold across her nerves. The white grew to fill her vision and then, everything stopped.

Della felt the motorcycle drop out from underneath her, but didn't sense the drop in her stomach. It was like driving into the water, the air around her somehow thick enough to keep her aloft. All around her was white and featureless.

She was adrift in an ocean of milk, though she didn't feel the fluid and had no difficulty breathing or seeing. She felt like she was still careening forward, but slowed by whatever heaviness there was in this strange air.

For a moment, a searing pain drove into Della's skull and she felt herself move. She looked around. Up and down, there was just that endless, smooth white. But then, she realized she couldn't see her nose. You can always see your nose, you just don't think about it.

Casting her gaze to one side, she saw one of her gloved fingers, too close to her eye to focus on. Feeling no pull of resistance from her muscles, Della spun her gaze further; a strigine half circle.

Casting her look so, Della found herself looking down the length of her arm towards her body. She was indeed floating, arms and legs splayed out, in her boots and jodhpurs and leathers, helmet and goggles still on her head.

Somehow, her sight had been taken from her eyes—which gazed ahead above an impassive mouth—and transferred to one of her fingertips. She couldn't blink, couldn't scream; only gaze in horror at herself, her senses somehow divorced from her body.

Another pain and her vision changed. She was staring up at the toe of her boot, blurry for its proximity, but unmistakable. Della turned her disembodied gaze to see the boot floating beyond her bare foot. The laces floated freely in the air, as did her socks and jodhpurs and everything else.

Della viewed her naked body—exposed against her will for the first time in her life—with her clothing floating above and below. Some unearthly power had undressed her like a paper doll and laid the pieces out neatly to be observed, one at a time.

Far ahead, it seemed, her hair was spread out like a nimbus. There was no movement in it, no current of air or water, no gravity to pull it in a single uniform direction.

From this vantage point, she seemed to be floating face down, yet her breasts did not dangle from her chest, nor slouch towards her feet, nor melt towards her shoulders. They remained where her brassiere—now a foot away from her chest, still clasped—would have held them.

The pain struck again and the vision shifted. Della now beheld the nimbus of her hair fanned out around her face. An eyeless face with a mouth half open revealing no teeth or tongue.

She tore her gaze away only to see her eyes floating in the strange air a foot below her skin. Tendrils of living fiber still attached them to her brain, which lay uncovered and unprotected in empty space. Her skull floated along with the rest of her skeleton a few feet below that.

Whatever power had stripped her, had now deconstructed her body itself; separating skin from nerves and organs, from muscles, from bones without any apparent dissection. Far below the point where her gaze was fixed, her blood hung in the air, unbound by veins, unmoved by heart, yet tracing the same paths it ought to inside her; some red and some a deathly purple.

Beyond the tight web of her blood, a hundred feet below her, it seemed, was her motorcycle. It too was in a state of utter deconstruction. Every bolt and screw floated beyond the larger frames of metal. The gasoline still flowed and burst into tiny gouts of flame, despite it being outside its hoses and separated by an arm's length from the sparks that ignited those little fires.

Then, a terrible sense of falling overcame her. Like an old sailor with an itch in his peg leg, Della could still feel her body, all of it, despite seeing it spread out into its component parts in front of her. And she felt like she was falling in on herself; the gravity not coming from the earth, but from her own gut, pulling all her extremities in with the same force as the unyielding ground rising up to meet her.

Her vision went dark and the engine of her Excelsior

roared back into her ears (she hadn't noticed its silence before). Gravity dropped out of her stomach and her body followed after it. Her shoulder collided with dirt that had been packed almost into rock. Her chest pitched forward, but she couldn't roll as her leg was pinned under the weight of the motorcycle. So, instead, it dragged her across the dust and pebbles.

Every inch of Della's skin burned and there was a horrible pressure beneath, as if a million tiny things were trying to claw their way out of her legs, her arms, her scalp. The deeper pain of hitting the dirt ached quietly, disappearing into the harrowing fire, then asserting itself again every few seconds. Trying to scream, Della's mouth refused to open, a strange stiffness holding her lips in place.

The pain was overwhelming, but also made her alert. She heard the other motorcycle approach, expecting Ryan to free her. Instead of the weight of the bike being lifted, she heard him opening the saddlebag. He was going for the envelope, completing the mission. Even as one part of her mind cursed him, another knew she would have done the same.

For a few minutes, she despaired for herself, wondering when the pain would end her and she would die alone on this desolate back road. Then, she heard footsteps. The bike was lifted and two pairs of hands lifted her out of the dirt. There were voices, but they sounded distant, as if at the bottom of a deep well. Darkness was encroaching.

There had been a car behind her, a fact which had slipped her mind until she heard the door open. Her body was jostled as the hands got her inside and laid her down on the bench seat. Through the fire on her skin, she registered the comfort of the seat, though it was little relief. The last thing she heard before succumbing to the darkness was the thump of a closing car door.

Part 1:
CRANSTON

Chapter 1:
The Golden Headed Eagle

August 15th, 1917.
Quincampoix, France.

The door clicked shut, the car sped forward, and the general began talking immediately. Cranston had never met an Englishman, much less an officer, as gregarious as General Cavan. The general was some kind of nobleman, which made it either more or less surprising that the man grinned continually at him; but Cranston was far too unfamiliar with British peers to know which.

"I want to say how grateful I am that you are here, Captain Walker," the General said. "I understand you boys have become something like free agents since Flanders."

"It has been an adjustment," Cranston admitted. "The allies were asking for Praetorian units as soon as Wilson announced we would be deployed to the western front. Funston was adamant that we remain part of the NAEF structure, but Pershing seems to feel we'll do more good this way; racing around the front, answering the calls for aid from anyone with a star on their shoulder."

He kept smiling, trying to match the general's demeanor, but Pershing's order last May felt less like an act of Allied cooperation than an attempt to wash Uncle Sam's hands of the Guard.

"Lucky for these stars, then," Cavan said, jovially tapping

his own shoulder. "That you weren't too close to the front."

"I was until April," Cranston said. "I had a close call, you might say, and they ordered me to recuperate in England for a month. Since I got back, I've hardly said two words to NAEF command. I'm getting all my orders from the switch girls."

"There are worse things than taking orders from a girl with a switch." The general nudged Cranston with an elbow.

Cranston laughed because he needed to. "Like taking orders from a boy with a switch?"

Cavan gave a single, ear-splitting "Ha!" then said: "I went to Eton, so..."

"I have heard tales."

"How is merry old England faring, these days?" Cavan asked. "It feels like a dog's age since I was there last."

"Hospitable," Cranston said, a sense-memory of baking strawberries coming to him. "I was put up in a cottage in Birchington-on-Sea."

"That's near Canterbury, right?"

"Yes, sir."

"I'm from Hertfordshire, myself. Haven't spent much time in the low country."

"It's lovely." He felt the salt breeze on his cheek, recalling the walks along the sea wall, constrained by public decency, and the desperate indecency that followed the shutting of the cottage door.

"And where do you hail from?"

"Silkhaven."

"Is that right? So, you're Canadian?"

"King Charles Island is under the joint sovereignty of Canada and the Federated States, so I'm both Canadian and American. Bourassa was not as tenacious about recruitment as Wilson, so I ended up fighting for Uncle Sam."

"Well," Cavan said, spying the house approaching. "Thanks to Pershing, you're fighting for the entire Entente."

"Yes, sir."

Cranston's eyes were heavy. He hadn't had more than a couple full nights of sleep all summer. Most nights he needed a dram of *pinard* to get any sleep and, during the day, he often had to rely on Forced March tablets to keep himself up right. The only real rest he got was when he was somewhere near a hospital. There was always an overworked nurse in need of intimate release and Cranston, technically an officer, was somewhat cleaner than most of the available men. Those were the most restful nights he had. Failing that, he could usually trade a few exotic cigarettes for a dose of morphine.

The one benefit of being sent all across the western front was access to a variety of cigarettes. Wide distribution of anything took a concerted effort during wartime and cigarettes were a low priority, so the supplies of a given brand got concentrated into one or two places. As a Praetorian, Cranston spent more time in port towns than the trenches. This meant he could get the spare cartons off sailors from the Mediterranean in exchange for whatever was available in town; a good deal for the men who couldn't get leave to step outside the harbor gates.

Trade, it turned out, really was in his blood. Even after spending his youth dodging the responsibilities of the family shipping business, Cranston had wound up doing import/export, anyway.

The driver brought the car to a stop and Cavan practically bounded from the car, replacing his cap on his head like a cricketer taking the field. Cranston hurried to join him. He wanted everyone's first sight of him to be at the general's elbow.

The farm house was a declining, two-story building of mismatched and often uneven stone. The doors and shutters looked new, though. A faint, but distinctive bovine smell was on the wind and Cranston thought he heard the clunk of a cowbell from somewhere beyond the trees that bunched up close to the house.

There was a big, canvas-covered truck in front of the barn and two other cars in the driveway. Three men in infantry trousers and undershirts were sitting in the grass by the barn, playing cards on a crate.

They watched Cranston and the general arrive. One of them saw the gold eagle embroidered on Cranston's shoulder and said something to the others. Their idle curiosity transformed to scowls.

Old man Wilson had thought the Praetorian Guard would be "the fulcrum of allied victory". American soldiers were going to win Europe's war for them, was the idea. He envisioned the Guard leading charges out of the trenches and shouting Jerry into submission. Hence the decision to cover the right shoulder of their uniforms with an ostentatious eagle's head.

If the "gold" thread had been cheaper or the seamstresses faster, they may have had the wings sweeping down the front, as well; so intent was the War Department on making Praetorians a beacon. That tune had changed in the first six months of the war. Now, it was considered an act of espionage for a Praetorian to wear any other uniform, even an FS Army coat sans eagle.

Up ahead, a guard was at attention by the door to the farm house. He saluted the general as he crossed the threshold, but pointedly glared at Cranston without raising a hand.

Cavan stopped halfway through the door. "Lance Corporal." He wasn't jovial, anymore. Now, he sounded like a general.

"Yes, sir." The guard answered.

"Do you see the bars on this man's uniform?"

"Yes, sir."

"Count them for me, would you?"

"There are two bars, sir."

"And what does that tell you, Lance Corporal?"

"He is a captain, sir."

"And what does a lance corporal do when he sees a captain?"

"He salutes, sir."

"Very good, go on, then."

The guard raised his hand to his brow and looked ready to spit. Cranston returned the salute quickly, wanting to put the kid out of his misery.

Cavan turned to Cranston. "I apologize for the lance corporal's breach of manners, Captain Walker." He stepped closer to the guard, speaking directly into the lad's ear. "Childish superstition has made him forget himself. It shan't happen again."

"No, sir!" The guard said, eyes dead forward.

Cavan continued into the house. "Is there a kettle on?"

Cranston paused, though. "We are on the same side, Lance Corporal. In a trench, I know which way to point my rifle. I hope you do, too."

The kid's lip quivered towards a snarl. "And if I forget, sir?"

Cranston shrugged internally; he had tried. "You wouldn't be the first; and yet, I am still here." He marched into the house.

The aging home had been converted into a field base. The front room was taken up by a large, wireless receiver-transmitter. The great, modern radios teetered on rough-hewn tables of unfinished wood that might have dated from Charlemagne. Two engineers manned positions with headphones on, pressed against a wall with barely enough room for one to pass behind the other should the need arise.

"Gentlemen," Cavan announced as another corporal brought him a cup of tea. "Our other guest of honor has arrived. Please welcome Captain Walker with proper English hospitality."

One of the engineers turned in his chair to face Cranston. "Cop a fag, guv?"

A chuckle rippled through the room. Cranston smiled and reached into his coat, producing four cigarette cases, each in a different style. He pulled the second one from the top into his free hand and replaced the others.

It was a tin case in want of a polishing with a worn down relief of King Edward on the top. "Player's?" He offered, popping the case open.

The engineer gaped in delighted surprise. "Good enough for me, Captain."

"Is there anything you need," Cavan continued. "Before you go in?"

"Two more cups of tea." Cranston said. "One for me and one for the foreign dignitary."

"We have sugar," Cavan added.

"Cubes or grains?" Cranston asked.

"I don't rightly..." Cavan turned. "Corporal, do we have sugar cubes?"

"Yes, sir." Came the reply from the kitchen.

Cranston raised his voice so the man could hear him in the kitchen. "Good, one cube in each cup. Do not stir it."

"Yes, sir."

Cavan gave Cranston a quizzical look.

"Know thy enemy," Cranston replied.

The tea was brought and someone found a tray to set them on. Cavan indicated a small radio set up, only about the size of a doctor's bag. It was unfolded on a collapsible table of the kind found in trench offices, with three pairs of headphones laid out in front of it.

"We'll be listening from here," he said, reassuringly. "No need to jot anything down."

"Do you speak German, General?" Cranston asked.

"Not I, sorry to say." He pointed to two of his men who were preparing for their part in the interview; one old enough to be the other's father. "Green, there, has been translating German since Wilhelm became Kaiser."

The older of the pair gave a small bow. "Wilhelm the second," he added, self-conscious about his age, apparently.

"And Kästner was born in Berlin."

The younger man looked apologetic. "My father is a Catholic professor." He explained, sounding every inch a Dubliner. "They moved to Ireland as soon as I was old enough to travel." It was a well-rehearsed speech. Cranston had heard similar stories, told in that same intonation of the oft-repeated, from a dozen Canadian soldiers of German extraction.

"I'm listening in," Cavan said. "Just out of curiosity. It's fascinating what you do. I have long wanted to witness it in action. Green assures me we'll be safe, listening through the headphones."

"Yes," Cranston assured them, taking his turn at looking apologetic. "The Voice doesn't work through electric receivers."

"Jolly good," Cavan clapped his hands. "Are you ready to go in?"

"Yes, sir. Though, I'm afraid it won't be half as exciting as you're anticipating. It's little more than very efficient hypnotism."

"And a hypnotist can fill a circus tent. I dare say, I'll be dining out on this story for a month, once the war's over." The general clapped Cranston on the back. "Now, go work your magic."

The Brits took up their positions round the collapsible table. Evidently, the vacuum-tube contraption was not a radio. It was now he saw the wire going up the wall and through a narrow hole that had been bored through the wood;

a microphone.

Cranston took up the tin tray of slowly cooling tea and balanced it on one hand, then opened the door to where they were keeping the first "guest of honor".

It was a bedroom. The bed lay against the far wall, under a window, where a man in the trousers of a German and not much else was sat, gazing out on the clear, French, summer day. The man swung his bare feet to the floor as Cranston entered. His boots were against the wall, below a peg where his coat was hung.

The German's bare arms had no significant bruising and there were no marks on his feet. But for the heavy and decidedly ungentlemanly growth of beard, he seemed to be in fine condition.

"<I brought you some tea.>" Cranston announced in German.

"<Thank you,>" the German prisoner said, rising and crossing to the small table and chairs that had been arranged to facilitate the interview. "<It is the only food the British make well.>"

"<I agree.>" Cranston said, setting down the tray. "<They are entirely too fond of beans.>"

The German smiled. "<Which one is mine?>"

"<It doesn't matter. Please.>"

"<They are not poisoned, then?>" The prisoner asked in the subtle tone of German humor.

"<They are, but I have a strong constitution.>" He replied with the straightest of faces. Cranston needed the prisoner to be receptive. Copying the man's attitude was an important step in that direction. He extended a hand as he sat down. "Captain Cranston Walker."

"Oberst Armin Eisenhuth," they shook and sipped their tea. "<Your accent is very good.>"

"<Thank you,>"

"<May I offer some advice?>"

"<Please.>"

"<You extend the final schwa too long.>" Oberst Eisenhuth demonstrated. "<You said 'cup-uuuh'. It is 'cup-uh'.>"

"<Cup-uuh,>" Cranston attempted.

"<That is better. Cup-uh.>"

"<Cup-uh,>" he tried again.

"<Yes, that's it.>"

"<Thank you,>" Cranston saw what Eisenhuth was doing. He was playing like this was a social call, building a rapport, making friends. It was how clever prisoners avoided the worst of their internment. It played right into Cranston's goals and so he ran with it.

"<There is one I struggle with.>" Eisenhuth continued.

Cranston nodded. "<Please.>"

Eisenhuth switched to English. "*Colture,*" he attempted in an almost convincing American accent.

"Ah," Cranston said. "<The vowel is too round.>" He switched to English for the word, as well: "*Culture,*"

"*Callture,*"

Cranston considered. "<Have you ever been to Chemnitz?>"

"<No, but I know something of the dialect.>"

"<Good, it is like the way they say 'make'.>"

"<Make,>" Eisenhuth said with a Chemnitz accent.

"<Yes, it's the same vowel.> *Culture.*"

He stretched out his jaw and loosened his tongue for a moment. "*Culture.*"

"<Yes, you have it.>"

"<Make>...*Culture*...<that's the first time I was glad to have dated a girl from Chemnitz.>"

Cranston nodded sagely. "<Where are you from?>" Now that they were pronunciation pals, they could get acquainted and bring some barriers down.

"<Rothensee, but it is part of Magdeburg, now.>"

"<Did Germany invade itself?>"

"<No,>" Eisenhuth replied. "<Nothing changed, really, but it is a little sad to lose the name. The irony is not lost on me. I am sympathetic to the French people.>"

"<Many things are changing for them, though.>"

"<This is true.>" Eisenhuth finished his tea. "<Where are you from?>"

"Silkhaven, King Charles Island,"

"<Ah, yes, I have heard of it.>"

"The Jewel of the Atlantic," Cranston recited the motto in English.

"<It is part of Canada and America, correct?>"

"<Yes,>"

"<How does that work?>" Now, the German was trying to get inside Cranston's defenses, which was fine. Eisenhuth was playing a strategy for a much longer game than Cranston was.

"<Most of the time, we are neither.>" Cranston said. "<In peacetime, America lets us be Canadian and Canada lets us be American, so long as everyone is making money.>"

"<As it is in Alsace.>"

"<Yes,>" Cranston started fishing in his jacket. "<Cigarette?>"

"<Please.>"

"<Dimitrino?>"

"<Yes, gratefully.>"

Cranston produced a cigarette case covered in the expressionistic vines and flowers one found in Muslim art. He opened it and held it out to Eisenhuth, who plucked one and took a deep sniff of it.

"<I have not had a Dimitrino in five years,>" Eisenhuth said.

Cranston put a cigarette in his own mouth, then clicked

on his lighter. He extended the flame to the German before lighting his own.

"<In London, I traded for three packs from an American sailor who got them in Egypt.>"

Eisenhuth took a full breath and held the smoke in his mouth, savoring the taste—eyes closed—until little tendrils began escaping from his nose. "<Yeah, that's good.>"

Cranston nodded.

"<You're going into smuggling?>" Eisenhuth asked. "<I have a cousin who can get you Killepitsch by the crate for a good price.>"

"<I never tried that before.>" Cranston replied, putting an intrigued note into his voice.

"<It is very good.>" Eisenhuth assured him. "<There are many Germans, in America. They will pay luxury prices for it.>"

"<I must remember that.>" Cranston said, seriously. "<My family is in shipping.>"

"<I apologize,>" Eisenhuth leaned forward. "<What was your surname, again?>"

"<Walker.>"

"<Are you one of those Walkers?>"

Cranston nodded. "<The Walkers of Silkhaven, yes.>"

"<Oh my goodness, I really should give you my cousin's name. Do you have pen and paper?>"

"<I'm sorry, I do not.>"

"<Nothing I could stab you with, yes?>"

"<I suppose.>"

"<So, his name is Jorgen Eisenhuth. He is not a patriot, at all. For years, he has wanted to make partners in America.>"

"<Jorgen Eisenhuth?>"

"<Yes, he lives in Hamburg. He owns Sea Eagle Shipping.>"

"<Sea Eagle,> okay." Cranston was genuinely committing

all this to memory.

Eisenhuth chuckled. "<This is the most pleasant interrogation I have ever been in. Of course, I am not suggesting that the British have been cruel. I was worried when they separated me from the other prisoners, though.>"

"<It's true,>" Cranston said. "<That is rarely a good omen. But this is not an interrogation, per se.>" The mention of interrogation had been Eisenhuth putting one of his own walls back up. Cranston reckoned that he regretted being so open about his family.

"<Is it not?>"

"<You may be turned over to the Americans,>" Cranston lied. "<My job is to see if you are in your right mind. The Americans do not want prisoners that the English have tortured into madness.>"

"<I see. I am quite mad. In a moment, I shall start frothing from the mouth.>"

"<Crazy like a fox. That will go in my report.>"

"<I am damned by my own good manners. So, the stories about your kind are not true?>"

"<The Silkhaven Walkers?>"

"<No,> Prätorianers. <There are so many rumors about you.>"

"<Ah, all false.>" Cranston smiled, seeing another chance at common ground. "<Half of the things they told us in boot camp turned out to be lies.>"

"<That is the army for you.>"

Cranston picked up his empty tea cup and inspected it mournfully. "<If I still had a drink, I would toast to that. What are the rumors on your side?>" Cranston knew the answer and saying it out loud would put Eisenhuth on the back foot, maybe even apologetic.

"<The provincials say you are witches. Reasonable people say you have some kind of mesmerism.>"

"<We were supposed to be bodyguards.>" Cranston shrugged. "<We were trained to see assassins coming. I suppose that gives us an advantage in interrogations, reading people.>"

"<What did they tell you in boot camp?>" Eisenhuth asked. "<The lies.>"

"<That we would single-handedly win the war.>"

"<You are awfully far from the front.>"

"<As I said. So, the Brits have treated you well?>"

"<Yes, they have been gentlemanly. I could not shave, but I understand why.>"

Cranston looked at the ceiling, as if trying to remember any other questions he needed to ask, letting Eisenhuth anticipate the end of the discussion and one notch less alert. "Oh," he snapped his fingers to draw the prisoner's attention and then his voice changed. It took on a strange, unearthly quality, so that it sounded like two deep voices talking at once in an intonation lost to antiquity. "<Where is Generaloberst von Falkenhayn?>"

Eisenhuth's eyes glazed over. They were still pointed in Cranston's direction, but it no longer seemed as if he were looking at him.

"<He is in Romania.>" Eisenhuth replied.

"<Why?>"

"<It is punishment for failure.>"

"<What was his failure?>"

"<Verdun.>"

"<Who replaced him?>"

"<Generaloberst von Hindenburg,>"

Cranston clapped. "<Thank you very much, Oberst Eisenhuth.>"

The German tipped forwards in his chair, overcome by a sudden bout of dizziness. "<I think I am going to vomit.>"

"<Probably not.>" Cranston gathered up the tea cups. "<I

only asked you four questions. I have never seen vomiting after less than seven.>"

Eisenhuth just groaned.

"<Jorgen Eisenhuth, Sea Eagle shipping, right?>"

"<Fuck you in the knee!>" The German replied.

"Quit your bellyaching." Cranston said In English. "You'll be fine."

Back outside, Cranston was met with stunned looks. Even the previously gregarious General Cavan was ashen faced. It wasn't the first time Cranston had seen that; seeing the Praetorians in action had that effect on people.

"Should I wait outside?" Cranston asked the general.

"No, my boy, not at all." He pulled himself to his feet and straightened his uniform. "You did fine work today. It was a pleasure and an honor to have you as part of this operation."

Cranston suddenly felt like he was about to face a firing squad.

The general, seeing his confusion, reached over to a square of paper that sat on the table. It was stamped in French, an old telegram card, evidently salvaged by the boys running the radio. Today's date was at the top, printed in steady handwriting. Followed by a message from NAEF Central Command.

General Cavan put a hand on Cranston's shoulder. "I'm sorry for your loss, lad."

To Praetorian Captain Cranston Walker, the missive said. *We regret to inform you of the passing of both of your parents. Arrangements for your discharge to begin forthwith.*

Chapter 2:
The War Is Too Much With Us

September 7th, 1920. Silkhaven.

The Walkers had been in Silkhaven longer than it had been called Silkhaven. The shipping company had been founded in 1734, when Captain Henry Walker retired from privateering for the English. He had three captured Spanish treasure ships and set up shop in Nova Scotia. The company received a royal warrant from Charles III for Henry's support in the 1745 War of Restoration.

Two generations later, James VIII would call on the Walker Company to help evacuate his cousin, Louis XVI, to the New World. When Louis established his new home on Île Saint-Jean, it was Walker Company ships that brought in the materials for the new estates, and they were the first shipping company to establish a permanent office in the tiny port town of Marieville. The luxury goods being brought in for the survivors of Louis' court earned that port the nickname 'Silkhaven'.

The town was officially renamed after Louis and Marie had their revelation that the rise of the French Republic had been a judgment from God. While the king and queen took vows of poverty, their nobles did not follow suit; Silkhaven continued to be the capital of luxury trade in the New World, and the Walker Company established itself as the premiere shipping company of that city and, indeed, the continent.

In 1811, Louis died and the crown of New France passed to his last surviving child, Queen Mary-Theresa, wife of Charles IV of Great Britain. British rule had begun to weigh heavily on the New World and the Napoleonic Wars offered the colonists fresh leverage. The Treaty of New Versailles established Canada and the Federated States of America as independent nations, while promising continued military alliances with Great Britain. As a gesture of good will, Île Saine-Jean was renamed King Charles Island with sovereignty over the island shared by America and Canada.

Through all of this, the Walker Company maintained its headquarters on the northern point of Marché de la Soie, a confluence of five streets a stone's throw from the docks. Cranston's great-grandfather had torn down the old office to build the twenty-story monolith that stood there now. It was a triangular building of red brick with arched windows and busts of great men from history set into the exterior walls; a tribute to the Palace of Versailles.

Cranston Walker, striding through the front doors at 10:30am was the nominal CEO of the company. The board of directors had appointed him, in absentia, when his father had died, but the actual business of the company was handled by his sister, Vivienne. She had been their father's assistant for a decade when the war started, and no one in the family knew the business better. Despite Cranston's presence, Vivienne was still styled as the Acting CEO, since Cranston refused to take the reins from her.

He had never had much interest in the company, but today, he had a mission. After much cajoling from Vivienne, Cranston had spent the last six months seriously familiarizing himself with the business; at least, on the days when he had the energy to do so. Last Friday, he had been reviewing shipping records and noticed a pattern of discrepancies dating back to November of the previous year. The affected deliveries were all for various liquors, and America had passed its prohibition on liquor in October. Cranston was certain that there were bootleggers now operating within the company.

He had planned to begin investigating it personally on Monday, but he had had one of his bad days and couldn't bring himself to leave the penthouse until dinnertime. However, he had sought remedy for this downturn in his favorite consort: Pearl, a hostess at the famed Mermaid Club. The frisky minx hadn't let him out of her apartment until 8am. Then, he had had to go home to get a fresh change of clothes and wash the olfactory evidence of his dalliance off himself.

Still, 10:30 was better than nothing and he had all the vigor he needed to begin hunting bootleggers. Stepping out onto the 19th floor, Cranston gave a few waves to those already at work and was slightly disappointed that Vivienne was not there to witness his near-punctuality.

The 19th floor was a terrible waste of space, and that was the point. Coming out of the elevators, you were greeted by a spacious lounge area. A half dozen very comfortable chairs surrounded a small table where copies of the official Walker Corporation history (15 years out of date) were to be found, along with a history of Silkhaven itself. Biscuits sat in glass dishes on the three small end tables, and there were two young ladies on staff to bring fresh tea and coffee on demand and to clean out the spittoon. The idea was that you might be waiting a long time. You were important, hence the comfortable furniture, but you may also have time to make progress on one of those history books.

The offices of every department head lined the sides of a narrowing hallway until you reached the arrow's point, where Cranston and Vivienne's offices took the east and western sides, respectively. The offices were not arranged by seniority, but rather by how much time the occupant was expected to be inside. The Chief of the Line and the Head of Quebecois Affairs were nearest to the elevators, as neither actually worked in this building.

It was all very intimidating, the 19th floor you saw from the elevators; a display of power meant to both cow and reassure clients. "Behind" the elevators, though, was an entirely different kind of power. The hidden office of the board's chairman, as well as the meeting room for the board, were places where even Cranston and Vivienne became supplicants from time to time.

Cranston made for his office and the matronly Mrs Shields. At 58, Mrs Shields was the youngest female employee Vivienne would allow near Cranston and a closed door.

"Good morning, Mr Walker," Mrs Shields said, rising from her chair. She wore a brown, high-necked dress with a lace fringe on the collar. It was a very good brown for her, as it gave more color to her hair and made her seem more energetic. Said auburn tresses were piled high on her head and held firmly in place by an invisible army of pins. Over the dress, she wore a plaid apron in white and green with matching sleeves pinching at her wrists and her upper arm. A few black streaks of ink stained the sleeves, and yet she was the only lady in the office who still wore them.

"Good morning, Mrs Shields," Cranston replied, hanging up his hat on the tree just outside his office door. "Has that shipping report I asked for arrived?"

"It did." Mrs Shields made one of her infamous faces. It was a face that informed you that she had deeply-held and readily pronounceable opinions on a matter that she was not in a position to make known. "The report was...*intercepted* by Mr Cabot."

"That's one way to ask for a meeting." Cranston momentarily wanted to throw something. "I don't suppose he offered anything in the way of explanation."

"The spirit moves in mysterious ways," Mrs Shields said. "And it learned it all from Mr Cabot."

"Is there any hope that you squirreled part of it away?"

"None, sir. We stand at the river Styx and Mr Cabot asks us for our coins."

"I do love a woman who reads."

"Well, my son would be none too happy about me taking up with a man younger than he, so you'll have to try your luck at the library."

Cranston furrowed his brow and looked off into the middle distance. "That's not at all a bad idea." He collected himself. "Anyway, it seems I have been summoned."

"Best of luck, sir."

Cranston turned away and began the long walk back towards the elevators. He opened the door off the lounge into the much more practical space devoted to the board. A single, curving hallway wound from the lounge door, around the hidden machinery of the elevators, to another door that opened onto the opposite side of the lounge. At the apex of the curve was the office of Jonathan Cabot, chairman of the board.

Cabot had been ancient as long as Cranston and Vivienne had been alive. When their father was alive, he had seemed like a buffer between the CEO and the board. Now that Cranston was dodging his responsibilities and a woman was gladly taking them on, that role seemed to have shifted.

Cranston knocked and listened to the shifting of weight on the other side of the door. The door was opened by a man with a shaved head, wearing a brown wool cloak with a cheap length of rope tying it closed.

"I'm here to see Mr Cabot." Cranston told the man whom he did not think was really a monk. "I believe that I am expected."

The monk said nothing, only bowed and stepped to the

side, allowing Cranston to walk past him. A few feet from the door was an antique writing desk with a large book open on it, next to several pots of colored ink. The book was open and one of the pages was entirely blank, while the other was half filled with blackletter writing. The desk was lit by a number of candles.

The room extended off to Cranston's right. Five sets of long windows were all curtained, save one that was open but a sliver. In the dim light, Cranston could see several high piles of books; an extensive library with no shelves. At the very furthest end of the room was a plain desk with a phone next to a pad of paper and a pen.

The center of the room was dominated by a tile labyrinth. There was Cabot, walking the twisting path. He wore a suit that had been cut for a larger man. It may have been cut for Cabot, before age had withered him. It was threadbare enough.

"Almost finished with the great work?" Cranston asked, politely.

"Book 4," Cabot told Cranston. "Still some ways to go."

"I was told that some records I requested..." Cranston continued.

"Yes," Cabot cut him off. "That is not your work."

"As the CEO of the company, isn't that my decision?"

"Are you the CEO, now?" Cabot asked.

"That's what it says on my door," Cranston answered.

"Do not be coy. You are no schoolgirl." Cabot shuffled forward a step. "I was heartened to see you taking a tangible interest in the company. But the CEO has larger things that he must think of. Vivienne thinks of them, but she is the stone crying out while the disciple is silent."

"Indeed," Cranston walked a few steps towards Cabot's labyrinth. "She cries out that you keep pestering her about how little responsibility I'm taking. Now, I am trying to take it upon myself to discover potential bootleggers within the company and you take it away from me. You can imagine my confusion."

"That is work for the sixteenth floor." Cabot explained. "If your suspicions prove valid, it will rise to your desk."

"And who decides if they are valid?"

"Someone on the sixteenth floor."

Cranston had a sudden urge to accuse Cabot of being part of the theoretical smuggling ring. However, it was difficult to accuse a man wearing a suit from the last century of graft.

"Alright," Cranston forced himself to breathe. He could feel his calm beginning to slip and needed to avoid real conflict. There hadn't been enough good days in a row for him to fight like a gentleman. "What would you have the CEO do?"

Cabot looked up at him, as if surprised. "Reach out to Saint Moon. They have been stalling on the contract they proposed for six months."

"Vivienne has that well in hand," he said, hoping to obscure his real hesitance.

"Six months with no progress is not 'well in hand'. Make no mistake, Vivienne is the firmest hand that has lain upon this company's wheel in my lifetime, but she remains a woman. Injustice that it is, this closes doors."

"I shan't have better luck opening it than she."

"The board is not asking you to negotiate the contract yourself. That is for the lawyers. Your job is to make them friendly. We have no illusions about your lack of business acumen, but you do excel at a night on the town."

"Yes," Cranston sucked on his lower lip. Glad-handing clients made up the bulk of his official duties. "Well, the hands at Saint Moon won't be glad of mine."

"What makes you so sure?" Cabot asked, returning his

eyes to his feet and shuffling forward on his well-worn track.

"Our contacts there were in the army."

"As were you."

"I was a Praetorian." Cranston told him and his voice cracked on the last syllable.

"And?" Cabot asked, waiting for something he didn't know.

Cranston couldn't say. He couldn't say 'we were pariahs', 'we were hated', 'our own allies tried to kill us'. It sounded too much like 'boo-hoo, the other boys were mean to us.'

"We were not fighters on the line." Cranston managed this half truth, but the sentence came out too quickly. "There was resentment for our station." He felt like he was losing control of his mouth, so he made a tight fist behind his back and gave himself a thump. It was enough of a distraction to stop himself from saying more.

"That was over there." Cabot creaked out his reply. "None of you is wearing a uniform. You're just men, now."

"You don't know," Cranston heard himself say, as if it were someone else's voice. "You don't know."

"Then, explain it."

Cranston was too busy fighting to stay in control of his tongue to think of an answer.

"I see." Cabot resumed. "I don't know what folly this is: pride or sloth or maybe wrath. It does not matter. The Rose and Chain requires you to make friends with powerful people. Not because of who you are, but because of the chair you sit in. The duty of the CEO is to bring in money. Money is what keeps us in the halls of power and that is where the society does its real work. Never forget that you are not the society's work, you merely hold open the door.

"If that door is too heavy for you," Cabot looked up again, "there are other Walkers. Less capable, but willing to do their part."

Before he knew what was happening, Cranston belted out a laugh. "Do you mean Martin?" The laugh was high, maniacal. It terrified even him to hear it, but he couldn't stop himself. "Lawd, you really are desperate, if you think you can threaten us with that. Have you even met Martin? Not only will he pilot the ship straight onto the sand, that sniveling cretan doesn't give two figs for the Rose and Chain's work."

Inside his head, Cranston was screaming at himself to stop. He didn't know what he was going to say next and the train steamed on: "He will paint his hair gold and declare himself the king of all Silkhaven, then laugh about the doddering old coots who think they can control him. The Rose and Chain will be a punchline at dinner parties where he tries to humiliate all the big wigs that won't give him the time of day, now."

Cranston sucked in a breath. "Threaten us with Martin? You might as well tie yourself to train tracks, Snorkey!"

"Are you finished?" Cabot asked.

Cranston bit into his lip and bowed to hide it.

"If this bootlegging suspicion of yours has any merit, you will be notified. Until then, the great and the good await you."

It felt like ants were crawling up his neck, but Cranston managed to say: "Of course," and no more.

"*Nuovissimi primi*," Cabot said, dismissing him.

"*Et primi nuovissimi*," Cranston answered.

He did his best not to run back to his office. No one was to be alarmed. The meeting had gone poorly, that could be known, but all continued to be well. Mrs Shields stood as he approached. That itchy tightness that accompanied the shudders was coming back to his arm and he couldn't have her seeing him twitch.

"I need a moment," he said as he whizzed past her.

"Of course, sir," she said as he disappeared behind his door.

That was alright. She could think that he had had a fight with Cabot and lost and nothing would change. There would be no fuss; consolatory tea, perhaps, but nothing more. She would assume that he was angry and that was alright. There was nothing disturbing about a man being angry in his own office. Everyone knew what to do about an angry man: give him some space and let the old boy cool off. That simplicity made anger such a desirably 'manly' alternative for more nuanced emotions.

Cranston braced himself against his desk with his left hand and allowed the right to convulse for a moment. It was his fight-or-flight response causing him trouble. The part of his brain that was meant to dampen that primal, chemical urge had been taxed too fully and too often. Spending days on end fueled by little more than cocaine had not helped. Attempting to keep the primal survival instincts in check now caused a variety of undesirable responses.

Thank god for Pearl. If he had gone to see Cabot without the invigorating effects of a night spent with a charming woman, the reaction would have been stronger and set in much sooner. There was a small liquor cabinet and Cranston carefully poured himself a single shot of Four Roses. Just enough to settle his nerves.

The shot poured and drunk, Cranston set the bottle back and eased himself to the floor. It wasn't difficult to stand, he simply didn't see the point in that moment. He didn't see the point of much of anything.

Cranston closed his eyes, not to sleep, merely to reduce the amount of stimulation his mind received. He let the feeling of warmth in his stomach fill his mind. Imagining the whiskey bathing his muscles gave a psychic restoration to the genuine physical release. It returned none of his strength to him, but it made the horrible confusion of the episode tolerable.

He spent nearly an hour sat like that. Once the dizzy

confusion of his nervous system's war with itself had passed, he was left feeling poured out. A feeling which reflected itself on the world around him. In such a state, it was easy to think the world around him was cheap, painted plywood; that his life was no more than an opera and all the other players about him violently opposed to looking through the fourth wall.

While that feeling lasted, Cranston found it very difficult to act of his own accord. Being led about, however drearily, was manageable; but left to his own devices he would find a place to sit and remain there until his mind was able to recover itself. That recovery began with the knowledge that he could get up, consoling himself that this was not a permanent situation. Once that was established, suggestions for things he could do began to trickle in.

Sitting on the floor of his office, back against the liquor cabinet, the first suggestion was to move to his much more comfortable chair. He didn't, but the suggestion was a sign of improvement. Next, he considered calling on Pearl, but he knew it was too early for that. Not only would Pearl be in bed for at least two more hours, but his driver would be unreachable even past that. The thought that got Cranston off the floor was about his suit: it was certainly creasing ever deeper as he sat there. It was too early to be seen that way.

Cranston began to pace slowly about the room. It was the best way to work out a crease. After a few turns about the place, he noticed he was hungry. He took off his jacket—relieved to find no serious wrinkling—poked his head out of the door, and asked Mrs Shields to have toast and butter, along with whatever fruit juice was on hand, brought in for him.

Not yet prepared for any real thought, Cranston leaned against his desk and took in the view from his windows. Nineteen floors up, the cars and horses were still large enough for their movement to be discernible. Cranston let himself get lost in it, the way he might do with the bubbles in a champagne glass at a particularly dull party.

Chapter 3:
Lucien Gabrielle

September 7th, 1920. Silkhaven.

Mrs Shields knocked on the door to bring him his toast and apple juice. "Are you free to see someone?" She asked, setting the tray on an end table.

"It's not the monk, is it?" Cranston asked.

"No, sir," she replied. "He gave the name Lucien Gabriel."

"Lucien?" Cranston felt warmth radiate up from his feet. "Where is he?"

"I asked him to sit by the elevators. You do know him, then?"

"Yes, Mrs Shields, pardon me."

Cranston nearly ran out of the room. He took the widening hallway with his longest strides. When he caught sight of a pair of shoulders twice as wide as the chair attempting to support them, he couldn't help but bark out a laugh.

"Lucien?" he called.

The man who sat with his back to Cranston rose, and his colossal size dwarfed all of the oh-so-intimidating furniture. He turned and grinned.

"I was worried you might have forgotten," he said.

Cranston didn't bother going around. He hiked one foot up onto an end table and went straight over the furniture barrier, arms wide.

"Nonsense, old boy!" His feet touched carpet and his arms closed around the big man. The two embraced tightly for a moment, Cranston's face pressed into Lucien's chest.

Lucien Gabriel stood nearly six and a half feet tall and had shoulders so wide that doors were occasionally difficult. He wore an impeccably tailored grey suit with a pale blue bow tie.

"When did you arrive in Silkhaven?" Cranston asked, making a mental note about the suit to be discussed later.

"The island? About two months ago." Lucien answered. "The city? Just now. I feel awful showing up like this, without a letter or anything."

"What you should feel awful about is showing up so late!" Cranston felt ready to burst. "We could have been painting the town red!"

Color rose in Lucien's face and he looked at his shoes—which gleamed with polish. "I wasn't actually sure you'd want to hear from me. Some of the others, you know, they'd rather leave the whole thing behind them."

"Yes," Cranston said, some of the wind falling from his sails. "I suppose they would. But that's neither here, nor there. Come along to my office. Have you had breakfast?"

"I ate before I came," he said.

Leading the way back down the narrowing hallway, Cranston added: "You really couldn't have chosen a better day. Tuesdays are frightfully dull at the best of times and a project I was working on has abruptly moved down the line. I have absolutely nothing to do all day. Your timing is impeccable!"

At the door, Cranston asked Mrs Shields for another tray, then ushered Lucien inside. There were two luxurious chairs against one wall, where Cranston could grease important clients. They were wide enough for even Lucien to sit comfortably.

"You seem to have done well for yourself," Cranston said,

as they sat, gesturing at Lucien's very fine suit.

"On the boss' dime." He shrugged. "She needs me to blend in."

"Good god, where? The Travers Stakes?"

"Not yet," Lucien said plainly. "Though, I was at Saratoga to see Man O' War lose to Upset."

"You what? I lost seventy-five dollars on that race."

"I lost ten. But there's talk that maybe we'll head down for Travers, this year. It's gonna be a rematch."

"Oh, yes, I hear he's been drawing crowds like Babe Ruth, this year."

The train of conversation was interrupted by the arrival of Mrs Shields with another tray of toast and apple juice. She transferred the dishes to the first tray, then bustled out of the room.

"Alright, enough suspense, what have you gotten yourself into?"

"I'm a bodyguard," Lucien said.

"You don't say! Well, you are certainly worth your weight in gold for that work."

"And yet...I think I might be in over my head."

"Those Saratoga crowds can get rowdy." Cranston grinned, but Lucien was too burdened to join in.

"Have you heard of Rosamund Syme?" he asked.

"Of the Boston Symes?"

"Yeah, probably. Her mom lives there and her uncle is running for congress, representing Massachusetts."

Cranston did know her, but didn't let on, as he wasn't sure if or how fondly she might remember him. There were few things more embarrassing than touting an acquaintance who threw a drink in your face when next you saw them. So, he did what old families did and played as if he knew of her and little more. "Henry Syme, yes. His brother, William, is a doctor; runs a sanitarium of sorts on the American side of the island."

"I know, that's where I've been the last two months."

"You're bodyguarding Rosamund Syme?"

"Yep."

"That explains the suit. How much trouble could she be, though?"

"Did you know she's been lecturing?"

"In an official capacity?"

"I guess." Lucien shrugged. "Dr Syme put out this big report two years ago. He studies the effects of dimensional pockets on people. This report he published was a big deal in the medical community, but it was too difficult for regular people. So, Rosamund wrote a book explaining it for Joe-on-the-street, and then she started touring. It's been a big hit, but it's ruffled some feathers."

"As literate women are wont to do."

"That's not half of it." Lucien shook his head. "There have been quite a few women lecturers making names for themselves while we were off in Europe. Most of them promoting domesticity and clean living."

"And Rosamund is instructing the nation on good etiquette to the chagrin of Dorothy Dix and her adherents?"

"No, Rosamund's on the other side of the clean living folks."

"She recommends filthy living?"

"That's how some see it. Okay, so you remember those guys that got EDAD?"

Extra-Dimensional Affective Disorder had been one of the scourges of the trenches. Not as common as the lice-borne illnesses, but it decommissioned more men than gas attacks. It was what came from being too near a dimensional pocket for too long; pockets like the one that kept Cranston awake at night.

"Yes, of course." Cranston replied.

"Well, Dr Syme has been looking for a treatment. He helped with the first manitaurine cigarettes, but he wants to move past prevention and find a real cure. He's not there, yet, but that report he published had some ideas about how to do it. The main thing is that the report expanded on the prevention side of things and that's what Rosamund's lectures are about.

"What Dr Syme has found is that people with a lot of..." Lucien closed his eyes, trying to remember the word. "Oxy... oxytocin? Yeah, people with a lot of oxytocin are less affected by the pockets. So, Rosamund goes around teaching people how to keep their oxytocin levels up. One of the things she says is that people should hug their loved ones for eight minutes a day. Not all in one stretch, obviously, just over the day. Cumulative."

"Go on," Cranston smirked. "Get to the scandalous part."

"Right, so blue petting is a prime way of getting oxytocin. Rosamund has even gone so far as to say that women should take themselves around the block twice a week."

"In public?"

"No! In their bedrooms. Or the bath, I suppose."

Cranston stared at him for a moment. "You said she was lecturing."

"Oh, yes, I see. Yes, she has said it in public. She spent most of the last eighteen months telling packed rooms of people that women can protect themselves from the worst effects of dimensional pockets by shucking their oyster."

"I can see the feathers, now." Cranston whistled.

"John Kellogg wrote a whole piece for the World calling it decadence masquerading as science."

"As damning as that sounds," Cranston raised his apple juice, "I think you could take him."

"It's the CHJ that has me worried."

"Who?"

"The Church of the Hero Jesus," Lucien said.

Cranston scowled, again searching his limited memories on the subject. "Oh, yes, they're the ones with that horrible statue out front. It's on...um...Water Street, I think."

"Yeah, the Silkhaven branch, but their HQ is just outside of Boston. The guy who started it, Reverend Charles Campbell, is running for that same congress seat as Henry Syme. So, he's got all his people foaming at the mouth about it. Trying to win the election from the moral high ground."

"I imagine there are plenty of other denominations willing to follow that particular flag."

"Mmhmm, the Seventh-Day Adventists are on the bandwagon. The Baptists are up in arms, but more because a woman is lecturing than anything she's said. Weirdly, the Pope weighed in, back in January. He published this whole thing saying that he wanted more research done."

Cranston boggled at the thought. "The Pope is supporting Dr Syme?"

"Kind of." It was Lucien's turn to try to remember. "He said there was nothing wrong with encouraging married people to 'couple', but said that men couldn't use mercuries."

"Naturally,"

"Rosamund is very much in favor of mercuries. Uh...and then he said something about masturbation being wrong only when there was lust involved and that lust was irrational, but if it was a health matter, that was rational. Anyway, the Catholics have no idea what to think and the protestants are treating that like an alliance. So, not only is Rosamund spewing filth, she's spewing Catholic filth."

"This does sound a bit out of your league."

"And it wouldn't be any of my worry, but the CHJ is getting 'rowdy'. We were down in Baltimore, back in June. Rosamund was speaking at a medical conference in this hotel. We were just walking through the lobby when this family jumped us. A boy hit me in the family jewels and the parents grabbed hold of Rosamund and tried to drag her into a car."

"Shit," Cranston replied.

"That's what brought us up here. Dr Syme wants Rosamund off the lecture circuit until after the election. He figures things will calm down, then. But, like you said, the CHJ has a branch up here and I'm not convinced that the sanitarium is gonna provide enough security."

"You think I could?"

"I need help." Lucien said. "I didn't have that many friends before the war and even fewer after. And that was back home. Up here, you're the only person I know. Mind, if I could ask anyone for help on this, you'd be it. I mean, you're Rosamund's kind of people, for one." He gestured at the plush, high-rise office around them. "And then, there's what we can do." Lucien gave an apologetic look.

Cranston dug his teeth into the end of his thumb for a moment. "Right. It is what we were trained to do."

"It was what we were supposed to be doing the whole war."

"Until Pershing hung us out to dry."

Lucien picked up the second glass of juice and raised it in a toast. "May his ass be forever fucked."

Cranston touched his glass to Lucien's and they drank.

"Two months," Cranston said thoughtfully. "The attempted kidnapping was in June and you came to King Charles Island, right away, but it took you two months to call on me. What happened? Why come to me, now?"

Lucien nodded. "Rosamund's been doing counseling with women suffering from EDAD. She has a new client that gives me the cold cockles. Something is off and I'm thinking she's a spy."

Cranston looked at his feet, at the polished leather that he could just about see his face in. They never felt right, always seemed a bit wobbly. The word 'spy', however, had him remembering those knee-high boots; the ones he had ground down into the exact shape of his foot.

"When does Rosamund expect you back?" Cranston asked.

"Soon, I think." Lucien shrugged. "I told her I was running into the city, but that was it."

"Do you think she'll be put out by one more for lunch?"

Chapter 4:
Rosamund

The Syme Retreat sat on the end of a small peninsula, where the Knox and Valleyfield rivers met to become the more famous Montague. Montague, the town, had done well for itself since the turn of the century, with a couple of enterprising real estate men marketing the place as 'the Lake Placid of the North'. At the height of summer, there were a thousand extra residents in the town.

Cranston had been to his fair share of parties out this way, but they got tiresome very quickly. Montague was on the American side of the island and people bought or rented houses there either because it was cheaper than in the shared sovereignty zone or because they bristled at being even slightly under Canadian rule. The former tended to be social climbers and the latter were fascists, at best.

However, all of that was on the other side of the rivers. The Syme Retreat proper comprised a dozen buildings, including "guest" lodgings, special treatment facilities, a dining hall, etc. The house where Rosamund was staying sat apart from the retreat, fenced off by a wide copse of pines. It was a two-story great house built to look like a Roman Emperor's idea of a log cabin. The exterior walls were all built from enormous tree trunks laid on their sides, but the veranda that ran the length of the facade was supported by vertical logs with long grooves cut in them and carvings in some lighter wood at the top to mimic the Corinthian style.

Each of the facade's arched windows had a few decorative panes of stained glass at the top. They seemed a bit silly, under the veranda, but Cranston supposed that they caught the setting sun beautifully.

Lucien had taken a bus from Montague, so Cranston offered to take him back. Mrs Shields had found Cranston's driver, and recalled him and the Packard to the office early. Lucien had told the chauffeur how to get to the retreat, then got out to open the gate to the great house, known as Syme Lodge.

As Lucien guided the Packard into a disused horse stall, retrofitted into an automobile shelter, a woman walked out onto the veranda. She wore a sage-green dress that fell to mid-calf and achieved the effect of being pleated without actually being so. It cinched at the waist, but billowed in the bodice and sleeves. As she walked out, she rested a very wide-brimmed hat of deep blue straw on her complexly done-up hair.

Apparently satisfied that Cranston's chauffeur could handle parking on his own, Lucien walked up to the veranda. He touched the woman's hand quickly, then took it away. It was curiously Victorian of him. Cranston had spent enough time around very rich old people to be able to read the brief gesture for what it was, but suspected others might miss it. That, of course, being the point.

Once the car stopped, Cranston took a moment to adjust his own dark green suit, trimmed in brown; not wanting to look over-traveled. He suddenly wished he had brought his cane, just to look a little more grown up. Stepping out and putting on his own hat, Cranston took a moment to very intentionally not look at the house—letting himself be seen—

before turning to the woman on the veranda and calling out: "Rosie!"

The woman lifted the brim of her hat and squinted in the early afternoon light. "Cranberry?" She called back in a voice that suggested he would not be getting a drink to the face.

Cranston took a bow and then strode quickly up to her. As he approached, she reached out with both hands to take hold of his face and place a large, affectionate kiss on his cheek.

"Whatever are you doing here?" Rosamund asked.

"I've come to personally chide you," he replied with a smirk. "Two months you've been on the island and I've heard not a peep from you. Your man had to track me down and break the news in person."

"Wait a moment," she said, casting a look at Lucien—who was directing the chauffeur to the staff entrance. "Have you two met?"

"At the academy," Cranston answered, though Rosamund was still intent on Lucien.

"The academy?"

"Yeah," Lucien said, catching up to them, brow furrowed. "Praetorian Guard training."

"What about that?" Rosamund said, looking at Cranston as if he had grown a tail. "Our Cranberry, a Praetorian Guard."

Lucien barely restrained his amusement. "Cranberry?"

"Just a pet name from when we were younger." Rosamund said, taking Cranston's arm. "Back when he thought Cranston was too grown-up sounding."

"We were all terrified of adulthood," Cranston replied. "Weren't we, Rosie?"

"Careful with that," she began leading him into the house. "Or I might start calling you 'Mr Walker.'" They continued a few steps with Cranston saying nothing and Rosamund suddenly stopped short, a hand flying to her mouth. "Oh dear, I shouldn't have said that. I was so sorry to hear of your parents' passing. I did write to Vivienne when I heard."

"Think nothing of it, Rosamund." Cranston replied. "I get called 'Mr Walker' rather a lot these days."

"Well," she continued into the house, arm firmly around his. "It seems we have an awful lot of catching up to do. Firstly," Rosamund said, "I want to hear everything about how you two met."

Lucien, coming up behind them, added: "I was just about to say that same thing."

The foyer was small, not much wider than the large front door. After two meters, it split into a hallway leading deeper into the house and a stairway going up to the second floor. They passed a sitting room on the left on their way down the hall. Past the stairs, they turned right into another hall and left into a simple kitchen with a breakfast table. The real kitchen would be in the basement; this room being just functional enough for the lady of the house to indulge in some American self-reliance.

Rosamund insisted that the men sit while she made sandwiches for them: cold ham and cheddar with a slice of tomato. It was a fashionable thing for women of her generation. Ladies' magazines were full of advice columns from women out west, peddling the romantic notion of the country hostess who does not rely on household staff for the needs of her guests; at least, not at lunchtime.

Lucien's protectiveness of her was apparent, but that greeting at the door had shifted some of that in Cranston's direction. A part of him saw one of Rosamund's old boy friends as a threat. To allay this, Cranston immediately began telling Lucien about how 'Rosie' had been mother to their little gang, back in the summer of '06. It was the first year that her mother had allowed her to spend the entire season on King Charles Island.

"Not mother by choice," Rosamund added. "After Ethel went back to Washington, you were running around like a pack of wild dogs."

"Ethel?" Lucien asked.

"Roosevelt," Cranston replied.

"No one could keep the boys in line like Ethel," Rosamund continued, "not even Vivienne. Have you met Vivienne?"

"No, I don't think so," Lucien answered.

"Cranberry's older sister. She was already working in the office by then."

Cranston nodded. "Vivienne became father's secretary when she was twenty."

"Gosh, but I envied her." Rosamund said. "My father didn't put that kind of trust in me until the war was on." She brought them the sandwiches. "Coffee?"

"Milk is fine for me," Cranston said.

"Do you need to brew a new pot?" Lucien asked.

"No," Rosamund answered him. "There's still some in the kettle. I just need to heat it up."

"That's alright." Lucien said. "I don't mind cold coffee."

"I do." She shrugged one shoulder at him, then turned to go back to the stove.

"I can light it." Lucien said, getting to his feet.

"Not at all," Rosamund replied. "There's still good wood in there from breakfast. Sit."

He did, dutifully, while she opened a wicker basket set on a high shelf. From within, she removed a handful of dry grass which she threw in the stove before striking a match to get the fire going.

"Now, Lucien," Rosamund called as she heated the coffee. "Before you start thinking I was a matron as a girl, you should know what kind of beasts Cranberry and his pals were. I once caught them throwing rocks at a family of ducks who were just trying to cross the street."

"In my defense," Cranston interjected, "we had every intention of cooking and eating one if we could hit it."

"You didn't have guns?" Lucien asked.

"It was an extemporaneous thing." He shrugged. "A whim."

"It was ghastly!" Rosamund corrected. "Most of the ducks were hardly out of their down."

"And you made good and certain that we understood the error of our ways." He turned to Lucien. "She came screaming at us like a bothered goose and wouldn't stop until she had all three of us holding our hats."

"Ethel wouldn't have had to scream," Rosamund sighed.

"She was in France, you know," Cranston said. "During the war. Her husband had a hospital out there and she was a nurse."

"Poor dear, marrying a doctor."

"Spake the doctor's daughter."

"Exactly. Working with Father, I've seen more of him in the last two years than in the ten before that."

"Yet, you're here, instead of Boston."

"Because, here, I can do some good. There, I'd be a very pretty piece of furniture until some congressman's son wore me down enough to marry him." She snapped her fingers and began searching for the milk.

"Not running some ladies' auxiliary?"

Rosamund found the milk, then took the coffee off the stove. "If I was very obedient, by now, I might have risen as high as Mother's assistant's assistant." She brought the drinks to the table, one milk and two coffees. "So, to what do I owe the pleasure of your visit? Lucien isn't trying to recruit you, is he?"

Neither man replied immediately.

"Lucien!"

"I need an extra pair of hands!" he protested.

"Rosamund," Cranston interjected. "Lucien told me about

what happened in Baltimore. I'm more than happy to assist with information gathering and being a little extra muscle, if it comes to that."

"Don't you have a company to run?" She asked.

"Not at all. Vivienne handles all of that and we're both very happy with that arrangement."

"Well," Rosamund raised her eyebrows. "I certainly wouldn't want to stand in her way, but really, Cranston, it's not half so dire as Lucien makes it out to be."

"All the better. I could use some time out of the city. There's nothing so refreshing as country air."

"Fine." She huffed. "Maybe you can get him to see sense."

They spent the afternoon catching up. Cranston chose his most innocuous and charming stories from the war, as veterans always did, glossing over the unavoidable allusions to the war's darker subjects. Rosamund, likewise, narrated her path to working with her father with only obscure references to the associated divide with her mother. It was impossible to say whether Rosamund's work with her father was cause or effect of this divide, only that her mother disapproved of it. No doubt, a woman of Mrs Syme's social standing bristled at her daughter displaying diagrams of pudenda in public halls.

Eventually, Cranston steered the conversation into Rosamund's therapeutic work. He dressed it in the guise of polite interest, the way that Rosamund did her questions about his current role in the Walker corporation. It was a fine line to walk. He wanted to hear details of the treatments she prescribed. If he seemed too aloof, she would omit such details. If he seemed too keen, she might think he was rubber-necking, or worse: suspect the truth.

Doctors were well-versed in spotting sneaky attempts at consultation, especially when the condition was embarrassing. He felt he was on the verge of the information he wanted when Rosamund got a serious look.

Lucien had excused himself, by that time. He knew all of the stories, already, and the tangential stories about Cranston and Rosamund's mutual acquaintances kept him out of the conversation.

Rosamund put her elbows on the kitchen's table and leaned in, quietly asking: "Do you mind if I ask about the Voice?"

"Oh, I don't suppose so." Cranston answered, realizing that the discussion of treatments was over for the time being.

"I know it is a delicate matter."

"It is," Cranston nodded, pushing aside his disappointment. "So, I'll reserve the right not to answer."

"More than fair." Rosamund continued, her voice low. "I only ask because I wonder if the hypnotic state it incurs might not be helpful in treating psychological illnesses."

"In that case, by all means. Anything I can do to help the great work being done here."

"Thank you," she said. "I know what has been published: that it is a specific modulation of the vocal cords and that only a small percentage of people have the construction to do it. But is it purely mechanical? That is, do you find that there is a psychological component?"

Cranston thought for a moment. "One could say that there is a psychological component, yes, but only in as much as there is also one in long-distance running. It requires focus, so your mental state does influence its effectiveness. However, we were expected to use it under grave circumstances. We needed it to be almost second nature to us, but that was what the training was for."

"What sort of training?"

The two men exchanged looks, as if deciding which of them would start it off. Really, they were silently debating how much of the truth to let her in on.

Chapter 5:
Over There

October 7th, 1914. Fort Jackson, New Jersey.

It was evident that the FS Army was already having second thoughts about the Praetorian Guard. The Guard had been born during the Philippine War, but did not become a distinct branch until 1907, before the Russian Revolutionaries were put down. They were occasionally touted as a kind of luxurious elite in military service: enjoying the comforts of an officer's life (something exaggerated in the press), but also the tip of the national sword.

It was a honeypot. Get a lot of hopeful young men to sign up, then ship them off to the infantry when they didn't have the right vocal cords.

Back in July, posters with the Praetorians' motto—Shout Forth Thunder—had been plastered all over Silkhaven. It was an Adolf Treidler and vertically oriented. High and center was a golden silhouette, dark lines showing his mouth wide open and his finger thrust ahead of him. Around him, more silhouettes in khaki green rushed forward as, near the bottom, grey silhouettes in pickelhaube helmets retreated.

Something had happened between then and September, though. When Cranston arrived at the academy, in New Jersey, a new poster was being plastered over the old Treidlers. This new one was a Sydney Riesenberg, so you knew they meant business.

"The Voice is for the enemy" proclaimed the new poster glued longways over the Treidler. In the center was a boldly silhouetted, but lightly detailed man with an eagle embroidered on his shoulder. He was holding out a hand as a German soldier handed over his rifle. Behind the eagle-shouldered man, looking on approvingly, were three, realistically detailed Americans: a soldier, a sailor, and a marine.

Cranston might have spent the better part of his young adult life avoiding the responsibilities of the family business, but he had learned enough to read the hidden message in the advertising. The rank and file had lost trust in the Praetorians and it needed, desperately, to be won back.

For the first 30 days of training, drills had been light. They ran five miles before breakfast and spent another three hours a day on the range. However, the main piece of kit they worked with was their Duden dictionary. Every single one of them had to be proficient in German or they were next to useless in the field. There were three second-generation immigrants in Cranston's class and a fourth who had been born outside Munich, then brought to America as a child. They understood the posters, too; desperately needing to build trust was already on their minds.

After thirty days, they had their big German exam. Anyone who failed that was sent to the infantry. Only then did the Voice training begin. You had to have the right kind of vocal cords to do it at all and doing it properly required an incredible amount of control. The cadets trained with opera coaches to build the base level of control, then came the scientists to explain the minutiae and get you controlling the right thing. Finally, a dozen "laureates" came in; a previous generation of Praetorians with wooden legs or missing hands.

Finally, on one Wednesday morning, the cadets were called out to the parade ground and put in two lines, facing each other. Cranston ended up across from a man he had only heard referred to as 'the giant' before then. He was, indeed, the largest man that Cranston had ever seen.

"Cranston Walker," he introduced himself quietly as the sergeants were otherwise focused.

"Lucien Gabriel," the other man whispered back. Gabriel was 6'4" and, when the two shook hands, Cranston's not unmanly hand disappeared inside Gabriel's great mitt.

As they made their way down the lines, the sergeants handed out small tins with the words "ear defenders" stamped into the lid. Opening the tin, Cranston found a pair of over-sized pawns that he was ordered to stuff into his ears. His pulse became the loudest noise in the world and, cast into that almost-silence, there was nothing to do, but wait.

He looked straight ahead, right at Gabriel's broad chest. Gabriel was not especially dark of complexion; he had the color of the men at markets who made their living in the sun. Still, Cranston thought, there had to be some of the negro or the Polynesian in him to get that big. While he wondered about this, he noticed a man step out of line and walk out of his peripheral vision. Suddenly, Cranston worried that this was the German exam all over again, and that there was a truck waiting to carry the failures off to be cannon-fodder.

After several minutes, a sergeant stepped up behind Cranston and tapped him on the shoulder. "Defenders out!" The sergeant shouted. Both Cranston and Gabriel pulled the chess pieces from their ears. "Private Walker," the sergeant—still wearing his ear defenders—continued shouting. "You will use the Voice on Private Gabriel. This parade ground is the only place where you will use the Voice on a fellow member of the FS Army or any other ally."

"The Voice is for the enemy, sir," Cranston and Gabriel called in unison.

"Very good. Private Walker, the command is: *gehst ins Bett.*

Begin."

Cranston straightened his back and lifted his chin. He shifted his body according to the checklist he had drilled with the laureates. This was his first time actually speaking words. Drills had always used single vowels.

He looked the big man in the eyes. Gabriel was nervous, too. One breath out, then one in. "*Gehst ins Bett!*" Cranston barked, his voice coming out in an eerie echo of itself, like he were speaking with two voices at once.

Gabriel teetered in place and Cranston watched as the big man's eyes glazed over, like he was thinking of something far away and curious. Then, with no word from the sergeant, Gabriel broke rank and walked away—purposeful, yet unhurried—towards the barracks. Cranston watched him go for a moment. No one tried to stop him.

"Good work, Private Walker." The sergeant shouted. "Replace your ear defenders."

May 17th, 1915. Half way between Itxassou and the Spanish border.

Spain was not, technically, in the Great War. They were, however, still upset with the Federated States over the loss of their final colonies; a loss which made them an empire in name only. The proliferation of their language and their status as trend setters for the bourgeois of their former colonies was little consolation. They wanted revenge and, with so much of the FS's military resources dedicated to France's war, it was the perfect time to wage a war of attrition on the Navy.

With supply lines being interfered with, the North American Expeditionary Force commanders had decided that a reconnaissance unit should scout the Spanish border and determine the likelihood of Spanish land aggression and the possibility of an allied counter-assault. What they had found was the entirety of the Spanish artillery covering as much of the Pyrenees as they could. And then, a box of dynamite had detonated under suspicious circumstances. This was why Colonel Lassiter was sent to the forward camp and, with him, his bodyguard, Praetorian Lieutenant Walker.

It was a ramshackle thing, as these forward camps always were. A handful of tents that always had a few pieces missing from their kits, several canvas-covered trucks, and a dozen crates that were as likely as not to be mislabeled.

"Sir," an infantry lieutenant approached Colonel Lassiter. "We have Diego, Gomez, and Escobar in confinement. It was a patch job, but it will do, for now."

Cranston had yet to make his peace with the regular conditions of these forward camps. He shuddered to think of what sort of jail the soldiers would put together on short notice; even if they were engineers.

"Excellent," Lassiter said. "Show Walker where they are. He'll find our traitor."

"Excuse me, sir," Cranston interjected. "My orders are to remain at your side."

"Your orders are to follow my orders, Walker," Lassiter spat. "I know that's hard for a rich boy, like you, to grasp; but none of my real soldiers can control minds."

"Sir, am I to understand that you want me to use the Voice on Americans?"

"Are you deaf, man? Three men are dead because of a saboteur. One of those 'Americans' is working with the Spanish and I want to know who."

"The Voice is for the enemy, sir." Cranston recited the line with mechanical speed.

"I thought you spoke French. A 'saboteur' is a kind of enemy. Now, go find him."

"Sir, I cannot use the Voice on our men."

"One of them is a traitor!" Lassiter was shouting directly

into Cranston's face.

"And two of them are not." Cranston drew in a breath as he watched a bead of sweat form on Lassiter's brow. "Sir."

There was no interrogation that day. Lassiter had the suspected saboteurs loaded into a truck to be driven to the nearest command post. They were all Puerto Rican and their hands and feet were tied for the journey. Bound and, additionally, gagged beside them was Lieutenant Walker; off to face a court-martial.

June 19th, 1915. Outside La Bassée, France.

General Parker had been quiet for the entire briefing. Lucien had arrived at the trench base with him late the night before. Rough planks of wood held up and held back the mud that the base had been cut out of. Lanterns were hung from nails wherever the light was needed most. Fragile things, in Lucien's mind, ready to crash to the ground and engulf the whole place in flames if a shell landed too close.

Parker was replacing a sour-faced Canadian who was painting a very bleak picture of the problem. It was just the three of them in the cramped little room. Lucien squatted against one wall because he was too tall to stand up straight.

The North American Expeditionary Force had been charged with breaking the German line at the northern end, so that the British could gain a better position for their artillery. However, a concrete-reinforced parapet on the German side was holding up the entire offensive. The Canadians wanted the artillery to take out the parapet, but the British believed that this would only draw greater defenses to that part of the line, undermining the entire purpose of the operation.

"We need to get on top of it," Parker said, finally. "All we need is to get five men inside that parapet and the whole line will collapse like dominoes."

The Canadian looked at Parker like he had started speaking Greek, then guffawed. "It's so simple. Why didn't I think of that?" he mocked. "I've lost an entire squadron trying to get explosives in range of the parapet."

"Sure." Parker nodded. "But you didn't have him." He jerked his thumb at Lucien. "He's one of our Praetorian Guards. Worth fifty men in the field, I'm told."

The Canadian eyed Lucien's mountainous bulk of muscle. "Is he going to punch it into dust?"

"Nope," Parker grinned. "He's going to tell the Germans to surrender and they'll do it."

"I'm sorry, sir." Lucien interjected. "I don't think I know what you're suggesting."

Parker turned and looked up into Lucien's face. "It's simple: we put you with a squad of our best and they get you close enough that you can do your voice trick."

"Sir, my job is to keep you safe," Lucien almost stuttered, still getting the hang of talking to superior officers.

"Yes, and just think how safe I'll be once that parapet is under our control."

"But, as from what the General has said," he gestured at the Canadian, whose name he had forgotten. "All attempts to get that close have failed."

"How close do you need to be?"

"Close enough that they can hear me, sir. If they're firing a machine gun, I'll have to be right in their ear."

"Don't be ridiculous!" Parker said. "You're supposed to be able to turn a charging line back."

"That was...um...poetic license, sir. On the Army's part."

Parker narrowed his gaze. "I'm beginning to wonder what good you are, at all, boy. But there's a sure fire way to find out." He rose to his feet and stood at eye-level with Lucien's elbows. "I see the fear. I didn't think a man like you would be fearful. Just the same, the fires of war will always reveal exactly what a man is worth."

Parker crossed to the map that the Canadian had used. "You're going to take that parapet." He said, slamming his fist against the rough drawing of the machine gun position. "You're going to show the world that the Praetorian Guard are a force to be reckoned with."

September 14th, 1915. Outside Ostreville, France.

The Ostreville camp was well behind the line. Artillery was being amassed there in preparation for what would be called the Battle of Loos. Hundreds of engineers and artillerymen milled about, very few having immediate orders, and not one of them would risk being seen fraternizing with a Praetorian. Cranston kept an intentionally irregular schedule and walked varying, often circuitous, paths to the radio tent, the latrine, and the mess.

The looks and whispers had always been ubiquitous, but now that Cranston didn't have an officer to stand beside, it was worse. At first, he had supposed it was his imagination, feeling exposed now that he had been deprived of his official duties. Then, someone had spit on him. The man had been Belgian and, as Cranston reeled at the unprovoked aggression, the spitter had shouted at him in French: "I don't speak English or German! What can you do?"

Cranston, fluent in Quebecois, had replied: "You should not ask what I can do, but what I will do." That had shut the man up and, at first, it had felt like a victory; but he quickly discovered that it only stoked the fire.

It was enough to make him wish for a frontline assignment. Bored soldiers were far worse than edgy ones.

He arrived at the mess at the very end of lunchtime. A

civilian ladies' organization ran the kitchen, so he knew no one would tamper with his food, but he made sure that he was the last—or very nearly—to get food. Any sign of deference was to be given when the opportunity arose. The ladies didn't say much to him, either, but that was out of piety. These were good, Christian women and everyone knew what soldiers were like far from home.

Cranston carried his small helping of lamb and cold vegetables to an empty table, far from the entrance; a place he could almost disappear. Today, though, it was not remote enough.

Two tables down, a pack of three Irishmen—thin and ragged-looking, almost emaciated—whispered together and occasionally cast a poisonous glance at him. The Americans and Canadians were in this war to honor the 1812 treaty; they were allies drawn into the fight by a signed agreement. The Irish hadn't signed a damn thing. Every day that they had to follow British orders was like having another tooth pulled. Combine that with the suffused boredom of Ostreville and they were devoid of empathy for the American pariah.

"Hey, you!" one of the Irishmen shouted. "You with the fancy eagle!"

Cranston wore his uniform, at all times. The golden eagle stitched onto the shoulder gave him away at thirty yards, but going without was worse. Too many people knew his face. A vain attempt at hiding his status would only encourage them.

"Aren't you supposed to be tellin' Jerry to run home without his supper?" The trio laughed. Cranston said nothing. "Oy!" The heckler stood. "I asked you a question! You too high and mighty to answer?"

"I apologize," Cranston said, not making eye contact. "I did not think you expected an answer. I cannot speak to why my orders are what they are. I only know that my orders are to be here."

"Ah, sure," another of them said. "If any of us gets uppity afore the battle, he's gon' set us straight. Is that right?"

"Nah," added the heckler. "I'll bet there's nothin' to it, now. It's just misdirection and all. I'd put down money that if we turned over this table and all took him in hand, there's nought he could do for it." The heckler put both hands on the table, palms down, to invade Cranston's view. "Would you have anything to say about that, would you?"

"You are free to speculate," Cranston said, his pride winning a minor victory over his good sense. "For now, I would like to continue with my lunch." It was a foolish thing to say and he knew so the moment it left his lips.

The heckler rolled his cheeks, then spat a small wad of saliva onto Cranston's carrots. It sat there, a meager collection of bubbles, and Cranston wondered if there were a defiant way he could eat them.

"That's all your voice is," the heckler continued. "Just a posh lad without a horse."

"We don't need the Voice to snap a twig like you," came a voice.

Cranston looked up, as did the Irishmen, to see the towering figure of Lucien Gabriel in his own eagle-shouldered uniform. He loomed over them like a mounted cavalryman only, like Cranston, without the horse. Two of the conscripts, standing shoulder to shoulder, were hardly wider than he was.

"Mother of god," one of them whispered.

"You done flapping your mouth?" Lucien asked the heckler.

It was to the Irishman's dubious credit that he didn't back down. "Oh, I still got air enough in me." He reached out and pushed Lucien with both hands. Nothing happened.

"Lucien Gabriel," Cranston smiled for the first time in a week. "You are a sight for sore eyes."

"Cranston," Lucien grinned. "You're the first truly friendly face I've seen since July."

"Where did they have you stashed?"

"The other side. Some old fool believed the propaganda and I got captured by the Germans."

"Lawd," Cranston breathed.

"Apparently, getting me back was a big fuss, but no one seemed especially cheerful about it. Gotta say, I think my good manners are still back there."

"I'm afraid I lost my bad manners in the Pyrenees," Cranston sighed. "Someone wanted me to interrogate three of ours and I refused. I came out of the court-marshal alright, but I haven't had much fight in me since."

"That's sure enough," interjected the heckler, reminding them that he was there. "Posh boy's going to do you no good when we drag you out of here."

"Drag *him*?" Cranston asked, feeling a surge of courage. "You three? There are horse teams that would struggle to do that."

"Now, that you've got your mate backing you up," the second said, "now, you can talk?"

"There are three of you," Cranston reminded him.

"Aye, and Ulster boys to a man," the second conscript said. "You look like your fist would crack on a stiff cushion."

"That reminds me," Lucien said, reaching for his belt, which had been out of Cranston's sight, thanks to the Irishmen. "Took this off an Oberst. Cranston, I suspect you're a fairer hand with it than me." Lucien raised a curved cavalry saber over the Irshmen's heads and tossed it.

Cranston stood to catch it. He unsheathed it, gave it a flourish to feel the weight and then held it in a low pret position. "I trained with a foil, but I think I can manage."

"Now," Lucien cracked his knuckles. "Gentlemen, am I getting my lunch now or later?"

"To hell with you," the heckler said, and the three made to leave.

"Didn't you hear?" Lucien said. "I just got back."

February 7th, 1916. Outside Troyes, France.

A one-hundred foot gap of bare earth, dubbed 'the river', separated the main body of the NAEF camp from the eagle-emblazoned tent and the truck with the broken axel. A thin trickle of smoke rose from the ad hoc chimney that had been cut into the roof of the rusting truck's bed. Cranston, bundled head-to-toe in what passed for winter wear in the army, stepped out of the truck and closed the padlock behind him.

Halfway across the river, he saw a woman making her way back to the camp. She too was well-bundled and he could really only be sure it was a woman by her boots. That would be Laura, the civilian that brought him and Lucien their meals. Or, rather, the ingredients for their meals as nothing cooked would survive the trek between the kitchens and the Praetorian tent.

It was a large tent, from the earliest and most optimistic days of the Guard; big enough for two generals and four guardsmen to sleep, as well as storing all of their equipment. Housing two under-supplied guardsmen, it looked bleak. In the French winter, when a small stove had to be kept lit at all times and venturing five feet from it was no different than fifty, the huddled circle of cots and rucksacks looked positively haunted.

Lucien had the tin pots on the stove, defrosting the items that they would dump into a single bowl for their dinner. They had found a few good, flat stones, which they kept under the stove to hold the heat. That was where their forks, plates, and the pot of ink were.

"How is he?" Lucien asked, as Cranston entered.

"Still reciting Goethe." Cranston replied, lifting the lid on what turned out to be mashed potatoes with a few carrots.

"Did you try the echoing idea you had?"

"Not yet." He checked another tin and found a block of ice that would become beef broth. "If I stumble on it, it won't work and I don't remember *Hermann and Dorothea* all that well. If it was *Faust*, I probably could have."

"I have a feeling they're going to demand he be tortured soon."

"Damn fools, a soldier in pain won't give you a thing you can actually use," Cranston said, briefly forgetting who he was talking to. "Do you remember that song you learned from the boy in Nevers?"

"Not really," Lucien said. "But I don't think it would make a difference. I think the nostalgia would strengthen him."

"What's next, then? Humanizing ourselves?"

Lucien shrugged. "We have to get him to stop reciting Goethe somehow."

"It doesn't hurt that I'm the one who would have to do it."

"It's not my fault you both bleed blue."

There was motion at the tent's entrance, the impotent afternoon light casting the shape of a Brodie helmet and the man beneath on the green canvas. They kept the flaps closed against the wind and whoever this was couldn't quite find the break. Since he hadn't announced himself, the two Praetorians just watched his fumbling search.

Finally, a young infantryman stepped through. He planted his feet just inside the entrance and took off his helmet, holding it with both hands. "Sirs," he gave a small bow. "I'm Private Henry and I was wondering if I might speak with you."

He was English, from the West Country, but that was as fine a point as Cranston could put on his accent.

"Alright," Lucien said. "Speak your piece."

"I thank you, sir." He gave another small, awkward bow. "It's just that I've heard stories, like. Stories about your powers and where they come from."

Lucien and Cranston exchanged a look.

"It's alright, sirs." The young soldier insisted. "I have no quarrel with it. I'm a theosophist, myself. It's just, you see, that my old Dad has passed on. Passed on while I was over here, he did, and you know what the army is like. They can't be sending home every man who has to bury a family member. I dare say, if they did, there would be a right plague of nans going off. Folks would be inventing a new religion what demands funerals go on for six months; just wanting to keep their boys at home, like."

"We're very sorry for your loss," Cranston said, hoping to get the kid to his point.

"That's right kind of you to say, sir. Like I said, I heard tell of where your powers come from and I wondered if they might extend beyond getting men to tell their secrets."

"The Voice is for the enemy." Lucien told him.

"I understand that, sir, and I'm grateful for it. I wouldn't ask you to use it on me or nothing. Wouldn't do no good. No, sirs, I was wondering if you might perform a seance for him, my old Dad. Just so's I could say my goodbyes, you understand."

"I apologize," Cranston said. "You mentioned the source of our powers. What exactly is it that you've heard?"

The young man went pale. "Well, the men...they do speak in dark terms, like, but I understand it's not at all like they imagine. I'm a theosophist, as I said."

"What sort of 'dark terms'?" Cranston said. "I don't mean to put you on the spot. It's just that very little of what is said about us is said to our faces."

"What they say," Private Henry stuttered, "and this is

what I've heard. I don't believe a word of it. That is, I know
that they're speaking of things they don't rightly understand.
But what I've heard is that your powers—you speaking to the
enemy and getting them to tell you things—well, sirs, the men
say it's from the devil."

Part 2:
VIVIENNE

Chapter 6:
Father's People

"Thank you," Vivienne Walker said, benedictive to yet another faceless mourner. Few of their words reached her, masked by the scrape and thump of the gravediggers' shovels raining ashes and dust upon the coffins. She was resplendent in a veil and high heels, like someone's Lady of Mercy. Vivienne towered in most situations, through a combination of good posture and long legs, but today, she seemed a colossus.

The company's employees had been the first to go. Their condolences had been strained since they knew her better as Mr Walker's secretary—and their new boss—than as his daughter. People Vivienne would have to see on Monday were followed by those she only saw on occasional weekends: society ladies weeping and kissing Vivienne's hands and their polite husbands tipping their hats. All that remained now were members of the board and the remains of the Walker clan.

Vivienne was not allowed to mourn here. Her duty, this day, was to accept condolences. She was the vessel of their words, spoken so that they could know that they had done what was required of them and could begin the orphic journey out of grief. As the daughter of the deceased, only she could be such a repository. She had never wished her brother was by her side more, if only to stand behind her and bear her up an inch. As it was, there were none here that she could share the burden with.

Father's people were beside the graves. His sister, Lydia, stood beside Mother's grave. Mother's family was all in the old country or dead, and perhaps Aunt Lydia felt she should stand in for them. A few members of the board also held their vigil at Mother's side in an act of vague chivalry.

Aunt Lydia wept still, clutching her youngest daughter like a crutch. Lydia's husband, Uncle Herbert, stood a little ways from them looking furtive. Perhaps he felt responsible for the rain which had slicked the road that had sent her parents' car into that tree. Or, perhaps, he needed money. Whatever it was, it didn't look like he and Lydia were on warm terms.

Vera, Aunt Lydia's eldest daughter, was at the foot of Father's grave with her family. There was a time when Vera had been Vivienne's most beloved relative. But Vera had taken the path of motherhood while Vivienne became Father's secretary, and the two had drifted apart.

Father's sister-in-law, Ethel, hung back from either of the graves, surreptitiously drinking from a flask. She had attended the funerals of her first son and then her husband, so the liquid courage was all she needed.

Such was the tableau and so it remained until Aunt Ethel teetered over to stand at Vivienne's shoulder.

"It's a tragedy," she said. "But it's how things are supposed to be. Children burying parents, I mean. It's a horror the other way around."

"Yes," Vivienne kept her voice even. "I remember."

"No, I don't imagine you could forget. Buck up, girl. James and Lolita are getting a Christian burial." She took a drink. "Nowhere on the island takes a suicide." Meaning her husband.

"I remember that," Vivienne replied. "Father signed the check, but I made the arrangements."

Aunt Ethel gave single, spiteful chuckle. "Oh, we all know you arranged it."

She took another dram of her liquor and wandered off towards the car that was waiting for her. As she did, the priest—standing between the headstones—watched intently. He made what eye contact he could with Vivienne through her veil. It was time, then. The last of the outsiders was gone.

One of the board members, who held his hat with both hands, looked over his shoulder at Vivienne and nodded to her. When she did not reciprocate, he turned to the priest. He gave the man a nod and the man replaced his hat and began walking towards Vivienne.

He was about her father's age and had the broad frame of a man who had once been quite muscular, but had allowed age to fatten him. His suit was well-made, but not tailored, and his hat was in need of shaping. No one on the board wore tailored clothing; everything was ready-to-wear and often, she suspected, second-hand.

She didn't know his name. The members of the board changed frequently and no one had ever thought that she, the daughter, would need to deal with any of them; excepting the chairman, of course.

Coming to a stop close by her, the humbly-dressed board member said nothing, but only reached into his coat and presented Vivienne with a rose bound with a silver ribbon.

The board members were equally distributed between both graves, though not out of chivalry, she realized. They were paying their respects to Lolita as much as to James. Vivienne's parents had been part of something greater than the Walker Corporation. Indeed, generations of her family had been part of the Rose and Chain. She had suspected that the other members would reveal themselves, here, but she hadn't realized it would be the entire board. The priest was one of them—probably the gravediggers, too—and that look had been a request for privacy.

Vivienne, only initiated into the lowest levels of those mysteries, sought through her father's stories trying to remember what the correct thing to do with these symbols was. The silver ribbon was long. She began tugging at the knot and looked to the messenger for confirmation. He only offered a sad smile, which she took as an affirmative.

She untied the ribbon and held it in her right hand, changing the rose to her left. The rose and the chain, read from left to right. Again, she looked to the messenger and, this time, he nodded. So armed, she approached the graves and held the rose up a little. Now, she checked with the priest, pointing the bloom towards her father, then her mother.

The priest tilted his head as if to say: *Either will do.* She let the rose fall into her father's grave—being on her left—where it was immediately buried by a pile of dirt. When she held the ribbon over her mother's grave, the priest gave her a shake of his head. He stroked his neck with one hand. Vivienne considered that. Taking the ribbon in both hands she tied it around her neck.

The priest smiled and Vivienne nodded, then turned to walk towards her car. Uncle Herbert was waiting there for her.

"Vivienne," he said, raising his arms momentarily, as if to hug her, then thinking better of it. "It's an awful thing. It really is."

"Yes," Vivienne replied.

"Your father was such a kind man." Herbert crushed the brim of his hat in his hands. "It's a terrible shame, your brother not being here. A dirty thing, the army not sending him home, yet."

"Thank you."

"Listen, I know it's a dirty thing of me to be asking, but it's the only time I have, you see."

As Herbert made his apologies before the offense, Vivienne saw Vera coming towards the line of cars with her family. Her husband, Roger, saw Uncle Herbert and broke off to march purposefully towards him.

"It's not right to do these things in a telegram," Herbert continued. "And I wouldn't ask if it could be helped."

"Herbert," Roger said to his father-in-law in quiet, firm voice.

Roger was as much Herbert's junior as he was Vera's senior, but he had proven to be a stabilizing force in the clan since he joined; partly because of his strong, yet careful personality, but also because of his money.

Feeling Roger's hand on his shoulder, Herbert ceased.

"We will talk at the hotel," Roger said, steering Herbert towards his car.

Herbert made a milquetoast objection, then walked away.

"I'm terribly sorry for that, Vivienne," Roger said.

"Not at all," Vivienne told him. "It is a good reminder. My world is not the world and the world moves on unchanged."

"Well," Roger nodded. "I do hope your world continues to spin or...you understand."

"Yes."

Of course, she understood. Vivienne understood everything, today. These pilgrims brought her condolences and she blessed them with words of thanks. All was understood, all was accepted, all was forgiven. She held her own grief inside, as she held the grief of all others. If she were to cry before them, they would have to be tears of milk.

Roger gave a final condolence, then returned to his family. Vera offered Vivienne a knowing look. The look of one saint to another, knowing her feast day was still to come. They got Herbert into the car, then waited for Aunt Lydia.

Vivienne waited by her car, as she had by the graves, until

all of the family was gone. Then, she turned to signal that she was ready to leave. Williamson, her father's driver and now hers, rounded the front of the car to open her door.

As she turned her head to thank him, he shook his head. "No need, ma'am."

Beyond the little hill that separated the road from the graves, Vivienne heard the sounds of a hammer striking metal.

Williamson suggested a scenic route along the East River, which would allow Vivienne's guests to get situated before her arrival at the hotel. She opted to go straight home, though; she was not in a mood that could appreciate the beauty of nature.

When they arrived, he let her out at the main entrance, where Hornsby was waiting for her. Vivienne's great-grandfather had built the first ten stories of the hotel and envisioned the place as a British Great House. The staff were trained by eminent butlers and housekeepers from England. A tradition maintained by her grandfather when he added another dozen floors.

It was Vivienne's mother who had made changes after discovering that a former butler of the Ryumins was living in New York. She hired him to reinvigorate the staff procedures, and the current day and night managers had been trained by him directly before he returned south.

Hornsby let the doorman usher her in, then asked: "Any requirements, ma'am?"

Vivienne had been contemplating what her needs for the rest of the day would be on the drive. "Tell Ferrara that, for dinner, I would like him to follow his heart and send up a bottle of something to prepare my palate. I would also like a few breakfast glasses brought to the penthouse, immediately. Just the simple, cheap ones. Also, call Madam Joho and tell her I will be making an appointment for a fitting some time this week. Apologize that I can't say when, but that I will, at least, be needing a new hat."

"Is that all, ma'am?"

"Yes, Hornsby, thank you." Those two words felt heavy coming out of her mouth.

He turned and started off towards the penthouse elevator, leaving Vivienne to catch up at her own pace. It was quiet in the lobby, quieter than it should have been. Vivienne did not look around, but knew the staff was watching her. A week ago, she had been one of them to a degree. For all that she was James and Lolita Walker's daughter, she was also James' employee.

When her father entered the kitchen, for example, everyone greeted him and then immediately returned to their work in earnest. They expected to hear nothing from him. When Vivienne had entered on her own, only a handful of them would greet her and someone—usually Ferrara—would set aside what they were doing, knowing she had a task for them.

There had been jokes about her mother's strange requests; shared sighs of frustration when Father had one of his bouts of indecision; and gossip with the maids. The staff had helped her sneak gentlemen into the hotel without her parents knowing and she had been the one to smooth it over when someone needed to take more than a single day off.

She had lived in the penthouse, but had also worked in the hotel. Now, it was just the former.

Vivienne began her procession towards the elevator. Her shoes—a fresh pair, changed in the car—clicked loudly on the marble flooring, with few other sounds to mask them. Ahead of her, Vivienne heard Hornsby clear his throat aggressively and the sounds of work being done picked up, letting her steps pass unnoticed.

Once in the penthouse, Vivienne waited for Hornsby to shut the door. Alone, she slipped off her shoes and let her feet sink into the Persian rug. She just stared down the hallway, past the doors and into the silent living room. The last week had been taken up with preparations and the silence had felt like a waiting. With that gone, this was the sound of her home, now.

She picked up her shoes and headed for her room. Until a week ago, the first floor had been her parents' domain and the second her own. Now, she noticed how dark the corridor of vacant bedrooms was.

Vivienne changed out of her funeral clothes and into a slip under a housecoat. The housecoat had been a Christmas present two years ago, when the family had donated the bulk of their silk to the war effort. It was luxurious, Virginian cotton—marketed, now, as "Victory Silk"—with fox fur lining.

In her private bathroom, she removed her makeup while trying to avoid looking at herself in the mirror. When she returned to the small dining room, the dumbwaiter flag was up. She slid the door open and found a bottle of 1882 merlot with the proper stemware, plus a half dozen cheap juice glasses; all on a silver tray.

Vivienne took the tray to the table, closed the dumb-waiter, and opened the wine. She took her glass of merlot to the railing and looked out through the two-story windows at the city of Silkhaven at 2pm on a Friday.

It was exactly the same view it had been her whole life. Perhaps, if she gave it serious thought, she would remember a building that had been torn down and rebuilt four or five years ago. But, on the whole, nothing had changed. Not in thirty years or three years or three months or one week.

The city of Silkhaven, from her family's home down to the docks which were her family's business, continued as it always had.

Finishing the merlot, Vivienne turned and put the wine glass back on the table and picked up one of the juice glasses. Holding it low, she whipped back around and hurled it at the giant windows. The glass smashed against the wall, ear-splitting in the silence of the penthouse.

Vivienne reached back for another glass. "Fuck you!" she shouted, sending the next glass flying after the first.

The third glass was accompanied only by a throat-ripping screech that utterly drowned out the sound of the shattering.

Chapter 7:
Cousin Martin

The elevator doors opened and Vivienne stormed up the center aisle of the 19th floor. The secretaries recoiled from the furious aura surrounding her. Esme, Vivienne's colored personal secretary, stood as the boss approached, but Vivienne said nothing. She strode into her office, leaving the door open. A combination of sounds followed all at once. Vivienne grunted, the bell inside her desk telephone clinked, and something snapped.

When she returned to the hall, calmer but not much, she was holding the telephone from her desk. The one with the specially made, 10-foot cord on the combined receiver. She had forcefully disconnected it, herself.

"Esme," Vivienne said. "Did you succeed in contacting Bell?"

"Yes, ma'am," Esme replied. "They said they could have an inspector here this afternoon."

"An inspector? Contact them again. Remind them who you work for. Tell them that if the telephone lines on this floor aren't functioning by the end of the day, so help me God, I will launch a competing service next year, and all of my friends will use it. Tell them that I will open a free engineering college for women only, give all of their daughters jobs, and none of them will get married until they're forty. And trousers! Every one of the lady engineers at the Walker Telephone Company will wear trousers!"

She started to march back to the elevators, her fury stoked anew, but she stopped and turned to Mrs Shields, across the aisle from Esme.

"Is Cranston here?" Vivienne asked.

"He was, ma'am," Mrs Shields said, standing. "He left with someone."

"Please tell me it was a man."

"Oh, yes. Biggest man I have ever seen."

"Thank God. Did he see Cabot?"

"Yes, ma'am."

"Okay, one less thing to be cross about."

Now, she walked to the elevators, her own trousers swishing as she went.

At work, Vivienne had been dressing like a man since she was twenty. Not in the sense of those patriotic women who had insisted on fighting in ancient wars, but in the way of the most daring flappers. For many years, she had been bringing the most fashionable of men's suits to her modiste and having the irrepressible old Parisian copy and alter them to Vivienne's measurements.

It was not that Vivienne wanted to shock the men she worked with, it was subtler than that. For one, it set her apart from the other ladies in the office; bifurcation communicated the seriousness of her work and her opinions. For another, any suits she wore had to be tailored, which meant money, which meant power.

That power was at full force when she stepped out again onto the 17th floor. Her heels clacked through the rank and file of accountants and logisticians, telephone in hand, to the office of Mr Olson, assistant director of Canadian Accounts. By linear footage, this was the closest office to hers that had a clear connection to the switchboard.

One of the padded chairs from reception had been brought in. Vivienne looked at it disdainfully. She thrust her desk telephone at Olson.

"Connect this, please," she said, then stepped back out into the desk pool. "I need two men," she announced. When four presented themselves, she continued: "I want that big chair out." With a glance back into Olson's office, she said: "And the coat rack. Apologies, Mr Olson, but I need the room. In fact, take the day off. Someone will punch out for you."

"Are you sure, Miss Walker?" Mr Olson replied, unhooking his own phone from the line and getting the cable into hers.

"Of course," she smiled. "There's no telling how long this will take and if you're not going to get any work done, you may as well do it outside."

"Oh, I can still get things done," he insisted.

"Fred," Vivienne countered.

"Yes, ma'am. Thank you, Miss Walker."

The boys cleared most of Olson's office out, even pushing his desk back a foot. Then, they left the Acting CEO to her own devices. Alone in the office, Vivienne considered taking off her shoes but there was no carpet and she was still at work.

"Hello," she said into the receiver. "Please reconnect me with Toronto."

"Yes, ma'am," replied the switch girl.

Even as she waited, Vivienne began to pace. Sitting while talking on the telephone didn't suit her. It was far too easy to get distracted. The cord on Mr Olson's phone was not even two feet long. She could hardly stand up while using it, much less keep her mind focused with the subconscious business of walking back and forth; thus bringing her own down.

"Vivienne?" The phone grumbled.

"Martin, so sorry to keep you waiting. The technical troubles continue. I'm considering starting a phone company."

"Of course, you are," Martin replied.

Martin Walker was the director of Walker Transport in Canada. It was a semi-autonomous branch of the Walker Corporation. The position had been given to him by the board in 1917, after he failed in a bid to take over the whole nine yards.

Martin's father had been the President of the Walker Corporation before his death in 1903. James Walker, Vivienne's father, had taken over. He had offered Martin a position when he finished university, but the boy had refused. Martin had then used up his inheritance trying to go into business for himself. When James died and Cranston was named his successor, Martin had attempted to get the chair back. The board decided that his independent business record disqualified him, especially since Vivienne was intimately familiar with the company, already. They had given Transport to Martin as a consolation, but also as a reserve position.

If Cranston hadn't returned, the matter would have been revisited. Now that Cranston was back and avoiding his duties, Martin saw an opportunity. One big failure on Vivienne's part would give him grounds to organize a no-confidence vote.

"As I was saying," Martin drawled, "this latest extension of the Volstead Act is the last straw. Hiram Walker & Sons, Seagram & Sons, Gooderham & Worts...they all want to renegotiate their contracts. Fillion over at Seagram said they would make more money rumrunning than renewing their contracts with us."

"Tell them they'll have to wait until their contracts are up. How much longer do those contracts have?"

"Hiram & Sons is up next month. Seagram is just before Christmas. We have until next summer with G&W, but they are trying to leverage the bankruptcy clause against us."

"Okay, tell Uncle Edward that his current contract has a family discount on it and if he's going to be a stinker, we'll just treat him like anyone else."

Martin sighed. "We knew this was going to happen. We should have been strategizing about this months ago."

"No one was stopping you from strategizing."

"I have trucks, Vivienne! What in God's name am I supposed to do with trucks full of liquor during Prohibition?"

Vivienne wheeled, as if she could turn to face her cousin. "These are your relationships! I have been dealing with exporters in Great Britain, Jamaica, Italy, France…Japan! Have you ever tried to read a contract translated from Japanese? It's like hearing one side of a conversation a man is having with himself."

"So, our domestic partners can go hang while you kowtow to Orientals?"

"Walker Trading didn't make its fortune taking beaver pelts to the world."

"Do you have any idea how influential Seagram is? If we lose them, a third of our produce revenue will follow. Without our domestic partners, there will be no one to sell our imports to!"

"I am fully fucking aware, Martin."

"Then, why have you let this sneak up on you? It can't take that long for your nails to dry."

And that was Martin showing his hand.

"Maybe you're right." Vivienne grinned. "I can put together a strategic team and have them start drawing up contracts. We'll bring Uncle Edward and the chairs of Seagram and G&W out to Silkhaven. We'll make a summit of it. That way, I can rectify the situation myself and you can go back to playing with your trucks."

"Now, hold on a minute!"

Gotcha, Vivienne mouthed. Of course, now that Vivienne saw that was the game, she could play to win. "Yes?" she asked her sputtering cousin.

"As you say," Martin struggled to find the words. "These are my relationships."

"Does that mean you've stumbled onto a strategy to keep them in line?"

"I can't formulate any strategies before I know what latitude I have."

That's right, puppy. Vivienne thought. *Remember that you're on a leash.* "Of course," she said out loud. "Put together some meetings, the fun kind. Take them hunting or golfing, whatever it is they like. Find out what they want and draft me a report. I'll see what we can spare and you can begin negotiating with Hiram & Sons by the 20th."

Martin wasn't quite ready to roll over, though. "That will be too little, too late. We're practically in last minute negotiations with them already."

Vivienne felt her brow begin to furrow. She pressed two fingers into her skin to smooth it without smudging her foundation. "Offer them an investment on a small batch." She was furiously trying to remember exactly how much they had made on Canadian Club in 1919. "Tell them I will personally bankroll a thirty barrel batch of blended rye aged ten years. Start at ten dollars per gallon, but don't agree to more than thirteen. Payable over three years, but only if they renew and exclusivity is non-negotiable."

"Vivienne," Martin said shortly. "That's hardly a patch."

"It's a gesture. It will get them to the table. And remind them that Quebec has already repealed its prohibition; and King Charles Island and Nova Scotia have been wet as fish since April of last year. Domestic sales will all return in the next two or three years. No one, and I do mean no one, can guarantee them sales to both Japan and Quebec. No one but us. Sales to Japan brought in nearly seventy-five percent of our whiskey sales to Britain, last year."

"Still, they can't stay in the black with sales as they stand."

"Start with the small batch, Martin. Thirty barrels, blended rye, ten years; start at a sawbuck, but no more than thirteen. That's the deal you make on the green. Once they are at the table, you can offer them up to an extra three dollars per gallon, but remember that it's your warehouses that'll hold what we can't sell."

That three dollars came out to twice what anyone else could offer for overseas shipping. Vivienne could hear Martin chewing his lip over the wire. He wanted to push her into a bad deal, but he had not the first idea what Walker Trading's books looked like.

"Alright," Martin sounded deflated. "I'll get Uncle Edward on the phone."

"Do. Let me know how the game goes." She almost threw in a barb about his handicap, but decided to let him walk away with his ego intact, this time.

Chapter 8:
Saint Moon

When Vivienne returned to the 19th floor, a small army of men in cheap, but crisp brown suits were standing about. They had bags over their shoulders and were in the process of receiving tea from the various executive secretaries. Vivienne made her way to her office accompanied by a chorus of 'sorry, ma'am's to rival Handel.

Once she got to her door, she found Esme sat at her desk very pointedly writing something while Mrs Shields talked with a man about Vivienne's age wearing a small bowtie with a flat cap under his arm.

"Here is the woman you want to see," Mrs Shields told the man, gesturing at Vivienne.

The man turned and reached automatically for his head, only to remember where his hat was and grin at his own mistake. He did a sort of Buster Keaton pantomime of tipping his hat, then extended a hand. "Ira Blank," he said. "Bell Telephone. And you are?"

Vivienne, primarily concerned with why her secretary was sitting, pointed at the door to her office. The ground glass of the door had her name clearly printed on it. When Mr Blank seemed unclear on the meaning of her gesture, she said: "Vivienne Walker."

Blank fished in his jacket pocket and pulled out a paper folded into quarters. He consulted this. "V. Walker?" he asked.

"Yes," Vivienne replied, then thrust her phone with its long cord into his hands. "Come with me." She led him into her office where, to her surprise, Mr Cabot was waiting. The old man was standing at her book shelf, casually reading something with a blue binding. "Mr Cabot," she said. "What a surprise."

He folded the book closed and held it reverently with both hands. "Yes, I came looking for your brother."

"His is the other door," she said. "Mr Blank, please reconnect that phone."

"I know," Cabot replied, ignoring the engineer. "He is not in at the moment. I thought you might know where he is."

"I haven't seen him. Did you speak with Mrs Shields?"

"Yes, she said he left with a very tall man a couple hours ago."

"Then, you know as much as I do. Excuse me," she turned and called Esme. When the young, mulatto woman was inside, Vivienne continued. "Esme, this is Mr Blank. Mr Blank, this is Esme, my secretary. She will be handling the client side of your visit. Is that a problem for either of you?"

"No, ma'am." Esme answered giving Mr Blank an I-told-you-so look.

Blank, still untangling Vivienne's long cord, sputtered for a moment.

"It was a yes or no question, young man," Cabot added.

"No..." Blank managed. "No, I suppose. It's just...well..."

"It's just that you were so struck by Miss Esme's beauty that you forgot yourself," Cabot continued sharply. "Is that it?"

"Alright," Blank conceded. He turned to Cabot, who gestured towards the women. "I'm very sorry, Miss Esme." Blank said. "I was out of line, before, but I'm at your service, now."

"Leave that," Vivienne pointed at the phone. "Go let the rest of your men know."

"Yes, ma'am." Blank hustled out of the room and Esme followed him, closing the door behind her.

"What can I do for you?" Vivienne asked Cabot, crossing behind her desk. Outside, Blank was calling for the attention of his engineers.

"I met with your brother earlier," he said, putting the book back in place. "It did not go well."

"Oh, dear, what did he say?"

"Something impertinent, but the details are unimportant. The board is very concerned about the lack of progress regarding the Saint Moon contract. It is our collected opinion that things would go smoother if he were to become more involved."

"I shouldn't think so. They would much rather deal with me."

"That was Cranston's opinion, as well. How is it that you have reached this conclusion?"

"The both of us met with their representatives back in March. You could have cut the air with a knife. They flat out refused to discuss any terms of the contract with him in the room."

Cabot moved to the small chair facing the desk. "May I?"

"Of course."

Cabot sat. "It was Saint Moon that proposed this partnership. Why would they refuse to deal with the CEO?"

"I can't say for sure, but it seemed to be because Cranston had served in the Praetorian Guard."

"Yes, he mentioned that. Do you have any insight on why that would matter?"

"Why would he tell me? I'm just his sister."

"He seemed reluctant to explain it to me, as well." His eyes fell on the still disconnected phone. "You understand why we need Cranston to take a more active role in the business."

"I understand why it seems we need him, but we have done just fine without him. The Walker Corporation has recovered from the loss of its wartime contracts faster than any other company in North America. Even with the losses we are sustaining, now, due to the Volstead Act, our investors could do no better."

"You have performed your duties admirably, so far, but the board is concerned with the future. During these chaotic years, people have made allowances on account of the war, but we fear those allowances may come to an end, any day."

"You mean, with all the men back from Europe, they won't be so patient with a dame running things?"

"Indeed, and then there are much further future concerns." Cabot snapped his lips for whatever reason it was that old men did so. "The sudden loss of your parents goes to show just how fragile a thing life is. We were fortunate that James had a child as capable as yourself to take his place. Neither you nor your brother are in such a position."

Vivienne drew in a long breath. "The board would like it very much if I were to find a gentleman to impregnate me?"

"If you insist on being blunt, yes."

"What about Cranston?"

Cabot fixed her with a serious look. "Cranston can't be impregnated."

"Mr Cabot," Vivienne chuckled. "A bon mot! I never thought I would see the day."

He held out his hands in a faux showman's bow. "That's my one for the year. To answer your real question, the board would be most pleased to see both of you starting families. However, the duties of motherhood would keep you from the office for some time. During those years, much of the day-to-day would fall on Cranston; a burden he is not ready to shoulder."

"I see," Vivienne nodded. She had her doubts about any gentleman being able to impregnate her. There was more than one drunken indiscretion in her past and nothing had come of any of them.

"So, you see, there is a need to bring Cranston back into the fold. Yes, attitudes about your gender are an inconvenience, but you have proven apt to keep the ship moving forward. However, there are seas on the horizon that will demand Cranston's captaincy. That aside, we cannot lose this opportunity with Saint Moon."

"I understand." Vivienne nodded. "And I do know what's at stake."

"No, you don't." Cabot retorted. "None of us do and that's just the point. Whatever Saint Moon is planning with its vaccine project, the Rose and Chain needs to know sooner than later. The eugenicists are gaining ground in North America. They must be thwarted." Cabot nodded to himself then eased up onto his feet. "*Nuovissimi primi,*" he said.

"*Et primi nuovissimi.*" Vivienne answered.

At 4pm, the 19th floor was still swarming with Bell technicians coordinating with the building's handful of on-sight fix-it men. Vivienne stood outside her door watching the young men in their brown suits carefully dismantle the wainscoting and bits of floor to get at the telephone wires. She had considered taking the rest of the day off when it became clear that this enterprise would last the rest of the business day. However, she had an indecent attraction to men being useful.

The charm was, no doubt, lost on the sort of women who married that sort of man; but Vivienne was daily surrounded by men who earned the price of a horse by doing nothing more than debating the relative qualities of Mary's Pickford and Minter over gimlets before shaking hands on the price of rubber or sugar or parrot feathers. A man earning fifteen-hundred a year on little more than elbow grease and know-how was exotic perfume to her.

Vivienne caught herself glancing at Cranston's door like it would change something. He had come in, today; she reminded herself. He and Cabot had met and, presumably, settled whatever bug was in Cabot's ear. She hadn't heard a peep from behind the elevators all day, which was as good as dealings with the board ever got. Yes, Cranston had found some excuse to leave, but it was a male excuse, this time.

All of these things were improvements. It had taken almost a year to get Cranston to set foot in the building. Naturally, he never spoke to her about what had transpired in the war. For the first few months, he hadn't spoken to her about much of anything, not even his breakfast order, but things were improving.

If he had been here, though....

If Cranston had been here, he could have put Martin in his place without needing to promise several thousand dollars to a supplier who may be bluffing. If Cranston had been here, the telephone technicians would have come after the first call. If Cranston had been here, she wouldn't be alone.

No sooner had she allowed the words to articulate in her mind, than Cranston came striding out of the elevators.

"Vivienne!" He called jovially. "Get your coat, we're going to Condé!"

Vivienne straightened up. "I'm not dressed for dinner." She called back across the floor.

"Okay," Cranston replied with no loss of exuberance. "Get your coat, we're going home! And *then* we're going to Condé!"

Chapter 9:
Three Christmases

Christmas, 1912. Silkhaven.

"It *is* practical." Lolita Walker forced a smile that accentuated her already prominent, slavic cheekbones.

Cranston was looking down the length of an umbrella, plain black and cotton. The handle was mostly cork, which felt flimsy in comparison to the weight of the metal making up the thing's skeleton. His father suddenly lunged at the umbrella, snatching a small price tag off the cap. James Walker glared at his daughter for a moment.

"Thank you, Vivienne," Cranston said, polite and unperturbed. She might have actually gotten this from a drug store. He had three others, all of much finer quality, and it almost felt like she was trying to tell him something with this gift. But, if she were going to put that much thought into a gift, it would have been easier to buy him something he actually wanted. There must have been a sign at the drug store suggesting these made good Christmas presents.

They were all gathered in the living room. Father and Cranston had gone out a week ago to chop down the tree, themselves. Mother had draped it with lengths of silk. And Vivienne had made sure everyone at the hotel got their appropriate Christmas bonus. Lolita had insisted that the tree be placed in front of the piano; not actually blocking the keys, should she feel the desire to play, but obscuring them enough that she wouldn't feel obligated to. Hornsby had arranged for a dozen red and green candles to be brought in and had seen to it that the cord of wood by the fire was fresh pine.

With the sofas pulled into a semi-circle around the fire, the family had laid all their presents to one another on the big, driftwood table that had been in the hotel since before it was a hotel. The table where Cranston's great-great-grandfather had had his solitary meals, trying to get the new office for the Walker Trading Co. profitable before sending for his wife and son.

Mother had brought everyone new pajamas on Christmas Eve and they wore them, now, to see what new treasures were to be added to the family's collection, this year. Cranston was unmoved in any direction by the drug store umbrella and Vivienne pretended not to notice her parents' disapproval, knowing it was going to swing the other way when she unwrapped her gift.

The poorly folded paper and uneven bow were forgivable coming from a man of Cranston's age. Vivienne read the folded square of paper tied to the misshapen bow with a bit of twine: "To Vivienne, love Cranston." She looked up at him through her pale eyebrows. "You sentimental old fool."

Cranston smirked and gave a theatrical sort of shrug.

The rankling of paper temporarily drowned out the sound of James grinding his teeth. Inside was a box and in the box was a pair of moccasins. They had good leather soles and were in her size, but were nonetheless moccasins.

"Honestly," Lolita said under her breath.

The rest of the presents went swimmingly. Vivienne got Father a beautiful quire of stationery for his personal letters and Mother a set of silver throwing knives. ("Now, who's being sentimental?" Lolita had said to her daughter.) Cranston gave Father a bottle of 1865 Glen Garioch that he had won in a poker game, last summer, and to his mother, he gave a mink stole.

Still, it wasn't quite large enough a patch on their parents' ire.

It was after lunch and Cranston was in his bathroom, face lathered, when Father knocked on the half-open door. "Mind if I review your technique?" James asked. He was in his trousers and undershirt with a towel over one shoulder.

"By all means." Cranston stepped aside to give his father room at the sink, while he gave his straight razor a couple strokes across the leather.

"Will we see a mustache from you in the new year?" James asked.

"It's still vexingly thin," Cranston replied.

"If it's any comfort," Father said, "thin of hair about the face means thin of hair about the back. Your Uncle Petro looked like a timberwolf with his shirt off. Be grateful you got your hair from my side and not your mother's."

"I suspect they're going out of fashion, anyway."

"Always going out or coming in." James used Cranston's brush to lather his own face. "Your mother and I do wish that you children would put a bit more into each other's gifts. Christmas is a time for family. I can't help but think if I had doted on your Aunt Lydia a bit more, we would have had more settings at lunch."

Cranston made a noise, signaling his intent to respond, as he ran the razor up his neck. "I don't think Vivienne particularly wants me to dote on her."

"Only because you haven't." James dipped his foamy razor in the sink's milky water before preparing his next stroke. "Women never really appreciate a man's attention until they get used to it. I just don't want you two sending each other polite letters at Christmas in thirty years' time."

"Nor I," Cranston nodded. "I suppose."

"Some effort is all." James said, bringing the razor to his chin. "You'll use the umbrella."

Mother always insisted that Vivienne help clean up meal settings. She needed to be intimately familiar with them. The lady of the house may not set the table, but she was responsible if anything was wrong with it. After the Christmas goose was cleared and the new linen put down, Vivienne was brusquely ushered into her parents' suite; the door conveniently opposite the entrance to the main dining room.

The first room of the suite was, officially, Father's study. A denser collection of bookcases lined the innermost wall than in the living room. Father's desk and his good chair—much cozier than the antique one in his office—were on the north end and two reading chairs sat on the southern end.

Lolita pointed, wordlessly, at one of these. Vivienne smoothed her day skirt before she sat and Lolita shut the door. "You shit on your brother!" Lolita declared, allowing her Novgorod accent to come out in full force.

"He got me a child's costume!" Vivienne snapped.

"You are older! He plays games with you because you do not treat him like a man!"

"Perhaps, next year, I'll get him a whole prostitute. He'd like that."

Lolita wheeled and slapped Vivienne across the face. "You do not say that word on a holy day."

"I apologize, mother," Vivienne said quietly, pointedly not reaching up to touch her cheek.

"A cheap umbrella." Lolita crossed her arms and shook her head. Then, she went to Father's desk and lit one of his cigarettes. Just one.

Vivienne looked out the window, cheek throbbing. She had been twenty the first time her mother had struck her on the face. A reminder that womanhood had not changed their relationship: 'I can't put you over my knee, but I am still your mother.'

"A cheap umbrella," Lolita repeated. "You don't love Cranston?"

"I do. Not every day, but on the whole."

"And what would you buy him on a day that you love him?"

"Something funnier." Vivienne shrugged.

"Where did these children come from?"

"It's our way, Mother," Vivienne said vaguely.

"He gave you flowers for your birthday. I saw them."

"He *sent* me flowers. He couldn't have borne to give them to me, in person."

"So, you shit on him because you must look him in the eyes?"

"I promise, Mother: Cranston took no offense."

"Of course, not!" Lolita said, marching back across the room, trailing a line of blue smoke. "You taught him that 'shit' is a sister's word for 'love.'"

Vivienne looked at her hands; folded, involuntarily, in her lap.

"In the house," Mother continued, "you will wear the moccasins. I want him to see you wearing them."

"Yes, Mother."

Lolita reached down, handing Vivienne the cigarette. "A whole...." She didn't say the word because it was Christmas, but she did say the rest with a Silkhaven accent. "As if you could buy him just a part."

"I know," Vivienne said, drawing in a tobacco breath. "I was disappointed with myself as I was saying it."

"I would have said: 'Perhaps, next year, I'll get him a cooch dancer.' Same idea, but it rolls off the tongue better and none of those words offends God."

"The other word is in the Bible."

"There are parts of the Bible that one reads in church and some that one does not. The point is: you really must work on your bon mots. A good hostess is always prepared for a drunken cad."

Christmas, 1913. Silkhaven.

Vivienne's gift was not in the sturdy, manila stock of last year. Instead, it was bound up in a silk kerchief emblazoned with the Quirk's Department Store crest. The Quirks were cousins of the Walkers that had been partners in the business for a hundred and fifty years. After Captain William Quirk retired from privateering, he had opened a curio shop, specializing in the less practical of exotic goods brought in by the Walker Trading Co. The Walker Corporation had acquired the Department Store line in 1897, when that generation of William's descendants had needed capital for a mining venture.

Wrapped in his new pajamas, Cranston watched Vivienne pull apart the expertly knotted kerchief—all Quirk's employees were taught sailing knots—to reveal a bottle of l'Heure Bleu. *So that's what it's called.* Cranston remarked to himself. Mother smiled at him and Father gave an approving nod. There had been reminders not to repeat last year as early as October.

"Do you know?" Vivienne said, eyeing the bottle with nothing akin to surprise. "I'm almost out of mine."

Cranston shrugged. "Mother let that slip."

"I did no such thing," Lolita interjected, indignantly.

"Who else?" He said.

"I..." Mother took a moment, trying to remember when she might have said anything about perfume. She furrowed her brow at him. "Or maybe you went poking around in her room."

"Cranston!" Vivienne feigned scandal. "If you ever go poking about in my things again...do keep an eye out for my pearl earrings. I haven't seen them in a month."

"Such accusations!" he replied. "And from my own family."

Father chuckled. "You better pray there's never a murder in this hotel. These viragos will throw you to the detectives with a ribbon tied on."

Mother batted him on the shoulder.

Vivienne leaned forward and picked up a fat, black envelope of some heavier cousin to paper and handed it across to her brother. It was similarly decorated with the Quirk's crest; gold on black. Inside the envelope was a leather envelope-like case with a snap on the fold. Opening this, Cranston extracted a pair of soft, brown driving gloves that flared dramatically above the wrist.

"Oh, Vivienne," he said, taking a moment to drink in the sight of them. "These are beauties."

"I borrowed yours a while back," she said. "I found them of little comfort. Williamson recommended those."

Father studied the gloves from across the driftwood table. "Williamson has expensive taste in gloves."

"Well," Vivienne said coyly. "I suspect they are an aspiration."

"Hmm," Father pursed his lips. "Maybe he deserves a pair of his own."

There were no disturbances to the rest of the day. At ten, they dressed for lunch. The goose was carved, consumed, and cleared. They spent the afternoon preparing Boxing Day gifts for the domestic staff.

Father was seeing to a pair of Canadian Club bottles in tissue-lined boxes. One was 12-years and the other 20. Placing the cards on the lids, he was nervously checking that he gave the 20-year to Hornsby. With that sorted to his satis-faction, he called: "Viv."

"Yes, Father?" she answered, looking up from the ribbon she was tying around a copy of Pollyanna.

"What were those gloves you gave Cranston?"

"Driving gloves," she answered, truly knowing no more.

"Yes, yes, but what kind?"

"Oh, I don't remember." She cast a look at her brother. "He wrote it down for me."

"Here, Father," Cranston said, fetching the leather case from the driftwood table.

"Very good," James said, taking them out and inspecting them. "My, they do look comfortable." He found a blank card and copied the details onto it before handing the gloves back to Cranston. "I think I'll make the old boy's Boxing Day a proper treat." Then, went in search of his shoes.

Vivienne gave Cranston a wide-eyed expression and he tugged at his collar in jest.

"Darling," James called. "I'm going to stop in at Quirk's. Do you need anything?"

"It's Christmas. They'll be closed."

"Perks of owning the place, my dear: I have a key."

Night fell and Cranston was adjusting his white bow tie when a soft rapping came at his door. There was Vivienne, in a voluminous fox fur below the daring, bear-fur hat she had acquired a decade ago when they had visited Moscow. There had been a vain hope of getting to Novgorod and perhaps finding some of Mother's people, but it was not to be.

"That was an awful trick you tried on Mother," she said.

"I was on the spot," he answered. "I don't think any harm was done."

"It was still dirty."

"l'Heure Bleu; is that your usual?"

"For black tie and better, yes."

"Millicent was asking about it last summer. She'll be pleased to finally know."

"Are you seeing her, tonight?" Vivienne asked, amused.

"It's likely. She loves the Mickmack. And where are you off to?"

"The *Marie Antoinette* to watch the fireworks."

"Escorted by?"

"Ricardo."

"The bull fighter? Is he still around?"

"Until spring, yes."

"Wouldn't it be a gas if he asked you to marry him?"

"Ha!" Vivienne ejaculated. "He'd end up in the St. Lawrence."

Cranston set his top hat in place and pocketed his watch. "The poor devil."

As he fetched his coat, she asked: "Aren't you worried that Williamson will tell Father he knew nothing about the driving gloves?"

"No, it's a gift," Cranston said, folding his greatcoat over one arm. "Neither of them will be keen on discussing the particulars."

"Next year, we should coordinate a bit more."

"I suppose. It got dicey down there." He held out his free arm, she took it and he led her down to the elevator. "We're on our way!" He called through the open door to their parents' suite.

"Have a good night," Father called.

"Be home in time to get some rest," Mother added. "You need to be in good spirits for when the staff arrive for lunch."

"Yes, Mother," the siblings said in near unison.

Hornsby was waiting for them in the elevator. It dinged as they descended, floor by floor.

Back in the study, Lolita looked at her husband over the

top of her book. "You almost rumbled them."

"Do you think I should have let it be?" James asked. He was at his desk, writing his sister, Lydia, a polite letter.

"They're conspiring, but they're doing it together. In the end, that's what we wanted."

"Alright, I won't poke at it, next year."

"You can poke a little." Lolita smiled. "We wouldn't want them getting indolent."

Christmas, 1914. Silkhaven.

Vivienne had been the one to buy new pajamas for the family, this year.

She hadn't slept more than three hours. Restless, she had gone down to the living room at 4am and began unpacking the box of decorations that Hornsby had set by the fireplace a week ago. The tree—a purchased one, for the first time that Vivienne could remember—had an angel on the top and a few lengths of silk, but still not even half finished. No candles had been put out, no garlands hung.

Yet, when Mother and Father emerged from their suite, they found the living room in full yuletide regalia. Festooned like any other year. Vivienne was pacing a little, a plate of toast in one hand.

"Toast?" she said, covering her mouth. "There's cinnamon and ginger on these." She swallowed her mouthful and pointed at another plate on a side table. "Those have jam."

Mother and Father, in their usual dressing gowns, looked at the decorations with uncertain emotions. Lolita sniffed, looking as if she had done a good deal of crying, already. Neither of them said anything and Vivienne stood in the midst of the yule trimmings, dressed in her new pajamas, and holding a cooling plate of seasoned toast.

The frost on the tall windows creaked.

"Yes," James said, his voice soft. "Toast with jam for me." He wrapped an arm around Lolita and tried to push her forward, but her feet only moved a half step closer. "Oh, dear," he continued in a more usual tone of voice. "We've forgotten our new pajamas. How silly. We can't very well do Christmas without our new pajamas, can we?" He shifted his arms and began ushering Lolita back into their suite. "Come along, dear, we must dress."

The door shut and Vivienne ran back up to her room. She hadn't been sure if they would do presents; Mother had not brought any out, last night. However, Father seemed to be of a mind for them. Her gift for Father was in a handsome, wooden box and Mother's was wrapped in green tissue. She brought both of them down from her room and placed them on the driftwood table.

While she waited for the re-emergence of her parents, Vivienne fetched the tray of eggnog ingredients from the bar in the small dining room. Usually reserved for a lunch-time aperitif, she thought they might start a bit sooner. It also occurred to her that Mother might not be in a condition to mount the stairs, today.

Father came out first, bearing two packages. From beside the driftwood table, he said: "This one is yours." He held one package up, then set it on the end of the table where Vivienne was accustomed to sit. "And this is for your mother." He set it opposite the first. Four packages was a meager thing in their house. Surveying the empty-looking table, James muttered: "Damn it, I should have got you two each."

"I have a third," Vivienne said, tears forming at the corners of her eyes. "I didn't bring it down because I thought it might upset Mother."

James opened his arms and Vivienne—a grown woman of twenty-eight—fell into her daddy's embrace. She didn't cry, just sighed heavily into his silk shirt, feeling the waning strength of his aging arms around her. He kissed her hair.

"Go get it," he said.

"Are you sure?" she asked, blinking back nascent tears.

"Yes. And go into his room. I left a package for him there. Bring that down, as well. We're only counting the days."

Vivienne nodded, then rushed up the stairs and opened Cranston's door.

Chapter 10:
Condé

Vivienne had a long history with exciting men: matadors, auto racers, two of the Oyster Bay Roosevelts. Hardly an actor or singer of any renowned could pass through Silkhaven's Dauphin Street without at least having dinner with her; provided they were bachelors. Vivienne was no one's little vacation from their wife and, with a hotel full of maids, she could be sure to get the finest intelligence on any man worthy of notice.

The trouble with exciting men was that they were used to women being excited by them. Experience of easy success gave them expectations. For this reason, Vivienne's collection of evening dresses was largely unexciting. The necklines were a little higher than fashionable and her ankles barely exposed; nor were the older pieces fitted for expansive corsets. Her smaller, *a la mode* collection was reserved for society functions where she needed to impress entire rooms and whatever escort she scrounged up knew he wouldn't be getting much attention.

Going to dinner with her brother, however, unbound her completely.

Vivienne had commissioned the violet dress three months earlier, but had not had an occasion to wear it. It had a narrow, square neckline that fell closer to her waist than her collar bone. It was trimmed in carnation pink. The line of the collar continued down the full length of the dress with Vivienne's bare skin being replaced by a pattern of white flowers. Making the neckline even more daring was a broad, pink, lace choker that covered more of her throat than one of her grandmother's blouses.

There was a matching cloche hat into which she tucked her hair, save a pair of blonde curls. She finished with a voluminous, but sheer black frock with black gloves and boots.

Cranston had been vague about his afternoon activities on the drive over. An old friend had stopped by and they had gone out into the country for lunch. There was a thread of giddiness to him, tonight, and Vivienne knew she was being buttered up for something. He was going to tell her something he thought she wouldn't like and a dinner at Condé was there to soften her up. Little did he realize that seeing him this animated for the first time in six years was more softening than any dinner could manage.

When they arrived, Cranston gave the name 'Bakurov' for their reservation. It was their mother's maiden name and one they used for reservations to avoid gossip columnists. The maitre d' was a man that Vivienne didn't recognize and who didn't seem to recognize them. From his accent, he was Quebecois. From the precision of his manners, this was not his first posting.

Their table was on the second floor near a window and the restaurant's band. The window, which was more like a glass door, was open onto the restaurant's balcony and the last of the warm summer nights. The band was doing their usual thing, playing sweet renditions of Irving Berlin and Fred Fisher tunes.

Cranston immediately cracked open the menu and began surveying their options.

"Are you going to tell me what this is all about?" Vivienne asked.

"Let's order, first," Cranston replied.

"You're being obtuse." She told him, opening her own menu.

Cranston looked over his menu with the devil in his eyes. "Espionage demands it."

The word gave Vivienne a pleasant little shiver. "What, now?"

"Let's order," he said. "People always order before they talk."

"*Men* order before they talk. For women, everything in a restaurant is garnish."

"Yes, well, do let me play my part, then."

Vivienne could hardly focus on her menu. The idea that they were embarking on some kind of espionage was too thrilling a prospect to attend to anything else. She had read the soup options three times without registering what either of them was when a woman's voice behind her called out: "Cranston?"

Well-mannered, Vivienne inclined an ear, but did not turn her head. Cranston stood and smiled. "Abi!" he said, taking a step away from the table.

Abigail Monroe was a cousin of the Bourbons and had married Charles Monroe of the Gouverneurs. (Charles' grandfather had changed his name when he entered politics, intending to one day become governor of Virginia and wanting to avoid the whimsy of nominative determinism.) The Monroes were a Virginia Conservative family and lacked any of the iconoclastic tendencies of the Atlantic Virginians. Charles' father, Andrew, had moved to King Charles Island in the 1880's to found a bank with his friend, Arthur Cabot. Andrew had married one of the Toronto Blakes and the son was continuing the tradition of moving up in the world.

Vivienne turned slightly in her chair as Abigail approached. Abigail and Cranston exchanged kisses before she turned to notice Vivienne. A look of surprise fleeted across Abigail's face.

"Vivienne?" Abigail grinned. "I was ready to give the old 'Here There Be Dragons' speech to whatever ingénue Cranston had roped in, this time, but...well." She laughed.

'Here There Be Dragons' was a speech that Vivienne had written back in 1907, when her brother was first becoming a danger to society girls.

"I'm surprised you remember it." Vivienne smiled back.

"I admit that the memory is a bit spotty, these days." Abigail rubbed her protruding belly.

"How far along are you?"

"Four months," Abigail said. "I expect I'll start to really balloon out any day. Oh, do say you'll come to the christening. I know it's a long way off, but you are such a busy woman, I don't know how else to get on your calendar."

"Of course," Vivienne replied. "I wouldn't miss it."

Vivienne had not been to a christening in a few years and was sure she was only being invited because of the situation. She fully expected the invitation card to be mysteriously lost in the mail.

Abigail turned back to Cranston, her smile widening. "I haven't seen you in ages, just ages!"

"Yes, well," Cranston nodded. "I was rather busy in France."

"Oh, you," she patted him on the arm. "I really wanted to invite you to our Christmas party last year, but Charles wanted to limit the guest list to family and business partners." She leaned in a little. "Between you and me, I think he was worried about his mother's family."

The Toronto Blakes and Silkhaven Walkers had been rivals once, with the matter firmly settled in the Walkers' favor.

"You may be right," Cranston said. "The last time I saw you was at your engagement party."

"It was not! We danced at the le Bon's Summer Welcome in '14."

"Did we?"

"You were spiffed."

Before Cranston could answer that, he noticed Abigail's husband approaching. "Charlie," he said.

"Cranston," Charles took a position behind Abigail and didn't extend a hand.

"Charles," Vivienne said, pointedly not extending a hand either.

"Vivienne," Charles gave her a small bow.

"Cranston," Abigail continued. "Did you know Charles was stationed in Italy? You two were practically neighbors."

"Yes, just the Keizer between us."

Abigail laughed the way girls always did at his jokes.

"You really must come around for dinner, sometime," Abigail went on. "That darned war delayed my wedding by two whole years and Charlie won't spill a single bean about it. Maybe if I get the two of you tipsy, I can finally hear what all the fuss was about."

"Tight lips are a hard habit to break."

"Oh, gosh. Vivienne, do help me, here."

"Dinner would be delightful," Vivienne told her.

"Come along, dear," Charles said. "We haven't seen our table, yet. The maitre d' is waiting."

She batted her husband's chest. "We still need to set a date with the Walkers."

"Say what," Charles smiled for the first time. "Cranston and I will work out the particulars the next time we're at the officers' club. Fine by you, Cranston?"

Cranston nodded. "Yes, that's fine."

"Alright," Abigail pouted. "We'll leave you two recluses to your dinner, but I was serious about my invitations." She reached out and straightened Cranston's tie. "No more being a stranger."

"I promise."

They said their good-byes and Charles whisked his wife away to the other side of the band.

"What was that?" Vivienne asked.

Cranston looked over at the band for a moment. "I think it was *Peg O' My Heart*."

"No, between you and Charles."

"I don't know what you mean."

"If he had been any less polite, you could have challenged him to a duel. And since when do you go to the officers' club?"

"I don't." He looked up at her, but only made it to her chin. "I'm not a member."

"But you were a captain."

"In the Praetorian Guard. It was a different chain of command."

"So, why is Charles taking digs at you? You didn't sleep with Abigail, did you? Tell me the child is not yours."

"Vivienne! Of course not." He folded his menu.

"Is it just because you were in the Praetorian Guard?" she asked, but received no answer. "First the Saint Moon boys and now the entire officers' club? What is this stigma surrounding you all?"

Cranston shook his head. "I'm not drunk enough to explain that. And I might ask why you are just now hearing about a society woman's pregnancy."

Vivienne sighed. "I don't have the time for that sort of thing. I have been thoroughly trussed up with running the company. That kind of news doesn't make it up to the nineteenth floor."

A waiter arrived and Cranston made the unilateral decision to skip the fish course. Vivienne hastily ordered the *tortue claire* and almost immediately wished she had gone with the *creme reine Hortense*.

"Alright," Vivienne said when the waiter was gone. "So neither of us have been attending our society obligations."

That devil's look came back into Cranston's eyes. "I have just the way to resume."

"Espionage?" She asked under the din or the band.

"Do you remember Rosamund Syme?"

"From Boston?"

"Formerly, yes. Her father has a sanitarium on the island, now."

"Yes," Vivienne nodded. "Where the elderly have orgies."

"Pardon?" cried Cranston.

"That's the rumor." She shrugged.

He shook his head. "I suppose I can imagine why." He explained, as best he could, how Rosamund had taken up the cause of bringing her father's research to the masses. "She quite openly encourages women to...encounter themselves intimately."

"You mean 'masturbate'?" Vivienne asked, saucily reaching for her cigarettes.

The band was not loud enough to give them absolute privacy, but Cranston took Vivienne's openness as a challenge. "Indeed, I'm not sure what the girls are calling it."

Vivienne lit her cigarette. "I read Rosamund's book."

"You could have said so!"

"Men dislike being informed that a lady already knows something he is explaining."

Cranston lunged forward quickly and snatched a cigarette from Vivienne's case. He stuck his prize between his lips and gestured for the lighter. "I'm not 'men.'"

"That's for sure," Vivienne replied, lighting Cranston's cigarette for him. "'Men' don't keep me waiting."

"Anyway, as you may already know, Rosamund has run afoul of the Church of the Hero Jesus."

"The ones with that awful statue out front?"

"The same." Cranston found his sister's cigarettes strangely sharp. There was something added for flavor, but he couldn't tell what. "Their founder is running for senate against Rosamund's uncle and is using her to tarnish his opponent."

"And this was your afternoon appointment?" Vivienne said, eyes narrowing. "Mrs Shields said you left with a giant."

"That was Mr Lucien Gabriel." Cranston picked a loose bit of tobacco off his tongue. "We met in the war. He was in the Praetorian Guard, as well. By a twist of fate, Lucien is working as Rosamund's bodyguard. He's the one that foiled the kidnapping."

"Kidnapping?" Vivienne exclaimed loud enough that the bass player looked over.

"Did I not mention that?"

Vivienne had her elbows on the table, eyes wide, and attention full on her brother. "You know you didn't!"

"Yes, a family of CHJ devotees attempted to bundle her into a car in Baltimore, I think it was."

"I'll be!"

Cranston smirked, gratified to have Vivienne hooked. "Lucien isn't convinced that they won't try again, hence coming up here."

"But they have a church here!"

"And that's why he came to me." Cranston leaned in, as well. "Keeping Rosamund at the retreat does increase her security, but Lucien is worried that the CHJ is secreting an agent into the retreat, itself."

"A spy?"

"He asked for my help in smoking them out."

"You're doing it, of course?"

"Of course. My first step is intelligence gathering and I could use your help."

Vivienne exhaled a cloud. "Me?"

"Tomorrow is Wednesday. I thought we could attend a prayer meeting."

"You want to go to church?"

"The Church of the Hero Jesus, yes. It's a reconnaissance mission. Two pairs of eyes are better than one, plus you'll be able to talk to the women."

The waiter brought them a plate of olives, celery, and salted nuts along with their wine.

"A protestant church?" Vivienne mused over their appetizer. "Whatever shall I wear?"

Part 3:
SPIES

Chapter 11:
Hotel Bar

September 8th, 1920. Silkhaven.

The ball of white was placid and all encompassing, filling Cranston's vision. It cast no shadows nor gave off any heat, but it felt like looking through a window into a brightly lit chamber awaiting decoration. It filled him with unutterable fear. Not of the ball, not of anything; just fear. Purely chemical, without higher reasoning to give it any direction.

The unrelenting sound of metal slamming against metal seemed a world away. The sharp thunder of artillery melded into a warbling hum that sank to the bottom of his consciousness like silt. And the bone-rattling explosion of the last of the engineers' tunnel bombs registered as little more than a moment's imbalance.

Transfixed in his fear, the whole world was falling away, except for the ball of white. Except for the pocket.

Then, in that halcyon white, something moved. Something not as white as the milky ocean its league-long tentacles propelled it through. He saw it and it saw him and then he heard the voices.

The krakens. The krakens.

Cranston awoke, still hearing distant machine guns. He scrambled up onto his knees and looked around for his trench-sweeper. There was no gun, though, and no battlefield. He wore no uniform, only silk pajamas that clung to the sweat on his back and belly. His hands shook and a part of his mind kept repeating "the krakens, the krakens" again and again.

He didn't bother to look at the clock. He stripped off his clothes and stumbled into his washroom. It was too small for a tub, but he could give himself a sponge bath, enough to remove the night sweat. Then, he put on a fresh pair of pajamas. The shakes had mostly subsided, appearing only as an occasional shudder that ran from his right hand to his shoulder and back.

Deciding there was no gallantry in trying to sleep with a manic arm, Cranston pulled on his dressing gown and the slippers that the hotel staff had gotten him for his birthday.

Cranston's room was at the south end of a corridor that had once led to his grandparents' suite, long-since converted to uncurated family museum space, thanks to that new JP Morgan building spoiling the northern view. The corridor let out onto a balcony of sorts, which had always been known as the small dining room.

A well-stocked bar dominated the eastern side. A dumb-waiter supplied food from the kitchens. Beside the bar was a small, round table, just big enough for four. The western side of the balcony area was devoted to coat hooks and shelves for handbags, suitcases, and shoes.

Cranston began pouring himself a whiskey when a shudder ran through him, causing him to smash the bottle into the corner of the bar. He leapt back, out of range of the glass and spilling whiskey. Cranston steadied himself against the bar and half-wished he could cry. It would relieve the tension.

He was, by no means, above cleaning up his own broken bottle of liquor. It was just that the prospect, in the moment, felt supremely daunting. If he could cry—about the dream, about the 20-year Macallan—perhaps he could get on with it and find a broom; be useful. The daunting feeling beget frustration, and that became one more thing he would-if-he-could cry about.

In the dead of night, all on one's own, and in one's own home no less, a man ought to be able to cry about whatever he pleased. Cry and get back to sleep. There was probably something about that in the Bible and, if there wasn't, there ought to have been.

"Are you coming or going?" Vivienne asked from the hallway.

"Neither," Cranston said, looking up and allowing himself to look frustrated.

Vivienne was wearing a thin dressing gown over a silk shift, baroque lace running down either side for ventilation; the kind Mother had been fond of wearing about the house. Vivienne was nearly as tall as he was and the narrowness of her frame made her seem even taller.

Leaning against the corner of the wall, face impassive, Vivienne surveyed the wreckage of Cranston's drink. "Does that mean I can expect you to be on time tomorrow?"

"That was the plan," Cranston said. "I'm afraid I chose rather too thrilling a story for bed-time. I was hoping a drink would still me, but I've only gone and excited my nerves further."

"Leave it," Vivienne said. "Hornsby will see to it."

"No, I should take care of it."

"You should get some sleep."

"It'll only take a moment. Where is the broom?"

"Wherever the maids keep them."

"Do we really not keep that sort of thing handy?"

She stepped forward, reaching a long and slender arm through the space above the broken glass and spilled whiskey to take the upper portion of the bottle from him.

"I can clean up my own messes."

"Not if you can't find the broom." She dropped the broken bottle neck into a bin, where it crunched under its own weight.

"I think I'll see if Cooper can supply me with a drink. I've shaken my trust in myself for the night."

"Don't get lost. I have too much on my plate to deal with the board complaining about your absence. Plus, we have that prayer meeting. You'll need to be bright eyed and bushy tailed for reconnaissance, Captain." Vivienne pulled her dressing gown around herself and then returned to her room.

He could have told her about the dream. There was a time when he couldn't; a time when he suspected she would think less of him for it. He knew better, now. And yet, there were just certain things one didn't confess to anyone but a lover.

It was nearly one o'clock. He could get to the Mermaid Club by one-thirty, spirit Pearl away and manage to actually sleep by three. But that would require dressing and he wasn't sure he could do up a tie with his hands trembling as they were. So, it was off to Cooper. He didn't change shoes. The slippers the staff had gotten him were perfectly suitable and it would do them good to see him wear them.

At the center of the small dining room was a flight of stairs leading down and east before a landing that turned them west. These stairs brought Cranston into the living room with its two-story windows, grand piano, and copious bookshelves (shut with stained glass doors, lest the sunlight harm the books).

A hall led north from the living room, past the doors to the large dining room and their parents' vacant suite, to the elevator. Reaching the door, he realized that he had not fetched his key. It was not necessary to go down—lest dinner guests become trapped—but it would required to come back up. The night manager could sort that, though.

The private elevator let out onto every floor of the hotel,

though it required a key to open the door, save the penthouse. There was a time when Father had employed a nightman for the family's elevator, primarily to stop Vivienne from sneaking out. When Father caught her using the staff elevator behind the large dining room, that had come to an end.

With the cage already at the penthouse, Cranston saw no reason not to operate it himself. He eased the lever down to begin his descent. He was a fair hand at the cage, but took it slow, tonight; watching the hallways rise and float away, becoming a little less luxurious as they went. Attentive to the dinging bell, Cranston managed to stop the cage only an inch above the first floor, proper.

The night manager, O'Reilly, was there to open the gates for him, having heard the elevator coming. "Good evening, Mr. Walker," he said. "Is there anything I can supply for you?"

"Not for the moment," Cranston replied. "I am merely availing myself of the bar, tonight. Cooper is on duty, yes?"

"Yes, sir."

"Excellent. Have you ever had one of his cocktails?"

"At the Christmas party, sir."

"That was a while ago, wasn't it?"

"In December, sir."

"Far too long. I'll tell him to expect you at the end of your shift."

"Thank you, sir."

"Also, O'Reilly, I failed to bring my key along with me."

"I have mine, sir."

"Good man,"

"Thank you, sir."

Cranston clapped O'Reilly on the shoulder and made his way into the hotel's foyer, waving to those on duty. He knew the night shift far better than the day-people. Most of his comings and goings were nocturnal and those trips he made during the day were utilitarian. Besides, he was far more gregarious after sunset, even on little sleep.

The Walker Grande Hotel bar was the finest public drinking establishment in Silkhaven, and had been so since its opening in 1825. It was on every tourist's guide to the city and, as such, was open twenty-four hours a day. Patronage had been a little irregular, this year, since America passed the Volstead Act. Those coming from the American side of the island were subject to all kinds of rumors about policemen waiting outside to catch drunk citizens.

The exact application of the Volstead Act on the city of Silkhaven—which was technically in America and Canada both—had been a sticky matter. Bourassa had intimated that Canada would be disinclined to assist with anti-smuggling efforts and that had put a stop to the conversation. However, with Meighen in and smuggling becoming a reality, that could change, any day.

One way or another, the bar would remain. It was an exquisite room of dark woods and gilded accents, intended to evoke the sense of Titania and Oberon's forest hideaway. The art nouveau style that the place had most recently been done in was considered to be 'nostalgic', meaning that they would need to redecorate, soon. The Louis John Rhead that Cranston's grandfather had commissioned had been taken down years ago.

Tonight, there were only a few people in. An older couple were sharing a booth and giving off an air of escape. A taxi driver was enjoying a dime beer by the window. And a woman in a charming dress and a half-deflated hair-do was sitting at the bar.

"Good evening, Mr. Walker," Cooper said as Cranston entered.

"How's tricks, Cooper?"

"Fine, sir, just fine. What can I get you?"

"A Macallan 30, please." Cooper knew how Cranston

took it. "Also, I told O'Reilly that he should pop in at the end of his shift. Take care of him, won't you?"

"I'll have a gimlet ready."

"Use the Gordon's."

The barman nodded approvingly. "I will."

Cooper handed Cranston his two-fingers of whiskey with a cherry and then busied himself elsewhere. Cooper was a good man, always knowing exactly where his business started and ended.

Cranston took a sip and considered the drink. He could still hear the whispers: "the krakens, the krakens." The whiskey might get him to sleep, but there was no guarantee that it would keep him there. In the three years since Vimy Ridge, only one thing had ever guaranteed him a full night's sleep.

"Would you like another?" Cranston asked the woman, five seats down from him.

"No, thank you," she smiled. "I mainly just wanted a place to sit."

"You're not a guest, then?"

"Oh, I am." She held up her key. "I just wasn't supposed to be alone in there, tonight."

"A fellow's done you wrong?"

"Six ways to Sunday."

"Where are you from?" Cranston asked, turning in his seat to face her.

"Virginia," she said.

"Well, now...I've never met a man who had the courage to stand up a Virginia girl."

"Then, you've never met a Virginia boy."

"Not since the war, no."

The woman cast an indicative look at Cooper. "He called you 'Mr. Walker.'"

"Only because it's my name."

"You're not a guest, then?"

"No, I am not."

"You're that Mr. Walker?"

He stood and crossed to her, extending his free hand. "Cranston Walker, at your service."

She took it. "Melissa Capshaw,"

"Charmed," Cranston kissed her hand.

"First time a man in a dressing gown has done that. Is this how you greet all your guests?"

"It's a special service."

Melissa turned in her seat, swinging her legs away from the bar and righting her posture. "What other special services do you offer?"

Cranston finished his whiskey. "I have been known to provide quality control inspections of guest rooms."

"Quality *and* control? That's a rare combination in a man."

"You like control?"

"I'm always in control." She sighed, feigning weariness.

"Perhaps I should inspect your room, myself, then. One less care on your mind."

Cranston kept his eyes on Melissa's and handed his glass back across the bar. Cooper took it and surreptitiously slid a paper-wrapped mercury into Cranston's palm.

Cooper was a good man.

Chapter 12:
Sanctuary

The Christ Triumphant was originally cast in 1902 by Andrea White, a student of Louis Amateis. The official story was that she had heard Charles Campbell preaching on the radio, one night, in 1896—the famed 'Victors in the Crown of a Conquering God' sermon—and been so moved that she began drawing the sculpture at 8pm and finished a four-sided sketch by 2am. She had used scrap bronze from her commissioned pieces—stones that the builders rejected—to cast it and presented the piece to the Reverend Campbell, coincidentally, just before the tenth anniversary of the founding of the Church of the Hero Jesus.

The ten-foot-tall sculpture depicted a version of Jesus that looked remarkably like Eugen Sandow with a full beard. He was on one knee with his left hand clutching the throat of the devil, who lay prone and writhing on the ground, while his other arm was raised in preparation for a final, harrowing punch.

As Campbell's church had spread through the Federated States like wildfire, copies of this sculpture had been cast so that every official CHJ temple could have one. It was an eye-sore, but Protestants had never been known for their aesthetic tastes and took any artistic criticisms as a form of religious persecution.

With the rise of mass media in the 19th-century, the faithful had seen an opportunity to preach their faith in new and exciting ways. The fact that this faith was already ubiquitous in the country in no way discouraged them from writing bad novels, worse plays, and occasionally good music that repeated their message almost exclusively for their own consumption; insulating it from any critique.

Children who had grown up with these paltry works, when confronted with things that were well-written, found the experience jarring; and yet, they had long been prepared for this. These other novels and plays and songs were "of the World". If they seemed more alluring, it was not because they were of a higher quality; it was just that sin was always alluring and sin was woven through the very fabric of "the World". Thus, these children carried on the literary and musical traditions set down by mediocre artists until it was a definable style.

The success of these artists was a sign that God's work was being done and the numbers of the faithful were growing. When these artists were financial failures, it was because the devil did not want their message to get out. No one imagined that there was any conflict between these two ideas.

Vivienne understood all of this and was still shocked when she finally saw *The Christ Triumphant* up close. She wasn't sure how faithful a copy this one was, but the notion of the Man of Sorrows contorting his face into a battle cry as he beat a fallen enemy into the ground was more disturbing than the odd proportions of that face. The bulging, overly-defined muscles didn't help.

Cranston, whose arm she held, shuddered as they stared up at it. "Well..." he said quietly, as though they were in an art museum and not a public sidewalk. "It is evocative." Then, a moment later: "Is that Eugen Sandow?"

"I was thinking the same thing," Vivienne replied.

"Do you suppose he knows?"

"He might."

The CHJ temple was three-stories high and occupied the entire block. A small lawn was set behind the violent statue and did nothing to make the building more welcoming, with its doric columns on every corner and thickly muscled stone angels peering down on the streets below. Rather, walking through the green gave Vivienne the sense that she was trekking into a valley, preparing to be swallowed by a dark cave.

There were two sets of doors at the front. One labeled 'Campbell Sanctuary' and the other labeled 'Freeman Sanctuary'. The doors were identical, as were the bronze letters above them, but Vivienne knew better. Segregation was illegal on King Charles Island, but there were ways around it.

The two sanctuaries had been a minor scandal five years ago when the church was built. (Dwarfed by the scandal of such an extravagant building being erected during wartime.) The negro preacher in residence had written a florid editorial on the matter. He cited the Apostle Paul saying "To the Jews, I am a Jew. To the Greeks, I am a Greek." And went on to make the argument that the temple was not segregated by any means. Rather, having separate sanctuaries allowed for Jesus to be "White to the Whites and Colored to the Colored". He followed this by stating that the sanctuaries, in their appointments, were completely identical.

Reading that, Vivienne had wondered why Jesus was never a woman.

She had dressed in a corset for the first time since the war ended. It was a longer style, synching her waist while also adding volume to her backside. This was essential for the dress, itself five years old, which fell strangely on her boyish figure without shaping assistance. While most women found age gradually pushing them ever further from the center of fashionability, Vivienne was among the chosen few whom the last decade had drawn in.

The previous era's silhouette had been a voluptuous one and designers had favored those women who merely needed shaping, rather than padding. The gradual slimming of that silhouette over the last decade had finally arrived at an angular figure, which Vivienne had inherited from her father's side. At last, fashion had turned its favor on her with the added bonus of minimal undergarments.

Cranston, for his part, wore a day suit in brown. It was tailored, but subtly. It was meant to give him the look of a working man. Their business being shipping, there were frequent meetings with seamen and his flashier suits—with their pinstripes, chevrons, and plaid—did not invite the cordial obedience of men wearing a layer of sea salt on their skin.

The Walkers were attending tonight's prayer meeting as potential supplicants. Vivienne smiled as they entered the Campbell Sanctuary doors and were greeted by a young and intentionally homely-looking woman. She wore an apron that had a half-dozen, pulp-paper pamphlets in the pocket.

"Welcome, friends," the Campbellite woman said. "Is this your first time at the Church of the Hero Jesus?"

"Yes, miss," Cranston replied. "First time."

"That's so wonderful! It's always a pleasure to meet future Heroes of Heaven at the beginning of their journey." She rattled off the sentence like a student actor would the To Be or Not to Be speech.

"A journey?" Cranston said. "Good thing I brought my driving gloves."

The Campbellite woman laughed the way that most women did at his jokes. "That's a good one." She took a clipboard and pencil from a nearby desk. "Can I get your names?"

"Thomas and Juliet Bakurov," he said. "Siblings."

Over dinner, Cranston had explained that the key to a good deception was to lie as little as possible. One lie, uncovered, could pull the entire charade apart. Deception was best done by presenting the facts in a misrepresenting order. If your target tried to verify what you said, they would only find truths and thus strengthen the greater falsehood. So, tonight, they went by their middle names and their mother's maiden name; the names they used for restaurant reservations. If they were recognized, they could easily explain that they were incognito. They were, after all, scions of the second-richest family on the island.

Vivienne had been disappointed by this, having hoped they could invent entirely new identities for themselves.

A family came into the foyer behind them. Vivienne turned at the sound of the door opening and saw the maître d' at *Queen Marie-Thérèse*, home to the finest Lobster Thermidor in North America. "Oh," he said, recognizing her. He fidgeted for a moment, flustered, but she smiled at him to soothe his nerves. "Miss Bakurova, I wasn't expecting to see you."

"Nor I you, Mikkel." Vivienne turned to shake the maître d's hand. "This must be your family."

"Yes, my wife, Ingrid, and our children, John and Ruth."

She shook the wife's hand and nodded at the children. "Your husband is very good at his job," Vivienne added to the wife.

"Look at that!" The Campbellite greeter said. "You've already got friends, here."

"Professional acquaintances," Mikkel corrected her. "But," he turned back to Vivienne, "I would be happy to take over the tour guide services, if you wish."

"It's your day off, Mikkel," Vivienne said. "Be with your family."

"This is what I tell him," Ingrid interjected.

"Go on, Michael," the greeter said. "Even God rested."

"It is no trouble," Mikkel protested.

"The ladies have you outnumbered, old man," Cranston added. He extended his hand. "Thomas Bakurov, the brother. I know the feeling well and it's an honorable surrender."

Mikkel chuckled. "Mikkel Jorgenson. Of course, you are right."

"Go on in," the greeter told them. Mikkel and his family went ahead in a cloud of niceties. "We do get the best people, here."

There was nearly a half hour before the prayer meeting started. The greeter, whose name was Mary, took them through a side hallway where she told another aproned woman that they had "novitiates," and this other woman took Mary's spot at the front door. As they were shown a great many doors and introduced to a handful of deacons, Mary talked about the various community volunteer "opportunities" the church offered. There were various "Bible studies" all through the week, each studying a different book, none of which were in the Bible. Then, there were "fellowship" events, lest any of their members be tempted to go to a club or the cinema.

As they walked, Vivienne took the time to read the posters that liberally decorated the walls. Most were blanket benedictions. "Show me your works" was written above a picture of a man lifting a barbell in one hand and a Bible in the other. Another depicted a runner with a cross on his shirt outpacing a man with a Star of David and another with the Papal seal, with the words "But one receives the prize! Run that you may obtain it!" A somewhat dated poster showed an American soldier killing a German with a sword, shouting: "I can do all things through Christ who strengthens me!"

Other, more topical posters included pictures of paternally-smiling Charles Campbell with the slogan: "Pray for Massachusetts"; a man standing gallantly atop a pile of broken kegs, with a crown and papal miter sticking out from the wreckage, stating: "Alcohol: the devil's sacrament"; and a relatively lavish portrayal of a gaudily dressed woman riding a red dragon that said, simply: "Rosamund Syme".

The tour brought them back to the foyer. "That's the dressing," Mary said. "Now, for the turkey." She opened the sanctuary's double doors and led them inside.

The sanctuary vaulted to the second floor, where a balcony allowed for more seating. It was shaped like a baseball diamond, slanting walls drawing the eye to the chancel and the great pipe organ at the back. Those walls were covered by floor-to-ceiling reliefs of realistic figures Vivienne assumed were the Apostles, all of them powerfully muscled.

Mary gestured to a row of pews, under the balcony, and at least a dozen rows from the chancel. "We ask novitiates to sit back here. I know that sounds terribly formal of us, but I think you'll see why when the service starts." She pulled two pamphlets from her apron. "You'll want to read these, too. Tonight's message is the third in a series, and these will catch you up."

"Thank you, very much." Cranston said.

"After the service," Mary looked Vivienne in the eyes for the first time, "there's a tea for the ladies and"—turning back to Cranston—"there are cigars and blessed beer for the gentlemen." She pronounced "blessed" as two syllables.

"Blessed beer?" he asked.

"Mmhmm," Mary grinned. "Less than 0.2% alcohol and guaranteed to be healthsome."

"Ah, of course! We called it 'near beer' in the Army."

"Well, ours is brewed right here on the island in a church-owned facility. But, don't worry, it's all complementary at church functions."

"That's very generous."

"I'll leave you two to catch up with those." She gestured at the pamphlets and returned to the foyer.

Vivienne and Cranston chose a spot on the otherwise empty pews. The members, at least thirty, were all much closer to the pulpit. The only other soul in these back rows was a lone man, reading a plain, blue book. Cranston decided to go talk to him, while Vivienne began her reading homework.

The pamphlet was cheaply printed and marked with the day's date. The title of the sermon series was "Prometheus Unbound", which turned out to be more literal than she expected. According to the Church of the Hero Jesus, there were many spiritual truths that could be found in other religions. Misinterpreted, of course, but God had ostensibly given Rev Campbell insight that allowed him to pull holy truths from pagan myths.

It turned out that Heracles was a prophetic vision of Jesus. The Greeks had made him the son of Zeus; a name derived from a pre-Greek word, "dewos", which meant "god". In their prophetic visions, the "blind" pagans could not see a distinction between "son of God" and "son of Zeus". Paradoxically, Zeus was also a demon. Prometheus was a symbol for all of God's prophets to the Israelites, bringing the word of God to men. The Greeks, jealous of the Israelites' enlightenment, concocted a story of their god binding the Israelite prophets. However, the Greeks' own prophets then saw Heracles freeing Prometheus, a sign that Jesus would unbind the word of God and spread it throughout the world.

If that was the summary of parts one and two, Vivienne couldn't imagine what would be in part three. She turned back to the front of the pamphlet and saw the frankly unlikely subtitle: "Part 3: Prometheus in the End Times".

The meeting still hadn't started, so Vivienne joined Cranston.

"Ah, Juliet," he said. "This is Mr Ryan Wolfe. Ryan, my sister, Juliet."

"It's a pleasure to meet you," the man said.

"Have you been coming here long?" Vivienne asked.

"No, only about a month, month and a half."

"It's..." she held up the pamphlet and glanced at the very Athenian reliefs on the walls. "It's awfully Greek, isn't it?"

"Well," Ryan shrugged. "The New Testament was written in Greek."

Several thoughts went tumbling through Vivienne's mind, more than one of which contained the word 'moronic'. "That is true," she managed.

"Look," Ryan pointed to the chancel. "That's the pastor."

"It was nice talking with you," Cranston said.

"You, too, Thomas," Ryan replied.

Vivienne and Cranston returned to where she had left her purse and he his hat.

"Are all protestant churches like this?" she asked quietly.

"I wouldn't know."

"Is spying always like that?" Vivienne asked from behind the bar in the small dining room. "It was frightfully tame. No one even had a gun."

They had returned home from the prayer meeting, which Vivienne felt was overstating things. Most of the night had been taken up by the pastor—who displayed every trapping of a skilled public speaker, except eloquence—delivering an energetic barrage of nonsense about Jesus, Prometheus, Odin, and another name that she didn't recognize being the four horsemen of the apocalypse. It had been dizzying.

"I'm afraid so," Cranston said, returning from his room without his jacket or tie. "It's a great deal of chit-chat and smiling. Do we have any ipecac?"

"Do you think they poisoned you?" Vivienne asked.

"Not exactly," he put his hand on his stomach. "But I am keen on getting that blessed swill out of me. A loaf of bread would have been less filling."

"If you're in earnest, you could call down. Hornsby surely knows where some is."

"I may." He sat at the small dining room table. "For now, something clear and straight."

Beyond the small dining room, the tall windows of the living room were darkening, point by point, as the city below put itself to bed. The living room lights were off and they drank by the dim lanterns of the small dining room.

"What exactly did we learn tonight?" Vivienne asked.

"Firstly, that Campbell's smear campaign has reached this far north. Philosophically, at least, this chapter is no friendlier to the Symes than any other."

"Your friend Lucien's fears are not unfounded."

"No," he sipped his vodka, letting it aid his digestion in small measures. "Secondly, we got names. If the CHJ is going to attempt another assault, it won't be half-cocked. They'll want someone with a history; someone who knows what they're doing. We have a few names; we can see if any of them have criminal records."

"And how do you intend to get those?"

"The Rose and Chain."

"You've been spurning them since you got back from France."

"I attend mass." Cranston said in his defense. "At any rate, you'll be doing the asking."

"I will?" Vivienne swirled her cocktail dubiously.

"I thought you wanted to help."

"That's not exactly what I had in mind."

"You were hoping for a shootout?"

Vivienne looked down at her drink. "I suppose not."

"I'm afraid it really is desperately boring." He said. "Until it very suddenly isn't and that is usually because someone made a mistake."

Vivienne had not had a clear idea of what this venture

was going to entail. She had only imagined that they would be undertaking it together, shoulder to shoulder.

"And what will you be doing?" She asked.

"Tomorrow morning, I will return to the Syme Retreat and let Lucien know what we've found."

"Tomorrow morning? You're not coming to the office?"

He laughed. "To do what?"

She didn't have an answer. Not a specific one, anyway.

"All I do," he continued, "is entertain big clients. We aren't scheduled to see any of them."

"Next week," she said gravely, "we do have the representatives from Saint Moon coming in. They are reviewing the changes we requested to the contract. I know you have your differences with them, but a show of effort on your part might get Cabot off our backs about it."

"I'll be back by then."

"Alright," Vivienne said. "Give me the names and I'll try to get a meeting with The-Men-Who-Know-Things."

"Excellent," he finished his vodka. "We'll be creating our own code words in no time."

That childish sentiment warmed Vivienne more than the cocktail, not that she would tell Cranston so.

Chapter 13:
Hot Iron

September 9th, 1920. Montague, KCI.

After reconnoitering the CHJ, Cranston had gotten perhaps two hours of real sleep. The vodka had gotten him one, but the white ball of light that cast no shadows had broken through. After that, he had only been able to achieve half-sleep; that liminal place where thoughts are not quite dreams, but also terribly vivid and difficult to control. He had existed there for most of the night, only to have the conflicting and twisting thoughts escape him upon deciding to wake up.

Around 6am, he was ready for his day and in the lobby of the hotel, waiting for a chauffeur. Not Williamson; Vivienne required him, but Cranston knew that the ride would tempt him to sleep. He wouldn't get it, he knew, but best not to risk it from behind the wheel.

Sitting in the back seat, the cool air helped him stay alert for a while, but his eyes got heavy, eventually. As he drifted down into that darkness, the white ball emerged and the clattering of gunfire shook him back awake. He looked around, adrenaline flashing through his system. There was only sparse forest and vast meadow around them. The guns were in France.

The chap behind the wheel had the good sense not to comment, but Cranston caught him looking.

As much as his senses could tell him where he was, the sounds of machine guns and the whisper from within the pocket lingered well after he awoke, suggesting that maybe the passing trees and sunshine were the dream and he was still on his knees in the blistering snow at Vimy Ridge.

When they arrived at the Syme Lodge—separated from the Retreat proper by a copse—Lucien opened the gate for them. He wore another tailored suit, this one with a knee-length jacket, to cover the pair of pistols strapped to his waist.

"Rosamund is finishing breakfast," he said, after the chauffeur had parked. "Your driver can go in through the staff entrance." Cranston nodded to the chauffeur and the man wandered towards the back of the house, taking in the view along the way. "Come on," Lucien told Cranston, leading him away from the Lodge.

Near to the front gate, closer to the road than the main house, was a building that Cranston had initially taken for a barn. It may have once been—an artifact from the property's former life—but had been refitted as a servants' quarters.

"I've pretty much got this place to myself," Lucien said as they entered. The ground floor was taken up by a great room for dining and reading. A kitchen and bathroom were attached.

"Rosie doesn't let you sleep in the house?" Cranston asked.

"Usually, I do," he shrugged. "But that's not always possible. Whenever she entertains, the staff are relegated to this place."

"It's not bad," Cranston said sincerely. "Better than our tent in France."

The kitchen was separated from the great room by a half-wall. There were three barstools, there, in case eating lunch-counter-style was more convenient than the dining table. Cranston took a stool, while Lucien cooked him some bacon from the ice box. Cranston walked Lucien through his evening at the CHJ.

"So, I was right," Lucien said, traying the bacon. "Toast?"

"Only if you're having some. And, yes."

Lucien returned to the stove.

"What do you want to do about it?" Cranston asked.

"Not much I can do. I've only got the one body and it needs to stay as close to Rosamund as possible."

"When is the election?"

"November," Lucien said. "But they'll make their next move before then."

"Right," Cranston took up his knife and fork and sliced off a square of the bacon. "On Tuesday, you mentioned that Rosamund has a new client. You think she's a spy."

"Della Caine," Lucien said. "Supposedly the most advanced case of EDAD ever recorded. But I've seen bad cases—we've seen bad cases—and they don't talk much."

"Or move," Cranston added.

"Exactly, I don't know where that condition advances to after locking you up inside your own body."

"When does this Miss Caine arrive?"

"Tomorrow."

"Good lord!"

"Rosamund is the strike-while-the-iron-is-hot type. Once she decides to do something, it gets done pretty quickly. Miss Caine's car will drop her off tomorrow, early afternoon, then pick her up on Sunday morning. There's a secure hospital in Murray; that's where she's staying. Supposedly, anyway."

Cranston chewed thoughtfully. "Drop her off?"

"Yeah, there's a whole procedure. They claim she's easily disturbed, which makes sense for EDAD, so the car will arrive and go directly to the garage. Miss Caine will enter the house from there. No one is supposed to be in the house, except for Rosamund. The cooks are on a strict time table so that Miss Caine doesn't have to see them."

"And you?"

Lucien raised his arms to indicate the servants' quarters. "I can patrol the grounds, but only during certain times."

"Right...that sounds an assassin's dream."

"I don't think it'll come to that."

"I told you about the poster, didn't I?" Cranston said. "The one where Rosamund is the Whore of Babylon riding the Great Red Dragon."

Lucien brought toast to the counter. "Assuming they take that seriously, they still wouldn't kill her. They aren't going to try to screw up the apocalypse: half of them are chomping at the bit for it to happen."

"And the car," Cranston jumped back into the old train of thought. "Will it stay in the garage all weekend?"

"No, the driver is staying at a hotel in town. We shouldn't see him again until Sunday."

Cranston snapped his fingers. "That's our next lead, then. Can you get me a car? Something plain?"

"Sure."

"I'll take the car to the crossroads. When the driver leaves here, I'll follow him into town."

Lucien nodded, then tended to the stove. "It's the best plan we've got."

The door opened and Cranston turned on his bar stool to see Rosamund walk in. "I smelled bacon!" she said, stepping into the kitchen. She sidled up behind Lucien, close enough that he'd feel her corset against his back, and took a long whiff. "I can't touch the stuff, but I adore the smell."

She was wearing a slightly old-fashioned dress, the kind that had been falling out of style when he returned from the war. He assumed it was, in part, a play to look more whole-some; her morals being a matter of serious controversy. At the same time, she certainly did not have the boyish frame that was all the rage, nowadays. The older style was much friendlier to her proportions than anything he had seen on a fashion plate, recently.

"Cranberry," she said, coming out to sit beside him. "You look dreadful. How spiffed were you, last night?"

"Hardly at all," Cranston sighed. "I just couldn't get to sleep."

"Is that why you're here before breakfast?"

"It was a contributing factor."

Lucien carved a couple more pieces off the wrapped bread loaf and threw them on the pan. Rosamund propped one elbow up on the counter and looked at him. "That man would have an entire regiment watching this place, if he could manage it." The way she said it, and the softness of her eyes as she did, told Cranston exactly where Lucien was sleeping, when he stayed in the main house. "So," she returned her attention to Cranston. "There's a conspiracy to kidnap me again. And a woman who has been in a secure hospital since 1917 is at the heart of it. What are you going to do about it?"

"Very little," Cranston said. "I'm with you: Lucien is being paranoid."

"I never said that!"

"Yes, you have," Lucien added, eyes still on the toast.

"I never said it to him." She pointed at Cranston.

"You aren't especially circumspect, dear," Cranston told her. "At any rate, if your guest is plotting anything, her driver will be in on it. I'm going to find him later, and have a talk with him, just to make sure he's on the up-and-up."

"You're going to interrogate some poor orderly?"

"Gently," Cranston nodded. "Lucien, old boy, is there coffee?"

"Sure thing," he replied.

Turning back to Rosamund, Cranston said: "Despite

what you may have read in dime novels, a good interrogator befriends his subject. Torture is a complete waste of time. Get a man to like you and he'll reveal just about anything."

"The Voice helps," Rosamund added.

"The Voice is for the enemy," Cranston said, instinctively. He shook his head to clear it. "Imagine that you're walking down the street and a man grabs you by the arm and shoves a knife in your face. He demands to know your home address. Firstly, the fear you would then be experiencing would make recalling even such a small fact more difficult. Secondly, the danger this man poses would motivate you not to give him that information. If he's willing to stab you, what greater evils will he commit with the knowledge of where you live?

"I really don't know where people get this idea that fear and pain are the road to the truth. Men being tortured, if they tell you anything, will lie. They'll lie just to spite you, if nothing else."

Rosamund looked at Cranston with a sort of awe. It was an equal mixture of fear—imagining what events had given him this intelligence—and relief that he meant what he said about befriending Miss Caine's driver.

"Alright," she said, sounding overwhelmed. "Just make sure you get some sleep beforehand."

"I will do my utmost."

"Should I have a room made up for you?"

"I can bunk here." Cranston said with a dismissing wave. "I don't want to trouble you."

"You'll sleep better on one of the guest beds."

"Do you know, I got something of a taste for sleeping rough, during the war. Too soft of a mattress and I feel as though I'll drown."

Rosamund shook her head. "Men..."

Lucien brought hot coffee and cooled toast.

"At least," Rosamund continued, "Come to the house later

and play chess with me. This one"—she pointed at Lucien with a slice of toast—"always lets me win."

Lucien looked gravely at Cranston. "I am not good at chess."

"I have never seen you play."

"You can come through the front door," Rosamund said, standing. "Both of you."

Cranston waved, then turned to catch the look on Lucien's face as he watched her go. The poor devil was in deep.

Spending the weekend at the Syme Lodge demanded a trip into town to get a couple changes of clothes. He only had his check book and it was unwise to write too many of those in a short period of time. Eventually, someone would recognize the name and that would start rumors. Every check he wrote increased that likelihood and, once the whispers started, the more people who had seen the checks, the more outlandish the rumors would become. So, he had to be choosy.

He made the trip with his chauffeur, then sent the man back to Silkhaven when he was done. Being a summer colony, no one paid much attention to a luxury car in August. The town had a pair of tailors, who advertised mending above bespoke clothing, and a half dozen retail clothing stores. These were evenly divided between catering to the renters and the locals.

Cranston had a semi-social relationship with the staff of the Walker Grand Hotel. It was understood that he was their employer, but the intimacy of their employment required more reciprocity than with the people on the second or even sixteenth floor of the office. At work, he needed only strike up For He's a Jolly Good Fellow on important days and shake a few hands. At the hotel, he needed to remember birthdays, children's names, and even hobbies.

When he was quite young, Cranston had been brought along to one of his father's business dinners. Afterwards, he had undressed with his father. Father had congratulated Hornsby, his then valet, on several points of his wardrobe. Once alone, Father had explained that the way Hornsby dressed him was a key part of his business success. Any success he had was also Hornsby's success.

"Remembering that," Father had said, "is the key to creating loyalty. Loyalty can never be bought."

Cranston had not stopped into the shop for locals—no doubt, they all knew each other and would immediately and cynically recognize him as a tourist—and, instead, had settled on one that specialized in gentlemen's sporting clothes. He found three outfits of well-heeled hunting attire. Upon returning to the house, one of the maids insisted on giving the clothes a wash before he wore them. Lucien then insisted that they familiarize him with the grounds.

The property was set on a sort of inland peninsula, with two tributary rivers converging at the Retreat's eastern point. This posed the greatest security risk, in Lucien's mind, as giving chase by boat was a difficulty. If Lucien had boats ready at either river, invaders could sabotage them. Having the boats stored increased the head start of fleeing ne'er-do-wells. With that in mind, he had drawn up a map of patrol routes that would give them the best coverage of the north bank; the south bank being on the other side of the main road.

Ideally, though, anyone intending to molest Rosamund would come at night. One of them could be in the lodge, then, and the other in the staff's quarters. That would consolidate their manpower and keep them close to the road. If an attack did occur, Lucien's Plan A was to get Rosamund into a car and evacuate her. Cranston readily volunteered the Walker Grand Hotel—a two or three hour's drive—as a safe house.

Plan B was messier. In the staff quarters, Lucien had stockpiled a significant armory in a room that he dubbed "the broom closet". He had a pair of Winchester 1897 Trench

Guns, shotguns with shortened barrels that had been dubbed "trench sweepers" during the war. They were so effective in close quarters that Jerry had tried to have them banned while they, themselves, poured mustard gas into allied trenches. The Winchesters were complimented by four Colt .45's and a pair of the new Thompson submachine guns.

Rosamund refused to keep guns in the lodge, so Lucien had stashed a number of trench knives in accessible, but counter-intuitive places. If they were facing no more than a handful of angry parishioners, those would likely deter more violence than they facilitated. But Lucien and Cranston needed to be prepared for a mob with more bullets than scruples and they could not afford to wager that they would be the only—or even best—trained soldiers in the fray.

The evening was not half as foreboding as the afternoon. After dinner, per his own protocol, Lucien retired to the staff quarters and left Cranston to catch up with his childhood friend. Rosamund immediately challenged him to a game of chess. Their conversation wandered far and wide, concentration breaking between moves.

"The problem isn't really religion," Rosamund said of the CHJ. "At least, not in the pure sense of the word. It's tradition that I'm up against."

"You encourage people to pleasure themselves," Cranston retorted while trying to decide if taking her queen's knight was worth the risk. "Not that I'm one to cast stones, but isn't the Bible rather clear on that?"

"It's not! That's just the thing!" Rosamund got up, this point striking a passion within her. "The doctrines on masturbation are based on two highly spurious interpretations; one vague and one patently ridiculous. For starters, that the argument is based on interpretation at all is a chink in its armor. The Book of Leviticus has a veritable roll call of which family members qualify as incest. It's all of them, but the author felt he needed to be specific.

"It mentions your father, your mother, and your father's wife; just in case Junior had designs on raiding the harem when Papa passed on. Aunts, uncles, siblings are all in there. It even goes so far as to specify siblings 'born at home or abroad'. I'll own that I'm not expert enough on ancient Mesopotamia to know exactly why that might matter, but it is a terrific amount of detail."

She refilled her wine glass and continued. "The Bible is explicit on incest. And adultery and bestiality while they're at it. Yet, there is no explicit prohibition on either masturbation, nor premarital sex. Why would it be explicit on bestiality— surely a rare occurrence—and not on the surely common matter of self-pleasuring or youthful indiscretion? Because they are not sins!" She made a grand gesture which nearly slopped merlot onto the rug.

"Do you know?" she went on, not seeming to have noticed her brush with red wine staining. "God didn't invent marriage? Humans devised that all on their own. The Lord blessed it, of course, but he never prescribed it. At least, not until after it had been practiced for time immemorial."

Cranston considered endangering her king's rook, hoping she would protect it with her king's knight and make taking the queen's knight a safer move.

"What are these interpretations you mentioned?" he asked, taking his hand off his queen's bishop.

"The first," she said, calming herself and returning to the table, "is the flatly ridiculous interpretation of the story of Onan. Onan's older brother was married, but died before impregnating the lady. Onan was tasked with impregnating his sister-in-law, so that the child could inherit the older brother's land. If no child came along, Onan would inherit the land, so he 'spilled his seed on the ground'. For which, God struck him dead." She moved a pawn between his bishop and her knight.

"That is, firstly, not even masturbation and, secondly, clearly a story about the evils of greed. How anyone could see that as a prohibition on self-pleasure is beyond me. When you point that out, though, the traditionalists will tell you that one cannot masturbate without lusting. But lust is uncontrolled sexual desire. Masturbation can be an excellent aide in bringing the libido under control."

She slouched back in her chair and took another drink.

"It's men," she added. Then, leaned forward to point at him with the hand holding her wine glass. "You men want to be martyrs to your erections. Throwing yourselves on your cocks every time there's a woman you want that won't have you."

Cranston blinked at her. "That is an image which will not soon leave me."

"You're all horrible little gremlins." She squinted at him, but grinned beneath it. "Putting words in the Lord's mouth so that you can make your sexual frustrations our fault."

Cranston took her queen's knight, suspecting they wouldn't reach the endgame, anyway. "And yet, you seem awfully fond of at least one of those gremlins."

She scowled at him. "That's the filthiest trick of them all!" Rosamund declared. "You're so wonderful when you aren't horrid that you're almost impossible to give up."

"Almost," he winked at her.

They did finish the game, at Rosamund's insistence, despite her moves becoming increasingly erratic until victory was mere chance. When she finally declared herself ready for bed, two maids appeared and helped her up to her room. A third guided Cranston to the room he had previously declined, then excused herself, leaving him with a candle and the distinct impression that Miss Syme's libertine ideas did not extend to her staff.

Chapter 14:
Ocean of Milk

The night was full of the white orb. It was utterly smooth, less like a dome of frosted glass around a light bulb than a porthole looking down into an ocean of milk. It was bright, but not luminous and it took the eyes several minutes to adjust to it. Once they did, one could see shades in the white; soft, curving lines of a darker shade. Not grey, though, but shadowy; like the edge of ripples of a ship's wake that face away from the sun.

There were things in that ocean. Things that felt enormous to look at despite having no sense of distance. Things that could speak to you inside your own mind with voices like grinding steel. Things that wanted you to do something for them, if only you or they could learn the other's language.

The visions came almost as soon as he closed his eyes. Cranston heard the rhythmless beating of the machine guns like notes on a piano drifting up the stairs. He willed the pocket not to appear, to leave him in darkness with the chaos clatter of steel on steel. The white would not oblige. Those creatures that swam through the ocean of milk would no more obey him than he would they.

The fear was as palpable as if the pocket had opened in his room. It was not the fear of danger nor surprise. It didn't make you scream or run or try to defend yourself. It was apocalyptic; the unveiling which ends the world. It was the fear of discovering your home is made of painted plywood sets and, if you walk through the wrong door at the wrong time, you will find a stage manager whispering for you to get on with the show and, when you turn away, you see the audience awaiting the next line from a script that you've never seen. It was the fear of your friends, one day, deciding that they cannot keep up the charade any longer and breaking down into maniacal laughter at the ridiculousness of your dress, your manner, your every choice of words. It was the fear of seeing the enormity and sublimity of God and knowing, deeply and inescapably, that he loved you as a collector loves butterflies and that your eternal reward is a pin through the stomach and an eternity in a divine shadowbox.

Cranston awoke. The blankets were lighter than his own and the bed much wider. The shades of the walls and curtains in the darkness were wrong. His mind was full of a whispering voice repeating—"The krakens! The krakens!"—and that drowned out every memory of where he was or how he had gotten there; a demon sitting on his brain, while his chest was unburdened.

On instinct, he rolled over and reached for his manitaurine cigarettes. They were not where they should have been, touching only the cold metal of a candlestick. He frantically crawled out from under the strange blanket and landed on the floor heavily; the bed was too high. His trousers were a black rectangle across the lighter shape of a chair. His knee smarting, he got up and almost ripped the trousers apart trying to find the pocket where he kept the manitaurine, only to find it empty.

Back on the floor, on his hands and knees, Cranston groped about the wooden floor for his lost box of Baby Blues. His fingers found the grooved silver of his cigarette case and snatched it from the shadows. The case seemed to open by itself and he tore one out and bit it as he fought for the hazy memory of where his match box was.

The other pocket. They were always in the other pocket. His left hand would reach for the cigarette case and his right for the match box. He would remove both at the same time, keeping the match box in his palm as the fingers of his right hand gripped the cigarette. All the time wishing that he could still get the patches.

Back to his trousers, he found the match box exactly where it should have been. He opened it, removed a stick and stopped. If he struck it, there would be light. In that fog of terror and freshly doffed sleep, he thought that maybe, this time, when the red bulb scraped along the friction strip, it wouldn't be fire that bloomed from the tip, but that white orb.

"Guten Abend, gut' Nacht," he sang to himself in the Voice. "Mit Rosen bedacht..." He was trying to hypnotize himself with it. That hadn't been part of the academy training. It was one of the little improvements that naturally come from the frequent use of a tool.

He struck the match and breathed deeply. The manitaurine flooded his body and he could feel it blanketing his sympathetic nervous system. All the panic drifted back to join the echoes of the machine guns and the ringing silence that followed a volley of artillery.

"The krakens," he whispered. "The krakens." The words escaped him like old air leaving a room when the windows opened.

That thought led him to the window of his room. Summer night air mixed with the manitaurine smoke in his mouth, clearing out the vestiges of sleep from his head. Still, the world felt thin and he was haunted by the feeling that he might fall through the floor and find that he was a ghost replaying the moments before his own, now past, death.

It made him wonder what Della Caine experienced. Rosamund claimed that she was the worst case of EDAD that had been documented, but Cranston had seen the pockets lock men inside their own bodies. They were senseless creatures, unresponsive to any stimulus that the doctors dared subject them to. What could be worse than that?

After the message had come informing him of his parents' death, the army had hastily granted him a discharge. By that time, America was taking any opportunity to divest themselves of the Praetorians without causing a scandal. The people back home needed to continue trusting the government, and a thousand healthy men all sent home without explanation would erode that. So, any excuse was seized upon.

Walker Trading had been volunteering ships to the war effort since the beginning. Hearing that the President had died, sending his son home looked strategic. Managing that valuable resource—delivery ships supporting every man at the front—was far more important than anything one man could accomplish in the trenches.

Discharge was a simple matter, just a rubber stamp. Actually arranging Cranston's passage home was another thing. The letter informing him of his parents' death, received a week after the funeral, ordered him to report to Amiens. That's where he was given his discharge papers and his back-pay by a Colonel's aide-de-camp who told him that he could get a ship home in Calais.

Cranston knew there would be trouble when the NAEF office in Amiens couldn't provide him with transport to the coast. He ended up having to hitch a ride on an empty cargo truck. In Calais, he was told that he would have to wait for a medical discharge ship. When he asked when the next ship would be available, he was told "when we've got enough live bodies to fill it."

Needing to make himself useful, Cranston volunteered at

a nearby hospital. He used some of his back-pay to buy a suit, knowing that even wounded soldiers would be loath to speak with a Praetorian Guard. At first, the head nurse had nothing for him to do, as he lacked medical training. When she found out that he could read and write in both English and French, though, he was handed a box of clerical supplies.

The wounded and the dying needed letters written. Some were illiterate and others too weak. There were blind men and amputees, shellshocked men whose hands shook too much to use a pen. Cranston sat by their beds and wrote their words, sometimes their last.

Among those he could help were those who were beyond contact. Dimensional pockets appeared on battlefields all the time. Rarely in the towns or the desolate staging grounds, but in no man's land, they were plentiful. No one knew why. But too often they opened so suddenly and so close that the soldiers didn't have time to apply their manitaurine patches before the fear those balls of white exuded froze them. A lot of those men never unfroze. They lay in their beds, catatonic or gibbering, unable to respond to the world around them; only the endless nightmare of that milky ocean that now lived inside their minds.

Cranston had watched the nurses bathe them, when things were quiet. He had seen the pity in their eyes. Even the men suffering from shellshock had pitied them: 'there but for the grace of God go I'. The EDAD patients were looked on like old dogs that the owner knew would soon need to be put down. It was wretched.

After nights when he couldn't sleep, when he felt the fear and struggled to speak, Cranston wouldn't turn up for his letter-writing rounds. If he showed the least symptom of exposure to a pocket, he had been sure, the staff would know. They would know that he suffered, though less acutely, from that same condition. The idea of being looked on that way was sickening.

Still, he hid it. If the board knew, they would have cousin Martin in his chair before week's end. If Vivienne knew...he couldn't even imagine. His first go at an honest romance after the war had ended when the woman began to question his continued use of Baby Blues. While it was true that many old soldiers had come to prefer them over tobacco, many people who had never habitually consumed manitaurine—especially in the concentrated patch form—found it suspect.

Divesting himself of Vivienne simply wasn't an option, but neither was living with her pity.

Feeling self-pity begin to well up, Cranston reminded himself that whatever happened to him, it was worse for Della Caine. There was hope in that. If Rosamund could find a way to help her, it might prove to be a cure for him. It would require more than self-pleasuring she recommended in her lectures; Cranston had been pleasured in myriad ways over the last two years and the relief was decidedly temporary.

That was all he had ever hoped for. Even now, the Symes spoke of a cure the way certain eccentrics did of Atlantis or the City of Z: convinced that it existed, but unsure of how to find it. Cranston wanted to believe. On those days when his oxytocin was high, he thought he did, but on a night like this—when the fear was so close at hand—it was hard to imagine anything so overpowering ever being truly gone.

Chapter 15:
Purple Book

Rosamund turned Cranston out of the house first thing, handing him a stack of paper-wrapped egg and sausage sandwiches.

"Be sure to share some with Lucien," she said. "He's a growing boy."

"That's a terrifying thought," Cranston replied, blearily. He had barely slept and no coffee was yet on offer.

"Is it?" Rosamund looked off into the distance. She softly bit her lip.

"Alright," Cranston turned to leave.

"I have some calls to make. Lucien will explain" was all she said before closing the front door.

"She needs absolute quiet," Lucien explained. He was cleaning one of the pistols when Cranston brought their breakfast into the staff quarters. "She thinks telephones are uncanny. You know, talking to someone and not seeing their face, so she closes her eyes and imagines them. Other sounds distract her. When she's on the phone, the staff have to sit in another room and be completely still."

Cranston was only half listening from the kitchen, fetching salt, pepper and ketchup. He also set the coffee to brew. "I never took her for the neurotic kind."

"I wouldn't say neurotic," Lucien answered. "And I certainly wouldn't say it where she could hear. No, she's more of a luddite. If there's a natural way of doing something, she'll take that first."

"Hence the masturbation?" Cranston asked, returning to the table with condiments.

"It's more than that." Lucien said. "In fact, she's pretty clear that sex itself is preferable. Though, she does strongly encourage using mercuries."

"So, not a complete luddite."

"Not when nature can't do better."

Cranston returned to the kitchen for the coffee. Back at the table, Lucien had the beginnings of sly grin on his face.

"Did she show you the blue book?" he asked.

"No, why?"

"You brought up masturbation, so I can guess what you two talked about over chess."

"The Bible."

"Oh, you got the angry version."

"What's the blue book?"

"There are three of them, actually," Lucien got up and crossed to a cupboard near the fireplace, situated opposite the kitchen. "Dr Syme commissioned a great many short stories to aid his patients in their treatment." From within the cupboard, he retrieved a purple, hardbound book. He sat adjacent to his dismantled gun and handed the book to Cranston before unwrapping a sandwich.

The book's cover read *The Syme Institute Library of Therapeutic Tales, Volume 2*. Opening it to a random page, Cranston was greeted with a detailed, prose description of coitus being performed on a kitchen countertop.

"My my..." Cranston said, drawn in by a paragraph explicating the weight and firmness of the woman's breast in the man's palm.

"Apparently, all the writers are famous, but the stories are all anonymous." Lucien poured some ketchup onto the sandwich paper, salted it, then stirred with the corner of his sandwich. "Which one is that?" He craned his neck to see the spine.

"Good lord!" Cranston said, recoiling slightly and closing the book.

"What?" Lucien asked, amused.

"That was a story about a young man violating his mother," Cranston said. "She was very encouraging, but nonetheless."

"Volume two," Lucien nodded. "Those are the 'forbidden' stories. Volume one has the more sentimental ones; men and their wives, boys losing their virginity to pretty widows, young women being seduced by handsome strangers in Italy, that sort of thing. Volume two has a bunch of cheating wives, miscegenation, and incest. Volume three is full of English women being ravished in captivity by Arab sheiks, men being hypnotized by vampire women, lots of people getting tied up."

"*Therapeutic...*" Cranston said, eyeing the cover.

"It's something to masturbate to." He shrugged.

"One's mother?"

"I don't think that's the real fantasy. It's just not allowed. Breaking the rules is the fun part."

Cranston picked it back up, looking to the table of contents. "Miscegenation, you said?"

"Yeah, there's one about an Englishman becoming a raja, but it mostly takes place in the harem. I'm pretty sure it was written by Rudyard Kipling. Really tightens the trousers."

"Does it, now?" Cranston scanned the titles, hoping for something that would give it away.

"The big finale involves three women at once! Can you imagine?"

Cranston didn't have to. The reality was that it was a logistical nightmare and he had felt like an amateur ballet

director after about five minutes. Although—he supposed—
in a harem, the women might plan out the whole thing ahead
of time. Choreograph themselves, as it were.

"There's an index," Lucien added. "If you're looking for
something particular."

During breakfast, one of the maids brought Cranston's
laundry to the staff quarters. He dressed and prepared for
the morning's patrol. He took the trench sweeper, partially
because he was familiar with it and partly because the
Thompson wasn't suitable for hunting. Not that he was doing
any hunting, just that such was the air of his costume. He also
took a pistol, which he could secrete under his sport coat.

Lucien started first and Cranston watched from a second
floor window for him to appear on the west end of the house.
At that point, Lucien took a short break while Cranston
began his route. Thus, they maintained a two-point survey of
the grounds.

Cranston's costume—meant to disguise his purpose,
rather than his identity—was a dark, but vibrant red, tinged
with blue. It wasn't purple, but it had the subversive effect
of purple. He wore a blue tie with it, which increased the
effect at a distance, but decreased it up close. It looked like a
burlesque of hunting clothes from a distance, but respectable
up close. He imagined members of the stuffier, older generation turning up their noses at his approach and then feeling
the need to apologize as they shook his hand. It pleased Cranston immensely.

He wore a brown leather cap and matching, knee-high
boots with it. The waistcoat was also brown, but the difference in fabric made it seem darker in most lights. That was
unfortunate, but a leather waistcoat was out of the question;
certainly in ready-to-wear, but Cranston suspected that his
own tailor would refuse to make such a garment.

Each turn of the property took about an hour at the

languid pace that he and Lucien had agreed to, if they maintained it the whole time. Every thirty minutes, it had been decided, they would take a break for fifteen. Not a proper break, just a sit down or a chance to smoke.

On Cranston's third rotation, he saw Lucien wave at him from one of the lodge's windows. He gestured to the staff quarters, meaning Lucien would be having lunch in the house, and Cranston would not. Cranston lit up a Baby Blue. The unease which had kept him fitfully awake most of the night had not entirely subsided. The dulling fog of the manitaurine, paradoxically, helped him concentrate.

As he approached the renovated barn, Cranston caught sight of a woman walking out of the copse that separated the Syme Lodge from the Syme Retreat. She wore an apron and a pillbox hat over a blue dress—evidently, a nurse—and was carrying a platter. He trotted up to greet her.

"Need a hand?" he called, taking the cigarette out of his mouth.

"I won't be offended if you open the door," she called back. She was Irish, but he couldn't put a finer point on her accent than that.

He had heard a spectrum of them in the war, but had never been on friendly enough terms with the speakers to find out where they were from.

Cranston stood by the entrance to the staff's quarters and waited for the nurse to get close enough before opening the door. He felt his sleep deprivation fade, just a degree, when he got a good look at her deep red hair.

"Lunch for two," she smiled, as he opened the door.

"It's just me, I'm afraid," Cranston replied. "The other fellow is in the house."

"And you're expecting me to graze on the lawn?" she said in a neutral tone as she passed.

"I didn't expect a lady of your education to deign to dine

with the likes of me," he answered.

"You're younger than the men I'm used to eating with." She put the platter down on the long dining table. "But I think I'll manage." She extended a hand. "Lily O'Doherty."

"Cranston Walker."

They shook.

September 9th, 1920. Montague, KCI.

Mr Connelly moaned as Lily dug the ball of her hand through the fat layer on his back to get to the knotted muscles beneath. He was face down on the table, wearing only the thin summer trousers male patients were given.

"Now, you keep a civil tongue," Lily chided the man, thirty years her senior. "Or I'll start using my American accent with you."

"Perish the thought." Mr Connelly—three generations removed from Ireland herself—grunted as Lily's massage interfered with his breathing. "It was entirely involuntary."

"Glad to hear it."

The massages were part of the daily regimen for increasing oxytocin levels in the patients. As such, it was important for the patients to have a masseuse that they were on friendly terms with. Though, not too friendly.

Mr Connelly hadn't the slightest trace of his supposed ancestral home of Dublin in his voice. But he claimed that Lily's rich Dubliner brogue was the most soothing sound for his nerves, of which he had very few left.

During the day, Mr Connelly was a chipper, even gregarious man. He seemed to have memorized everything Oscar Wilde ever wrote and had a quote for almost any occasion. He was always after a game of cards, at which he cheated; though, he cheated very badly, so it put no one off.

When the sun set, though, he had terrors. Left alone, he

would stare into the night, seemingly against his will, and shudder until he began to scream. The only way to keep him calm was to hold his hand. Doctors, nurses, male and female patients all took their turns holding Mr. Connelly's hand between sunset and bed time.

Mr Connelly's room had a large metal plate with a single candlestick on it. He could only ever get to sleep if a candle was burning and the large plate secured it from starting a fire.

He had been fishing, two years ago, when a dimensional pocket opened just beside his little boat. The ball of white light which cast no shadows had enveloped one of the oars, making it impossible for him to row away. Since then, night-time had thrown him into an awful fear. He said there were giant squids flying through the air, horrible and impossibly big, whispering to him in a language he could not understand.

This was week three of his treatment and Lily knew, with pity in her heart, that no one was to hold his hand on Monday; not until he had a full episode. Dr Syme needed to see how long it took. It was the only way to measure the progress of his treatment.

At lunchtime, Lily didn't join the others in the cafeteria. She got a covered tray from the kitchen and walked from the main building—cafeteria and kitchens on the first floor, offices on the second—to the Green House. It was a long, single-storied building with five rooms joined by a hallway lined by storage closets. Each room had a single large window that looked out on Montague River and caught the sunrise each morning.

Lily brought the tray to Room 3, where Alice North waited.

"Good afternoon, Mrs North," Lily told the middle-aged woman sitting straight up in her reclining bed.

Mrs North said nothing, but followed Lily with her eyes

as she unfolded the tray's legs and laid it across Mrs North's lap.

"You smell lovely, today," Lily continued. "Sarah put a bit of perfume in your bath, did she?"

Under the cover was steak, mashed potatoes, and steamed carrots. Lily speared one of the carrot medallions with a fork and raised it to Mrs North's mouth. The woman opened her mouth slowly and Lily gently pushed the fork between her teeth, then waited for her lips to close before removing the fork. Mrs North chewed slowly and Lily grinned.

"You are doing so great at that, now!" she said. Lily had been there, two weeks ago, on the last day they had used a feeding tube for Mrs. North. "And it's almost noon! Let's get your radio on."

The retreat had its own radio transmitter and from noon until three o'clock, it broadcast records that could be heard anywhere on the grounds.

Back in December, Alice North had been sent to her employer's vacation home to prepare it for the family's arrival at Christmas. A repairman had found her collapsed in a hallway. She was taken to a hospital where she was found to be catatonic, though no cause could be discerned. The prevailing theory became that she encountered a pocket in the house, and her employer had graciously sent her to Dr Syme for treatment.

With her prescribed duties finished for the day, Lily treated herself to a bottle of beer—the mere 2% alcohol hardly touching her formidable, Irish constitution—and found a canvas chair from which to watch a game of ten-pins some of the gentlemen were playing on the lawn.

There were two doctors in their number, so she was not immediately alarmed when Teddy Holmes, a 35-year-old columnist from a publishing family, began twitching. The sound of the clattering pins seemed to be setting it off. Letting patients approach their limits was part of the treatment, if only to see whether treatments were succeeding.

When he began smiling and gesturing his good-byes without saying anything, Lily knew something was wrong. She expected one of the doctors to do something, but they just set up the pins and carried on with the game.

Teddy walked away on his own, not towards the dormitories or any other building one might expect. Lily went after him, giving the doctors a dirty look that they failed to notice. Ten minutes later, she found Teddy under an upturned canoe by the retreat's launch. His knees were pressed to his chest and one hand was snapping over and over in rapid succession.

"Teddy?" Lily crouched and extended her half drunk bottle of beer to him. "Would you like some of my beer?"

He looked at her, tears standing in his eyes. "Com...c...c...c..." he grunted in frustration and pressed his eyes into his knees.

"It's alright, Teddy." She inched closer and touched his shoulder, hoping to lure him out from under the canoe. "Just say what you can."

"Coming," he said, tearfully. "Coming...com...coming through the murk. Coming through the murk. Coming through...coming the murk and the darkness. Coming... coming...coming through the murk and the darkness." He kept repeating it again and again, apropos of nothing.

He collapsed, weeping into her lap, just repeating that meaningless phrase, over and over. Lily stroked his hair, hoping to ease him through the episode.

Retiring to her room, Lily stripped off the white and blue striped dress she was put upon to wear and collapsed onto her bed in her underthings, thinking she might fall asleep instantly. She could feel a headache coming on and hoped to just close her eyes and awake refreshed.

After a few moments, it became clear that this would not happen. So, she propped herself up and reached for 'the blue book'. This one being volume 3.

Someone—possibly Dr Syme and possibly his daughter—had commissioned several short works which explored a wide variety of erotic topics in narrative form. It was made available to all staff as part of their personal oxytocin regiments.

Lily's current favorite was a reimagining of Leda and the swan. In this version, Zeus used the swan shape to get close to Leda before taking on a human form. The author spent a very satisfying amount of time describing how Zeus kept Leda restrained and gave thrilling insights into how helpless Leda felt.

After just a few minutes, Lily had the book propped open with one hand against her left knee as both legs were spread wide. Shortly thereafter, the book was no longer needed.

September 10th, 1920. Montague, KCI.

Lily emerged from the copse that separated the Syme Retreat from the private residence carrying the, now, empty platter. She had received a phone call, that morning, from Rosamund Syme, a woman she had heard of, but never properly met. A gentleman, newly in Miss Syme's employ, seemed to be showing signs of EDAD. Rosamund wanted an expert opinion on his condition and a recommendation for treatment. Now that she'd conducted her examination, cursory as it was, she needed to report back.

Walking towards the kitchen to return the platter, she was amiably accosted by Mr Connelly. He wondered if she might read some Yeats to him, for which she had to give him a raincheck.

Inside the dining room, which she needed to cross to reach the kitchen, Dr Perkins wanted to know if Teddy Holmes should be back put on full therapy, after his breakdown. She left that to his expertise, as Teddy was not one of her charges.

After dropping off the platter, she made for the main office to phone Miss Syme. Before she could get to the phone, though, another nurse, by the name of Sally, hoped that Lily could write out a report for her; Lily having the loveliest penmanship. Lily was sorry, but she needed to talk to Rosamund Syme, right away.

One of the secretaries excused herself, leaving her phone to Lily. It took ten minutes for the connection to be made, which was twice as long as it would have taken to walk back to the lodge; but, then, Mr Walker might wonder what her business in the house was.

"Hello, Lily?" Rosamund answered.

"Good afternoon, Miss Syme," Lily replied.

"I saw you come through."

"Yes, ma'am,"

"Alright, how is he?"

"He was smoking a blue cigarette when I met him," Lily answered. "I could smell the manitaurine."

"I've heard that's a soldier's habit."

"Aye, the ones suffering from EDAD are known for it."

"Are they?"

"At least, around the hospitals in France, they were."

"I see."

"He looked sleep deprived, as you thought. I would need more time to be certain, but he could very easily be in long-term stage 1."

"I spoke with his sister," Rosamund added. "She says that he frequently seeks out female companionship."

"He's otherwise healthy, then."

"What do you recommend?"

Lily was trying to be objective, but selfishness kept nosing its way into her thoughts. "Further observation would be best." That was true, she reminded herself. One lunch was hardly sufficient for a full prognosis. Then, she added: "But it wouldn't harm anything if he began a rigorous course of oxytocin treatments." Lily chided herself for having said it.

"How much of that could you do, yourself?"

Lily knew what she wanted to say, but forced herself to say: "I don't think my duties here will allow for it."

"I can sort that out, if you would prefer. Excuses could be made for your regular presence in the staff quarters. There are...specialists in town, if you are uncomfortable administering the oxytocin treatments, yourself."

Lily had become a nurse to take care of others. It made her happy and she knew, in her heart, that what she wanted from this situation had very little to do with the well-being of Mr Walker. Certainly nothing to do with his condition. The right thing to do was say 'no', to recuse herself; but then she saw Sally, still not writing the report, waiting to ask Lily once more.

"I can take care of him," Lily said.

"I'm glad to hear it. I'll arrange everything and you'll have a new duty roster by this evening."

Chapter 16:
Chevy 490

Della Caine arrived at the Syme Lodge just after 1pm. An hour before, Rosamund had called both Lucien and Cranston into the house to remind them of the protocol—unnecessarily, as it was the frame upon which Lucien had built their guard duty schedule—and to remind them of how important it was not to violate that.

Miss Caine was psychologically fragile in the extreme. Whatever treatment she had been receiving, meeting with Rosamund was the next, perilous step. Catching sight of unknown quantities could do her serious harm. Protecting her from that was paramount.

Lucien didn't protest, but Cranston could feel that he wanted to. Rosamund could, as well—though, perhaps, she had already heard the protests—and that was why the meeting was happening.

One of the house maids waited at the gate for half an hour to let the car in. The maids were a known quantity, apparently, though they weren't ever supposed to be in the same room as Miss Caine. The car was a Chevrolet 490 that had been modified for additional privacy for the rear seat. Among these modifications was a hard top that, despite the matching paint, was obviously made of wood. The rear windows had been covered by wood panels, as well; the bolts and clasps holding them in place were clear to be seen. From a safety perspective, it would have made more sense to put the wood on the inside of the glass. Cranston couldn't account for why that hadn't been done.

The 490 went straight into the garage—Rosamund's Chandler had been moved to the Retreat in the care of that nurse, Lily—and the house maid shut the door from the outside and waited. As soon as the door was shut, Cranston left the staff quarters and raced through the copse.

He didn't have long to take in the Retreat. It was a collection of rustic, but comfortable buildings spread out between the two tributary rivers. People—many in dressing gowns, despite the early hour—milled about. There was a game of ten-pins happening. It hardly looked like the seat of debauchery that it was rumored to be.

Cranston skirted the edge of the copse, towards the main entrance, which let out onto the road into Montague just before a bridge. The Chandler was there, but there was no sign of Lily. As he came up alongside the car, he found her, ducked down under the level of the rear doors. She was pulling on a pair of trousers with her uniform dress draped over her for privacy.

"What are you doing?" Cranston asked.

"Changing clothes," she said. "The dress is dead give-away."

"You aren't coming with me," he replied.

Lily smiled at him. "Do you have time to argue?"

"No, I don't."

"Smart men never do." She winked.

He moved to the front and removed the gloves from their compartment, then crossed to the driver's seat. Lily climbed over into the passenger seat a moment later, as he pressed the button to start the engine. She was wearing a double-breasted coat and matching, loose-fitting trousers that would have made her look like a police woman if the color hadn't been wrong.

"You know," he said over the roar of the engine, "even Annie Oakley wears a dress."

"Constance Markievicz didn't," Lily answered, as she set a feathered hat on her head.

Cranston had no idea who that was and so couldn't argue. He pulled out onto the road and began cruising slowly towards Montague at the speed of one taking in the view.

"Aren't we supposed to be following someone?" Lily asked.

"We are," he called back. "But, critically, we don't want to appear to be following him."

They were halfway across the bridge when the 490 appeared behind them. Cranston raised his arm out the window and waved for the Chevrolet to pass them. As soon as the modified sedan was past them, Cranston began to gradually increase his speed.

Rosamund had arranged for Miss Caine's driver to stay at the Friendly Inn, the most full service lodging in Lower Montague, she said. It was "Lower" because it was south of the river. By an unhappy coincidence or a cruel joke, Lower Montague held the majority of the all-year residences and the cheaper hotels. Upper Montague's hotels all being much finer than what one arranged for someone else's driver.

Several hours pouring over maps and Cranston knew the most likely route the driver would take to the Friendly Inn. When the 490 took a right off that route, Cranston did not immediately follow. He went on to the next block and turned there, continued two more blocks—at speed—and then made another right.

"Do you see it?" Cranston asked Lily as they sat at the intersection. They were both scanning the buildings and parking lots, as any tourist might.

"There!" Lily said, pointing up the street towards a Western Union.

Cranston dug into his waistcoat and removed his pocket watch. It was 4:37pm. "That's all I need," he said, with a grin, and then continued on through the intersection.

"That's all?" Lily asked.

"We are looking for evidence that Miss Caine is connected to the CHJ," he began.

"The what?"

"I'll explain that later. It's an organization that may have designs on Miss Syme. If something is being planned, we don't think it will happen this weekend. Most likely, this visit is to case the lodge."

"Case it?"

"Have a look around, get the lay of the land, reconnoiter. The point of following the driver is to see if he contacts anyone suspicious. Whatever he's doing in the Western Union, that will give us our best clues to his intent."

"How are you going to find out who he contacts?"

"I'm going to break in, later tonight," he replied, still grinning.

"And thus, I have fallen in with criminals!" Lily shook her head.

Cranston laughed. "Before you know it, you'll be smoking on the street corner and drinking whiskey."

She blinked at him. "You've clearly never been to Ireland."

"Drinking whiskey from the bottle, then."

"Not one foot on her shores."

"On a Sunday."

"Hasn't e'en seen a postcard."

Cranston made for the Friendly Inn, which had a restaurant that Rosamund spoke fondly of. The plan, now, was to see how long it took the driver to get there. In a town as light on street traffic as Montague, it was no good to follow him through more than one detour. However, the longer it took him to arrive at the Inn, the more generally suspicious the man became.

This part of the mission, as Cranston had begun to think of it, was when Lily's presence started to become a liability. Her clothing was noticeably cheaper than his. It was a rare thing for a lady's escort to be better dressed than she was. The gap was enough for Lily to pass as Cranston's maid. They would have raised fewer eyebrows if she were still in her apron. At least, then, people would have thought they were having an affair. As it was, even Cranston couldn't imagine what business they might have together.

Overtly adulterous was far better than overtly mysterious, under any circumstances.

The restaurant of the Friendly Inn was an addition to a large farmhouse; the farm long gone. There were new windows, as well, their frames of a slightly different shape than the older ones, spaced more widely on the house. Assuming each window was a single room, the lodgings didn't seem suitable for a vacation. It made him wonder who exactly was staying in them.

Cranston parked the car, then got out to open Lily's door. He offered her his arm. They walked in that way, a posture which could make them lovers or cousins. There was a strong scent of cooking meat in the air, too complex to be narrowed down further than that.

He chose a seat that would allow him to watch the parking lot. As soon as they sat down, the sleep deprivation slammed into Cranston like a boxer's fist. His whole body became very heavy. He blinked and, when he opened his eyes, he had the distinct feeling that he had closed them for too long. Lily didn't seem to notice; she was already perusing one of the menus left on the table.

That moment of weakness triggered a small jolt of panic. 4:37pm, he reminded himself. He couldn't forget that time. He tried to read the menu, but the letters blurred on the page.

"I've been meaning to ask," Lily said, looking at him over the top of her menu. "What is 'Victory Cabbage'?"

"Victory cabbage?" Cranston said vaguely, struggling to make either word meaningful.

"I see it on menus sometimes, but I haven't had the courage to order it, yet." Her eyes refocused on him. "Are you feeling alright?"

"Oh...um...yes, I've come over all worn, suddenly," he said. "It was my first night in a new bed, you understand. It made me a bit restless."

"Aye, that old barn you're staying in isn't the most hospitable, to look at it."

He didn't correct her. It didn't seem worth the energy.

The waitress arrived and asked Cranston what they would have. He struggled a moment too long to come up with a sensible answer, so Lily ordered the corned beef and cabbage.

"It's been a dog's age since I had any," she told the waitress.

"Oh," the woman replied, recognizing the accent. "A taste of the old country?"

"Almost," Lily smiled. "Plenty of cabbage to be had around here."

"And you, sir?" the waitress asked.

"Yes," Cranston said, still finding the menu difficult to read. "Terribly sorry. Um...what would you recommend with the victory cabbage?"

"Uh...sausage, I guess," the waitress answered, as if no one had ever asked her for a recommendation before. "It's a side dish, so we can serve it with anything."

"Sausage would be fine." Cranston smiled.

"Been on the road a while?"

"Yes."

"Well, we got rooms available."

"Thank you," he said. "Is there coffee?"

"Right over there," she pointed to a clean, but well-used tin pot at one end of the counter. "You can help yourself. It's on the house."

"Turkish tea," he said to himself, without having intended to do so.

"The bee's knees!" the waitress said. "I'll be right back with your food."

Lily reached out her hand and rested it on his. "Do you want me to get it?"

"That's alright," he patted her hand. "Stretching my legs will do me good."

Moving did help. He felt immediately more alert as soon as he stood, but he didn't trust it. It was that sort of refreshment where you couldn't remember feeling tired; a sure sign that your mental faculties were not at their best.

Locking his gaze on the tin coffee pot, Cranston found that object had lost all depth. Reaching for it felt like reaching into a photograph. Part of him was surprised to find that the handle was round and not a flat piece of cardboard painted— however expertly—to look like a tin coffee pot. It did feel flimsy in his hand and he involuntarily imagined himself smashing it against the counter to see it crumple and fold like newspaper. The shifting weight of the coffee within felt tired to him, the faux-coffee playing its role in the illusion but its heart was not in it.

He poured himself a cup. It wasn't all an illusion. He knew that without being able to convince his entire brain of this fact, but he could keep himself acting as if he were convinced. Looking at the liquid in the cup, he didn't see coffee. He saw water that had millions, even trillions, of tiny particles of coffee bean diffused throughout it. Some fanciful part of mind suggested that he could force the coffee to sink to the bottom of the cup like silt, leaving pure water on the top, if only he thought it with a sufficient force of will.

Cranston sipped the coffee and found it cooler than he liked it, but such was the nature of free coffee. He took a larger gulp and the rational part of his mind became a little more dominant. It still looked like water with flecks of coffee in it, sitting inside in a cup that was not really a cup, though it could do the job of a cup. But, he was rational enough to tell himself that this was an illusion of sleep deprivation and the thing which caused his sleep deprivation.

Turning to go back to the table, he saw the modified 490 park in a spot in front of the inn's restaurant. The driver got out and peered curiously into the restaurant, then faced forward and began walking.

Cranston watched the man's face for a moment, then a shock ran through his body. His sympathetic nervous system opened up and adrenaline flooded his body. It was the danger-ready feeling of hearing the first bullet whistle past your ear.

The driver was Ryan Wolfe, the man he had met in the back pews of the CHJ. The man who had said that he had been in Silkhaven for a month and a half, meaning June. Lucien and Rosamund had come in June. Ryan Wolfe had been right on their heels. He was the CHJ's expert criminal, but not a full member. It was less incriminating that way; easier to make it look like a rogue element and not anything to do with Reverend Campbell. A Wolfe in the fold, leading the overzealous astray.

Perhaps the attempt in Baltimore had not been a true attempt, but only a harrying party, getting a view of the enemy's defenses. Or even, more sinisterly, a flanking maneuver intended to get Rosamund back to the Retreat, getting her to stay in one place long enough for them to properly recon-noiter before the strike.

Very close, there was a sharp crashing sound. Cranston jumped back two feet and looked down. His coffee cup lay in pieces on the restaurant tile and the world returned very suddenly to itself; solid and whole and suffocatingly real.

Cranston grabbed his chest. There was something pressing down on it and he gasped for every milligram of oxygen. Blood pounded behind his ears and the sound of his own heavy breathing barely cut through.

"Cranston?" Lily said, her voice distant, despite her running to him.

"Is he alright?" Another voice came, far away and unimportant.

"He needs some air," Lily said. "Is it too late to cancel our orders? I'm very sorry. He was in the war, you see, and he has bad days from time to time."

"Of course, there's no one that wasn't affected."

"Thank you." Lily was holding Cranston's face, now, and filling his vision. "Cranston, we're going to go outside, alright?" One of her hands left his face and took in his hand.

She was pulling him. He had no reason not to go with her, but he couldn't make up his mind to actually do it. Slowly, he yielded to the pull of her hand, if only because it was the strongest force acting on him. In Cranston's mind, they arrived at the car without having gone more than a few steps and he viewed it the way he had Rosamund's guest room; the unique disorientation of waking up in an unfamiliar place. She got him into the passenger seat.

The fear was dissipating, replaced by a malaise. He had sunk into his own body and was watching the world happen outside of it. He knew that he could step forward and rejoin the world, but felt too tired to do so. Instead, he sat slumped against the door of the Chandler and watched Lily hit the ignition button and drive out of the parking lot.

There was clarity in that sunken perspective. He had

suspected that Lily could drive, but he hadn't seen her do it before and felt a toothless kind of surprise at how adept she seemed to be. Resting quietly in the back of his own mind, Cranston told himself that she must have learned in the war. She was Irish and a nurse and roughly his own age. Of course, she had served in the war. Plenty of nurses had ended up behind the wheels of ambulances.

Now that he thought about it—and without the slightest trace of emotion—it would have been irresponsible not to teach as many of the hospital staff as possible to drive. After all, if tanks had come rolling over a nearby hill, the patients would need to be evacuated. Ambulance drivers were liable to get shot as much as anyone else. You couldn't know who would be fit to drive, so it was only sensible to make sure everyone could.

This matter settled to his satisfaction, his attention fell away from Lily. Cranston thought of nothing. Objects presented themselves for consideration in the passing town, but he declined to expend the energy on any of them.

He didn't notice when they left the town and returned to the forested road. It came to him abruptly; perhaps he really had fallen asleep. He was drifting back into the world, knowing it would take effort to remain sunken and being unwilling to make it.

Returning made him more aware of a mild discomfort in how he was sat. Shifting himself into a more comfortable position was, evidently, the first outward sign of any change.

"Are you coming around?" Lily asked from the driver's seat.

"Yes," Cranston managed.

She waited a moment before asking: "Has that happened before?"

He took a deep breath. "Yes. I'm sorry. I know it can be alarming."

"I've seen much worse." When he didn't reply she said: "I didn't think you'd want to go back to the retreat, right away. So, we're on a bit of a scenic route."

"That's fine," he said, half-heartedly.

They continued on in silence for a few minutes. A turn in the road brought them within sight of a river, the trees thinning at the road's edge. Here, Lily stopped the car.

"I don't think I should drive," Cranston said, slowly.

"You're not going to," Lily said, getting out of the car. "Come along."

At first, Cranston thought he wouldn't, but then a small voice told him that he would have to argue and it was easier to just obey.

Out of the car, the after effects of one of these episodes came on strong. He felt perfectly relaxed. The process of the episode, whatever it was, seemed to flush all stress or concern from his mind. He imagined that this was what a train boiler felt like after some minor catastrophe blasted all the steam out of it; no energy, no, but no strain, either.

This relaxed feeling he carried with him on his return from the flat world was too lazy to recall much, which had the effect of making everything pleasantly new. He noticed the tinges of blue in the pine trees and the burbling whisper of the river ahead. Following Lily, he noted a swing in her step that he was certain he would have noticed before.

Driving a car would do that to you.

There was a short embankment, shored up by large stones, leading down from the road and into the river. Lily picked over the rocks carefully, until she was three feet from the water's edge. It was wide here. Cranston didn't calculate how long it would take to swim across, but only registered that it would be a good day's exercise to do so. The surface was placid and a twig drifting along nearby told him the current was slow; at least, at the top.

His attention was pulled from the river by the clomp of shoes on the rocks. Lily—with her back to him—had removed her double-breasted coat and her boots, leaving her in the loose trousers and the upper half of a shift. In his state of indolence, he watched her drop the trousers to her ankles. She stepped out of them, pushing her stockings down and off with her feet.

Lily reached up and slid the thin straps of her shift off and let it pool on top of her trousers. This action, even more than the sight of her coy bottom, began to burn away the indolence.

Without looking back at him, she swayed down into the water until it was almost up to her apple-shaped derriere. Only then, did she look back, careful to turn her neck only. "Are you coming?"

For a moment, he wasn't sure, but his body began to languidly strip despite the hesitation in his mind. He noted, amused, that he had more articles of clothing than she did. What a marvelous era the world had entered.

As soon as Cranston set foot in the water—the cold sending a second awakening surge through him—Lily dove into the river, disappearing beneath the surface. He waded out a few feet and then followed with a dive of his own. When he resurfaced, the lazy relaxation was gone, though his full faculties still lagged behind.

Lily was treading water ahead of him and he swam towards her. She let him get close and then suddenly swam to the side. He let her go, unsure of the rules of the game. Lily said nothing, only smiled at him with her chin just above the water. He swam towards her again, and again she moved only when he was close. Cranston waited for a protestation; that he was being fresh or that she wasn't that sort of girl.

Many women, following a coquettish impulse, found that they had unknowingly crossed one of their own lines. Only when the man in question felt he was vigorously accepting her invitation did she realize that she was in no mood to host him. His father had warned him of this fault of indecision so common in the fairer sex. No man of good character wanted to force himself on a woman harboring scruples about the coupling, but in the heat of their passion, might do so without realizing. For a young man from a moneyed family, that mistake could be disastrous.

So, Cranston let Lily swim away and watched her, waiting for some sign of regret. Not seeing it, he swam towards her again. When she next moved out of the way, he did not stop and the chase was on. It only took a few moments for him to get a hand on her ankle and pull her towards him. She let out a giggle as he did. Closing his arms around her, he felt her resist, but not in earnest. He tightened his hold, pressing her breasts into his chest, locking her in his embrace and Lily let out a small moan.

"You like being held, don't you?" he said with a half smile.

"Doesn't everyone?" she said.

"No, I mean"—he reached up to grab a handful of her hair and pulled her head back—"you *like* being *held*."

Lily whimpered in the affirmative.

So, she was that kind of girl. Not his favorite, but it was a game he was happy to play and, besides, he needed to sleep.

Part 4:
ROSE
AND
CHAIN

Chapter 17:
Cognostores

Vivienne didn't bother knocking on Cabot's door. It was 10am, so he would certainly be in there, meditating on the labyrinth and overseeing the copying and illumination of Paradise Lost. Entering unannounced was an act of authority, signifying that this building was hers; which it was, hers and Cranston's. Such exercises of authority which she already had, not overstepping or reaching for more, had always produced desirable responses from Cabot. He respected them, certainly, but she imagined that he saw them as signs of improvement in her; men who couldn't be kings, yet had frequent contact with kings, liked to imagine themselves as kingmakers.

The monk looked up from his table, startled. To his credit, the reaction didn't go any lower than his neck, and today's page remained immaculate. Cabot, who was shirtless for some reason, turned away from her to fetch his coat.

"Good morning, gentlemen," Vivienne said, acknowledging the monk while Cabot covered himself.

"Indeed," Cabot replied, draping himself in a second-hand overcoat. "To what do we owe the pleasure?"

"I need an audience with The-Men-Who-Know-Things."

"Oh? And what is it you would like to know?"

"Mr Cabot," Vivienne smiled politely, "my position grants me access to them whenever I have need of them."

"Yes, yes," Cabot replied, just as politely. "However, if it is something to do with the company, I should know. It is my duty to know."

"It isn't. It's a side project that Cranston and I are working on."

"Nothing to do with those suspected bootleggers?" he asked, confirming.

"None at all."

"Do you suppose this project will help bring your brother back into the fold?" He asked matter-of-factly enough, but added: "These are questions I will be expected to answer, later."

Vivienne stepped away from the door, crossing to the very edge of Cabot's labyrinth. It was the medieval design, laid into the floor as a mosaic of tiles only a few shades lighter than the rest of the floor.

"There is something that needs to be understood," she said, straightening her spine so that she loomed at her full height. "We cannot bring Cranston 'back', because we never had him. I know that the board hoped that he would pull a Prince Hal, but that's a thorough misunderstanding of who my brother is. He was never going to step up and be Father.

"So, no, this project will not invest him in the company. However, it could invest him in the society. As disappointing as it may be, I am the Walker you want in the big chair. Cranston will pay his dues, but you must find a position that suits him."

Cabot regarded her from under bushy, unkempt eyebrows. "On the one hand, you would know. On the other, you have the most to gain from this."

"Gain?" Vivienne allowed her weight to shift, cocking her hips to one side. "If I weren't in the CEO's chair, I would still have the check book. If I weren't here, I would be living a no less luxurious life."

"Hosting parties," Cabot said. "Having tea with other women of luxury. Curating artistic events."

"Exactly. So, what is it that I have to gain by continuing to run this company?"

"A set of duties you are more comfortable with."

"Hosting parties is a duty?"

"You must think very little of your sex," Cabot said, then turned his face down and moved to the center of his labyrinth. "What do you think your mother did for the society?" He began shuffling along the tiled path.

"She was on a vigilance committee for almost twenty years."

"Yes, but she did far greater service hosting parties. Your father ran the business, bringing in funds and creating channels of influence for the society. People will bend to the will of money and the whims of powerful men, but they do it grudgingly. Your mother talked to people, made them her friends. She made that will and those whims feel like they came from within, not without. Lolita won hearts and minds; as crucial a victory as any your father had."

Vivienne allowed that to sink in before saying: "Cranston can do that."

"Undoubtedly," Cabot replied. "If only he would."

"He has heartily entertained every client we have asked him to."

"Yes, but we have to wonder. We need a Walker in the big chair and we need another Walker finding the friends we need, not just keeping the ones we have. If Cranston refuses to do either, there are other Walkers who will happily fill the position."

Now, Vivienne crossed into the labyrinth, cutting across the lines to stand at Cabot's shoulder. "The-Men-Who-Know-

Things," she said.

"Mmhmm, posthaste."

She leaned down and kissed his head, leaving a faint lipstick mark on his bald scalp. "There are no other Walkers," she whispered, then she turned on her heel and left.

"Della Caine?" Vivienne repeated, writing the name down.

In a move that both pleased and disquieted her, Cranston had phoned from the Syme Lodge to tell her that he would be spending the weekend there. If all went well, he said, he would be returning on Sunday.

"Yes," Cranston said over the line. "Supposedly, she has been in a secure hospital since 1917. Lucien has his doubts, so we need to rule her out as a CHJ spy."

"Your friend sounds...above averagely skeptical."

"He's very serious about protecting Rosie," Cranston said. "*Very* serious."

Vivienne had read enough cheap romance novels to see that picture clearly. Mrs Shields' description of Lucien had bordered on the fantastical. Still, she could imagine a most compelling passion rising between the feisty heiress and the mountainous former soldier. His enormous hands wrapping around her thin arms....

"We should all be so lucky," she told her brother, pointedly.

"If a pack of zealots ever try to kidnap you," Cranston replied, "I'll have an entire vigilance committee protecting you day and night."

"As long as it's an all-male committee. The last thing I need is to get stuck with a woman in a leotard following me around in the name of propriety."

"Like Mother?"

"Exactly! Anyway, when I go to see The-Men-Who-Know-Things, I'll add Della Caine to the list."

"Lovely, I'll phone for a car on Sunday. The schedule, here, is delicate and yet vague."

"Like every woman you've gone out with," Vivienne smirked.

Cranston gave a long sigh. "Good-bye, Vivienne."

"Good-bye."

Vivienne took out the list she had prepared for The-Men-Who-Know-Things and added Miss Caine to it.

The cabal of researchers known as The-Men-Who-Know-Things were properly known by some obscure Latin word. Calling them by their nearest English translation had originated as a joke that was very funny to people who had studied Latin to fluency back in the 1890s. Since her initiation, Vivienne had only ever heard them called by the translation.

Their ability to produce information was formidable to the point of seeming magical. Any recorded document, so it seemed, could be found and found reliable. Once, she had been working with her father on locating a crate of very expensive brandy which had been loaded onto the wrong ship. The-Men-Who-Know-Things had been able to locate a manifest from a ship departing Hong Kong for Sydney, Australia, in less than three days. Following that lead, they had found the crate in a warehouse in Australia—where some eagle-eyed harbor master had noted it did not belong on any of his ships—and had it redirected to its proper destination.

Looking at the list of names, Vivienne allowed herself to feel a little thrill go through her spine. It wasn't disguises and gunfights, but it was still exciting wondering which name on the list would turn out to be plotting against Rosamund Syme.

The thought was interrupted by a knock on her door. "Miss Walker?" came the voice of Esme. She was pretty, which was risky so close to her brother, but she was entirely too good at her job to give up just because Cranston might try to take her to dinner. Besides, she was mulatto and Cranston was only really dangerous around redheads.

"Yes, Esme?" Vivienne called and the woman—who was a year older than Vivienne, but looked much younger—entered.

"There is a woman here to see you," Esme said, sounding uncharacteristically cowed.

"Send her in," Vivienne replied.

"Actually, ma'am," Esme continued with halting words. "She would like you to come out. She also says that you should get your coat."

"Does she?" Vivienne stood, did not get her coat, and went to the door. "Thank you, Esme."

The secretary went to sit, revealing Vivienne's guest. The woman was only 5'6" at the most, but her presence caused all other things around her to shrink from one's perspective. Her straight, dark hair was pulled into a tight bun, bound in a silver cage from which a tassel dangled. She wore a long, red and gold brocade jacket, with a high-collar and turned up cuffs, that fitted exactly to her waist, then swept back to reveal her legs. Pristine white jodhpurs fitted her slim physique with nary a wrinkle down to her well-polished, black leather boots. In one hand, she held a round cap small enough it would need to be fastened into her hair.

Vivienne recognized the uniform, though not the woman. "Chamberlain," she said, feeling a rush of blood as one might when seeing a large dog on an empty street.

"Miss Walker," the Chamberlain of the Rose and Chain answered in a continental French accent. "If you will get your coat, we can be on our way."

"Yes, ma'am," Vivienne hurried to get her coat, purse, and the list of names. "Esme," she said, herself flustered, "I'll be out for the rest of the day." She tried to say more, but words weren't coming.

"Okay," Esme said. "I'll take care of it."

"Thank you."

"Ready?" asked the Chamberlain.

"Yes, ma'am."

"I will lead," she gestured towards the elevators. "If you do not object."

"Not at all." She walked at the Chamberlain's shoulder. "May I ask what this is in regards to?"

"You requested an audience with the *Cognostores*. I am here to announce you at your appointment."

"Oh, thank you. I wasn't told when the appointment was."

"Unfortunately, it is rarely possible to inform before the interviewees. It is a question of security. The protection of their sources is crucial for the function of the *Cognostores*."

The Chamberlain never gave her name—Chamberlains never did—but said that she was unfamiliar with this part of the city. That meant she was unfamiliar with Silkhaven, in general, and likely a recent transfer. Silkhaven was not a stronghold for the society the way that Glasgow or Milan were. Outside of the Walker Corp., their largest interest on the island was the St. Lawrence Vigilance Committee; unless there were interests that were being intentionally kept from her.

Down the elevator and out the front door, a long, silver car was waiting for them. The car was two-thirds engine, by the look of it, with long wheel guards and a conspicuous absence of hood ornament. Vivienne had been out with enough motoring enthusiasts to know that the lack of ornamentation on such a vehicle was meaningful, though she couldn't guess what that meaning might be.

The Chamberlain drove and made remarks about the city as they went, letting Vivienne regale her with local knowledge off the back of those leading remarks. It was a shock, at first, having a Chamberlain engaging in such immaterial conversation. The Chamberlains reported directly to the elders and were, among the initiated, halfway to a campfire story. Vivienne knew she needed to be careful what she said, but she wasn't entirely sure how to be careful when talking about Silkhaven's entertainment district.

Neither woman revealed much personal information, at least, not overtly. Vivienne wondered if Cranston would pick up on subtle tricks that the Chamberlain might be employing. What would he think a careful answer sounded like? Which truths would he reveal in which order?

Eventually, the Chamberlain drove them into a working-class neighborhood; one story cottages with gardens and fences with dogs running along them to yap at the passing vehicle. There were still cars, but horses became more frequent sights. People, here, walked the sidewalks differently. They were slower, less purposeful, but by no means lost; the air of late afternoon constitutionals, rather than the necessity of reaching a destination.

The streets blurred together, their landmarks too small to be followed by an outsider. They turned down streets with letter and number designations until Vivienne was certain she wouldn't be able to find her way back. It was not the feeling of being lost that was giving her goosebumps, though; it was the isolation. Every other time in her life that she had been somewhere unfamiliar, she had had her own driver or her father or a suitor. There were stories of Chamberlains making people disappear and the cultish domesticity of near identical houses ordered from Sears, Roebuck and Co. started to feel like a threat.

At last, they pulled up to "a pretty little house" with a fine yard and a ceremonial wooden fence; straight out of the catalog. The car looked like an evening slipper among work boots, surrounded by boxy touring cars and unhitched carts.

The Chamberlain got out and Vivienne followed. The two women walked through the front gate into a yard flanked by victory gardens. The left side appeared to be recently harvested, while onions and pumpkin were half grown on the right. They stepped up onto a modest porch where a pair of cats eyed them indifferently. The Chamberlain didn't knock. She opened the door as if it were her own home; which seemed unlikely, given her costume, and made Vivienne feel like a burglar in the worst way.

Vivienne had heard piano music and, upon entering the home, found a young man practicing Schubert on an upright with a forest of scuffs along the side. The young man did not seem to notice them, as if they were invisible or he a very convincing mechanical Turk.

In the next room, they found two men sitting at dinner table. One of them looked up as they entered, so they hadn't turned invisible. He was dressed in overalls and his hat was on the table. The other man, in a simple suit, had a notebook in front of him and seemed completely oblivious to them.

"And for lunch?" the man in the suit asked.

"Oh," the man in overalls said, taking a cue from his host and shrugging off the appearance of two women in expensive clothing. "A sandwich. My wife made the bread...uh... with wheat flour. I get that for her every couple of days from the general store. That's Denny's general store, again. It had tomatoes that she grew at home with some corned beef we get from a neighbor; they're Scotch-Irish. She put some mayonnaise on it, with chives. She...my wife, that is...she grows chives, too."

All of this was dutifully recorded by the man in the suit. Vivienne did her best not to stare, but she made eye contact with the man in the overalls and got the impression that he was as confused by his own presence as he was by hers. There was sweat on his brow, despite the fine weather, and Vivienne felt herself begin to perspire, as well.

They continued into the kitchen where a woman stood over a basin of water with a pocket watch in one hand. Looking at the watch, she took three quick breaths and then plunged her face into the water, keeping the watch raised. Vivienne almost screamed.

The Chamberlain opened a door leading from the kitchen, having never said a word to the family who apparently lived here. The door led to a landing and that to a staircase going down into a basement at least twenty feet beneath the house. An aluminum railing was set into the cold concrete to assist them on the long walk down.

"I apologize for the cold," the Chamberlain said, breaking the silence she had held since they left the car. "They use a clever system of heating in winter, but it makes the house intolerable during the months that are warmer."

"It's alright," Vivienne said, trying to sound unshaken. "I don't catch chills easily."

At the bottom of the stairs was a plain, wooden door. The Chamberlain turned the knob and then heaved the thing open. As it swung towards them, Vivienne saw that the wood was only a thin layer covering a half-inch of metal. Passing through, they came to some sort of library. Bookshelves were spaced as closely together as would still allow a person to move between them. Each end, at least each that Vivienne could see, was carved with a bas relief depicting men and women in the style of medieval icons; a gallery of unknown saints. Looking down the nearest aisle, Vivienne saw the books stretch off for at least a hundred feet in either direction.

The Chamberlain led her deeper through the library. Vivienne quickly scanned the spines of the books, as they passed. Most appeared to be notebooks. Others were those three-ring binders with the finger hole on the side and catalogue numbers writ large on the spine.

After a dozen aisles, they came to a series of doors, separated by plaster statues of more anonymous saints. They stood around eight feet tall, reaching from floor to ceiling. The faces changed, some having beards and some even being women, but their poses were identical. Feet together, elbows in, and hands pointed downwards with the palms out; expecting to be given something.

The door immediately in front of them had a zero painted on it, like in a cheap hotel. The Chamberlain turned left and Vivienne saw the numbers counting up, but only the odds. Beyond the fifth door, there were more bookshelves, perpendicular to those they had just come through, but they stopped at door 3.

"Here," the Chamberlain said. "I will wait for thirty minutes. If the interview takes more time, someone else will take you to your home."

"Thank you," Vivienne said, as the Chamberlain opened the door.

The room inside was small and blank. A table cut through the middle, touching both walls, separating the door she had come through from another opposite. A padded chair sat on either side. Almost as soon as the door closed behind Vivienne, the one opposite opened.

A man with a mustache entered and smiled at her. The sides and back of his head were shaved, leaving a long coif of hair growing from the top and this was slicked back with pomade. He wore loose, blue trousers and a white shirt with the sleeves rolled up past his elbow, revealing forearms cluttered with tattoos. They were not the classic sort, which shared artistic roots with newspaper comics, but rather appeared to have been done by someone that had studied fine art.

"Miss Walker?" he said in a crisp, American accent.

"Yes, sir," she replied, sounding unpleasantly like a schoolgirl.

"The name's Brand." Stepping to the table, he extended a hand.

"It's a pleasure to meet you, Mr Brand." Vivienne shook

his hand, momentarily worried that they might be sweaty, but found a strange degree of comfort in the formality.

"Have a seat." He sat and produced a small notebook and pencil from his trousers pocket.

Vivienne sat, pulling out her own chair as the table prevented Mr Brand from doing so for her.

"Welcome to the archive," he said genially. "I am one of The-Men-Who-Know-Things."

"Thank you," Vivienne replied. "I am Vivienne Walker, Acting CEO of the Walker Corporation."

"I saw that." He said with a tone of curiosity. "Why 'acting'?"

"The board is still waiting for my brother to take over the position."

"Praetorian Captain Cranston Walker?"

"Yes,"

"Is that likely? The war's been over for a while now. I apologize if that's prying, but it is sort of my job."

"Cranston has shown no interest in the position."

"Hmm," Mr Brand wrinkled his mouth. "Would you like to have the 'acting' part removed?"

Vivienne was at a brief loss. This was not at all a question she ever expected to be asked. "Yes," she said, then summoning the force of her personality, added: "I am the Walker that will lead the company into the next era. I understand that this is a man's world, but I can do things, at the company, which no man living is capable of. I do not equivocate and I would prefer if my title reflected that."

"Hell, yeah," he nodded. "I'll make a note. I don't know if it'll help, but it couldn't hurt. You've got like a whole George Eliot thing going on; that's why I asked."

"A what?"

"You know, George Eliot?"

"The writer, yes."

He paused for a moment, considering his words. "If she were alive today, I think she'd dress like you."

"I shall take that as a compliment."

"As intended," Mr Brand nodded.

"If I may ask," Vivienne ventured, "where are you from, Mr Brand?"

"Virginia. New Atlantis, born and raised."

"I wondered."

"It's the dialect, right?"

"I'm afraid I am only familiar enough with it to suspect when I hear it."

He shrugged and nodded, amiably. "Sure. Alright, what say we get down to business?"

"Yes."

"What would you like to know?"

Vivienne took the list of names from her purse and handed them to him. "These are the names of members at the Church of the Hero Jesus, here in Silkhaven, with the exception of the last two. I would like to know if any of them have criminal records. The last name, Della Caine, is a different matter."

"Okay," he said, holding up a hand to pause her. "Let me note this." He drew brackets around the names, save the last two, and made a shorthand notation beside the bracket. "What do you want to know about Della Caine?"

"Hospital records. Supposedly, she has been in a secure hospital since 1917, suffering from EDAD. I would like to confirm that."

"Supposedly?"

"There is a degree of doubt around the claim."

He nodded slowly. "Fun." He made more shorthand notations. "And what about Ryan Wolfe?"

"Criminal records, like the others. He isn't a full member of the CHJ, but he does attend there."

"Is that everything?"

"Yes."

"Alright, wait here just a moment. I am going to run this by our sources and see what we can get." He stood. "This could take a while. Would you like coffee or tea?"

"Tea, please. Anything black with sugar."

"Coming right up."

Mr Brand left Vivienne alone in the blank room. The light was even and pleasant enough that she did not quite feel like a prisoner, though the feeling was very close. After a few minutes, Mr Brand returned with a tray. A large pot of water sat beside a matching cup and saucer with a tin of leaves and a bowl of sugar. He also brought her a newspaper and told her that her request had been submitted, they were just waiting on a reply.

In her reasonably comfortable chair, sipping her tea, reading the day's paper—and almost, but not quite feeling like she had been arrested—Vivienne passed a full half hour, getting regular updates from Mr Brand. None of them were especially meaningful to her, but it kept her from feeling forgotten. Finally, as Vivienne was considering the sports page and wondering if she could reverse engineer the rules of baseball from the report on the Senators-Indians game, Mr Brand returned carrying a thick, three-ring binder.

"Here you are, Miss Walker." Brand set the binder on the table. "Criminal histories on the names you gave us, plus the medical history of Della Caine up to the present day."

She stood and shook his hand. "Thank you very much."

"The Chamberlain will get this back from you in a few days."

"I understand."

"Have a good day."

"You as well." Vivienne picked up the binder and tucked it under her arm, then saw herself out.

In the main room, the Chamberlain had been replaced by a lean, athletic-looking man in a billowing pair of striped trousers tucked into black boots and a loose shirt with no buttons, revealing half of his hairless chest. He wore a domino mask under a bandana cap.

"Miss Walker?" he said with a flourishing bow.

"Yes," she said.

"I am...El Tiburon!" He straightened his back and puffed out his chest dramatically. "Sent for you by the St. Lawrence Vigilance Committee. I'll be driving you home today."

"Oh," Vivienne smiled at him. "An armed escort?" She eyed the cutlass attached to his hip.

"Only the finest for one such as yourself, madam."

"Very good, lay on."

She followed him back out of the house and into a boxy touring car. Tiburon didn't try to make conversation, which suited Vivienne. She was in a queer sort of mood.

The-Men-Who-Know-Things and the Chamberlain were deep elements of the society. Cabot, for all his wrangling, was little more than a messenger between the Walker Corporation and the society proper. She could argue with Cabot, even defy him, without consequence. Angering the Chamberlain was another story and she had no idea what kind of influence The-Men-Who-Know-Things could bring to bear.

What she knew was that she felt less powerful than them. She felt, without any real proof, that they could pull her out of Father's chair and toss her out onto the street with unchallengeable authority. That everyone in the building would immediately accept it with fear and trembling. Vivienne was used to dealing with men who incorrectly believed they were in such a position and dared them to make their move. Looking people in the eye who actually could was new. Having such people speak to her in cordial and polite, if not formal, tones was disorienting.

She was beset by the feeling that she was in control of nothing at all. This was beyond humility; this was helplessness. It was a feeling that would make her second-guess herself—a fatal action in her professional life—until it was purged.

When the Walker Grand Hotel came into view, Tiburon broke his silence. "If you don't mind me saying so," he ventured. "It's a real honor to be driving you."

"That's very kind of you to say." Vivienne replied.

"Really, it is. Your parents are legends at the vigilance committee. There hasn't been a lady like your mother since she retired. Not in the committee, that is."

His tone was deferential in an awed and sincere way.

"I still have her old uniform." Vivienne said. "The family has a kind of private museum. Would you like to come take a look?"

"Really, ma'am?"

"Of course," then, coming to the hotel, she directed him into the garage. "As a favor," she added as they parked. "For the next hour or so, continue calling me 'madam.'"

Tiburon looked confused, but didn't protest. "Yes, that will not be a problem."

"Good boy,"

Chapter 18:
My House

September 9th, 1920. Silkhaven.

The tradition of vigilantes had its roots in the French Revolution. In the early days, James VIII of Great Britain had been hesitant to lend military support to his cousin, Louis XVI, lest the British army be dragged into a war against Austria. As such, no aid was ready to be mustered when Louis was arrested in 1792.

Sending in the army would have meant a months-long campaign from Normandy to Paris, in which time, the revolutionaries would surely have executed Louis. Instead, James organized a squadron of fifty highland fighters to enter France in secret, where they were met by the Royal-Ecossais, a regiment of Scottish soldiers serving the French crown as a symbol of the two nations' ongoing alliance following the Stuart Restoration.

While the royalist regiment fortified positions in Vendée, the fifty highlanders made their way to Paris and stormed the Temple. During the attack, they wore masks and shouted revolutionary slogans to sew confusion among the guards. Once Louis and Marie Antoinette were out of the prison, the highlanders stripped off their masks and hid the deposed king and queen in crates of apples.

Throughout the Reign of Terror, British masked men

continued to operate in France, rescuing as many nobles as they could from Madame Guillotine. Collectively, they became known as Pimpernels, due to the flower being a code symbol for their safe houses.

A decade later, the newly independent Federated States of America faced a law enforcement crisis in its biggest cities. Gangs were rampant and police officers were frequently victims of revenge plots. Some volunteer police squads, inspired by the Pimpernels, began wearing masks to keep themselves and their families safe. In time, the gangs began masking themselves and wearing crude uniforms, often posing as volunteer police.

The volunteer law enforcers began trading their badges for unique costumes to distinguish themselves from the criminals and the first vigilance committees were born.

The Rose and Chain, as well as other secret societies, supported vigilance committees across the Federated States, Canada, and even a few in the Indian States. In Silkhaven, the Rose and Chain ran the St Lawrence Committee. This was how Vivienne's mother, a poor Russian immigrant, had gained entrance to the society and gone on to marry into one of North America's richest families.

She had been known as Mirror. Her costume had been an all white dress with a full cape—lined with sheaths for her throwing knives—worn over an iron corset, and her mask had been a Greek-style helmet with silver plating. All three pieces now rested on mannequins inside a glass box that stood along one wall of the room that had belonged to Vivienne's grandparents on the north side of the penthouse.

Simple boxes were stacked next to the museum-grade display cases all over the room. Turning this room into a family museum had been Lolita Walker's little project, one that she progressed on in fits and starts. Across from Lolita's costume was James'. James was the second Smoke, the first having been Lolita's brother, Petro, until his murder. Petro's costume had been lost.

James' grey suit and cape were hung neatly on their own mannequins. His fedora and face-covering scarf were situated on a bust of Alexander Hamilton that had long ago held pride of place in the living room. Smoke's trademark sword cane, however, rested on a custom-made wall mount.

None of that interested El Tiburon, though. He had gone straight to Mirror's case and hardly looked away since.

"Smoke and Mirror," he said, "were my inspiration to join the vigilance committee. I dreamed of meeting a woman as *fuerte* as Mrs Mirror."

"Is that so?" Vivienne asked, draping her coat on an old sea chest.

Tiburon, transfixed by the slightly yellowed costume, continued to muse about his favorite stories of the two vigilantes. He was completely oblivious to the sounds of Vivienne stripping down to her silk step-in; bifurcated, so she could wear it under trousers. She didn't bother with her stockings, never having met a man who preferred them off.

As Tiburon talked, Vivienne came up behind him and wrapped an arm around his broad chest, her hand slipping under his shirt. The vigilante froze, then let out a short groan as her fingers found one of his nipples.

"Miss Walker..." he said.

"Ahem," she replied. "What did we agree to in the car?"

"Madam."

"Good boy."

"I don't understand."

Vivienne chuckled, tilting her head up a little to breathe on his ear. "I have a job for you. I'm going to tell you how to do it at every step and you are going to follow my instructions to the letter. Do you have any objections to that?"

"None at all," he replied.

Tiburon was a puddle of a man on the floor of the family museum when a knock came at the door. Vivienne had kept his mask on him and nothing else. She, in nought but her stockings and garter belt, called out: "One moment!" Then struggled up onto wobbly legs to crack open a box and fetch a pair of old dressing gowns. To her dismay, they had a few holes in them, but nothing indecent.

She threw one to Tiburon and pulled the other on herself. Hornsby was waiting when she opened the door looking flustered for the first time in recent memory.

"A woman has arrived to see you," he said.

"Who is she?" Vivienne asked.

"She did not give a name, ma'am, but she arrived with a young lady in a very particular coat: red, double-breasted, with tails." Hornsby knew as much about the Rose and Chain as any non-initiate was allowed to and probably then some. In a pinch, he could likely pass for a member. "There were two men of the St Lawrence Vigilance Committee with them, as well. The woman insisted on waiting for you in the penthouse. I prevailed in keeping the young lady and the vigilantes in the lobby."

"Thank you, Hornsby." She set her hand on his arm for a moment. "Please tell my uninvited guest that I shall be with her shortly. I have a male guest from the vigilance committee here. See to it that he joins the others by the staff elevator."

"Yes, ma'am. Is there trouble? Should I call all hands to the lobby?"

"There's no danger, Hornsby. If it were that serious, they wouldn't have agreed to wait downstairs. The worst that could happen, today, is an attempted matchmaking."

Hornsby eased into a more relaxed posture. "Should it come to that, ma'am, I have a cousin here in Silkhaven. He's a confirmed bachelor who would not intrude upon your liberty."

"Well-heeled?"

"A veritable silk connoisseur, ma'am."

"I'll keep it in my mind." She smiled. "Now, I must dress."

Vivienne stepped into the small dining room in a fresh day dress and her house slippers. Looking over the railing into the living room, Vivienne saw a woman sitting on one of the sofas, busying herself with her knitting.

The woman wore a simple dress that had once been white, but had taken on a mild tinge through many wears and washings. It was high-collared and the shape of the bodice, the fall of the skirts, made it look at least twenty-five years old. Vivienne couldn't tell for sure, but she suspected that the lady wore a bustle. Black boots, well-polished but unmistakably worn, were only just visible beneath the flounce of her dress. A kerchief was tied over her hair and under her chin; while a round, brimless black felt hat—flecked with white lint—sat on the driftwood table.

Vivienne herself wore a trim, brown dress with an embroidered white sash that matched the square collar; under which she wore a linen shirt, buttoned to her throat. This was no time to look like a flapper.

As Vivienne came down the stairs, she saw a large canvas bag on the sofa beside the woman; no doubt where she kept her knitting. The hands working the needles were a young woman's; the dark blue veins only colors beneath the skin, not the soft ridge lines that had appeared years ago on Vivienne's own hands. The woman's face was of a woman older than she, but well preserved: cheeks that had lost all the shape, if not the texture, of youth.

"Miss Walker," the woman smiled. "I apologize for surprising you, like this, but I couldn't be sure when you would arrive and, besides, I had an open invitation from your mother."

"I'm sure you know that I am the mistress of the house, now."

"Of course, dear, I know I've taken a liberty."

"More than one," Vivienne said to the woman, still unsure of her name. "When you come to my house, you take off your shoes."

The woman stopped smiling, but did not scowl. She extended her foot out from beneath her dress. "Have you a button hook I could make use of?"

"I'll call for one." Vivienne crossed to the phone.

"I shan't be long, dear," the woman said. "The damage is done. No need to bother the maids."

The two regarded each other for a moment.

"But where are my manners?" The woman set her knitting down in her lap and extended a hand without standing up. "I'm Mrs Wilma Hopkins."

Vivienne went to her and shook. This close, she could see the woman's uneven hair line and greyed roots. "Shoreham?"

"No, Springfield."

"I see."

Mrs Hopkins reached into her bag and produced a rose with a grey ribbon tied around it. She set it on the driftwood table, between them, like a calling card; as if coming with the Chamberlain and two vigilantes wasn't evidence enough.

"Your brother was not at work today," Mrs Hopkins said. "Some find that concerning."

"He is visiting some old friends in Montague."

"The Symes?" she asked, they being the only permanent residents of Montague that might be old friends of Cranston's.

"Yes, Rosamund and he knew each other when William first opened the retreat."

"And the very tall fellow?"

"You heard of him from Cabot?"

Mrs Hopkins nodded.

"I gather that he knew Cranston in the war."

"The world is small, isn't it?" Mrs Hopkins said. "Two old soldiers spending their days with an embattled family? And this prompted you to visit The-Men-Who-Know-Things?"

Vivienne felt a ghost of Cranston's advice telling her not to reveal anything of that visit. Let the woman reveal what she knows on her own. "Yes," Vivienne said. "Cranston will do as he pleases; always has. If you wish to stay in his good graces, you help. Attempting to redirect him will only harden his resolve."

"Cabot said that you were indulging him."

"It is the reality of the thing." Vivienne suddenly wished she had pockets.

"And you believe that by assisting him, the society can prove itself his friend?"

"That is how Cranston defines his friends."

"What would you suggest?" Mrs Hopkins said, picking her needles back up. "What can the society do for him?"

Vivienne couldn't say what conversation she had expected to have, but this was not it. "I'm afraid you would have to ask him."

"Of course, but we had hoped to have an offer prepared."

Vivienne thought for a moment. The society was asking for something and it would behoove her to give them whatever she could. At the same time, she didn't want to reveal anything about her research, so far. She needed something from the fringe that, at the very least, appeared useful.

"What do you know about Benjamin Syme?" Vivienne asked.

"Not much, personally," Mrs Hopkins said. "He lives in Boston, I believe. I seem to recall that he is believed to be a member of the Order of the Fourth Fate, but I couldn't speak to the provenance of that."

"This matter with Rosamund seems linked to her Uncle Henry's run for senate. That sort of thing does tend to become a family affair. However, I have seen no evidence of Benjamin's involvement. It may be good to know why that is."

Mrs Hopkins nodded. "That should be easy enough to discover." She returned her knitting to the canvas bag. "Please let your brother know that the society is at his disposal." She rose.

The two women now stood eye to eye.

"Vivienne," Mrs Hopkins said, "if you really are the Walker to lead this family, you will need to find a place for Cranston in it. These flights of fancy of his simply won't do."

"Of course," Vivienne nodded. "I suspect that he is trying to find a place for himself. He is not the same boy that went off to France. It may be that he isn't entirely sure who he is, now." This information revealed nothing. It was a sentiment that Vivienne had seen in a dozen advice columns since the war ended.

"There are few forces as stabilizing in a man's life as a woman."

"I am doing my best."

"Not that sort of woman." Mrs Hopkins gave her a significant look. "I, along with some other members of the board, believe that what Cranston needs is a wife."

"Have you been communing with my mother's ghost?"

Mrs Hopkins shook her head, disapproving of the joke. "We understand if he is reluctant to take up with a woman of his own station; your father certainly was. We would prefer she not be a barmaid, but if it takes a rough sort, there are women in the society that can acquaint her with the duties of your set. The crucial thing is that Cranston adopts a predictable routine to his life. Unreliability is why your cousin Martin is in Montreal."

"Though," Vivienne squared her shoulders, "I suppose

his routine is more predictable than Cranston's."

"Significantly," Mrs Hopkins replied. "He has a wife, three boys, and is rarely late to work. Even more reliable than Martin, though, is your cousin Vera's husband, Roger. Did you know he was a member?" She meant of the Rose and Chain.

"I did not."

"Yes, his family was initiated two generations back. Not as storied as yours, but loyal and capable. Roger has a younger brother who is very active in their business and his father is yet living. It could be arranged for Roger to take an interest in his wife's family's company. The shareholders would prefer to see Cranston rise to the occasion, but the board is confident that Roger could win them over."

"I understand."

"You will see me again when the society has made its decision on this matter. Do well and I will gladly remove my shoes."

"And if I do badly?"

"Then, this won't be your house, anymore." She set her hat and gave Vivienne, as hostess, a small curtsy. "*Nuovissimi primi,*"

"*Et primi nuovissimi.*"

Chapter 19:
Pharmacy Dinner

September 12th, 1920. Silkhaven.

Kermit Walker, Vivienne and Cranston's great-grand-father, had taken over the family business in 1859, after the board of investors had become intolerant of the conserva-tive—and decreasingly profitable—decisions that Kermit's older brother was making. It was a matter of family lore; a cautionary parable in the Walker family's private oral tradi-tion.

Needing to demonstrate a greater ambition, Kermit had invested in a new soda fountain manufacturer. The invest-ment, on its own, provided only very small returns. However, Kermit had then had machines installed in all of the Quirk's Department Stores. In three years, the revenue from soda drinks covered the initial investment, while increasing the popularity of the cafeterias in the stores.

In 1866, cafeteria traffic in the Silkhaven Quirk's was approaching twice that of the sales floor. It was suggested that the cafeteria be expanded, but the Quirk's director worried that the construction would upset the environment of the store. It was also pointed out that much of the cafeteria-only crowd were youths and that their increased presence would further deteriorate the shopping experience of the sales floor. So, instead of expanding the cafeterias, the Walker corporation found two struggling drug stores and bought them out, installing soda fountains and lunch counters. The drug store food was cheaper than in the cafeteria and this helped siphon those who could not afford the sales floor out of Quirk's.

Walker Drug Stores were cleaner than other pharmacies, but only sold the most everyday medicines and related sundries; laudanum, soap, various forms of cocaine and, after 1905, manitaurine cigarettes.

For Vivienne and Cranston, the drug stores had been their first taste of fame. They had lines of credit at all five of the Silkhaven locations, making them a wonder to their peers who frequented the places. On good days, they were known to buy a round for everyone, the way Father might at the club. It was a place where people treated them the way adults treated their parents.

There was a time when Vivienne would plan her visits for the busiest hours. Tonight, though, it was empty. A phone call had cleared the place out at 7. She and Cranston arrived at 7:30 to find hot sandwiches waiting for them alongside a pair of freshly pulled pink slippers; the signature soda of King Charles Island made from cloudberry syrup, vanilla and sweet lupins to give it a milkshake consistency. They ordered sauerkraut and grain mustard and feasted like teenagers.

"She still calls me 'Cranberry'," Cranston replied. "Lucien's had the good manners not to go along with it, but I'm afraid he's starting to slip."

"I never approved of that nickname," Vivienne said, taking a sip of her pink slipper. "Somehow, it seemed too feminine."

"Really? I thought it was rakish, back then."

"As if you needed the help. When you walked through the park in October the leaves piled themselves."

He laughed.

"Actually," Vivienne continued, "and I do feel a big silly asking, but: do you have a girl?"

"No, but I can check my other trousers when we get home."

She pulled the corner off of her sandwich and threw it at him.

"Fine!" He said, checking for mustard on his jacket. "No, Mother, I don't have a sweetheart."

"What about Pearl?"

"Pearl is a hostess at the Mermaid Club. While her professional services end at the club's door, her other services are predicated on my patronage to the club. She's rather like me, taking clients out for drinks."

"That's all it is?"

Cranston sighed, put upon. "She's a pal, at this point, I suppose."

"You and I both know marriages founded on less."

"Is that what this is about? Getting me to settle down?"

"It's about getting you to show up for work," Vivienne winked. "Perhaps you'd have a more convenient sleeping schedule if you didn't have to seek your entertainment outside of the house."

He thought about mentioning Lily, who had all but taken up residence in the staff quarters over the weekend. "I won't say I don't see the appeal, but there are complications."

"Such as?"

"Any woman I marry will be expected to host dinners. Despite the job title, I don't think Pearl would be quite up for that."

"I wouldn't know."

"The sort of woman you're imagining is exciting. The sort of woman who could shoulder the duties of being my wife is not."

"I can host dinners," Vivienne scowled. "And I was proposed to by a matador."

"So, there are exciting women that can't host dinners, dull women who can, and then there are women who remind me of my sister."

"Now, that is a conundrum." Vivienne took a bite of her sandwich and silence descended until she swallowed. "On a separate tangent, I got that research you asked for. It's all at home for your perusal, but I couldn't find much of interest."

"No?" He asked.

"The CHJ members we talked to are all clean as whistles. However, I did find something very interesting in the files on Ryan Wolfe and Della Caine. I believe they may know each other."

"And why is that?" Cranston had surmised as much, but not in any useful way.

"Miss Caine has, indeed, been listed as a patient in one hospital or another consistently since 1917. She was initially brought in by two New York State policemen. According to them, they were following her down a country road because they suspected that she was involved in a burglary at Asclophare Pharmaceuticals. Both officers said that she drove her motorcycle—she was on a motorcycle, I forgot to say that—they said that she drove her motorcycle through a dimensional pocket."

Cranston furrowed his brow. "That's impossible. Nothing ever comes out of a pocket."

"So, I'm told, but that was the story the policemen gave. One of her doctors noted, last year, that the police still wanted to question her about the burglary; also impossible, they say, given her condition."

"What did you find out about her condition?"

Vivienne looked upward, fetching this lesser information. "Nerves, episodes of hysteria, and something about her hair."

"Her hair?"

"Yes, the doctors seemed coy about it; God knows why. Something about peculiar keratin growths is about as detailed as they got." Vivienne took a drink. "Anyway, the really big thing is that the reason the police still want to question her is because, at the time of the Asclophare burglary, Miss Caine was an employee of the Atlantic Network."

Cranston furrowed his brow, trying to recall. "Isn't that some kind of detective agency?"

"Sort of. They bill themselves as a private security firm."

"Mercenaries?"

"Almost. From what I could find, yesterday, they rather resemble the Pinkerton Agency but with fewer scruples."

"You just described the mafia."

Vivenne shrugged. "For some reason, the police think that the Atlantic Network was behind the Asclophare break-in. The Atlantic Network gets interesting because they are also the last listed employer for a Mr Ryan Wolfe."

"He and Della Caine worked together?"

"They worked for the same company. Beyond that, I can't say. What I can say is that Mr Wolfe's last recorded employment was in early 1918. It seems that neither he nor Miss Caine were employed much after the Asclophare incident."

"If they were suspected of a crime," Cranston said, "they might have been fired."

"Indeed. And the best part?" She took another drink, leaving Cranston in suspense. "The Atlantic Network is run by none other than Benjamin Syme, Rosamund's uncle."

"Hot damn," Cranston whispered. "Hot damn!" He slammed a hand on the table. "They must have been fired! They must have a vendetta against the Syme family! You see, Vivenne, when Miss Caine was brought to see Rosamund, I followed her driver into town." He paused for suspense, as well, but didn't take a drink.

"No..."

"Ryan Wolfe."

"No!"

"It was him! For certain!"

"Did he see you?"

"No, I saw him through a window. I was indoors and he hardly looked in my direction." Cranston was smiling, now. "I'll put good money on Mr Wolfe being the architect of this whole endeavor!"

"Wait, why would he be trying to kidnap Rosamund, though?"

"Well, he might be trying to get Henry Syme to drop out of the senate race. With a family emergency like that, it would be indecent of Henry to keep campaigning."

"True, but also, suspicion would immediately fall on Campbell. The Bureau of Investigation would swarm him."

"And find nothing." Cranston nodded. "The only reason we know Mr Wolfe is involved is that we saw in that church."

"But it doesn't mean he's involved in the kidnapping plot."

"Not conclusively," Cranston set down his sandwich and fished around in his jacket pocket. He produced a folded piece of carbon paper. "When I was following Mr Wolfe, he made a stop at the Western Union." Cranston handed Vivienne the paper.

"A telegram?" Vivienne said, unfolding the paper. "How did you get this? I didn't think the Western Union employed women."

"I'll admit, I had to resort to more brute force tactics."

September 11th, 1920. Montague, KCI.

The Western Union building was one of the few buildings in Lower Montague that Cranston was certain was purpose-built. It was a free-standing, single-story, brick construction with tall windows set into identical, arched frames. The ceiling looked to be almost twelve feet from the floor, making it noticeably taller than any other first story in town. This suggested that the Western Union expected to add floors and that made him wonder if they knew something about this summer colony that he did not.

After returning to the Syme Retreat, Cranston had filled Lucien in and then gone to bed, intending to nap. The nap had lasted six hours and he awoke after midnight, more refreshed than he had been all week. Now, he was standing at one of the more secluded windows wearing a tool belt and digging a hand drill through the wood at an upward angle.

The staff quarters had an extensive collection of tools for maintenance. Cranston had raided it before setting off.

When the drill hit the metal fastener that kept the window shut, he took a hammer from the belt. He lined the hammer up with the wooden handle of the drill and gave it the strongest hit he could. The collision wasn't as loud as Cranston had expected, but he still waited a few moments before landing the next one.

He reasoned that two or three loud-but-isolated thuds would draw less attention than a series of quieter ones. At any rate, they would be harder to pinpoint. That second hammer blow was accompanied by the sound of rending wood and a sudden give from the drill; followed closely by the quiet tinkling of the metal fastener hitting the interior floor.

Tools back in the belt, Cranston slid the window open and climbed inside. The interior was a large, open room with a dozen tables set in two rows. Each table was dissected into quarters by a low divider and each quarter outfitted with a ticker machine.

He stood still for a minute, letting his eyes adjust to the greater darkness inside the building than out. Once he could make out the subtle forms of the room's furniture, he found the broken latch, put it in a pouch on the tool belt, and then walked down the row to the counter. There were four windows set into a facade, each shuttered with a flimsy gate. The facade itself did not reach to the ceiling, so instead of damaging any more property, Cranston climbed up on the customer side of the counter, then hoisted himself to sit on the top.

Behind the counter, the darkness was absolute. From his seated position, Cranston launched himself forward so as to land on the floor and not risk the unpredictable surface of the teller's side of the counter. He landed in a crouch, stabilizing himself with his hands. Now that he was behind the counter, he pulled the flashlight from his belt.

Among the paraphernalia of the telegraph office, there was a large filing cabinet. Every transaction would be kept for a week or, perhaps, a month before being audited. Auditing the transactions was necessary for bookkeeping, but also for determining the demand for services. Telegrams were the bread and butter of the company, as a whole, but some offices did a greater trade in money orders. More money orders coming in meant that they would need to install greater, more expensive security; more money orders going out meant that they should bring more luxurious aesthetic touches to the customer area. There were easily dozens of other considerations to be made, as well.

Crucially, though, after an audit, the telegram copies would be destroyed and the financial documents stored somewhere more permanently. Cranston knew this because his father was deeply concerned about people breaking into the Western Union—just like Cranston was doing, now—to read his telegrams. James Walker had somehow learned the audit schedules for all three Western Union offices in Silkhaven. If he needed to send a telegram, he would go to the office that would be auditing the soonest and, therefore, destroying their copy of his message.

The filing cabinet's drawers were locked, but Cranston found the key after a cursory search of the counter. He memorized where the key had been so that he could return it when he was done. Handily, the drawers were also labeled and he found the one for the preceding day without difficulty. He flipped through the handwritten papers, keeping an eye on the 'time filed' box on the form.

4:37pm.

He found one labeled 4:36 and another 4:42. The 4:36 message was addressed to a Mr Ari Mayer of Nantucket, Massachusetts. The sender was notifying Mr Mayer that a lost pair of shoes had been found and said they would be in the mail, soon. The 4:42 message was stranger.

> August 6, 1920
> **To** Miss Patience Virtue
> **Street and No.** 474 Tamarack St. Apt. 7
> Place Silkhaven KCI
>
> Neon Jezebel in house. Instructions followed. Expect no msg fore meeting.
> Lancelot

September 12th, 1920. Silkhaven.

"Cranston!" Vivienne gaped.

He just shrugged and dipped his sandwich in the mustard before taking a bite.

Vivienne returned her attention to the telegram. "These codenames are ridiculous."

"True," Cranston said, covering his mouth. "But if the police ever got their hands on that, it would lead them nowhere."

"It would lead them to 474 Tamarack St."

"Apartment 7, yes," he nodded. "Which the landlord told me was empty."

"He did? When?"

"I phoned him. The operator said there weren't phones

for the individual rooms, so I asked the landlord to put me in contact with the occupant, but there isn't one. My guess is that the landlord is a CHJ member himself."

Vivienne finished her pink slipper. "Why 'Neon Jezebel'? The biblical allusion is obvious, but 'neon'?"

"Modernity?" he guessed, glancing out the window at the street full of neon signs. They were newfangled things that made it just that much more exciting to be out on the town. Not that CHJ people approved of such entertainment, much less trappings that made the experience more enticing.

"Alright, so we know that Mr Wolfe is behind all this. How certain are we of Miss Caine's condition?"

"Rosamund is convinced and she's the only one that's met with the woman."

"So, he uses his sickly old colleague to get access to Rosamund, then calls in the CHJ to do the dirty work?"

"That's the shape of it," Cranston agreed.

"Next, we need to figure out exactly what it is he wants."

"My money is still on sinking Henry Syme's campaign."

"It's awfully baroque." Vivienne picked up her knife and tapped it against her glass. The high-pitched sound drew the pharmacist out of his backroom sanctuary. "Another round of pink slippers, if you please!" She was happy, but she wished there was vodka.

Chapter 20:
Previous Engagement

September 15th, 1920. Silkhaven

Vivienne heard the door to Cranston's office shut at 10am. She knew he hadn't slept much the night before. She needed to speak with him about the Saint Moon representatives. Two of them were coming up from Murray tomorrow, but negotiations would happen on Friday. These were the same two that had refused to discuss business with him in the room before, but maybe, if the three men could spend an evening drunkenly carousing with each other, those scruples would be forgotten.

Still, she knew Cranston would resist and she had been waiting for a day that he was well-rested for it. That day, she now realized, had been Monday. Mondays were always extremely busy for her, so there hadn't been a realistic opportunity for it. Vivienne had thought that this whole thing with Rosamund had given him a sense of purpose that would give him equilibrium. Evidently, it hadn't.

His state had been degrading since he returned. Whatever it was that let him get a good night's sleep in Montague, he was bereft of, now. He hadn't gone out, which surprised her. He was a regular at the Mermaid Club on Mondays, but he had put himself to sleep with scotch, this week. She wondered if alluding to the possibility of marrying Pearl had put him off.

Vivienne got up and straightened her suit, then immediately felt silly for doing so. It was Cranston. But she was nervous. This conversation needed to happen and he was only going to keep getting worse. He needed to get himself together before tomorrow. If that meant taking the rest of Wednesday off, that was fine.

Outside, Vivienne asked Esme: "How did he look?"

"Tired, I suppose," Esme answered, trying to be polite, which was unhelpful.

"Mrs Shields?" Vivienne asked quietly.

The older woman frowned. "I don't think he'll be taking any meetings today."

"He doesn't get a choice with me," Vivienne replied.

She didn't bother knocking; it's not like he would be indecent. Instead, she found him with his head on his desk.

"You need to sleep," Vivienne told him, announcing her presence.

"And yet you are here," Cranston replied, then raised his head to smile, likely sensing he had been too brusque.

"I can't imagine you're like this at the Syme Retreat." Vivienne helped herself to a seat. "Is it the country air?"

"Something like that."

"No, really, Cranston. Why is it that you came home well-rested, but can't seem to catch a wink in your own bed?"

He looked down at his blotter. It was what men did when they were trying to decide whether they were going to lie to you. Vivienne couldn't imagine what he could have to lie about. It was sleep. The list of things that might help was short and none of it scandalous, not unless he was out murdering unfortunates to quiet his mind; which was something he would lie about, no matter what.

"No memories, I suppose," Cranston said, finally. "Being back in the penthouse, I just think about the past too much."

It was a lie. All women fancied themselves excellent detectors of lies in men, but very few actually were. If women, as a species, had a genuine knack for noticing when a man lied, men would have given up on the tactic thousands of years ago. Vivienne had thought she could always tell when her boyfriends were lying, until she became her father's assistant. It took a hundred hours in conference rooms for her to realize she was not half as reliable as she fancied herself, and a hundred to learn the skills.

Cranston wasn't being insincere about memories keeping him awake, but it was nothing to do with the penthouse. (That kind of distinction was critical in a contract negotiation.)

"Then, get yourself a love nest!" Vivienne exclaimed. "Buy a little place in New Versailles or something. There's no sense torturing yourself on my account."

He scowled at her, admitting that he'd lied and she had successfully called his bluff. "I'll look into it."

She huffed. "Fine, don't tell me. A grown man is entitled to a few secrets. But do what you must to get some sleep."

"I will."

"Tonight, now, I don't care," Vivienne pressed. "I need you at the height of your powers, tomorrow."

Cranston cocked his head as if he had misheard her. "I'll be in Montague, tomorrow."

"You'll what?"

"Yes, at the Syme Retreat. Della Caine has another appointment with Rosamund."

"No, Cranston! I need you here."

"For what?"

"The Saint Moon boys will be back."

Cranston scoffed. "Have you forgotten about last time?"

"I haven't, but I have a plan. No business, tomorrow, just you doing what you do best. Show them the absolute time of their lives and, come Friday afternoon, when the hangovers have worn off, whatever quibbles they have with you will be laid to rest."

"It's not that simple." He shook his head.

"Then, explain it! The complications don't daunt me: I'm smarter than you!"

"One night of drinks is not going to erase prejudices they spent years learning in the war."

"Good heavens, Cranston, what did you Praetorians do that you think everyone hates you for?"

"Our jobs!" he bellowed.

Vivienne winced. He had never raised his voice to her that way before. She saw him retreat into himself, seeing in her face that he had gone too far.

"I'm sorry, Vivienne," he half-whispered. "It doesn't matter. I already promised Lucien and Rosamund that I would be there when Della Caine arrived. A lady's safety is worth more than the off chance that I can win over a client."

Vivienne didn't entirely disagree, which was the worst part, but she couldn't agree, either. "So, I get to know nothing," she said.

"Pardon?"

"I don't know where you go. I don't know why you can't sleep." Her voice was escalating and she couldn't stop it. "I don't know why a company that came to us wanting a distribution agreement refuses to speak with you! You're the CEO, for goodness' sake! And... I don't know you!"

It was Cranston's turn to wince.

"I have been waiting for six years for you to come home and you still haven't! I held up mother and father every time more than a week passed between your letters. Your letters, which were always addressed to them!" She stood and began pacing. "I have been holding up this company for three years; fighting to be acknowledged by clients, fighting to be respected by the board, fighting to keep...everything I've known! Why won't you fight beside me?" she screamed. "Why won't you help?!"

Vivienne had run out of things to say. So, she just stood there, breath heavy, waiting for him to say something. Cranston stood and walked to her. His arms wrapped around her, momentarily pinning her arms to her sides. He smelled like Father and that melted her. She didn't cry, she just sank into the hug and embraced her brother in return.

After a few seconds, the catharsis had run its course, and Vivienne was more attentive to the situation. Namely that her brother gave very good hugs. She had always thought it was silly how women gushed over him, but she was starting to see their point.

"I thought you liked being in Father's chair," he said softly.

Vivienne laughed and released him, signaling the end of the huge. "I adore it! It's the most wonderful job in the world!" She allowed Cranston to guide her to a chair. She couldn't understand why men thought women would faint from strong emotions. That only happened to women in badly shaped corsets.

He left her sitting and poured her a glass of water from his bar. "Why is it you think you could lose 'everything'?"

"The board wants you to become Father and me to become Mother. They'll settle for me being Father and you being Mother, but either way, you need to start keeping regular hours."

"Or else what?"

"They'll force us out. Well, they'll force me out. With you, it will be more of a release, I suppose."

"And replace you with whom? They aren't so foolish as to give Martin the company."

"Not Martin, Roger."

Cranston's eyes lit up. "Roger. Well, that's alright, then!"

"Alright for you!"

"Vivienne, it's Roger. Even if he would agree to leave

the railroad business, he would never get rid of you. Firstly, unlike Martin, he has no vendetta against us. He knows you had nothing to do with Uncle Cecil's suicide. Secondly, Roger is the kind of intelligent that knows when he doesn't know something. He is passingly acquainted with trade, but knows nothing of ships nor of international relations; unless you count the Comanches.

"Roger would undoubtedly keep you on. He would know how valuable you are to the company and, if he ever started to forget, Vera would remind him. Of course, he would insist on earning his keep, which might superficially diminish your standing, but your work wouldn't change. You would simply have less of it.

"It's a splendid idea! Come on, let's go tell Cabot what a fine idea bringing Roger is."

"No, Cranston. Roger might not cuckoo me out of the nest, but the board would. Even if I were allowed to keep my office, they would tell me nothing. I would be excluded from every intelligence. Half of my day would be spent trying to find out what was happening in the company. The only tasks they would allow to cross my desk would be dinner parties."

"What about the clients?" Cranston ventured. "What if they were to refuse to deal with anyone but you?"

"No," Vivienne said. "Not enough of them actually like me. Most are looking for any excuse not to deal with me."

Cranston plunged his hands into his pockets. "Alright, then. I'll be Mother."

"You are going to host dinner parties?"

"Is that what they meant? Oh, dear."

"What did you think it meant?"

"Joining a vigilance committee."

"I don't think that will be enough," Vivienne told him.

"Alright, you prove to them that you don't need me and I'll meet with Cabot on Monday. Man-to-man, we will reach an accord."

"Monday? So, you're still going to Montague?"

"Do you love me, Vivienne?" Cranston asked softly.

She growled and said: "Yes."

"Would you love me so much if I wasn't a man who kept his promises?"

Vivienne groaned and marched to the door. Her hand hovered above the doorknob, but she couldn't leave things as they were. She didn't need to win, but she couldn't bear to lose. She turned around: "A grown man is entitled to *some* secrets, but not all of them. I need to know some things or my love for you really might start to slip."

That had sounded less weighty in her mind and she suddenly felt unprepared to hear his answer. Vivienne threw open the door and bolted for her own office before Cranston had the chance to think about it.

Saying it out loud had made it truer than she had realized it was. The stack of papers on her desk suddenly meant very little to her. All she was thinking about was the Praetorians and why Cranston couldn't sleep and where it was he went at night. She really did need to know.

Chapter 21:
The Mermaid Club

September 16th, 1920. Silkhaven.

Vivienne walked ahead of the boys from Saint Moon, not wanting the man on the door to think she was somebody's chippy. It had been a long day of negotiations and the Walker Corporation's guests were in need of a good time, on Vivienne's dime, of course. Hosts walked ahead of their guests as they approached exclusive clubs.

It wasn't just her ego; it was good etiquette. Though, most etiquette existed to protect someone's ego.

Negotiations would begin tomorrow. Tonight was just about greasing the two representatives up. Cranston had left a suggested itinerary with Esme the day before. He had suggested a fine restaurant and a club that had social dancing. Vivienne had made reservations at the restaurant, but had spent dinner distracted. All she could think about was the life Cranston had been living while she was trying to get him to live hers. And thus, social dancing had been scratched off the list. Instead, they were here.

The Mermaid Club was a six story building with a great, canvas painting covering four of those. It was done up in the old Mucha style, but nostalgia was part of the draw. The titular sea creature was leaping out of water the artist hadn't bothered to paint, save for a few looping waves at the very bottom.

Her hair covered her breasts, because this was a public street, but the suggestion of what was to be found inside was clear.

Vivienne had brought a second suit to work so that she could freshen up from the meetings before going out. The suit she had worn to talk about shipping routes and tariff distribution had a skirt. This one, the one she had chosen for a night of business drinking, had pants. Not that anyone could mistake her for a man, though, not with the top cut to look like a jacket with no shirt underneath. It was all scarlet silk with mustard and cerulean flowers embroidered deeply from the cuffs.

She had never hosted this way before. She had taken clients to plenty of lunches, but dinners and drinks had always involved Cranston in the lead position. The plan that he had laid out with her before returning to Montague had been a very business-like thing. The social dancing club had given her pause before Cranston explained that the owner brought girls in for those that paid for a table; the Saint Moon boys were unlikely to think that they ought to dance with her.

That plan, however, had gone in the waste bin the moment Cranston's back was turned. Their talk about Pearl had planted a quick seed in Vivienne's mind and she had resolved, through no will of her own, to visit the Mermaid Club. She couldn't say, even to herself, what exactly she was here to learn; there was just an irresistible nagging in her ear, telling her to come and see.

Knowing roughly what sort of place it was, Vivienne hadn't dared come alone. At the same time, she wasn't prepared to lead a solo expedition into this uncharted territory. Needing a male buffer between her and the Saint Moon boys, Vivienne had called on Mr Montblanc. Saint Moon wasn't part of his portfolio; he was the Head of Quebecois Affairs. However, he was in town and happy to come along to reassure the Americans that whatever they were drinking was better than anything you could get in Paris.

Montblanc had brought a new suit, as well. He was in salmon-colored trousers and waistcoat under a cream jacket with chocolate plaid. His bow tie was a shock of seafoam. Vivienne had thought her outfit was daring until he had stepped out of the elevator, swinging his silver-knobbed cane and tipping his cream-colored hat with a chocolate band. She wondered what Hornby's cousin would think of that.

The poor chaps from Saint Moon had been wearing the same clothes for twelve hours, at this point. One was in black—that was Briarson—and the other in navy—being Mr. Jones—and they were clearly from a store; obvious shoulder pads and loose in all the wrong places. The way Briarson's trousers tightened around his knee made him look like he was wearing knickerbockers.

Vivienne couldn't believe Briarson was married. Not because she didn't think he could attract a wife—he was upper management at the second-largest food manufacturer in America. Vivienne just couldn't believe that any woman would let her husband out the door looking like that. She wondered how many of his shirts had iron scorches.

The man on the door at the Mermaid Club looked to be married to a woman Vivienne would approve of. His suit was navy with white pinstripes and loose about the joints so he could dance in it.

"Good evening," Vivienne called when she was still ten feet away.

The man on the door tipped his hat, but said nothing.

"Vivienne Walker," she extended a hand.

He took it. "Bruno."

"First or last?"

Bruno just shrugged. "Only one I need."

"Do I call you 'mister' or 'darling'?"

"The girls, here, just call me 'Bruno.'"

"Yes, well, I don't feel we're on quite those terms, yet. I'll call you 'Mr Bruno', if that's alright."

"No skin off my nose." He shrugged again and eyed the three men falling in line behind her.

"Good enough."

"Any of these fellas on our guest list?" he asked in a way that said he already knew they weren't.

"No, but my brother is."

"Ma'am, I'm not supposed to let ladies in to fetch their family members unless they're in the breathing room, which is empty, right now."

"I'm not here to fetch anyone. I'm here for the drinks."

"Ma'am," Bruno was looking apologetic. "We've got a guest list and there's no ladies on it."

"Did you hear when I said my name was Walker?"

Bruno pondered for a moment and then a bolt of lightning shot through him. "You're Cranston Walker's sister?"

"Also known as Vivienne the First, CEO of the Walker Corporation."

Bruno put his hands together. "I sincerely apologize, Miss Walker. This will never happen, again. I promise."

"Quite alright, Mr Bruno; introductions can be sticky things."

"Thank you, ma'am." Bruno opened the door and took a step inside. "Oceane!" He called and a girl in a strapless, blue dress embroidered to look like fish scales came over. "We got Mr. Walker's sister, here. Take her and her guests up to his oyster." He turned back to Vivienne. "You can follow the girl, ma'am."

"Very good," Vivienne started in and called over her shoulder: "Montblanc, do thank the man for me."

Montblanc hung back and handed the man on the door a ten before striding to catch up with the rest of the group.

The Mermaid Club was mostly one, enormous amphitheater. Walking in the front door and through a shimmering, blue curtain, one found themselves near the center of a concave space that rose another two floors up and one floor down. On the descent was a crescent of tables on tiered steps, surrounding a big stage. Above, box seats gazed down, the underside of each carved and painted to look like a clam shell.

At the center of it all was a big stage. A fifteen-piece band was playing at the back, while a line of girls in sexy sailor costumes were tap dancing. Under the stage was a dimly lit fish tank where more girls, nude ones, swam about, taking occasional gulps of air from bubbling pipes.

As soon as the shock of that fish tank had passed, Vivienne's first thought was: How long is one of those shifts?

"Wow," Montblanc said, coming in behind them "There really is nothing like this in Paris."

"Bon soir et bienvenue a le Club des Sirènes," the girl Oceane said. She reached out and touched the silk on Vivienne's suit. "J'aime le way qu'à hang!"

"Merci," Vivienne replied. "C'est nouvelle."

"La chemisière ou l'expérience?" Oceane grinned.

"Tout ça."

Oceane nodded, still grinning. "Suivez-moi. Ça s'ameliore."

She led them to an elevator, upholstered in light blues and silver. Predictable, but Vivienne respected the commitment to the theme. Less predictable was that Oceane knew how to operate the elevator.

They rode up a single story and into a curving hallway lined with traditional fish tanks and floor-to-ceiling black. Every twenty feet or so along the inside of the curve was a door with a single light above it. Each light had a number painted on.

Oceane took them to number 4 and opened the door.

The box seat was done up like a huge shell. A semi-circular padded bench, low enough that you could rest your arms on the edge of the shell itself, surrounded an open space. Small tables for drinks were arranged about a foot from the edge of the bench.

"S'assassiez," Oceane said, staying in the doorway. "Camme toé. La sirène vous rejoindra bientôt."

With everyone settled, Oceane closed the door and left them to gaze out over the spectacle of the club. Briarson, in his black suit, and Jones, in his navy, took seats at the center of the curving box and watched the tap dancers. They were turned halfway in their seats, knees up on the bench, and Vivienne became certain that these boxes were not intended to be used this way.

She looked out at the other boxes and noticed that most only had one or two occupants. In the nearest occupied oyster, a gentleman was getting a very close-up cooch dance from a woman dressed only in what appeared to be large bubbles.

"Hot damn," Briarson said, shifting forward in his seat. "This place really is something else." He nudged Montblanc. "You come here a lot?"

"No, not me." Montblanc laughed. "It is as new for you as for me. No, this was all Vivienne's doing."

The Saint Moon boys turned to her, where Vivienne was sat trying to look like this was all quite usual for her. "My brother highly recommended it."

"Now, why didn't he come out with us?" Jones asked. "That is, I wouldn't want you to offend your sensibilities on our parts."

"No fear, Jones," Vivienne reached into her faux jacket and withdrew her cigarette case. "I see at least one naked woman every day. A few dozen more won't make a difference."

She watched them turn back to the show. It took them a few minutes to notice the bubble woman's dance, happening mere inches from the other gentleman's face. The girls on the stage tap dancing to make their tits tremble was the sort of thing she would have guessed at. Having girls come to the box seats was something she had gathered from Cranston's scant stories, but she had imagined them as the dainty creatures businessmen brought along to fancy dinners. Dizzy things with sufficient sense to laugh at their escort's jokes or little enough to think they were actually funny. She had always guessed such women were professionals at that sort of occasion and that these clubs consolidated the process; a place to have a fancy dinner that also supplied the girls.

Up-close cooch dancing was unexpected, yet surprised her not at all. If anything she was disappointed in her imagination for not having thought of it. Then again, she didn't even foxtrot, so maybe that was the problem.

"Good news, Vivienne," Montblanc said, holding up a menu he had found somewhere. "They have 'drinks for ladies.'" He had seen her drink straight whiskey often enough to know she would find that amusing.

She leaned forward, a hand extended, and he passed her the menu. Sure enough, at the bottom of the cocktail menu was a section of Drinks For Ladies. It offered such things as orange juice and black tea at prices slightly higher than the cocktails, which made her think there was some baroque code at work.

Shortly thereafter, the door opened and a buxom woman in a gauzy robe entered. The robe obscured the more exciting aspects of her figure, while shamelessly advertising them. Her hips could make you seasick and her crooked, little grin could make you feel all better. She had dark hair rising above a jeweled band tied over her forehead.

The new woman's gaze swept the box and landed on Vivienne. "You know, doll," the woman said, "if you wanted to gossip about your brother, you shoulda come on a Tuesday."

Charming impertinence out of the way, she extended a hand. "Name's Pearl."

"Pearl," Vivienne reached out and shook without rising. "Vivienne. I've heard a good deal about you."

"Likewise. I wasn't kiddin' about Tuesdays."

Pearl was American, that much was obvious, but Vivienne wasn't familiar with the accent.

Pearl stepped a little closer to Vivienne and welcomed two more girls into the oyster, similarly dressed. There wasn't much light, but Vivienne caught quick glimmers of something shiny underneath the gauze. The other girls, Daphne and Ariel, sat among the men, while Pearl took drink orders.

"Will you be drinking with us?" Briarson asked Ariel.

"Oh, sure," the blonde replied in a voice that made her sound twelve. "If you wanna order me something."

"Alright," Briarson said. "How about champagne?"

Ariel giggled. "Silly, mermaids don't drink alcohol. Tell you what; how's about we just chat for a little bit and you order me something later?"

"Fine by me, I just didn't want to be rude."

"No sweat, mister, so what do you do?"

Waiting for her scotch and soda, Vivienne watched Ariel trick Briarson into thinking that all of her favorite foods were made by Saint Moon and that she was just tickled to be talking to him. She was starting to reel Jones in, as well— Daphne attending to Montblanc—when Pearl returned with the drinks.

"Pearl," Daphne said as the dark haired woman handed Montblanc his cabernet, "Isn't his accent just to die for? He got it in France and everything!"

"As long as that's the only thing he got in France," Pearl said, loud enough for everyone to hear and laugh about.

With the drinks distributed, Pearl sat close to Vivienne. The mermaid took on Vivienne's detached posture and leaned in close enough to speak quietly. "What's the skinny, sister?"

"22 inches three weeks a month," Vivienne replied.

"Damn, I can just get to 25 if I eat like a rabbit. But, come on, who are these mugs?"

"The one in the good suit," Vivienne said, "works for me and the other two are representatives from Saint Moon. We are in round three of contract negotiations with them."

"I take it that Cranston is still out of town?"

"He is. What did he tell you about it?"

"A war buddy needed help with something."

"That's all he told you?" Vivienne asked, expecting Pearl to get more news than she did.

Pearl shrugged. "He don't talk about the future to me, much. Music, pictures, that's his sort of thing."

There was truth in that. After his second drink, Cranston had some very firm opinions on the topic of Eddie Cantor.

"How does this all work?" Vivienne asked.

"We get the boys excited and then they buy us drinks. If we start feeling thirsty, we make our excuses."

"I take it from the welcome we received that Cranston keeps the girls well hydrated."

"Mostly just me; he's easy to listen to."

"Mostly?"

"If he's in a very bad mood or a very good mood, he'll ask if I can bring a friend along."

"None taken, I'm sure."

"Nah, I'm happy to spread the wealth a little. I get him all to myself after my shift ends."

As their conversation dropped into silence, Vivienne heard Daphne tell Montblanc that she was thirsty. He picked up the menu and began perusing with her.

"What will you have?" Montblanc asked.

"It's up to you," Daphne shrugged. She pointed over her shoulder at a nearby oyster. Two men in suits were seated with their arms spread wide on the edge of the oyster. Each had a mermaid pressing her cleavage into the men's faces and shimmying. "They're having milk."

Montblanc nodded, realizing how the system worked. Then, he looked up at Vivienne, who shrugged. That didn't seem to do much.

"I'm sorry," Montblanc told Daphne. "I think I need to see a more detailed menu."

"It's alright," Daphne said. "A lot of first-timers feel that way." Then, she turned to Pearl. "Hey, Pearl, I'm getting kind of thirsty."

"Go for a swim," Pearl told her.

"Thanks," she stood and turned to Montblanc. "If you change your mind, Pearl knows how to send up a signal."

Montblanc just nodded awkwardly. Vivienne looked over at the Saint Moon boys who looked to be in a similar position. It was quite clear that both of them were ready to buy a whole bottle of something, but didn't feel at liberty with Vivienne there.

"Mr Montblanc," Pearl called across the box, over the band. "I can get another friend of mine up here. We got a Japanese girl; she don't talk much, but she does a flexibility demonstration that is really something. And I know a couple negro girls, if you want to see the latest ragtime dances."

"It's alright," he shouted back with a smile.

Pearl leaned back and spoke to Vivienne. "He's not... you know? Because he looked like he was getting sweet on Daphne."

"No, he isn't," Vivienne replied.

They were all minding their manners on her account. Not that she blamed them. Places like this were built for men to escape women like her and she knew it. She had come here for her own, nebulous ends, but still needed them to enjoy their evening. She needed this Saint Moon deal to work and she needed a more effective way to give the boys permission than a nod.

Vivienne reached out towards Montblanc and gestured for the menu. She opened it for Pearl. "What's something my brother has never ordered?"

Pearl looked impressed. "Black tea," she replied. "He likes looking me in the eyes."

"The blue pair or the brown?" Vivienne asked.

Pearl winked.

"Ariel, dear," Vivienne said loudly. "Could you get Pearl a black tea?"

Ariel got up. "Right away," she said and was gone.

"Who's the lucky guy?" Pearl asked.

"They can buy their own." Vivienne told her.

Pearl got to her feet and addressed the box. "Alright, seeing as this is your first time here at the Mermaid Club, I'll go over the rules with ya. Now, when a lady's dancing she likes some encouragement, but we mermaids got sensitive ears, so mind your language. Also, as tempting as it surely is, the gentleman needs to keep his hands to himself." She turned to Vivienne. "But, seeing as you're not a gentleman, I guess that one don't apply to you."

The expression on Pearl's face said she was waiting for a reaction, but all that came was an increase in the already distinct tension of the box.

"Give the band just a second," Pearl told the tightly wound bunch. No one had really been paying attention to the music, but now that they did, it was clear that the current song was winding down.

The tap dancers trotted off and a trio of women bundled in harem-girl costumes came slinking on as the band kicked off a new song. It was darker than the last one and slower, but with a distinct swing to it.

Pearl took her cue and began turning languorous circles

with her shoulders and hips. The gauzy robe she wore clung to her in places and draped in others. As she danced, this effect was amplified. Her hands floated at just the right height to obscure the shifting gap in material across her chest.

Once she had settled into the rhythm of the music, Pearl moved closer to Vivienne. It wasn't a long distance to cover, but just that foot or two was enough to fill Vivienne's vision. Jones—of the navy suit—shifted up the bench, away from Vivienne, to better observe the dance. This put all the boys squarely on the other side of Pearl's derriere from Vivienne's perspective.

She assumed the pose she had seen before, arms spread wide on the edge of the clam shell. The comment about touching might have just been sass and Pearl surely had to deal with enough handsy clients as it was.

This is the right thing to do, Vivienne felt the need to reassure herself now that another woman's barely clad bottom was rolling back and forth in front of her face. *Once she is finished, I can tell the boys it is their turn and they'll have no reason not to enjoy themselves.*

Then, Pearl began running her hands down her bottom and then back up her sides. It was something Vivienne had never seen before and she immediately understood the appeal. She started feeling twinges of jealousy: *Golly, I had never even thought about doing this.*

Pearl was as graceful as any other dancer, she simply wasn't using her feet. *How much practicing does she do?* Vivienne wondered. As the robe pulled tight against the inner curve of Pearl's waist, she thought: *Is there a special exercise to get that figure or does one need the hips?*

The hands slid down again, this time continuing to the legs as Pearl bent herself in half. It was probably the first time the boys envied her view. Pearl's hands flipped up the back of the robe and Vivienne was treated to a look at her mostly bare bottom. Black, glossy fabric ran between Pearl's thighs.

There wasn't a single bump on Pearl's skin. She had a couple of cute, little freckles, but her skin looked flawlessly smooth. Vivienne knew for a fact that she had some sort of mole on her own rump. The robe came back down and the dancing continued, as before. "Gee whiz," Pearl announced. "I can't tell how I'm doin', you all bein' so quiet."

"You are splendid!" Montblanc called back. "We are rendered speechless by your performance."

"Well," Pearl replied. "Show a little effort." She twisted around, keeping her bottom swinging inches from Vivienne's nose. "How about you, doll? Enjoyin' the show?"

"I wish I had your bottom," Vivienne blurted.

"I get that all the time." She smiled. "This is nothin', either. You ready for the real show?"

"Why not?"

Pearl hiked a leg up behind her and onto the bench. Without ever tuning her hips away from Vivienne's face, Pearl somehow managed to mount the bench. *She has certainly practiced that!*

The robe rose up again, this time falling behind Vivienne's head. She was in a tent of gauzy fabric with another woman's wonderfully round bottom. Her thin underwear was mostly of a flesh-toned fabric and had big, glass beads sewn into it. The strip of black was only along the bottom-most part.

Vivienne wondered, for half a second, if Pearl had sewn the underwear herself or if there were shops that made such things. The thought was cut off by Pearl pressing her derriere right into Vivienne's face. The slightly alarming move was elevated when Pearl began shimmying her hips, so that Vivienne's face was gently pulverized by Pearl's copious lower cheeks.

It was such a strange moment that Vivienne had to try very hard to keep herself from laughing. It made entirely too much sense that men would enjoy this. *How disappointing it would be, she thought, if I were to attempt it.*

Vivienne really felt she was at a turning point. Never in her life had she envied hippy women, having always felt at home in her own boyish body, but now she felt she understood why her grandmother had worn a bustle. This led to a vague image of Grandfather Walker burying his face in Grandmother's cleft and Vivienne was fighting another bout of giggles.

Pearl's robe crumpled around Vivienne's shoulders and the dancer slid her body down across Vivienne's chest. Vivienne shifted her shoulders, trying to keep her deeply cut faux jacket from being pulled open.

Feet still on the bench and knees bent high, Pearl was lewdly perched atop Vivienne's lap. The boys, whom Vivienne now had a clear sight of over Pearl's shoulder, were besides themselves clapping and cheering.

Pearl's satin-smooth bottom began to churn against Vivienne's own hips. A maneuver created with a man in mind, clearly, but not at all unpleasant. Pearl arched her back, resting her head on Vivienne's shoulder to press her derriere deeper. This gave Vivienne a look at Pearl's chest.

More glass beads—stitched into a wide-woven, skin-toned mesh—glinted in the light and covered the dancer's areolae. The mesh appeared by glued onto the flesh of her breasts. It did nothing to offer support and Vivienne was left staggered. Pearl's breasts were like two halves of cantaloupe and they sat on her chest as pert as a teener's.

"Come on, doll," Pearl said quietly—her mouth being right at Vivienne's ear. "Live a little."

She reached out and grabbed Vivienne's hands and placed them on her thighs, then reached up over Vivienne's shoulders to brace herself against the edge of the clam shell. Seeing one woman's hands on another's thighs, the boys were instantly silenced. That effect was not new to Vivienne—sapphic play having been fashionable for her entire adult life—and the staggered looks, as they always did, emboldened her. She began sliding her hands gently along Pearl's skin in a way she imagined herself enjoying. All the while, Pearl's abdomen was rolling her bottom against Vivienne's lap.

Vivienne looked up at the boys. Their eyes goggled and their mouths hung open and, in that moment, Vivienne was having the most fun she had had all week.

Below, the band ended their song and, with it, Pearl's dance. The dancer grabbed the robe that lay slack around Vivienne's shoulders and dragged it across Vivienne's coiffure—releasing a shower of perfume—as she got to her feet.

Dressed again, Pearl turned to Vivienne. "Oh no!" Pearl exclaimed, hands on cheeks. "Oh, doll, I'm sorry."

"Not at all." Vivienne said, uncertainly.

"I mean, I really made a mess of your makeup."

This was no surprise. "Really? You must show me to a powder room."

At some point in the dance, Ariel had returned with a collins glass of water.

"Ariel, sugar," Pearl said. "Can you take over for me? I gotta take Miss Walker to fix her face."

"Three boys," Ariel squeaked. "All for me?"

Briarson looked Ariel over. She was not as overall womanly as Pearl, but certainly buxom. Briarson fumbled to get the menu in his hands.

"Um..." he said, looking at the euphemistic drink names, not at all certain what any of them meant. "What's your favorite?"

"The orange juice is always a hit," Ariel replied.

"I'll take one of those, then," Briarson said.

Pearl laughed. "I'll send a couple more mermaids up to scrape you boys off the floor. Come with me, Miss Walker."

She opened the door as Ariel began her warm-up dance.

Montblanc's eyes followed Vivienne, which Pearl noticed as she guided Miss Walker out ahead of her. "Don't wait up." She winked at him.

"What is orange juice?" Vivienne asked out in the hall.

"The way Ariel does it," Pearl replied, "A fire hazard."

Not far from the door to number 4 was a cleverly hidden entrance to a well-lit green room. There was a full bar with a man dressed as a merchant sailor behind it, cutting down on elevator trips. Beyond that was a row of well-stocked vanities, racks of clothing, and a few chairs where a handful of mermaids were refreshing themselves.

"Coral, Misty," Pearl addressed two of the mermaids. "Ariel's drinking orange juice in box 4 and there are two fellas not getting a sip."

"Uh oh," one of them said and quickly finished reapplying her lipstick.

"Are they drunk, yet?" The other got to her feet, looking genuinely urgent.

"Not a bit," Pearl said.

"She's gonna start a riot!"

The bartender had a glass of water ready on the bar for one of the girls to take to Ariel as they rushed out to prevent some libido-driven disaster.

"We don't usually get lady customers," Pearl told Vivienne. "So, there's no washrooms for you in the public area. You can use mine." Pearl pulled a chair out for Vivienne.

Looking in the mirror, Vivienne nearly recoiled. Her lipstick had been spread well across her cheeks. Pearl produced a small bowl of water and a towel that appeared to have many years of makeup removal service to its name.

"So," Vivienne said, wiping at her cheek. "Is Pearl a stage name, or is the owner merely adept at finding beautiful women with aquatic names?"

"Rebecca," the dancer said, extending a hand.

"Vivienne," they shook.

"Mind if I call you Viv?"

"Deeply."

"Vivienne it is."

"How long have you worked here?"

"It's goin' on four years, now, which makes me the old lady."

"The mermaid business has a high turnover rate?"

"Oh, yeah," Pearl/Rebecca said. "Half the new girls we get are out after six months. They're the ones that can't work a box."

"Nerves?"

"Nah, the nervous ones don't make it up to the boxes to find out. You gotta get fellas buying drinks on the floor, first, and jitters don't make anyone thirsty."

"Ah, they don't know how to pull a man's strings."

"They don't listen too good. The fastest way to a man's heart is just payin' attention to him."

"Is that so?" Vivienne had a carefully crafted playbook in her mind designed to make a man chase her down. In her experience, men would go on talking no matter if the woman on his arm did.

"They're starved for it. The ones who come here are, anyway."

"I rather had you pegged for a seductress of the highest order."

"Oh, I am. My secret is that I like it."

"Seduction?"

"Listenin'."

The lipstick was gone and Vivienne began looking through the collection of cheap colors in front of her.

"Here," Pearl/Rebecca said, picking one up. "It's just about the exact color of your suit."

"Thank you," Vivienne replied, making a mental note to have a case of higher-end things sent to the dancer.

"Cranston's troubled. You know that, right?" Pearl/Rebecca said it with unmistakable concern.

"Yes," Vivienne said, eyes fixed on the lipstick. "It was like a stranger came back from the war." She had said it without thinking and regretted doing so.

"I've seen a lot of fellas who got scrambled by the war. They just need someone to be their mother and it sets them right. It's not war troubles that Cranston's got. It's a whole other kind of trouble on his mind and it beats me what kind of dame he needs to get his keel even."

When Vivienne returned to the box, she found Briarson nigh catatonic as Ariel sipped her water and reclined against his shoulder. They remained another two hours, with Jones calling in one girl after another.

He, at least, didn't seem to need an attentive ear. Montblanc spent much of the time chatting with Coral, but bought her a parting glass. Briarson never quite recovered himself and generally looked as if he had seen the face of God—the one from the Old Testament—for the rest of the night.

She didn't entirely blame him; though, she was more than a little curious to see Ariel in action, herself.

Vivienne had expected the Mermaid Club to be full of sad, little girls hoping a millionaire would come rescue them from a life of licentious degradation. She left with the impression that the club truly belonged to the mermaids and the gentlemen were but guests; not so much paying customers as supplicants making offerings.

Exiting the club, Vivienne felt a heaviness in the world around her. Everything was hard and intent on its own greatness, out here. In there, all the rules were different. Nothing insisted on greatness; it simply was. And more than great, it was mythic. It was a place where a man could be a hero and a woman could be a goddess, yet there wasn't a monster in sight.

She wondered if the world always felt this heavy to Cranston. If so, it was no wonder he couldn't sleep. Vivienne wasn't sure she would be able to, either.

Part 5:
ROSAMUND

Chapter 22:
Her Most Explicit Guidance

September 16th, 1920. Montague, KCI.

As expected, Miss Caine had set another appointment with Rosamund; the same days and the same protocol. Considering Cranston's new intelligence on Mr Wolfe and Miss Caine's connection to the Symes, they determined that the smartest plot was to kidnap Rosamund on Sunday. The protocol for Miss Caine's arrival and departure required Rosamund to be alone with the two women in close proximity to the car. If Miss Caine could, for example, slip a sleeping agent into Rosamund's tea, they could carry her sleeping body into the garage and depart with her in the backseat without raising any alarms. The abduction would be quickly discovered, but Mr Wolfe would have put some distance between them before chase could be given.

Rosamund balked at the suggestion, as she did any suggestion that Miss Caine was involved in a kidnapping plot. According to her, Miss Caine was extremely candid when she was certain that no one but Rosamund could hear her. She couldn't imagine the poor woman caring about the CHJ's prudish zealotry. Miss Caine's condition, Rosamund had once let slip, left her feeling disconnected from society; which was no revelation considering she arrived in a car with blocked windows.

That was as specific as Rosamund was willing to be. The only other aspect of her ailment that Cranston knew of was a deep fear of most people. She seemed to expect some violence from strangers. This didn't really align with Cranston's experience of EDAD. Soldiers in hospital had clung tightly to doctors, nurses, comrades, when the terrors came over them.

Upon Cranston's arrival at the Lodge, Lucien had quickly informed him that nothing had changed since last time, then left him to unpack.

Cranston had left the hunting costumes in his room, here, but had returned with a suitcase of more versatile clothing. The week before, Cranston had seen that Lucien kept his Praetorian Guard uniform with him. It was possible that the old boy simply had nowhere else to keep it, but Cranston had decided to bring his own. Ryan Wolfe might think better of his scheme if—upon leaving the garage—he found two of the army's famed hypnotizers waiting for him.

Cranston had brought an evening suit, the better to blend in, should Rosamund wish him to accompany her into town. He had also brought pajamas and a dressing gown for the usual reasons.

On a more practical line of thought, he had packed his Colt M1917 revolver, the one he had been issued in the war. Lucien had assembled a fine arsenal, but nothing compared to the weapon with which one had survived No Man's Land. Less practically, more totemic, Cranston had opened up the display case where his father's old vigilante costume was kept and taken with him Smoke's old sword cane. It was a heavy beast, more sword than cane by the feel of it.

Cranston had taken fencing as a boy and had put those skills to practical use more than once in a trench. Ammunition could run out, and the longer push across No Man's Land, the more likely that became. Trench fighting, more often than not, had been a desperate brawl. Long guns were just about useless, even when you still had bullets for them. Sure, you could try scavenging for them off the fallen, but that was a long process with your eyes turned away from those who wished you dead; much better to sling your rifle over your shoulder and draw steel.

Lastly, at the bottom of his case, Cranston had brought a dress for Lily. It was ready-to-wear, since he unfortunately did not have her measurements, but it was the height of fashion otherwise; black with floral embellishments and daringly low cut, with a mesh of pale fabric across the chest to maintain a certain minimum of decency.

He hid the dress away, so that he could have one of the maids prepare it before he gave it over; then, set about oiling his revolver. Cranston was vigilant about keeping it in working order; but with a potential return to use looming, a fresh oiling was in order.

This was how Lily found him: sitting on his bed with the end table pulled away from the wall, his gun laid out. The door was open and Lily leaned against the frame to say: "Oh dear, a man cleaning his gun. Perhaps I should come back later."

"Not at all," Cranston said, putting down his long brush. "Come in."

"I don't know if I should," she said, the beginnings of her love game evident in her voice. "It's not proper for a simple girl like me to be entering a man's room, unchaperoned and all."

Cranston pushed the table a safe distance from the bed and stood. He moved slow, decisive; like bubbling aggression sans anger. "You misunderstood," he said, eyes boring into her. He came face-to-face with her, close enough to smell that she was freshly showered. "I was not making a suggestion." He reached up and grabbed her by the hair, then pulled her violently into the room and tossed her onto the bed. Cranston kicked the door shut behind him, loud as a gunshot.

Two hours later, Cranston went down to the great room—with the long dining table and adjoining the kitchen—to find something to eat. Lucien was sitting at the table with a copy of Tarzan and the Jewels of Opar.

"Is she alive?" Lucien asked, as Cranston descended the stairs, wrapped in his dressing gown.

"She's having a wash," Cranston said, trying not to appear proud of himself. "I didn't expect to see you again, this evening, old man. My apologies for the ruckus."

"She's a volume three sort of girl, huh?"

"A gentleman would never say, but I can assure you that whatever sounds you heard were not made in protest."

"Have you taken a look at volume three of the Purple Book?"

"I read two stories which were recommended to me."

"The first time I went through it," Lucien said, dog-earing his spot in Tarzan, "I thought it was sick. Some of them have the women getting damned close to death and being grateful for it. I thought 'it's one right bastard that fantasizes about that'. I actually went to Rosamund about it, wondering just what kind of men the doctor was catering to."

"Not the men?"

"Nope." Lucien shook his head. "I mean, I heard fellas talk about 'pincushion girls', ones that liked you to rough them up, but I figured they was just making excuses. Rosamund set me straight, though."

"Yes, I learned about that rough kind of game in the spring of 1909." Cranston took a seat. "There was a lady, who shall go unnamed, widowed by a failed expedition to the arctic. She was not old enough to be my mother, but advanced enough in years that our companionship did not appear to be a court-ship. And it wasn't, at least not in the strictest sense. She was lonely and I curious about the charms of experience."

"Pincushion?"

"At her most explicit guidance, I enacted violence upon her that I hadn't thought myself capable of."

"Holy shit."

"Nothing permanent, of course, and I only drew blood once."

"Oh," Lucien visibly relaxed. "My imagination went wild on me, there."

"Sorry, again. I was raised to handle the weaker sex with kid gloves."

"You talk dangerous." He chuckled.

"Oh, yes. I suppose I should choose my words more carefully with Rosamund about."

"Speaking of which," Lucien leaned forward, "I talked to Rosamund about what you found and what it might foretell. We came to an agreement. When the car leaves, she'll be the one to open the gate for it. That way, we'll know she's not been taken."

"Just Sunday, or tomorrow, as well?"

"Tomorrow?" Lucien's raised an eyebrow, then both as realization dawned. "Shit, right. Taking her right away tomorrow is a real danger. Harder to subdue her, perhaps, but it would take us a lot longer to discover it."

"It occurred to me after you left."

Lucien picked up his book, preparing to leave.

"One moment," Cranston stopped him. "What did she say about her uncle?"

"Not much, just wondered how you knew they'd worked for him. That'll keep until breakfast, though."

"Naturally,"

"I'll say this, though." Lucien stood, tucking the book under his arm. "I've been ringing the alarm bell on Della Caine since the first day Rosamund mentioned her. Every step of the way, I've had my qualms and I've made them each known to her. Today, though, when I mentioned her uncle; first time I've seen a lick of concern from her."

Cranston weighed that. "I do believe we're onto something."

"And no question." He knocked once on the table. "I'm gonna tell Rosamund about tomorrow. This time, you shouldn't expect to see me again."

They shared a chuckle and Lucien left. Cranston made some toast, quickly, then carried the butter, jams, and knives up to his room. Lily was still about her ablutions when he arrived and began setting up their evening snack.

The staff quarters had running water, baths, and even toilets attached to the rooms. Each bathroom could be entered from the bedrooms on either side, with each room having access to one.

Lily came out naked and damp. She got up on the bed on all fours and crawled towards him like a hungry lioness. "Cranston," she said in a sing-song voice. "I'm still horny."

He was sat with his feet on the floor, so she wrapped an arm around him and licked his ear.

"Can we do something...special?" she asked, her voice high, younger.

"And what did you have in mind?" he grinned, expecting her to say 'something Greek' or ask to be blindfolded.

"Well, I heard stories and I know they aren't all true, but...I was wondering if you could use the Voice on me."

"What?" Cranston recoiled from her.

"You were in the Praetorian Guard, right? Like Lucien."

He got to his feet. "The Voice is for the enemy."

"It's alright," she said, sitting on her heels. "I'm asking. I'm giving you permission."

"That's not..." he did not have the words. This was unthinkable. He was utterly unprepared and that feeling, the dark surprise of it, made him want to lash out. "No," he said, not looking at her. "I won't."

"Why not?"

"Does it matter?" he snapped.

A cowed expression spread across her face. "I didn't mean to push you. I was asking sincerely."

His instinct was to tell her to leave. It would be easier, to make the offense known and shut her out; but then there was what Vivienne had said. That instinct needed to be checked if he were to have any sort of relationship approaching marriage. He had known that; it was why he had not pursued any kind of long-term arrangement before, despite the horrors of his insomnia. Not that he was considering making an honest woman of Lily—a phrase Rosamund, no doubt, objected to—but instincts were animals and this one needed to be starved.

It was only once he had resolved himself against throwing her out that he remembered how far from home he was. Without Lily, he would be useless come Sunday.

Evidently, this act of resolve took too long. Lily got up from the bed and began gathering her clothes.

"Wait," Cranston said, softly.

She did. Lily stood at the foot of the bed, holding her corset to her chest.

"I was rash, just now," he said, looking at the floor. "I apologize for that. No one has ever asked me that before." Cranston took a long, deep breath to steady himself, but also to compose his words as he stared off towards a dark knot in the wooden panels of the near wall. "I know the stories make the Voice sound like magic. Even the reality of it seems like magic to some. And who would not want to do magic if they could?"

He summoned his courage to turn and face her, feeling tension mounting behind his eyes. She stood watching him, keeping herself covered with the flattened corset.

"Everyone was afraid of us. Everyone." His jaw began to

tremble. He breathed slowly, willing himself not to cry. "They thought we…. It made us pariahs." He sucked in a breath between his teeth. "Every one of my school chums did their service, mostly as officers. We were supposed to be their bodyguards; at the beginning, anyway. So, they knew better than most." Cranston tightened and released a fist quickly, again and again; it steadied him in that moment. He didn't know why. "Those that came back…" his voice cracked. He took two breaths to control it again. "They'll have nothing to do with me. I'm still a Praetorian and they are still afraid."

Quiet sat between them.

He knew what Vivienne would do. She would try to buck him up by putting them down and reminding him that he was a Walker and what that meant. Perhaps she would tell him to get his coat and they would paint the town red, hitting all of the most exclusive places, proving to him that he was no pariah.

That was why he had never told her.

"I didn't know," Lily said quietly.

"Of course," Cranston replied, his throat tightening. "How could you?"

Lily folded the corset and put it on the end table, beside the plate of toast. She walked over to him and put her hands—slowly, tentatively—on his dressing gown. Silently asking for permission, she gently pulled it away from his chest and down his arms.

They kissed, softly. She took his arm and guided him to the bed, leading him like a dance partner to sit with his back against the headboard. Lily knelt beside him, then opened her legs to straddle his. She held his face with both hands and kissed him again, just as gently. Then his forehead, then his cheek, then his neck, his chest.

And all was quiet.

Chapter 23:
Whore of Babylon

September 17th, 1920. Montague, KCI.

Just after 1pm, Ryan Wolfe pulled the modified 490 up to the gate of the Syme Lodge where a maid, in apron and bonnet, opened it for him. Rosamund herself opened the door to the empty garage and shut it behind them, obscuring the disembarkation of Della Caine. Cranston was on the second floor of the staff quarters with a rifle that Lucien had added to the armory. Lucien, himself, was hidden inside the tall shrubs that lined the street sides of the property.

A minute later, Rosamund opened the garage door and led the car to the gate. Cranston prepared to shoot out a tire the moment anything unexpected happened. But the 490 rolled out onto the pavement and Rosamund shut and latched the gate without incident. She looked up and saw the rifle, trained protectively in her general direction, and blew it a kiss, before walking back into the house to begin her counseling with Miss Caine; whatever that might entail.

Rosamund had carefully laid out a schedule for herself and Miss Caine, detailing where they would be in the house. This would allow for Lucien and Cranston to patrol the grounds without Miss Caine seeing them. Lucien had further adjusted the patrols, opting to walk along the outside of the shrubs, giving him more patrol time.

A half hour into the visit, Cranston strapped on his revolver and covered it in the green hunting coat he had purchased the week before. By this time, Lucien would be halfway to the northern end of the property, where he would push through the shrubs and back onto the lawn, eastward along the river. He and Cranston would meet there, just north of the lodge. Cranston's route took him across the copse that divided the property.

Over the previous weekend, he had come to love the patrol. The quiet suited him in a way that he hadn't expected. He fully understood, now, the romance of the country gentleman. The patrol, due to the restrictions of Rosamund's movements, required him to sit for extended periods at the edge of the copse or along the North River—the South River being on the other side of the road. These pauses were ideal for reading and, in moments when he was sunk much too deep into the environment, he considered taking up poetry. He imagined something like *The Lay of the Last Minstrel* or, considering who was likely to read it, something obliquely erotic.

He rendezvoused with Lucien by the river. There was a fine rock that accommodated them both and they took out their cigarettes, the tobacco kind. Tobacco was one of the great equalizers. Cranston's were much more expensive than Lucien's, but there was no need to be embarrassed about that. Smokers were true loyalists, always convinced that their preferred brand was the finest available.

"What happens after the election?" Cranston asked, as the two men watched the tributary river pass.

"Rosamund will go back to lecturing," Lucien said without having to think about it.

"Job security is a weight off one's mind."

"So you've heard." Lucien laughed.

"I should find some of the other guardsmen that are

hard up," Cranston mused. "They'd make a fine vigilance committee."

"Maybe," Lucien nodded. "I saw a couple familiar faces on the tour. They didn't much want to relive the experience."

"No, but it doesn't hurt to ask."

"What about you?" Lucien asked. "How many weekends are you going to spend down here? What happens after that?"

"I'm not sure. There are days that I feel like a stranger in my own life. I suppose I shall have to make its acquaintance or demand that it make mine."

Lucien took a long pull on his cigarette. "What the fuck does that mean?"

Now, Cranston laughed. "In practical terms?"

"Please, please, yes."

"I think I'll need to make a real effort to fall in love."

"Do rich people actually do that?"

"What else is money for?"

"Having." Lucien shrugged. "Having more of than other rich people."

"Oh, yes," Cranston nodded. "There is that. It's gauche to speak of, though; far better to wallow in the existential mire." A moment passed. "You could have contacted me, when you needed a job."

"What would you need with a bodyguard?"

"I have a shipping company," Cranston said, as if the next part was obvious. "At the very least, I could have gotten you working security on the docks. That would be immediate work. Eventually something else would open up. House detectives for our hotels make enough to support a family. If you wanted a bit more adventure, I could get something on a ship with a couple phone calls."

"Yeah," Lucien drawled. "Like I said, I wasn't sure you'd want to hear from me and, besides, I was in Brockton. How was I going to get up here?"

"You still could have chanced it. If disaster struck and I found myself suddenly destitute, I would be cabling every acquaintance I had and I dare say I have fewer qualifications than you do."

"Didn't you go to college?"

"The only thing I learned in college was how to mix drinks."

"There you go! If Rosamund ever gives me the boot, you and me are opening a bar."

"Absolutely! I'll be the bartender and you'll be the bouncer."

"We just gotta find ourselves someone who can deal faro and we'll be gilded."

They finished their cigarettes, debating the merits of faro vs. baccarat, then agreed to retrace the routes they had just taken, rather than continue forward, respectively.

At half past three, Rosamund's schedule put her and Della Caine in a guest bedroom on the west side of the house. The windows opened towards the front gate and the staff quarters. Cranston's own room faced east, meaning that the ladies could potentially see inside. With the common area on the first floor having very little in the way of windows, this was a poor time of day to be in the retrofitted barn.

Cranston had found a spot a little ways into the copse. He still had a good view of the grounds, but the trees and their shadows made him quite difficult to see if he didn't move; especially in the green jacket. He pulled out his copy of *The Ballad of Golgotha County*, the epic poem which marked Oscar Wilde's flight to Virginia and return to the Christian allegory of his early career. In school, Cranston had had a professor who called it "the English Inferno" combining, as it did, political commentary through the lens of religious philosophy the way Dante had done.

Sat in a comfortable crux of tree roots, Cranston continued reading of the progression of the cross-bearing Christ through Ireland, witnessing the crimes that the Protestant British committed against the Catholics. A quixotic knight in rusting armor had just appeared, declaring that a beggar was a dragon, when Cranston heard the roar of an engine and a rending from near the house.

He jumped to his feet as he saw what appeared to be a milk truck break through the front gate and turn in as tight a circle as it could manage before coming to a stop. The rear of the truck opened and two figures ran out and into the lodge.

Cranston burst from the tree line, dropping the book, and sprinted for the servant's entrance to the lodge, some 200 feet away. He threw open the door to a bare landing with stairs down to the basement kitchen and a door into the smaller kitchen, where he had had breakfast that morning. He paused for a moment to control his breathing and draw the revolver. Into the kitchen and he listened. There were cries from the second floor; Rosamund was berating someone.

"Let her go!" Rosamund screamed. "No! No! Della! Stay calm!"

Cranston opened the door to the hallway quietly. Ten feet away, the hall turned left into the vestibule of the house. Just beside the kitchen door was the small table and chair for the phone. Under the table was one of the trench knives that Lucien had secreted away. Cranston reached down and pulled it free of the leather loops with his left hand.

There was a chaos of footfalls near the front door. Cranston ran around the corner, revolver extended. He saw one man with his head covered by a burlap hood, hauling a woman in a blue dress into the back of the truck. The man's back was turned to him. He could only see the skirts and the strangely wide boots of the woman, but assumed this to be Della Caine.

"Do not move!" Cranston shouted.

The man looked over his shoulder. "Crumbs," he said from under the hood, which left his eyes and nose uncovered.

A gunshot erupted in the vestibule and Cranston heard the bullet whistle past his ear and splinter the wainscoting. He dove back around the corner and pressed his back into the wall. It was not wooden anymore. Instead, Cranston felt the cold earth of a trench press against his neck. He could smell French rain. The muddy floor gave a little under his boots.

Cranston grunted, willing himself back into the present; the floor and walls dry and sturdy wood. He turned around the corner again and fired, aiming high to avoid Miss Caine. The hooded man in the truck ducked as the bullet pinged off the metal roof. Della Caine lay face down inside. Two more shots rang out, hitting the floor near him. They were coming from a high angle; the stairs.

Opposite the hallway was a door into the sitting room. Cranston backed away from the corner, took a long stride and threw himself across the vestibule, crashing through the door and rolling into a crouch. He moved quietly to the other sitting room entrance closer to the front door, which stood open.

Through the open door, he could see the foot of the stairs, but no assailants. He held up the revolver, balanced on his left hand, still holding the trench knife. Two sets of feet came slowly down the stairs. Cranston saw the dark red of Rosamund's dress first.

The second man, also hooded, had his back to the wall and his pistol to Rosamund's head as her body shielded him. "Drop the gun!" the second hooded man said.

"No," Cranston replied. "If you shoot her, there is nothing stopping me from ending you where you stand."

"But the whore of Babylon will be dead."

"You're wearing a mask. That means you didn't come here

to die. You're a man who imagines he has a future. Surrender yourself and you may have one, yet."

"Or this." The second hooded man turned the pistol on Cranston and fired into the sitting room.

As soon as Cranston took cover, feet clamored towards the truck. Cranston ran out through the hallway door, hoping to catch the man in the back, but the door was shutting just as he came around. He didn't dare fire blindly.

Cranston ran back into the sitting room, dropping the trench knife and grabbing the first heavy book he saw. He threw the book through the stained glass window at the front of the house. The truck's engine had never stopped, but now thundered into gear. Arm out the window, Cranston fired at the truck's tires.

Two of his four bullets hit the hub of the rear tire. As he shot his last round, the passenger window shattered and he heard a feminine scream from the truck's cab. It was almost immediately drowned out by two more bullets pelting the front of the truck, attempting to damage the engine.

Lucien was sprinting down the lawn. He stopped to fire three more shots, then sprinted again, hoping to get closer. The truck rumbled over the crashed gate and onto the road, behind the shrubs.

Cranston holstered his revolver, left the window and tore into the vestibule and out the front door. "Move the gate!" He shouted to Lucien, running for the Chandler, parked in the old horse stall. The top was down and he vaulted into the driver's seat and pressed the ignition. He reversed into the driveway and then began rolling towards the entrance. Lucien didn't wait for him to stop. Once the big man had hauled the gate clear of the path, he jumped into the moving vehicle. Cranston turned onto the road, then gunned the engine.

The truck was already out of sight, but this was a long stretch of road.

"You out?" Lucien asked.

"Yes," Cranston said, feeling the steering wheel beneath his gloveless hands begin to heat.

Lucien reached across his chest and pulled out the revolver. He emptied the spent casings onto the floor, then refilled the moon-clip with .45 rounds he produced from a pouch strapped to his leg. Reloaded, Lucien put the gun back in Cranston's holster. Another pouch contained magazines for his M1911 pistol, which he reloaded next.

"Fuck," Lucien growled as the road became an intersection.

Cranston stopped the Chandler in the middle of it, so they could watch for any sign of the truck. There was nothing.

"How did it get over the gate?" Lucien asked himself, eyes closed, his face tight and analytical. "That was a White truck and it was riding high, but the wheels were almost scraping the sides of the wheel wells."

"Bigger tires," Cranston added.

"And a lifted suspension. Some engineers did that when the roads got too bumpy." He meant in the war.

Cranston checked his watch. It was 5:23. "Wolfe left an hour and fifteen minutes ago. He wouldn't have had time to phone someone. They rendezvoused somewhere."

"There's a garage in town. If anyone noticed a modified milk truck around, it would be the mechanics."

Knowing Montague better, Lucien took over driving. He pulled a pair of driving gloves from his back pocket and took them into town.

A police car, siren wailing, passed them on the way. No doubt someone at the retreat had heard the shots and phoned them. Cranston thought suddenly of Dr Syme. He had not actually met the man, yet, and wasn't sure if he was physically at the retreat. Despite living in the same home, Cranston could remember times when days had passed without seeing his father. Dr Syme might just as easily disappear into his own work. He felt strange, abruptly, that the old man had never been consulted—as far as Cranston knew—about the security of his daughter.

And now this.

The Chandler pulled up to a garage with a large, hand-painted sign out front declaring Milton Sons Auto Shop. The spacing was a little strange and the colors of the paint sharp where an ampersand had been recently painted over. The building was free standing with three bays for automobiles to pull into and a customer shop.

"They might be involved," Cranston said before they got out of the car.

"It crossed my mind."

"Which means they won't be forthcoming."

"No, that crossed my mind, too." He knew what Cranston was suggesting. "We don't do anything we don't have to."

Cranston scanned the shop. "I see one at the till and two in the garage. You take the till."

Lucien didn't argue.

They got out. Cranston wandered with a sort of aimless curiosity towards the open bay doors, squinting into the relative darkness. Just a looky-loo.

"Is that a Rolls-Royce?" he asked, taking off his hat and stepping into the garage, his eyes indicating a car sitting atop a large jack.

"Yep," said one of the mechanics, wiping his hands on a rag. "We get all kinds in here. It's the best part of the job."

"Yes," Cranston smiled, knowingly. "I suppose you may need to test them out, to ensure quality."

The mechanic grinned and nodded. "Just around the block."

"I'd expect no less. Why should the valets have all the fun?"

"Your Chandler going queer?" He gestured at the car.

"No, it's running fine, as far as I know." He turned and gestured through the window between shop and garage. "My friend has some questions, is all." Cranston took a step forward, extending his hand. "Cranston Walker, and which Milton are you?"

"The son," the mechanic smiled as they shook. "The second one." Behind him, the man Cranston took to be the first was observing from the security of a pile of tools. "Tom Milton."

"It's a pleasure." He gave the man a once over, now that they were standing so close. He had a scar on his neck, gone white with age. Cranston pointed to it. "I hope the Rolls-Royce didn't do that to you."

Tom touched the scar reflexively. "Nah, but Jerry just about got me in Ypres."

"You served?"

"Didn't we all?" he said, challenging the class distinction clear in Cranston's accent.

"Indeed," Cranston nodded. He slouched off one shoulder of his jacket, casually revealing the revolver. Undoing the top buttons on his shirt and pulling his undershirt aside, Cranston revealed a long scar of his own. "Shell fragment, Artois. The damn thing landed fifty feet from me. My ears were ringing and my entire body hurt. It took me almost an hour to even notice the blood."

Tom smiled. "Always happy to meet another doughboy who made it back."

Cranston made a sheepish face. This was exactly where he wanted the conversation to go, but he couldn't let on. "I was an officer, in fact."

"Same bullets," Tom shrugged. "Which battalion?"

Cranston cleared his throat, feigning discomfort. "The Praetorian Guard."

Tom's face went white. The older brother shifted, his hand coming to rest on something large and metal. "Sorry," Tom said, forcing a chuckle. "I never saw any of you over there. Kind of thought you were a myth."

Cranston smiled and laughed, himself. He was confident that the man was lying. Tom knew what kind of hell the infantry had put the guardsmen through. He wanted Cranston to think he hadn't been involved. Perhaps he hadn't.

"Were you in the engineering corps?" Cranston asked, changing the subject; the polite thing to do when someone becomes visibly uncomfortable.

"Yes, sir."

"I recall that some you put a lift of some kind on the chassis of the ambulances. You know, when the roads got too rough."

"Sure. I never did that myself. I was on the tanks."

"Cherries all over for you." Cranston smiled.

"Just lucky, I guess. But, certainly, I knew a couple fellows that rigged up the ambulances. It took some doing to get right, but once they did, you couldn't stop them."

"I ask because I saw a truck earlier today, a milk truck, that seemed to have the same sort of modification."

Tom looked confused. "Who would lift a milk truck?"

Cranston took a half step forward, leaning in. "Ne'er-do-wells."

Tom twitched. He looked over into the shop where the mountainous Lucien was talking with his younger brother. "We haven't done any kind of work like that," he insisted.

"Of course not," Cranston said, putting a not-reassuring hand on his shoulder. "But if anyone was going to notice such a vehicle trundling around, it would be a mechanic."

"I haven't seen anything." He chanced a look over his shoulder. "Mike, have you seen a milk truck on lifts?"

"No," came a rasping voice from the older brother.

Tom turned back to Cranston. "He served, too. Gas attack tore up his throat."

"I understand," Cranston stepped back. "I don't want to inconvenience you, or anyone. It is, however, very important that I find that truck, and quickly."

Tom looked back at his brother again. Mike walked forward, giving a protective look through to the shop. "We can give you a name." His voice was a rattling whisper. "But you didn't hear it from us. You never met us."

Cranston looked Mike in the eye. "Little birdies," he said. "They do chatter."

Mike nodded to Tom. "The Barnaby's," Tom said. "They're old fur traders, been on the island since before King Louis, supposedly. They take any old thing they can get their hands on, try to turn them into sports cars. They have a big house near Henriette's Crossing."

"I don't suppose you have a map."

"When you get to the Crossing, go north and follow the deep tracks. It's all dirt roads out there and they have petrol delivered by truck every couple of weeks."

"Anything else I should know?"

Tom's face darkened. "There's a bunch of them, but don't ask me how they're finding wives. And they're all anarchists, in their way."

"People go missing," Mike rasped.

"We'll be careful." Cranston said.

"I'd be strong," Tom said, then shrugged. "If I were you."

"Thank you," Cranston said. "Perhaps, one day, I'll meet you." He replaced his hat and turned to leave. As he did, he caught Lucien's eye through the window.

They met back in the car. "We should go back to the lodge," Cranston said.

"Sounds like you got farther than I did," Lucien replied.

"I got a name and almost an address," he replied, as they got in. "But I think we're going to need to raid the broom closet."

Chapter 24:
Blue Feathers

Cranston sat beside Lucien at the great dining table in the staff quarters. On the other side of Lucien, Dr William Syme was talking to a pair of local police officers who were out of their depth. They knew they were out of their depth and made no attempt to hide this fact, perhaps hoping to be let off the hook for this case.

When he and Lucien had arrived at the lodge, Dr Syme had been pointing out things that had been damaged around the front of the house. Then, the two bodyguards had given their statements about what had happened and concluded by saying that they had given chase, but not succeeded in finding the truck, and left it at that.

It was Cranston's first time meeting Dr Syme and there hadn't been time for proper introductions. The police had looked stunned from the moment Cranston had stepped out of the car. When he gave them his name, they visibly approached panic.

"Well," said one of the officers, as Dr Syme finished. "We will let you know if we get any further leads." He said 'leads' as if he was unsure if that was correct nomenclature.

"Mr Walker and I will be conducting our own investiga-tion," Lucien said in a polite tone that did not invite disagreement.

"You are her bodyguards," the other officer said, with some relief. "I guess that's part of the job. Like private detectives."

"If we come across anything more," Lucien continued. "We'll bring it to you."

"Quid pro quo," the first officer said.

As the police drove away, Dr Syme groaned. "They didn't even look inside."

"So, no one's disturbed it?" Cranston asked.

"I looked around, but quickly." He turned to Cranston and extended a hand. "It's nice to finally meet you, Mr Walker. I met your parents on a few occasions; fundraisers and the like. I was awfully sorry to hear of their passing. They were good people, community-minded." That might have been code for the Rose and Chain, but there wasn't time to explore it.

Cranston shook. "Thank you for saying, sir. At your leave, I'd like to investigate the house."

"By all means. You were trained as a sort of Army detective, is that right?"

"You could say so, yes," Cranston nodded. "I wish I had thought to say so during the war. It would have set certain people's minds at ease."

"I leave it in your capable hands, then."

Cranston's military training had been in interrogation, but the skills he would employ to investigate the house were older. A youth spent in very conscious and creative delinquency had taught him how to destroy and obscure evidence and, by extension, how to read it. Plenty of his peers had played their shenanigans and taken their lumps. For Cranston, there wasn't much fun to be had under the looming shadow of parental punishment.

Wanting to leave the vestibule as undisturbed as possible, Cranston went in by the staff entrance, again. As he did, he reflected that he should have gone to the truck directly. If he had taken the driver out of the equation, the whole thing would have been foiled. He pushed that thought down, though, and made his way through the kitchen and into the hallway.

Cranston checked for bullet holes, corroborating his memory of events. He scoured the floor near the stairs, hoping for a dropped item that would prove itself a clue. The only unfamiliar object was a bright blue feather near the front door. He put it in his coat pocket.

He traced the route from the entry to the guest bedroom that Rosamund had set aside for Miss Caine in her schedule for the day. The stairs and floor were well marked in fresh, black scuffs, as was the guest room. The room had a large bed, set longwise against one wall and, opposite that, was an armoire. There was a bureau and vanity against the near wall and an easy chair beside a small table by the window.

A rug beside the bed was in a violently disturbed state. There were two more blue feathers on the floor, near the armoire, which hung open. Clothes had been pulled down, some off their hangers and some dislodging the hangers in the process. Cranston rifled through the clothing and found more black scuff marks on the back and bottom of the armoire.

Someone had climbed inside the armoire and been forcibly removed. Cranston assumed that was Della Caine. Rosamund had made much of her delicate nerves. Knowing her, Cranston couldn't believe that Rosamund would be the one to hide.

The disarray of the rug suggested a struggle had occurred near the bed. There was a direct line of scuff marks between the armoire and the door, meaning that the struggle by the bed and the one by the armoire had been separate assaults.

Miss Caine had hidden in the armoire, then, and Rosamund had stood near the bed. When the men came in, they had gone for Rosamund. At some point, Miss Caine had given away her position and they had decided to take her as well.

Or rather, that was how it was meant to look. Cranston reminded himself that Miss Caine was a co-conspirator. She and Mr Wolfe had arranged this with their CHJ friends. It was curious that Miss Caine would keep up the illusion as the trap was sprung, but there were explanations for that. If something went wrong, keeping up the lie could help her escape justice.

It was also possible, given her medical records, that Miss Caine was unaware of Mr Wolfe's machinations. He wouldn't be the first to exploit the infirm for his own ends.

Cranston stood in the doorway, trying to reenact the event in his mind, and there was one question that he couldn't satisfy: why had they taken Miss Caine to the truck, first?

The sun was high, but taking on the warmer tones of late afternoon when Cranston went to find Lucien in the staff quarters. He had emptied the broom closet and laid their full arsenal out on the dining table. Lucien was busying himself with the process of filling every magazine they had with ammunition.

"Lucien," Cranston said quietly, as he approached. "We can't be sure what we will be facing at the Barnaby house. Even finding the house, at this moment, is an uncertainty."

"I know, Cranston," Lucien said, putting down one of the drum magazines for the Thompsons. "We should go before it gets dark." He smoothed his hair slowly with one hand, then twice more faster.

"We have no reason to believe that they'll hurt her."

"Yeah, Cranston, I know." His jaw began to quiver. His voice broke as he said: "It doesn't make a difference." Lucien squeezed his eyes tightly shut as his massive frame shook, sobbing quietly.

Cranston walked briskly around the table and put an arm around Lucien's back. Lucien, mindful of the difficulties of his height, sat. Cranston embraced him about the shoulders and Lucien buried his face in Cranston's chest. His great arms wrapped around Cranston's waist and he let the tears come in a cataract.

"I was supposed to stop this!" he wailed. "And not just... she loved me. She let me in...and when a woman lets you in, you know...you're supposed to protect her. And I didn't do a damn thing! I couldn't hit the tires...or the engine...nothing! If you weren't here...fuck...."

There were a dozen things that Cranston could have pointed out, in that moment. None of them mattered. This was not a moment for truth. This was not a crisis of faith or a faltering of hard-earned confidence. It was an over-abundance of pain. Pain could not be reasoned with or explained away, like doubt or fear. It could only be released. So, Cranston stayed silent, rubbing his friend's shoulder and letting his shirt absorb the man's tears.

In a few minutes, the storm passed and the rain stopped.

Lucien was empty of the overwhelming pain and, in its absence, rediscovered his resolve and returned to the Thompson drum magazine; he placed the bullets in the large slots around their spring-loaded wheel. Cranston grabbed another drum and a box of ammunition.

Half way through unscrewing the drum's fastener, though, he remembered something. Cranston reached into his jacket and withdrew one of the three bright blue feathers he had found.

"Lucien, does this look familiar to you?" he asked, holding up the feather.

Lucien squinted his puffy eyes at it. "I haven't seen any birds that color up here."

"What about in Rosamund's wardrobe?"

"No. Blue isn't her color."

Della Caine had been wearing blue, Cranston now remembered. The dress hadn't been this vibrant, but perhaps the collar or cuffs were. Lucien was right, though; plumage like this didn't belong this far north. This was a tropical color, a rainforest color. It was the kind of thing that got imported from Brazil or Adamaoua.

As much as Cranston had been a derelict scion of a shipping empire, it had behooved his romantic prospects to learn where certain luxury goods came from.

So, what was Della Caine—a woman who had been hospitalized since 1917—doing wearing imported feathers? Coming to that, who had paid for her extended hospital stay? It was hard to imagine a moneyed family allowing their little princess to work for the Atlantic Network.

The ammunition drums were full when Lily walked in. Cranston was holding a bandolier, loading it with shotgun shells and she came running to him.

"You're alright?" she said, holding him close.

Cranston set down the bandolier, so he could hug her back. "Yes, I'm unscathed."

"We thought we heard gunshots." she said and, only then, seemed to notice the armory laid out on the table. "What's all this, then?"

"Three men kidnapped Rosamund and Miss Caine," Cranston said, unsure of how much she knew or how deeply she would feel about it. "We are going to talk to some people who may know where she was taken to."

"Looks like you're planning a rather one-sided conversation."

"The hope is that it will be a quiet chat, but if they decide to yell at us, we don't want to be drowned out."

"Isn't that what the police are for?"

"We talked with them. They seemed to prefer that we

handle it ourselves."

"To hell with that! It's what they're paid for."

Lucien chimed in. "Ever heard of the Barnaby's?"

"The mad ones with the fast cars?" she asked.

"Sounds right,"

"You think they took Miss Syme?"

"No," Lucien said. "We think they made the truck that was used to take Miss Syme."

"And you suppose they'll be reticent about telling you who they made it for?"

"Reticence," Cranston said, "would be a stroke of good luck. At least, that's the impression we were given."

"Sure," Lily nodded. "One of the nurses, Alice, warned the rest of us not to dance with any of their like, in town. She said girls are known to go missing that way."

"We are not going to go missing," Cranston said. "We shall be on our best behavior, of course, but we shall keep our worst at the ready."

"I've seen them at the dance hall," Lily continued. "There's an army of 'em."

"Which would explain why the local police are reticent to deal with them," Lucien said.

"Fear not," Cranston kissed Lily's forehead. "The Keizer had several armies and we survived him."

Lily hugged him again and he could feel her doubts. "Eat something before you go," she said, pushing away from him. She ran into the kitchen and found it empty. "Shit! And the staff are all at the Retreat. I'll run over there and get you something."

Cranston went to her and gave her a kiss on the cheek. "Thank you," he said. She looked up at him, ready to cry. She understood, but she ran out of there and through the trees all the same. They weren't going to wait for her.

Chapter 25:
Peter

Cranston and Lucien were on the road by five-thirty, having lost a half hour to the waste of time that the police had turned out to be. They had decided to wear their Praetorian uniforms. If there were as many of these Barnabys as Lily had said, more than a few of them had certainly served in the war. They had no intention of using the Voice on anyone, but they wanted any potential aggressors to know they could as an incentive to mind their manners.

Henriette's Crossing was an intersection with a row of mailboxes nailed to an unfinished board, itself nailed to two old fence posts. A half hour's drive from Montague, these mailboxes were the only sign that there was anyone living in the area. There was only dense forest besides the roads. Either the people who lived out here were invested in their privacy, or the county had not taken them into consideration when making the roads.

People who liked this particular flavor of privacy were known to have a deep and abiding love for the Federated States' strict laws regarding trespassing. People who felt ignored by the local government frequently took the position that there was no moral reason that they shouldn't ignore the government right back. Both were of the opinion that trespassers deserved to be shot on sight.

Lucien turned the Chandler north and he drove slowly, watching for side roads; easily missed among the forest. The first left that they came to bore the deep tracks that Tom Milton had mentioned. A mile in, the trees gave way to fields of wild grass and weeds, the scent of livestock becoming unmistakable, though there were none to be seen. Shallow trenches also appeared, to channel runoff from the rain.

They followed the grooves cut by the petrol truck on rainy days gone by until the road forked. The grooves became shallower after that, buried by the tramp of hooves on dry ground. By the time they reached the next fork in the road, the petrol truck's path had vanished. All around them was more pasture, in various states of consumption and not a fence in sight. The livestock, of whatever kind, were driven along these roads too frequently for tire tracks to survive.

Lucien stopped the car and they both got out. Each of them followed a different road for a few hundred feet, hoping to catch sight of the grooves again. Cranston's route was a gentle hill. They had been gaining elevation consistently, but this was the sharpest rise they had encountered. Cranston reached the crest of the hill and squinted. The land continued upward, though not as perceptibly. He searched the line of the horizon for any interruption: the top of a windpump, a weather vane, a tree house, anything.

A gust of wind blew southward and cast grit into Cranston's eyes. The wind was like a wave, crashing against him and then fading away. It reminded him of the time an artillery shell had passed five feet above him and scattered everything that wasn't metal through the trench. The gust had smelled of water—fresh water—like the air after a rain or at the edge of a waterfall. There wasn't a cloud in the sky, though, and no roar of running water.

He had the feeling that something immense had just

passed over him. Something sublime. He felt its magnitude and a feral instinct cried at him to run, but a higher reasoning told him he didn't know where to run to.

Time seemed to slow. Cranston was suddenly more attuned to everything, his focus heightened, but without direction. A light of thankfulness flared in his mind for Lily; without her, this anxiety would be consuming him. He turned back towards the car, keeping an eye on his shadow, lest something come at him from behind. Ahead, he saw an aged and olive-skinned man in a white suit, bent over to inspect the Chandler. He wore a full beard so long-greyed that it would look white, if not for the suit which abjured the stain of the dirt road.

The man was not a Barnaby, Cranston was certain. From what he had heard of them, he imagined them to be Gaulish, if not Anglo-Saxon. This man could have been Italian, though very slim for that race. He might also have been a fair-skinned Arab or Turk. Cranston might have pegged him for a Jew, except he did not have the forelocks of the men in Silkhaven's Little Kiev.

"Excuse me," Lucien called from the other side of the fork as Cranston approached the car. "Do you live around here?"

The old man stood and tipped his boater hat in greeting. Getting closer, Cranston saw the man steadied himself on a cane. His suit was so white in the late day sun that it was a little hard to look at.

"No," the old man called back to Lucien. "Just passing through. That's a real nice car." His accent was francophone, but not Quebecois or continental.

Passing through? Cranston wondered. It's private property.

"I've heard there's folk with nicer about," Lucien replied with protestant self-effacement.

"Oh, surely," the old man grinned. "But I like this one

all the same. I remember when trains were really something. These automobiles, though...oooh!" He gave a mock shudder. "Thrilling!"

"We're looking for someone who lives out here."

"Wouldn't surprise me." The old man grinned.

"Good day," Cranston said, walking close enough to shake hands.

"And a very good day to you, too." The old man's hand looked papery, but gripping it felt like shaking hands with a statue. The motion opened the old man's jacket a little and Cranston saw a large ring of keys hanging from the man's belt.

"Could you help us find the Barnaby house?" Lucien asked, also noticing the keys.

"Might could." He nodded. "Say, I don't suppose I could trouble you boys for a treat, if you have one? My sweet tooth is aching, today." He chuckled.

Something swept over Lucien, then. His friendly, neighborly demeanor exchanged suddenly for one that teetered close to fear. "Yes, sir." Lucien ran to the passenger side of the Chandler and opened the glove compartment. He retrieved a Peter's chocolate bar, still in its brown wrapper. Hurrying back around, he gave it to the old man with both hands.

The old man chuckled. "That's my favorite one!" He turned to Cranston. "You wouldn't happen to have a dime on you, by chance? An old one, if you have it. I collect the old ones, is all."

Lucien gave Cranston a very serious look, the kind you got from someone at gunpoint, and Cranston fished out his wallet. Opening it, he had three dimes, one of which had the head of Mercury stamped on it. The government had discontinued that design after the name became synonymous with prophylactics and gave the phrase "mercury head" an unsavory connotation.

That alert focus returned. Cranston became unnaturally

aware of his fingers, watched them move almost as if they belonged to someone else. The mercury dime expanded in this focus, made his fingers seem enormous. He watched as his hand held the dime out, suddenly feeling as if he was offering a slab of meat to a salivating guard dog.

"That's mighty fine," the old man said as he accepted the dime. "Now, who is it you looking for?"

"It's a family," Lucien said, "by the name of Barnaby."

"Mmhmm, I know them, but that ain't your final destination, is it?"

"No, sir. We are looking for a woman, our employer. She was kidnapped earlier today, and we were hoping that the Barnaby's might be able to tell us where she was taken. That is, unless...respectfully...you could tell us that."

The old man reached up and patted Lucien on the cheek. The big man braced himself as he saw the hand coming. "It's best that you ask old Jeremiah Barnaby about that. He live up thatta way." The old man pointed up the left-hand road. "It's a big house, you won't miss it. The Barnaby's, they've been out here a long time; got blood in the soil, them. Thick and thin, they never budge. It was real thick for them not too long ago. Mr Barnaby—that's the sitting Mr Barnaby—his grandpappy built hisself a real fine house. He had his boys clear acres of pasture, thinking they was gonna be cattle barons." The old man said the word 'baron' in a way that would have been unrecognizable to a non-French speaker.

"Didn't last," the old man continued. "That's the trouble with dreams. They only take you so far before you gotta work to keep dreaming, and clear water ain't always safer than brown. Jeremiah, now, he put in a pump for gasoline to run his motors. That's the new dream. It won't take him too far, him, but maybe one of his boys, if they're smart.

"But, if you're going up there, you best keep your wits about you. Old Mr Barnaby—the sitting one—he does not live in a house of truths. Don't trust the fortune teller; she'll say whatever gets you to pay a dollar more. You gotta read the cards for yourselves if you want to see the truth. On your way, you oughta keep in mind who you are, because what you do comes from who you are. If'n there's something you want done, you gotta be the sort of person that does it. Think on that as you drive." The man eased himself against his cane, signaling that he was done.

"We will," Lucien said. "Thank you, sir."

"Notatall. Godspeed, now." He tipped his hat to them.

Lucien gave a small bow and got in the car. Cranston gave a nodding bow and crossed around to the passenger's side. The old man stood at the fork in the road and waved to them as they drove away.

"Trusting him, are we?" Cranston asked.

"Damn right," Lucien replied, his breath quick. "If we do anything other than what he said, we're liable to end up a ghost story."

"Why? Who was that?"

"Cranston," Lucien sighed, "you wouldn't believe me if I told you."

And, with that, the matter was settled.

Chapter 26:
Oneiromancer

Money—real wealth, not the kind you used for a piece of taffy—was like a farm dog. It knew who it belonged to and mostly preferred to stay where it was supposed to be, but every so often—once every seventy or so years—it saw a squirrel that it particularly hated and would chase it to the very edges of civilization. The owners would get very nervous and go looking for it. Sometimes they found it, right away, and sometimes it lived with another family for a while.

The Barnaby's were an old family, but a working-class one; or what had passed for working class back when Europeans thought of the Americas as a great expanse of derelict farmland. As such, they had been lucky enough to have the money dog wander into their lives more than once. It was back home, now—with people like Cranston—but vestiges of those heady days remained in the land that they occupied. 'Occupied' because there was room to doubt how much of it the Barnabys legally owned.

Past a few hundred acres of grazing land, there was a large, iron gate with an emblem of a capital B, ornamented across the top by a quarter circle, at the center of the frame's arch. The fence it was attached to was made of wooden posts and barbed wire and the gate, itself, was open. Some kind of foreboding weed had wound its way around the iron.

The driveway up to the house had once been cobbled, but the stones had been pulled up since and thrown to the side. It curved up to the house and became a loop. In the center of that loop was a gas pump. A thin metal circle topped the pump, but the maker's logo—printed on domes of glass—had been removed and replaced by a single piece of weather-darkened wood with the ranch's brand painted on it.

The house itself was two stories, but not very expansive. It was the sort of house one ambitious generation built, thinking it would be added onto, spread out. A veranda occupied two-thirds of the facade. It looked humble on such a narrow building, but would have served to mark the more guest-friendly wing of the house, had such a wing ever been built. As it was, a large section of the veranda's roof had caved in and ragged bits of it still hung down.

The lawn was overgrown in patches, suggesting that the Barnaby's trusted their landscaping to the livestock, but not for extended periods of time. The area around the veranda's side of the house was dominated by three cars in various states of deconstruction. One of them appeared to be a Mercedes, the rear half crumpled from an impact, but the front half had been picked too clean to be certain.

Two boys, shirtless in overalls, were at work under the hood of a surplus King armored car. As the Chandler pulled up the drive, they stopped to look up. One of them held a boxy engine component in one hand. Cranston supposed that the easiest way to build a sports car was to take the engine from something heavy and put it into something light.

It was a warm day and Cranston had unbuttoned his jacket and draped it across his shoulders. No doubt, the boys were shirtless for the same reason; not to mention wanting to spare their shirts the washing.

The two did not have a family look. The one holding the

boxy something in one hand—and a wrench in the other—
was a long, skinny teener with very black hair that was raised
up on one side from his pillow. The other boy was shorter
and broader in the shoulders with brown hair that might have
once been blonde. Seeing the Chandler, the stout one picked
up a screwdriver and held it like an icepick.

Lucien brought the car to a stop and they stepped out.
The guns were all well below the edge of the car's body, but
Lucien had thought to add Cranston's father's sword cane to
the arsenal. This Cranston held under his shoulder when he
stepped out.

"Howdy," Lucien said, in his still buttoned Praetorian
jacket, the golden eagle head embroidered onto the right
shoulder. "Is this the home of Jeremiah Barnaby? We were
hoping we could talk with him."

"A' we spectin' guests?" the stout one asked.

"Nawp," the long one answered. "Naw one said a thing
abo't guests, today."

"We are uninvited, I'm afraid," Cranston added. "It is
urgent, though. Is Mr Barnaby in?"

"Mmhmm," the long said, putting down the boxy engine
part and taking a step towards them, hefting the wrench. "He's
he'yah, but maybe ya shouldn't be."

"It's alright," Lucien said. "We aren't looking for trouble."

"Y'ar trouble!" yelled a third voice.

Cranston turned to see a young man, older and more
muscled than the other two, though with the stout one's once-
blonde, brown hair. He was walking with some speed towards
the visitors with an axe over one shoulder. A wagon carrying
a fresh cord of fire wood lay abandoned behind him.

"Now," Lucien called back to the one with the axe, "we
can still be neighborly."

The long one bounced his wrench in one hand. "Nah
neighbuhs round he'yah."

"Alright," Cranston said, drawing the sword from his cane. "Who wants to go first?"

The long one charged, swinging the wrench back and up to get a strong down swing while the stout ran out, screw-driver held high. Lucien sprinted out to meet the stout one, caught him by the wrist and swung him, letting the boy's momentum do the work, into the back of the long one. Both boys collapsed in a pile, but quickly got back to their feet and focused their aggression squarely on Lucien, despite his being at least a foot taller than they were.

"I'll take the big one, I guess," Cranston said and saun-tered off the driveway, into the uneven grass.

The one with the axe was in a full run, weapon held with both hands over his head. Cranston shrugged off his jacket, then reversed the sword in his right hand, so that blade ran along his arm. As soon as the axe started to come down, he planted his left foot and swung the cane to deflect the axe. With that forward motion, he spun, trying to hook the sword into the woodsman's back. However, the young man kept up his speed and was out of the sword's circumference too quickly.

They squared up, Cranston turning the sword forward while the woodsman widened his grip on the axe. From this angle, Cranston could see Lucien wrestling both of the younger boys, primarily to keep them from using their weapons.

The woodsman charged in again, attacking from his right, knowing the sword to be the weaker blocking weapon. Cran-ston stepped back, swinging the cane down and behind the axe to block a back swing, then thrusting forward with the sword. The woodsman released his left hand from the axe and allowed the inertia to help him lean back out of the way of the sword.

He grabbed Cranston's right arm with his left hand,

then swung the axe overhand for a downward blow. Cranston pulled his arm against the woodsman's grip and stepped inside the young man's swing. The woodsman's wrist and axe handle collided with Cranston's shoulder while Cranston bashed him in the ribs with the cane.

That made the woodsman retreat a few steps, letting go of Cranston's arm. He prepared for another right-handed swing, stepping closer to get Cranston in his arc. Cranston brought the cane forward and the sword high just in time to see that the woodsman had not shortened his grip during the swing. As the axe's head reached the point where the cane would have blocked it, he pulled it back and then lunged forward. Cranston braced for the blunt impact on his sternum and stabbed downwards.

The axe head slammed into him and knocked him back a half dozen steps, but not before he had gouged a chunk out of the woodsman's left shoulder. The young man barked in pain and took a reeling step backwards himself.

"That's enough!" a girl's voice shrieked.

Everyone stopped. Woodsman shifted so that he could see the house, but kept his weapon between them and Cranston held the sword up with the cane in a low, protective posture. Over in the driveway, Lucien had the stout one pressed against his chest, holding that boy's arm so that he might stab himself with the screwdriver, while the long one was squirming face-down in the dirt under Lucien's boot.

On the veranda was a very skinny girl whose age Cranston could hardly guess. Her dress was a light, dingy beige that bore fainted traces of a pattern lost through many washings. "Grandaddy says 'Ayveryone in'na ho'se'!"

The woodsman gave Cranston a look, silently asking if he would agree to the armistice. Cranston pointed his sword out, exposing his chest. The woodsman replied by heaving the axe up onto his uninjured shoulder. Taking that as the most good faith he would get, Cranston sheathed the sword in the cane.

Lucien turned both boys loose and let them scamper back to the house, then shifted to watch Cranston's approach. Thus observed, Cranston walked ahead of the woodsman, waiting to see if Lucien gave any signs that the woodsman was on the attack; but none came. After picking up his jacket, he joined Lucien in front of the car and let the woodsman go ahead into the house.

There was a sort of upturned brush by the front door, which the woodsman thoroughly scraped the soles of his shoes against before entering.

"You too," the girl drawled at them.

They walked up the stairs and Cranston reached up to tip his hat to her reflexively. He hadn't worn a hat, partly because he didn't have one for the uniform and partly because of the impracticality of wearing one in the car; there was little enough headroom as it was, and the bumps of a country road decreased that considerably, though inconsistently.

When the girl waved them past, they both scraped their boots on the upturned brush. The inside of the house was not much darker than outside, thanks to the large, front windows facing east. A central hallway connected all of the rooms on the first floor as well as accommodating the stairway up to the second. The young men of the household had disappeared into some back room or perhaps, very quietly, up the stairs.

On Cranston's right, as he entered, was a pleasantly dim parlor filled with thinly padded sofas, upholstered in leather. It wasn't hard to imagine a tannery being somewhere on the property, though he hadn't smelled one. The sofas were arranged more like church pews, with just enough space between them for one to walk.

On the left was a much brighter room, without the veranda to block incoming light. A lone easy chair sat in the center of the room with a spare table a few feet in front go it. Along the far wall was another table—this one draped with a cloth—and behind it a less imposing padded chair.

The easy chair was occupied by an ancient man, wrapped in a coarse-looking blanket and hunched forward, staring blankly out the great window before him. In the far, back corner, a younger man leaned against the wall, his face obscured by the falling shadow of the aging day. There was a door near him, not near enough that it might hit him, but would hide him completely when opened.

This happened a moment later when an elderly woman wandered through it. "You must forgive the boys," the woman said in an accent more educated than any other in the family. "Unexpected guests and trespassers are hard to distinguish, out here. We keep to ourselves is all." She sat behind the cloth-covered table and produced a deck of long cards, which she began shuffling aimlessly.

"Misunderstandings do happen," Lucien replied. "My name is Lucien Gabriel and this is my associate, Captain Walker. We had a question or two about a truck we saw near town. People say you folks do quite a bit with automobiles— modifications and such—and we thought you might be able to tell us something about it."

"Oh yes," the old woman said. "The boys do busy themselves with their motors when they can. My name is Esther van Dyke and that's my brother"—she gestured towards the man in the blanket—"Jeremiah Barnaby." He turned her hand towards the fellow lurking in the corner. "That's my son, Shem, and the young lady keeping the pups on their leash is his daughter, Lydia." She set the cards down and folded her hands, leaning forward. "What's this matter with the truck?"

"From what we could tell," Lucien said, "it had a suspension lift and a bit more power in the engine than you might expect." They were still standing in the hallway, right at the entry's frame; not having been invited any further in.

"A'e ya lookin' for somethin' wi' real powah?" Shem sneered as he eyed the Chandler through the front window.

"Is that something you can do?" Cranston asked.

"Ah, yeah," Shem said in a condescending tone. "We build 'em fastah than that Miss Nancy, Ford, has the sand to do."

"I don't suppose the milk truck was your handiwork?"

Shem just shrugged and fished a toothpick from his breast pocket.

"Excuse me a moment," Esther interjected. "Lydia!"

The girl in the thin dress tapped Cranston on the shoulder. "'Scuse me," she said, turning to squeeze past him and into the sitting room. "Yes, gran'ma?"

"Go and tell the boys it's time for their milk."

"Yes, ma'am," Lydia said. "Levi is cut up. They'ah helpin' him with the bandage is all."

"It was his own fool self that got him that way. So, you tell them to be quick about it, then go and prepare the milk."

Lydia curtsied, then pressed back through the two guests.

"Never fear," Esther said. "Plenty of cuts on a farm. We know how to treat them."

"Naturally," Cranston said.

"Well, Jeremiah?" Esther raised her voice to address her brother, who had shown no reaction at all to the conversation thus far. Now, he shifted a bit. "Jeremiah, you know anything about a milk truck?"

"Humm?" the ancient man replied.

"A milk truck?" Esther nigh shouted.

"None for me," Jeremiah mumbled. "Martha needs it for the baby."

"I apologize," Esther said, picking up her cards again. "He's a bit slow towards sundown. If you'd come a bit later, he'd have introduced himself."

"That's alright, ma'am," Lucien said. "We only came so

early on account of this being a ranch. I worked a few of them, myself, and I know it can be hard to get anyone for a conversation after lunch."

They heard movement back in the kitchen, presumably Lydia preparing the milk; though Cranston could not begin to guess what that entailed.

"How long ya had it?" Shem asked, glancing at the Chandler.

"About a year," Lucien said. "It's reliable, but it might be nice to get a little more speed out of it."

"Sho'... sho'... it might take a few days. I don' think we've got anything in the right size, at the moment. An' we don' wo'k on speculation."

"Cash up front?"

"Yep," Shem nodded. "Business is too irregulah, you unde'stand."

"Have you considered opening a shop in town?" Cranston asked.

"It's no good," Shem replied. "Townies don' like havin' ah cahs growlin' abo't."

"Business is irregular," Cranston said. "But you don't remember if you did up that milk truck?"

Shem sucked a breath through his teeth. "Don' go talkin' abo't othah's business, ya unde'stand."

"I see, it's just that we were hoping to talk to one of your past customers before turning our car over to you. We aren't speculators, either."

"Ah, that's good sense. Ya like knowin' who ya' doin' business wi' before you pay. Quite right, quite right."

The sound of feet approaching from within the house made Cranston step away from the entry and closer to the front door. The three younger members of the tribe had put shirts on, the woodsman's noticeably bulging about the shoulder.

"Ah, boys," Esther said. "You go into the parlor. Lydia will bring you your milk."

Cranston watched as the three—all with bitter expressions—silently obeyed their ostensible grandmother. They found sofas and sat, waiting. Lydia appeared with a tray of tall glasses, which she distributed. The young men gulped down nearly a pint of milk each and then laid down, falling immediately to sleep; or so it seemed.

Lydia returned to the sitting room, taking a position opposite her father by the kitchen door. Cranston retook his position just outside the entry and noted that the room was darker than it had been a moment before. Perhaps a cloud had moved in front of the sun. Out the window, the sun didn't seem any dimmer, but it was hard to say.

"So," Lucien said. "The milk truck was one of yours?"

Esther said nothing, only began dealing cards onto the table.

"Not mine," Shem said.

Cranston squinted at the cards. They were tarot cards, certainly, but hand-drawn. Black ink on white card, none of the bright primaries one found in a usual deck. He had had a few readings in the past. Young women found them a delight between dinner and cocktails. The first card he took to be the five of wands or swords and the second was the Emperor. Esther laid down a third card, which had six ornate circles on it.

"Jeremiah," Esther said, studying the cards, "they're asking about a milk truck."

"Oh," Jeremiah said, rocking a little. "We got a truck." He turned and looked towards Lucien and Cranston, though not quite at them. "And you, ya get those new hands fo' the co'n? We need 'em by Thu'sday. Good rain, this ye-ah. Good crop. We need more hands fo' the co'n. Yeah. Need them by Thu'sday. Good rain. Good crop."

"It doesn't sound familiar to him," Esther said.

To Cranston, that sounded like an absolute understatement. Given the apparent condition of his faculties, Cranston was surprised that the old man's own name was familiar to him.

Esther dealt herself two more cards, one above and one below the initial spread; the four of pentacles and the Tower, respectively. "No, it looks like no one seems to know. Where was it that you saw this truck, again? There are some people over near Samkook—the Judsons—they do cars, as well."

Lucien stepped forward into the sitting room. He crossed in front of the table before Jeremiah to stand at Esther's table. Cranston followed him a few steps and noticed, for the first time, red curtains at either side of the great window. He was half certain that they hadn't been there before. Shem adjusted his weight and Cranston fixed him with a look.

"You face an opponent," Lucien told Esther, looking at her cards. "Someone stronger than you and they're asking for something. Failing to give it to them would bring disaster on your house."

"Ya makin' threats?" Shem sneered at Lucien.

"They're her cards." He told the much smaller man.

Cranston switched his cane to his left hand, holding it by the shaft.

"What do you want?" Jeremiah Barnaby asked, his voice clear. He was looking at Cranston with suddenly clear eyes.

"I saw a modified milk truck in town," Cranston told him, his voice polite. "We were just asking if any of your boys did the modifications."

"My boys?" Jeremiah's eyes faltered, flicking about the room. "No, my boys are stayin' right he'e. We need mo'e hands fo' the co'n. That wa', that's Europe's problem. No, my boys a'e stayin' he'e. We got a good crop of co'n, this ye-ah. Good rain. Good crops." He drifted for a moment, then snapped his attention back to Cranston. "Send some Micks! Red-hai'ed basta'ds love a fight. You send them. My boys a'e stayin' right he'e."

"Lydia?" Esther said, her voice betraying some uncertainty. "Your grandfather's getting confused. Help him, would you?"

Lydia went stiff. "Now, gran'ma?"

"Yeah," Shem said, lunging at her. One hand grabbed her by the arm and the other wrapped around the bulge of his belt buckle; ready to remove it at the next provocation.

Lydia nodded and scurried away from her father. She crossed close to Cranston and then daintily sat herself on her grandfather's lap. He seemed as shocked as Cranston, but the girl wrapped her arms around the old man's neck; a bit too stiffly to be loving. Jeremiah blinked at her.

"Shem?" He asked the girl.

"Yes, uncle," she answered in a voice that was higher, more childish than before.

Shem, for his part, eased himself back into the growing shadow of the room. It was certainly darker, now; the contrast between the light on Shem's chest and the darkness obscuring his face much lessened.

"And how old a'e ya, now?" Jeremiah asked in the voice adults reserved for children and beloved pets.

"Ah'm only just twelve," Lydia answered, despite being too womanly for that age.

"That's fine," Jeremiah grinned. "Fine."

Then, Lydia leaned in. She was still stiff, but not exactly fearful. He wondered how much, if any, of her obvious discomfort could be ascribed to the presence of outsiders. Dutifully, she brought her face close to the old man's cheek. Lydia opened her mouth and ran her tongue gently over Jeremiah's ear.

Cranston wanted to stomp his foot. He might have

shouted if words hadn't failed him. Shem, seeing him bristle, just chuckled.

"Wha's the mattuh?" the girl's father smirked.

Cranston took a long breath through his nose. "I fear that we are straining your courtesy."

"Don't mind Shem," Esther said. "That's just his sense of humor."

Cranston looked away from the family. The curtains were partially drawn, now, just an inch or so. Behind him, he could hear one of the young men snoring, but Cranston turned to make sure none of them were preparing a sneak attack. He could only see one, sound asleep by every indication, the others hidden behind the backs of the strangely arranged sofas.

Turning back to the sitting room, Cranston was met by the gaze of Jeremiah Barnaby. Jeremiah was wearing a velvet smoking jacket, which caught Cranston off guard. Perhaps it had been hidden under the blanket, which was now nowhere to be seen. However, Lydia's dress had taken on a distinct flower pattern and Shem, the light on his chest hardly brighter than the shadow on his face, was now wearing a sport coat.

"What can I do for you?" Jeremiah said, his back erect and his hands holding his granddaughter in too familiar fashion.

"We were asking about a milk truck," Lucien told him, drawing the man's attention away from Cranston. "It had some modifications and we were wondering if your family had done those modifications." He moved away from Esther and stood in front of the window. The sun outside seemed all the brighter for how dark the room had become.

Esther's face had gone slack, her eyes empty, palms down on the table.

"Oh," Jeremiah furrowed his brow. "Let me think. Uh... Shem?"

"Yes, uncle?" Lydia answered.

"Where's my pipe?"

"It's on the table," she said.

Sure enough, there it was, right beside a lacquered box of tobacco; though both had somehow escaped Cranston's notice before. Lydia reached out, never leaving the old man's lap, and pulled the table closer. When it was close enough, Jeremiah took up the pipe and Lydia helped him pack it.

"I apologize," he said without addressing anyone in particular. "I get confused, sometimes."

Lydia—who Cranston saw was now wearing makeup— struck a match that she had gotten from who knew where and lit Jeremiah's pipe.

"Mmm," the old man said, taking a few short inhalations on the pipe. "Yes, ya got business with those chu'ch fellas?"

"Yeah," Lucien said. "We want to ask them about a kidnapping."

"Ah, you' lookin' fo' the Jezebel. They didn't bring huh he'ah. Ah won' have huh corruptin' mah boys. She's the devil's songbu'd, ya know."

"I hadn't heard that one."

"Oh yes," Jeremiah nodded, speaking of the devil in a most conversational way. "Didn't ha'dly believe mahself, but they showed me the light. She's a beast straight from the pit of Hades, and no question."

"That much I have heard."

"Doin' the lawd's wo'k, they ah. Gonna expose huh to the wo'ld. Show them what mannuh of beasts it is that the devil has roamin' among us."

"Well," Cranston said, "my friend and I are always willing to assist in the Lord's work."

"Christians ah ya?"

"I believe in God the Father," Cranston said with the rhythm of practiced, congregational recitation. "The creator of Heaven and Earth. I believe in Jesus Christ, his only Son, our Lord, who was conceived of the Holy Spirit and born of the virgin Mary. He suffered under Pontius Pilate, was crucified, died, and was buried; he descended to hell. The third day he rose again from the dead. He ascended into heaven, where he is seated at the right hand of God the Father almighty. From whence he will come to judge the living and the dead. I believe in the Holy Spirit, the holy catholic church, the communion of saints, the forgiveness of sins, the resurrection of the body, and the life everlasting. Amen."

"Amen, indeed," Jeremiah smiled up at him.

"So, where did these churchmen take Jezebel?"

"I can' be sho'," he said. "Probably to that the place of they-uh's. It used to belong to the Fai'faxes. You remembuh, we used to have potlucks up the'e when you we'e just a boy."

"Thank you," Cranston said.

"Very helpful," Lucien added. "But, it's been awhile. I'm afraid we don't know these parts like we used to. Could we trouble you for a map?"

"Not at all," Jeremiah said. "Shem, you go fetch a pen and papuh and show these boys where to go."

"Yes, uncle," Lydia dutifully removed herself from the old man's grasp, then smoothed her immaculately white dress, embroidered with creeping green vines and bright red flowers. She walked past Cranston and down the hallway.

"Be back quick, now," he added. "We need to see to that co'n."

The room was brightening, as if the clouds had been burned off; though there had been no change in the light outside.

Lucien returned to Cranston's side. "We're much obliged," he said.

"We won't soon forget your hospitality," Cranston added, watching Esther blink against the rising brightness. Shem's coat had vanished, leaving him in a plain shirt and work pants.

Jeremiah was again wrapped in his scratchy-looking blanket, looking vaguely at the empty table before him.

Lucien pulled Cranston away from the entry and out the front door.

"Aren't we going to take the map?" Cranston whispered outside.

"We'll wait by the car," he replied.

"What was that?" Cranston asked when they got further from the house.

"I'm not completely sure," Lucien answered. "But I think I know why Peter sent us here."

Cranston took him to mean the old man, nicknaming him after the chocolate bar.

"Why would that be?"

"'If you want something done, you have to be the kind of person that does it,'" Lucien repeated. "What is it we want done?"

"To rescue Rosamund?"

"Yes, rescue."

They reached the car in time to hear the Barnabys' door open behind them. They both turned to see Lydia—her face washed of makeup and her dress dingy, only showing hints of a long-faded pattern—coming towards them with a piece of paper in one hand.

"I'm sorry," she said. "I couldn' find any ink. Do ya have a pen?"

"In the car," Lucien said, and Cranston went to search for it in the glove compartment. "Lydia, how old are you?"

She eyed Lucien nervously. "A'm nineteen."

"An adult, then. Which means that you can come and go as you choose, as far as the law is concerned. Would you like to come with us?"

"Pa'don?"

"I got the strong impression that you would rather be

somewhere else. I know a woman—a woman of means—who would happily give you a roof, a full pantry, and some assistance in making a life for yourself."

"Ah don' unde'stand."

Lucien eyed the house, nervously. "Do you like it here?"

"It's whe'e mah fam'ly is."

"A lot of people don't like where their family is."

"An' who would ah have to marry?" she asked, seeming to feel she had caught on.

"No one," he said. "Not unless you met someone you felt like marrying."

"But," Lydia swallowed. "If ah left, daddy would be awful angry."

"You're free to go where you like, under the law. This woman I know can take you places your daddy couldn't dream of getting to you."

"She wouldn' mind?"

"Not in the slightest. Use up all the hot water, eat as much as you want. She's generous like that."

"They'll follow us."

"They'll try. They'll fail."

"Ya sho'?"

"Lydia, dear," Cranston interjected, feeling the danger increase with every word they exchanged. "When was the last time that someone dressed like us came to your house and left unscathed?"

Lydia nodded. "Grandaddy don' like the govunment much."

"And yet, not a crease." Cranston stepped back and opened the rear passenger door, trusting that a country girl like her would be comfortable with numerous firearms hidden near her feet.

Lydia kept nodding, but didn't move. Lucien crossed to the driver's side and got in. He made eye contact with her as he pressed the igniter. The car rumbled to life and the sound seemed to trigger something in the girl. She bolted for the rear door and Cranston shut it behind her, leaping up into the front passenger seat without bothering to open his door.

Lucien pulled forward and shifted up a gear before they had even looped around the lonely gas pump. Cranston looked back to see Shem come running out the door. He wondered how long the younger men would be asleep on their haphazard sofas.

Before he could see what Shem would do, the Chandler's dust obscured the house completely. Lucien drove hell for leather down the unpaved back road. In only a few minutes, they reached the first fork in the road, where the old man stood watching. He waved to them as they sped past.

Seeing him, Lucien slowed to a more reasonable speed to wave back, then crossed himself as they continued on the road back to Montague.

Part 6:
VIGILANCE

Chapter 27:
Negotiation

September 17th, 1920. Silkhaven.

Briarson and Jones had spent the night at the Walker Grand Hotel, but Vivienne had decided not to bother them on her way out that morning. They phoned the office after eleven to apologize profusely for sleeping so late. Vivienne had told them it was no problem and that they should come in at four. An early dinner would be brought in and they could discuss the proposed changes to the contract when everyone's stomach was settled and filled.

It was just after five, now. The paper wreckage of a half dozen sandwiches lay on the mahogany table of Conference Room 3 on the twentieth floor of the Walker building. Now, they were picking at a large charcuterie board.

This was the smallest of the meeting rooms on this floor, situated at the southern tip of the building, just above Vivienne and Cranston's offices. Both exterior walls were taken up by picture windows with ornate, floral frames plated in gold. It had a commanding view of the city, reaching the rivers that marked Silkhaven's southern and western borders before feeding into the Northumberland Strait. It was simultaneously intimate and intimidating; a show of wealth and power that had the feeling of being reserved for the most important clients.

Negotiations were slow to get started. Briarson was still in shock over what he had seen at the Mermaid Club. The state he was in reminded Vivienne of the summer after Cranston had turned 19. The widow MacGregor had found in him a willing escort to social functions who had no designs on her deceased husband's estate. After two weeks of everyone-knew-nobody-said, Cranston had come home with that distant look of the holy pilgrim's revelation.

Vivienne knew enough of her brother's society life to know that he was no stranger to a lady's chamber. Whatever the widow MacGregor had done, it had been no ordinary awakening. Cranston had truly discovered something new; about himself and the world.

And Briarson was no less tight lipped about what Ariel had done for, perhaps to,him. Vivienne had never felt the need to watch a cooch dance before, but she was considering going back there that night.

Jones was less stunned by the experience, but didn't blame Briarson one bit, by all appearances. Once the boys had collected themselves, though, the negotiations had begun and it was the exact same as the last time they had talked.

What Saint Moon wanted was distribution in Canada. They needed a deal with Walker because they were an American company. On paper, they were headquartered in Murray, here on King Charles Island; but the president lived in New York and the Murray office was mostly a repository for rubber stamps. So, despite being officially based on King Charles Island, they did not have the recognition of the Canadian government as part of the island's shared sovereignty.

That was important because of the matter of reciprocity. America simply grew more food than Canada did. They had industrialized faster and were in a position to completely overwhelm the domestic canned food market, which would have a knock-on effect on farming in general. Canadians feared that unregulated trade would lead to America siphoning away all of Canada's money.

Walker could help in a number of ways. For starters, the corporation was friendly with a number of lawmakers and could convince them to raise import quotas, particularly for goods with no domestic competitors. Second, they were already part of the existing reciprocity scheme and wouldn't require additional licenses to bring goods into the country. Third, Walker could rebrand some of Saint Moon's goods, putting them in an import grey area that could be slipped past some regulators or, at least, shift the financial risk away from Saint Moon.

It was immediately clear, however, that Briarson and Jones were not here to finalize the deal. Though, Vivienne felt she was getting a clearer picture of why. All goods covered in the agreement had delivery dates and there were certain goods which, it seemed, Saint Moon wasn't ready to ship. Evidently, they had jumped the gun on coming to Walker looking for an agreement. Whatever it was they really wanted to sell in Canada, they couldn't put an availability date on.

What those goods might be, Vivienne couldn't really say because they were not on any of the lists that Saint Moon was handing over. But the prevailing theory amongst the board was that it was the products of Saint Moon's secretive "vaccine project". Medical products were not an existing branch of the company and nothing about medicines had been mentioned regarding this contract. However, this only fueled speculation that the vaccine project was something sinister.

Given that Saint Moon's president was a known supporter of eugenics, the imagination could darken dimly indeed.

So, Briarson and Jones had hunted through the proposed contract looking for things to quibble over. They began with wholesale prices for the items to be rebranded, which was a non-issue as the proposed agreement limited returned stock to 15%. As things were, Saint Moon could only ever break even. It was a sweetheart deal and they only brought it up so that Vivienne could remind them.

Next, was the issue of combined markets. They had advertising strategies for sets of products, with connections that were not always related, and they insisted that those be available in the same regions. It was not a mad demand. Recipes were one of the best advertising tools a food company had, particularly in urban markets. They allowed the company to advertise multiple products on the same broadsheet, saving on ad dollars. However, just as before, Vivienne could guarantee nothing until she had complete lists of goods, which she would then need to send to regional regulators. It was out of her hands and always would be.

Their third quibble was over rights of inspection. It was another issue that simply couldn't be negotiated and they knew it. Saint Moon did not have inspectors certified by the Canadian government and they wouldn't be able to get anyone certified until after they were licensed to sell products in the country. That meant either using government inspectors or Walker inspectors for the first year.

Vivienne had made, and continued to make, a point about government regulators being very slow, which wasn't entirely true. The Rose and Chain wanted to get their agents inside Saint Moon's operation and this was the easiest point of entrance. Besides, if there was some clandestine eugenics project in the works, the Canadian government wouldn't be looking for it. And, even if they did stumble onto it, there were elements within the government that would be more than happy to let it happen.

It was in the midst of this discussion that Esme interrupted them. "There's a call for you, Miss Walker," she said.

"Excuse me, gentlemen," Vivienne said, standing. "Esme, have the drinks cart brought back in. Indulge yourselves, gentlemen, I'll be back as soon as I can."

Down a floor, she picked up the phone at Esme's desk. "Hello, this is Miss Walker."

"Miss Walker, it's Hornsby," the butler said.

"Oh, dear,"

"Indeed, ma'am. A reporter phoned asking about your brother's whereabouts. It seems Miss Rosamund Syme has been kidnapped. I told them nothing, of course."

"Of course," Vivienne replied, absently.

"I thought you would want to know, right away."

"Yes, Hornsby, thank you."

"Is there anything I can do for you, ma'am?"

"Let me think."

Vivienne lowered the receiver to rest at her shoulder. She was experiencing a moment of clarity like none she had felt in many years. The negotiations had fallen from a tiresome formality to an utter waste of time; an insult, even. It wasn't Briarson or Jones' fault; they were errand boys. But she couldn't continue. She just couldn't.

Then it occurred to her how angry the board would be and she almost began to compose a counterargument before she imagined Roger, her cousin-in-law, walking through those elevator doors and was utterly at peace with the idea.

She had wanted to be Father's assistant because she had wanted to help the family, and planning dinners with her mother made her want to scream. Taking over had been an act of habit. She had invested so much in the company that continuing on with it had felt like the most reasonable thing to do. And there was the whole legacy matter to consider.

But her parents were gone. Their story was written and done. The company wasn't going anywhere and they would always be part of it, their legacies secured. What was left of the family? Aunt Ethel and Cousin Martin had turned against her long ago. Aunt Lydia could do no better than to see her daughter, Vera, become the first lady of the company. To Vivienne, they were nothing more than names on a list to be written to around Christmas.

Cranston was the only real family she had left.

Assuming he hadn't been injured in the kidnapping, he was running around somewhere looking for Rosamund. All Vivienne had was his last known location and...and what? What could she do to help? Well, she did have the full resources of the Walker Corporation at her disposal, for the time being, as well as a directive from the Rose and Chain to bring Cranston "back into the fold". Mrs Hopkins had told her to let Cranston know that the society's resources were at his disposal.

So, really, Vivienne had a multi-million dollar company and an international secret society at her service. She was the locus of two of the most powerful entities on the island and, perhaps, the continent. She could do whatever she wanted.

"One moment, Hornsby," Vivienne said, seeing Esme come down the elevator. "Esme, dear," she shouted across the nineteenth floor. "Go tell the men upstairs that I have a family emergency. Tell them that they will be put up at the hotel another night and that they can draft a counterproposal to the contract at their leisure. If they have further questions, direct them to Mr. Cabot."

Esme's eyes went wide and she faltered, but turned and caught the elevator before it could be summoned to another floor.

"Miss Walker?" asked Mrs Shields. "How bad is it?"

"I don't know," Vivienne replied. "But I don't expect it's anything I can't fix." She lifted up the receiver. "Hornsby? Terribly sorry to keep you waiting. I'll be back at the hotel posthaste. In the meantime, phone the St Lawrence Vigilance Committee and tell them I require a pair of volunteers."

"Right away, ma'am," Hornsby replied.

"Also, have a maid lay out a travel outfit for me. I'm going to Montague."

Chapter 28: Vigilantes

September 17th, 1920. Montague, KCI.

It was a quarter after seven and the sun was just touching the horizon when the Chandler turned onto the road that would take them to the Syme Lodge. The plan was to drop off Lydia, get a map to this 'Fairfax' place, and be on the road before twilight set in. That plan became immediately complicated by a throng of men and cars cluttering up the street in front of the gate. When they saw the Chandler, they immediately burst into activity, like a disturbed beehive.

"What fresh hell...?" Lucien said to himself.

Cranston peered ahead and recognized a camera. "Reporters," he shouted over the motor.

"So, I shouldn't run them over?" Lucien yelled back before honking the horn.

Louder still was a gun blast from up ahead. Lucien ducked his head and began scanning, determining whether to stop or speed up. Cranston scrambled for his pistol and then leaned halfway out the side window. The reporters all ran for cover behind their cars.

Through the space where the Syme Lodge's gate had been, Cranston saw a long, willowy, rifle-toting woman walking not so much like a gazelle as a lion out to the road. She wore a mustard-colored shirt and trousers under a long, light green coat and matching hat. From the way the reporters reacted, she appeared to be speaking to them. Apparently at her command, four of them started herding the others away from the entrance, pushing cameras down, as the woman waved the Chandler in.

"Who the hell is that?" Lucien asked.

Cranston sat heavily back in his seat. "I'm fairly certain that's my sister."

They rolled the Chandler into the driveway in time to see Vivienne hand off her rifle to a man dressed like a pirate straight from the cover of Argosy Weekly. He was standing across from a man in a boxer's leotard under a sort of long skirt held up by a fat belt. There was a turban on the second man's head and more that same fabric covered the lower part of his face.

Behind the two of them was a large, horseless carriage; the kind police used for hauling away groups of miscreants. An emblem had been painted on the side: a red star on a white banner with blue trim, a shorthand for King Charles Island's shared sovereignty between America and Canada. In a circle around the emblem were the words 'Saint Lawrence Vigilance Committee'. Above and below the circle of words were painted friezes, intended to keep the vehicle from looking too coldly utilitarian.

"Vigilantes?" Lucien said.

"Indeed," Cranston replied wearily.

"What's going on?"

"Remember the old man at the crossroads?" Cranston said.

"Yeah."

"It's like that."

"Understood," Lucien stopped the Chandler outside the old horse stall. "Can you handle this?"

"Of course,"

"Lydia," Lucien said. "Come with me around the back. We'll get some food in you and you can draw us that map."

They all got out and Cranston headed for the veranda, where Vivienne was lighting a cigarette. "Good evening," she called in the sharp, pre-dusk light.

"What are you doing, here?" Cranston called back.

"I'm helping."

"By bringing reporters?"

"Don't be silly," Vivienne replied, handing him a cigarette once he was in range. "Not much happens in Montague and the local paper has a young man on staff keen to break a story. He followed the police here, then got them to talk, and immediately began phoning papers in Silkhaven to see if they'd pay him for the story. Evidently, the police mentioned you, so I got a call asking if I knew anything about it."

She waved a hand at the reporters on the road. "I'm keeping this lot at bay the best I can. I know two of their bosses and they'll not be invited to any Walker press conferences ever again if they don't do exactly as I say."

"And them?" Cranston nodded at the pirate and bedouin-swami as he breathed out smoke.

"I also brought vigilantes." She smiled as if they were fresh oysters at a picnic. "How goes the search for Rosamund? The boys are more than capable of assisting."

Cranston had to admit that outnumbering the CHJ sounded nice and that was assuming the three who had come to the Lodge were the only ones at Fairfax. As Cranston weighed the situation, Vivienne leaned forward and kissed him on the cheek. "Best of luck. I insist that you return." Then, she whistled for the vigilantes to join them.

The pirate bounded up the stairs with his companion coming along at a more laconic pace. Vivienne took the gun from the pirate. "It looks like someone over there is getting bold," she said. "I'll take care of it." And she swaggered off down the driveway. The three men watched her with various forms of awe.

"Mr Walker?" said the pirate, finally. "I am el Tiburon and this is my partner, the Fighting Sheik. We represent the St Lawrence Vigilance Committee."

"Yes, I saw the truck," Cranston said more curtly than they deserved. "Terribly sorry." He extended his hand to shake. "Cranston Walker; and I've had a hell of an afternoon. Welcome to the team." Cranston turned to the Sheik. "Do you talk?"

In response, the Sheik lifted up the lower wrap of his turban to reveal a grisly scar across his throat.

"The Ottomans gave him that," Tiburon explained.

"You were a prisoner of war?" Cranston asked the Sheik.

The Sheik nodded. He pointed at Cranston's jacket, then at his own right shoulder.

"A guardsman?"

Again the Sheik nodded.

"That makes three," Cranston said. "My associate Lucien is Miss Syme's personal bodyguard. He served with me in France."

"I want to say," Tiburon interjected. "It's an honor to be given this assignment, sir. Smoke and Mirror are personal heroes of mine."

"Is that so?"

The Sheik gave Cranston a weary nod. Tiburon was already rolling up his sleeve to reveal a tattoo on his meaty bicep and Cranston was presented with an image of his parents in masks and capes, rendered in the cartoon style of tattooists; his mother looking more buxom than she had been in real life.

"I would have taken your word for it," Cranston told him. There was something seismic about learning that one's parents were the subjects of complete strangers' tattoos.

"Sorry, sir," Tiburon said, rolling his sleeve down. "I'm just excited is all. What's the game?"

"There is a house," Cranston said. "Locals refer to it as the Fairfax place and our best intelligence puts Miss Syme and another woman, Miss Caine, there. The men holding them are armed and members of a group of 'Christians' who like to imagine the savior as William Bankier. There are three of them, as far as I know, perhaps more."

"When do we set sail?" Tiburon asked, putting on a Spanish accent.

"As soon as we get the map," Cranston told him.

Tiburon laughed for a moment before noticing that Cranston was not. "Oh," the vigilante said. "A real map?"

"Yes. Our amateur cartographer is in the breakfast kitchen."

He led the vigilantes into the house, through the bullet-riddled hallway and into the breakfast kitchen. Lydia was sitting at the table with Lucien and Lily. When the latter saw Cranston, she jumped to her feet and threw herself into his arms. Almost immediately, she pulled back and recovered herself. Cranston reached down and gave her hand a squeeze.

Lydia was in the middle of explaining to Lily how she had met Cranston and Lucien. She had been outfitted with a pencil and paper, but hadn't made any progress with the map.

"Gran'motha needs the boys sleepin'," Lydia said. "'Cause she's an uh-nee-ah-man-suh."

"And what's that when it's at home?" Lily asked, sitting back down.

Lydia's face became thoughtful as she searched her mind for an answer. Suddenly, her face brightened and she turned back to Lily, confidently announcing: "Greek."

"If I may," Cranston said. "Lydia, you were going to draw us a map to the Fairfax place."

"Oh, yes," she said, putting down her sandwich and taking

up the pencil. She paused. "I don' know whe'e we a'e."

"Can you draw it starting in Montague?"

"Uh-huh," she answered brightly. "The big ma'ket?"

"Which one is that?" Cranston asked.

"There's only one," Lily replied.

Lydia began her cartography with a simple rectangle at the bottom of the page. "A'e ya really gonna help those church boys with the Jezebel?"

"No," Cranston said. "We are going to rescue the Jezebel. She's a friend of ours. In fact, this is her house."

Lydia looked up, startled. "She lives he-ah?"

"Indeed," he answered. "She's the friend Lucien spoke to you about."

"The church boys said the Neon Jezebel was a beast from the pit."

"Boston, actually."

"Have you hea'd huh sing?" Lydia asked.

"No, why?"

"They called huh the devil's songbi'd. Ah though' she migh' be a siren."

"They were being...metaphorical," Cranston explained. "Do you know what a metaphor is?"

"Doesn' e'ryone? It's a truth dressed up as a lie."

Cranston nodded admiringly. "I couldn't have said it better myself."

"So, she doesn' sing?"

"Not to my knowledge."

"Very occasionally," Lucien corrected. "And 'the devil's songbird' isn't far off."

Cranston shot Lucien a questioning look. Lucien just shrugged.

Lydia looked disappointed. "Ah always wan'ed to hea' a siren. Ah think if yuh on land ya could su'vive it." Then, she began to draw.

Lydia's map was graphically crude, but included a number of written details that made it quite specific. Both sides of the paper were well covered before she was done. She provided some oral history as she went, as well.

It seemed that, before the war, a number of families had tried establishing a more exclusive summer colony to the north of Montague. For all of Montague's amenities, nothing in it was truly luxurious. Families like his, coming to the island, tended to stay in Silkhaven county; the northern coast having homes belonging to the Roosevelts, Astors, and Candlers.

According to Lydia, the families behind this new colony abandoned it, shortly after the outbreak of the war. Cranston could only assume that their fortunes had not weathered those days particularly well. Irish and German interests, he knew, had suffered greatly.

The Fairfax house, in particular, was two-stories with a wine cellar. There was a lawn all around it, as the Fairfax's had hosted outdoor potlucks there. In the years since its abandonment, several of Lydia's cousins had used the colony's houses as places to take girls from Montague. This was, evidently, what put the 'church boys' in touch with the Barnabys; the Barnaby boys not knowing that the property had been sold had chanced on the group.

Under less urgent conditions, Cranston would have sought out the real estate agent who had made the sale and attempted to learn more. As it was, the most that could be gained would be finding out how many people resided there; but that only by a slim chance.

The plan was to first find the house, then take the cars to the nearest neighboring house and park there. Lydia's map indicated that there was forest around the house, which they would use for cover. Cranston and Lucien would watch the house itself, while Tiburon and the Sheik reconnoitered the perimeter. Once they had an idea of how great a force they were dealing with, they would decide how to proceed.

Chapter 29:
Fairfax

Not wanting to declare their presence, the vigilantes had pulled eight panels from the back of their carriage. The panels were wooden with large magnets affixed to the back. The fronts, when properly arranged—four to a side—were painted white with the face of a baby besides red looping script advertising an early childhood nutrition product.

It was city camouflage. Out here, it was suspicious. However, suspicious was a step up from openly announcing they were vigilantes.

Tiburon and the Sheik had sidearms, but nothing heavier. Lucien offered them their pick from the broom closet, after Cranston had claimed one of the trench sweepers for himself. Tiburon had taken the other shotgun, leaving Lucien and the Sheik with the Thompsons.

Lydia's map proved counter-intuitive, but once all of the details were taken together, it got them where they needed to go. The driveway of the Fairfax house went through two hundred feet of forest, before opening onto the lawn. Helpfully, there was a well-made, three-foot square wooden sign beside the road that read 'Fairfax House' with the proper street address below. All of the houses in the abandoned colony had them.

The Chandler and the carriage passed this driveway and turned off at a sign which read Lehmanhaus Green. The house on this property was, in fact, painted green, leading Cranston to wonder how many Lehmans had been involved in the colony. If the would-be town had hung its fortune too heavily on one family, their solitary failure might have sunk the entire endeavor.

They parked the cars out of sight from the road, buckled and slung on their firearms, then proceeded into the forest between houses. The four mashed through the forest, until the Fairfax house came into view. Cranston and Lucien found a place where the undergrowth was thick enough that it would hide them while allowing them to monitor the house. They were perhaps a hundred feet from the driveway on their right and thirty from the tree line. In the blue shadows of dusk, they were rendered invisible.

Tiburon and the Sheik began a clockwise patrol of the lawn, staying at least fifty feet from the edge of the grass. Their orders were to stay out of sight until they received a signal from the bodyguards. If they managed to make a full circumference of the house before being signaled, they were to cross the road a hundred feet from the house.

Belly down on the forest floor, Lucien took a pair of binoculars from his coat and began scanning the facade. There was no sign of the milk truck, from where they were positioned, which Cranston disliked. None of the windows betrayed any light and he was beginning to fear that they were too late.

"Movement," Lucien whispered. "First floor, near window."

"I can't see anything." Cranston whispered back.

"It's dark." Lucien was quiet for a moment. "One person... maybe assembling something."

Something occurred to Cranston, then. He raised himself an inch on his elbows and knees and crawled backwards until he could get behind a tree. From there, he crouched and peered up at the house's roof. The chimney was set to the rear of the house, but he could just make out a thin wisp of smoke coming from it.

He crawled back to Lucien. "Chimney smoke," he said.

"At least two in the house," Lucien whispered. "They'll be lighting candles soon."

They kept watching, waiting for some further signs, but those inside were giving none. There was, however, a growing rumbling noise from somewhere behind them. In a few minutes, it was clearly the sound of an engine and, then, several. Cranston's gut tightened as he looked through the shadows of the trees to the sharp evening light on the driveway. A small convoy of cars was making its way up to the Fairfax house.

He could feel—more spiritually than physically—Lucien tense beside him. There were four cars in all: none new and two of them appeared to have been cobbled together from the corpses of other vehicles, a la Dr Frankenstein. Before the first car stopped and the driver got out, both of them knew full well who was inside.

Shem Barnaby stepped out and walked towards the house. He planted one foot on the steps leading up to the house's porch and shouted: "Hey, Bible boys! Come on out he-ah. We need ta have a talk."

The cars were parked in two rows at diagonals. Likely an instinct one picked up through many long hours with automobiles. They were ready to get back on the road quickly and together.

"Ah said," Shem bellowed, "come on out! We gotta talk!"

As the clunking sound of doors opening and shutting filled the lawn, Cranston could only see one row of cars. There were four Barnabys on the near side, not including Shem. Three of them carried hunting rifles and the fourth— the oldest of those he could see, likely of Shem's generation—

had a pair of revolvers strapped to his hips. The younger men held their guns insecurely; their off-hands shifted and their trigger fingers traced the lines of the guard. Either they had very little experience with these weapons or they were frothing for a fight.

The one consolation was that, clearly, none of them had military training. At best, they were game hunters, but the unfamiliarity with which they carried their weapons suggested otherwise. Cranston prayed that this was the case and that they were now faced with a pack of nervous, rather than bloodthirsty, farm boys.

A further blessing was that the cars had parked in the bright, orange beam of the setting sun, while the rest of the clearing was in blue darkness. Those inside the beam would have a distinct disadvantage firing on anyone in the shadows.

"Ah know ya in!" Shem called at the house. "We'll come in the'e if we hafta!"

Finally, the front door opened and a man stepped out. He wore trousers cuffed half way up his ankles and unlaced boots. His suspenders were tight against his white undershirt and he had a knitted toque pulled low on his head. With the addition of a scraggly beard and the muscled bulk of his chest and arms, the man looked like a stevedore.

"I'm sorry," he said, coming to the top of the steps. "I was indisposed. You're the Barnabys, yes?"

Shem took a couple steps up and the stevedore met him half way. Cranston strained to hear their conversation. They gave names, but Cranston only heard 'Shem' because he was prepared for it.

"...couple men come..." Shem was saying, some of the words too quiet to reach the forest. "...my daughter...'em."

"No," he heard the stevedore say. "...here. We were ex... time. So, we'll be...oon."

"Thank...see 'em..." Shem replied.

"Hold...they come here?"

Shem answered him in a lower voice, his body language suggesting a kind of casual embarrassment.

"Hell's bells!" The stevedore shouted. "Who else have you told?"

"Nah," Shem straightened. "It's no good raisin' ya voice to me. Twas my uncle did the tellin.'"

"What did you think those men would do when they got here? We are struggling against the forces of darkness and the devil doesn't come to negotiate!"

"You best keep ya voice dahn!"

This escalation had the Barnabys shifting more than before. Cranston saw them start fanning out from the cars, as if they might try to surround the house. As one of them walked near to the tree line, Cranston recognized him as the woodsman. He had a rifle tucked under one arm in a way that suggested that he might really know what to do with it.

Cranston nudged Lucien, tilting his head towards the young man. Lucien nodded. The woodsman was getting too close for comfort. Outnumbered as they were, the best thing was to stay back and wait for the Barnabys to leave. However, if they were caught like this—on their stomachs without their weapons drawn—they were as good as dead. If there was to be a fight, they needed the initiative.

The conversation between Shem and the stevedore continued. They were calmer, now, and Cranston had missed what exactly had changed that.

The woodsman was at the very edge of the tree line, now. His eyes were sweeping the lawn beside the house, looking for an ambush, then he turned his gaze on the forest. He stopped, looking roughly in Lucien and Cranston's direction. Keeping his eyes on the forest, he knelt down and began fussing with his boot, tightening the laces; either to give himself an excuse for a lower angle or in preparation to run.

Whatever his intention, he did look down to tie the knot. Lucien took that moment to raise himself up into a runner's ready position. The Thompson slung across his back shifted and he adjusted it with his elbow. Cranston followed suit just before the woodsman looked up. The woodsman shifted his weight incorrectly and momentarily lost his balance. He kept himself from toppling over, but dropped the rifle onto the grass.

In that moment, Lucien bolted out from cover, letting the Thompson swing down to his side and into his hands. A half second after, Cranston followed, drawing his revolver and positioning himself directly in front of the woodsman.

"No one move!" Lucien shouted, aiming the machine gun as he moved closer to the house.

"Don't do it," Cranston said to the woodsman. "I see your hand touch steel, I'll burn you down."

The younger Barnabys all retreated to the cover of the trucks. The elder with the revolvers held up his right hand, signaling them not to fire, while his left floated above the grip of one pistol like a gunslinger in a wild west show. Shem was utterly undaunted. He walked off the porch steps and marched a few paces towards Lucien.

"Whe'ah's mah daughtuh?" Shem bellowed.

"That's none of your business!" Lucien called back.

"She's mah daughtuh!"

"And a grown woman! She can go where she likes! Speaking of which," Lucien turned a degree to his left to aim at the stevedore. "How about you be a pal and go fetch those two women you kidnapped? You tried, you failed, it happens. There's no need for anyone to get shot, today!"

The stevedore went to the railing of the steps and shook an enraged finger at Lucien. "The Neon Jezebel is a servant of the devil! She is a harpy and a harbinger of the whore of Babylon!"

"Yeah," Lucien called back. "She's got a tongue on her, but I've got a gun on you."

"You will not thwart the will of the Almighty!"

"That's between me and him! You know what's between me and you? A loaded fucking gun! Now, go get her!"

"Hypocrite!" Shem screeched, his voice cracking. "You kidnapped mah child!"

That's when the first shot rang out and the pace of the world slowed to a crawl. A cloud of smoke rose from behind one of the trucks. One of the younger Barnabys had gotten too nervous. His wild shot hit nothing, but the fight had commenced.

The woodsman whipped his hand out for his rifle and Cranston made good on his word. One bullet straight through his head. The back of the woodsman's head erupted and he toppled sideways. For a moment, the grass disappeared; the young man was dressed in a grey-green coat and trousers and lying in a field of mud, a pickelhaube helmet fastened to his ruined head.

Lucien released a burst from the Thompson as Shem went running for the cover of the cars and the stevedore threw open the front door and dove into the house. There were three shooters behind the cars, one of whom was firing well above anyone's head.

The gunslinger drew his left pistol, but didn't fire. Shem was moving through his field of fire and the gunslinger moved to get clear of him, drawing the right pistol as he went. Cranston let off two shots in his direction and the gunslinger turned and shot with both guns, not exactly aiming with either.

There was more gunfire erupting from the other side of the lawn, as Tiburon and the Sheik joined the fight.

Shem had a hand raised as he ran. One of the boys threw a rifle from behind the cars and the older man snatched it out of the air. He whipped around, sliding the bolt back to draw a round from the clip, then shoved it back into place. The whole action was smooth as clockwork and twice as fast.

Lucien released a second burst, catching Shem in the shoulder, which made his first shot go wild. A very young Barnaby stood up from behind his cover, holding his shotgun at the hip—the gun too heavy for him to lift fully—and tried to aim at Lucien. Shem stumbled from Lucien's bullet in his shoulder and tossed in front of the boy just as he fired. The shotgun blast caught Shem in the back and he pitched forward. The boy with the shotgun screamed as Shem landed face-first in the grass.

Cranston fired twice more at the gunslinger, hitting him once, but not stopping him. The hail of bullets from the gunslinger poured on and Cranston heard two whistle past his head before both guns were empty. In the moment after the last two bullets fired, the smoke cleared in front of the gunslinger and Cranston fired the last of his revolver, catching the older man in the gut and he dropped to his knees screaming.

The young Barnaby dropped his shotgun with a loud clattering on the car's hood, then dropped out of sight. Lucien stepped behind the corner to the house for his third burst. This time, he struck one of the boys engaged with the vigilantes. A rifle disappeared from behind the nearest car and one of the young men ran to his fallen kin while the remaining rifle pointed nearly straight up.

Cranston holstered his revolver and slid the trench sweeper off his shoulder. The gunslinger was crawling back towards the cars. Cranston broke into a run and slammed the butt of his shot gun into the man's head as he passed, then dropped into a crouch beside one of the cars.

Lucien fired a fourth time, hitting the one that was running towards the opposite line of cars.

"Bastuhd!" a young man shouted as he rose, rifle up to fire at Lucien.

Lucien dodged back behind the house as a hail of bullets tore into wood. Cranston saw him pop out for another burst, but Lucien didn't fire. Three more shots erupted from the cars and Lucien went running for the trees. The Barnaby boy had found a shooting nest between the cars, giving him much better cover than just the hood.

However, he was still in the harsh sunset light and Lucien was deep in the shadows of the clearing. Cranston's eyes were sufficiently adjusted to the dark that he could see Lucien crouch to switch from the Thompson to his pistol. The Barnaby boy wasn't waiting, though. He fired two more wild shots before his gun emptied.

An awful quiet settled as Cranston heard the scrape of metal as the boy switched weapons, checking that this new one was loaded. The new gun clunked against one of the cars and Lucien let off three rounds. The gun clattered to the ground and Lucien rose to his feet.

"Don' shoot!" A boy cried from inside the fortress of cars. His voice cracked with youth and emotion.

Cranston heard feet running towards him. The long Barnaby from that morning came around the back of the car where Cranston was crouched. The young man was holding a rifle in one hand and looking at the ground. He saw the gunslinger incapacitated, first, then Cranston. There was a moment where the two weighed each other. The boy's gun wasn't ready; he had a finger on the trigger, but the barrel was pointed at the ground.

He made a decision, eyes widening. As the rifle swung upwards, Cranston fired the trench sweeper, removing half of the boy's face and a chunk of his shoulder, sending him twisting backwards.

Quiet settled on the lawn. Cranston's ears were ringing,

but he could hear a young boy sobbing.

"Don' shoot!" came the boy's voice. "Please don' shoot! Please! Please!"

"Lucien!" Cranston yelled.

"I'm fine!" he called back.

"Head into the house," he said. "Tiburon! You two alright?"

"Si!" Came the affected Mexican accent. "A couple flesh wounds, but we're good, señor!"

That left Cranston with the two boys. The one he was talking to squeaked every once in a while. There was no way he was older than fourteen. Cranston had seen boys that young; French and geared boot to helmet in dead men's clothes that drooped and sagged from their narrow shoulders and skinny legs.

None of them had asked for quarter, but not out of bravery. They had simply done as the adults around them. The only difference between them and these Barnabys was that the French boys had died faster than the grown-ups.

These were children, not the enemy, but in the absence of adult guidance and the trauma of watching their kin shot down, there was no telling what they'd do. The bloody reality might have set in and base survival taken over. Or they might find a desperate valor when faced with their family's killers.

They were going to live, Cranston decided. He was not going to kill children.

"Bedecke deine Ohren!" Cranston called to the vigilantes, knowing the Sheik would understand German. "Barnabys! Can you hear me?"

"Yes," one shouted, voice frantic. "Yes, suh! Please don' shoot!"

"Are you armed, son?"

"No, suh! I threw dahn my gun."

There was one still crying.

"Who's crying?"

"Tha's mah cousin, suh! Ezra."

"Alright," Cranston said. "Is he armed?"

"No, suh!"

"Good, we're going to let you go. However, there's not a lot of trust between us. I'm going to put my gun on the hood of this car, alright?" Without standing, he slid the trench sweeper up onto the hood, the butt hanging a little over the side; ready enough if he should need it. "Do you see it?"

"Yeah,"

"Alright, I'm going to stand up slowly."

He raised his hands first, then slowly stood, looking down into the space between the cars. For a moment, the car disappeared, replaced by sandbags. The boys lying in their own blood wore gas masks. Cranston blinked and they were farm boys again. He saw the one he had been speaking to; his hands were folded on top of his head and his face was streaked with tears.

"What's your name?" Cranston asked.

"It's Luke."

"That's fine. I want you to come and get Ezra. Get him on his feet."

Luke ran over to the boy who had fired the shotgun from his hip. Ezra was no younger than ten and Luke only a couple years older, but the younger Barnaby clung to his cousin like a toddler would a parent. Luke struggled a bit with Ezra's arms around his neck, but he got the child to his feet.

"Look at me," Cranston said. "Both of you." The tear-soaked eyes of the boys did their best to obey. "I want you to know," Cranston continued, softly. "That I'm very sorry about what happened here, today. I never intended for anyone to get hurt. Neither of you has a weapon, now, so none of my friends will harm you. You are going to go home. You're going to see your mothers. Can I ask you just one favor, though?"

"Yes, suh," Luke said, then nudged Ezra, who nodded

rapidly.

"Okay," Cranston adjusted his throat in preparation. "Run." He said in the Voice. It was the first time he had ever used it in English.

The boys' eyes glazed over, their tears stopped, and they both turned and bolted down the driveway. Cranston watched them go and felt something shift inside him. He had never used the Voice in English before. He had broken a vow he had made a thousand times; crossed a line that he had dug deep in his own sand. He had done it for the best of reasons, but it had still been a violation; not only of their wills, but his own sense of self.

Cranston placed both hands on the hood of the car. Tears were coming and he pushed them out, giving himself over for just a moment, then recovering a moment later. He wiped the tears from his face and picked up the trench sweeper.

Circling around the cars, he waved to Tiburon and the Sheik, both plugging their ears with their fingers. When they saw him, they dropped their hands and exited the cover of the forest.

"Lucien is already inside and I'm joining him," Cranston told them. "You two, watch the perimeter. Stop any man who comes out. If you see a woman, let her go. It will be too much to explain yourselves, in the moment."

They both nodded. Before going off to find vantage points, the Sheik put a hand on Cranston's shoulder. He pointed to his chest and then his head. *I know.* Cranston felt the tears rising again. Only a fellow guardsman could understand exactly what Cranston had done and how terrible it had been. Then, the Sheik gave Cranston a thumbs up. He shook the thumb for emphasis and fixed Cranston with a serious look. The Sheik nodded.

"Thank you," Cranston said, fighting back tears. "I could do nothing else."

Chapter 30:
Della Caine

September 17th, 1920. Inside Fairfax house.

Cranston entered the house with his shotgun pointed low. The main door was open, but he pushed it gently wider until it touched the front wall. He was greeted with a wide, open room cast in harsh shadows by the final brightness of day. To his right was a dining area with a doorless entry leading into the kitchen ahead. On the left was what should have been a sitting room. There were sofas, only two chairs around a card table and a camera—the black accordion folded up into the box—on a tripod. A plain sheet of canvas had been hung against one wall, creating an ad hoc photo studio.

The two rooms were separated only by a staircase. Motion caught Cranston's eye and he looked up the stairs. Lucien was crouched near a door and waving him up. Eyeing the stairs, Cranston had serious doubts about getting up them quietly, so he quickly pulled off his boots and mounted the steps in his stocking feet.

The upper floor was an L-shaped hallway with three doors leading off of it, all closed. Lucien was posted outside the nearest of these three. As Cranston knelt down beside him, Lucien held up two fingers, then pointed at his neck: two voices. They both turned their attention to listen.

"We have to check," one voice whispered beyond the door.

"The Barnabys are dead!" whispered the other back. "They'd be shouting for us, otherwise."

"Those other guys didn't strike me as the quiet types," the first replied.

"They're in the house! I heard it!"

"So, we just wait for them?"

"Yes!"

"Maybe they're out of ammo."

"Maybe lots of things!" the second whisper said, gaining a touch of voice on 'lots'. "There's no way we get to the truck without them seeing us. We stay here where can defend ourselves."

"Until when?" the first asked.

"I don't know, but more than five gosh darn minutes!"

The claim that they could defend themselves suggested that they were armed. They were less confident with those weapons than the Barnabys had been, clearly, but that did not necessarily translate into less skilled. More importantly, it was impossible to tell—from their position outside the door—where exactly Rosamund and Miss Caine might be. A wild and blind gun battle in an enclosed space gambled the lives of anyone within.

Cranston tapped Lucien on the shoulder and mouthed the word 'negotiate'. Lucien lifted his eyebrows and tilted his back and forth in a gesture of yeah, what else can we do? Cranston shook his head. 'Me,' he mouthed. 'The Voice.'

Lucien's eyes went wide. On reflex, the same and as deeply trained as Cranston's, he said "The Voice is for...", but he stopped himself. For a long time, 'the enemy' had applied only to men speaking German while wearing uniforms trimmed in red. The war was over and they were retired, discharged. There wasn't supposed to be an enemy, anymore.

There was a thought that had been bubbling up in Cranston's mind since Lucien had first shown him the broom closet. It was a thought that he had forced down, silenced, relegated to that place in the mind where one buried thoughts that clashed with one's sense of self. It returned, now, and he couldn't deny it. His throat tightened as he allowed it to become words in his head: we have a new war, now.

'Me,' Lucien mouthed.

"Gentlemen," Lucien called before Cranston had the chance to object. "Let's talk about you releasing Miss Syme."

There was silence for a moment. "Who is Miss Syme?" came one voice.

"Rosamund Syme," Lucien replied. "You kidnapped her, earlier. We saw you do it."

"We don't see it that way." The man who was speaking, now, had a trained quality to his voice. This one had some experience as a public speaker. "What we did was more like an arrest. Ours is a government above any Earthly authority."

"I don't think there are any Earthly governments that will see it that way."

"The White Throne of Judgement concerns me more than any mortal court."

"Be that as it may," Lucien replied, "mortal courts almost always have mortal enforcers; men with guns. If you aren't going to fight us, I doubt you're going to fight them. So, how long can you run for?"

"Long enough," the speaker said. "Once the world sees the Neon Jezebel for what she is, our work will be done."

"She wrote a book, friend." Lucien nearly laughed. "How much more can you show anyone?"

"We have a camera! Her face will be on the front page of every newspaper in the world!"

"Hold on, you kidnapped Miss Syme to photograph her? Why not pretend to be journalists? You could have photographed her in her sitting room."

There was a pause. "What?" the speaker called back.

"Never mind. Listen, as it is, you are heading straight for jail. The longer you run, the closer you get to a cemetery."

"Paul was imprisoned. John the Baptist was martyred."

"You aren't acting like someone who's ready to be martyred."

"Our work is not yet finished."

"You want to show the world who Miss Syme really is? Go to court. Think about it, if you get taken peacefully—if you're arrested—you'll stand trial. They'll accuse you of kidnapping her and Miss Caine, which means both of them will be called up to the witness stand. The only better way to show someone to the world is to put them on Broadway."

"And you would take us to the police, I suppose?"

"Happily," Lucien said.

"You are murderers!"

"Hey now, they shot first. We just shot better. A man's got a right to defend himself." They had nothing to say to that, so Lucien returned to his previous line. "We're here, now. There are more of us outside. If you choose the sword, today, you'll die and your mission will go unfinished. If you give up, you'll go to trial and you'll have the chance to finish what you've started."

Still, they were silent behind the door. This was probably the most that either of them would show their bellies. Lucien nodded to Cranston, who began to gently hum to himself in the Voice.

"You can leave here with your lives to pursue your mission another day. All you have to do is open the door."

In the quiet that followed, they heard the sound of footsteps approaching. Lucien rose to his feet, pistol down but ready. Cranston followed, pressing himself against the far wall. The door knob began to turn.

Suddenly, a shot rang out. They ducked and three more bullets fired. Seeing that none of the shots were coming through the door or the wall, Lucien kicked the door, landing his boot just above the knob. The door swung wide and Lucien came face to face with the stevedore. Surprise and training kicked in. Lucien put two bullets in the man's chest, then swept the room, looking for another target.

There was no one visible. There were two cots with steamer chests at their feet and an old sofa behind a simple table. Lucien edged in, shotgun ready, and Cranston quickly entered behind him, making the same visual sweep. The cots were off to the right, the sofa and table ahead and slightly to the right. To their left was a wall; at the far end, another door stood open. From inside, a fifth shot was fired.

Lucien pressed himself against that near wall and began to approach the second door. Cranston pointed his shotgun at the open frame and walked in an arc, away from Lucien and towards the cots. As he did, he found the second kidnapper. The man was lying behind the sofa, clutching his neck as blood poured out between his fingers in evenly timed spurts. He was trying to gasp, but the gurgling sounds that accompanied each were a sign that he was fighting a losing battle.

Cranston waved his elbow to get Lucien's attention, then gestured with the gun towards the dying man. Lucien peered around the sofa to see, then turned his attention back to the open door.

As Cranston reached the exterior wall, he could see a small room beyond with two windows giving it the gentle illumination of indirect sunlight. At the far end was another open door, leading into a shadowed room that Cranston took to be a washroom. He stepped closer, to make sure that the spray of his shotgun wouldn't catch Lucien if one was called for.

Lucien, a foot from the doorway itself, called: "Who's in there?"

He was answered by a muffled cry, a single long vowel

coming through a gag or something similar.

"Rosamund?" Lucien asked.

They heard another muffled vowel, followed by the clatter of wood on wood. Lucien looked ready to cry, but he steeled himself.

"Who did the shooting?" he yelled. "Come on, I know it wasn't Rosamund, so who was it?"

Still, no one answered. It occurred to Cranston that the last report they had heard might have been a suicide's bullet. He crept closer to the open door. The door itself obscured the better part of his view of the room. Cranston got low to the ground; low enough that Lucien could stand behind and shoot over his head—though, given Lucien's height, that really wasn't much. Pressing the barrel of the shotgun against the door, he pushed it open further, revealing the room to him.

Another cot and steamer trunk stood along the far end. Two chairs were placed in the center of the room; one had several lengths of rope pooled around its feet and the other held Rosamund, still bound and gagged. Cranston stepped through the doorway and into the corner created by the dividing wall and the exterior wall. A move which signaled Lucien to enter.

Lucien stepped in, saw Rosamund, and raced to untie her. The windows were closed, which meant that whoever had fired that last shot was in the washroom.

"I know there's someone in that washroom," Cranston shouted. "I know you're armed. If I have to come in there, it will end very badly for you."

As soon as Lucien had the gag off, Rosamund shouted: "Do what he says, Della!"

"Et tu, Rosie?" a voice came from the washroom. It was a woman's voice and seemed to sing each of its vowels. There was no melody to it, just musical notes, which Cranston was ill-equipped to describe.

"You lied to me!" Rosamund spat.

"No, I withheld the whole truth," the voice half-sung. "There is a difference."

"What are you talking about?" Lucien asked.

"I'm not the Neon Jezebel," Rosamund growled.

"Put your weapon on the ground," Cranston ordered. "And kick it out."

Rosamund, released, fell weakly into Lucien's arms. She breathed heavily through her nose, not willing to cry, yet.

Cranston heard the quiet thud of the gun being placed on the wooden floor and then the weapon slid across the washroom floor, out of the darkness, and halfway into the bedroom.

"Now, step out with your hands on top of your head."

"Cranston," Rosamund said, holding back tears. "Brace yourself."

Cranston looked towards her for a moment, then back at the washroom doorway as Della Caine stepped out. She no longer wore the blue dress and wide boots he had seen the day before. Someone had dressed her in a man's breeches and a plain undershirt. She was tall, perhaps five-foot-seven, but even taller with the plumage.

There was not a hair visible on Della Caine's body. From her head grew a thick crest of bright blue feathers that turned a greenish hue closer to the center. Her arms and her legs sprouted the same blue plumage, but were bare skin along the inner curve. Even her armpits were filled with downy growths of a paler blue. Her bare feet were covered in scale-like plates of hard skin and split into three long toes that ended in talons which clicked against the wood as she walked.

Her face was nearly human. Under pale, downy eyebrows her eyes were a bright green; but her nose had flattened and joined with her upper lip into a triangle of stiff keratin that partially obscured the dark pink flesh of her lower lip.

She looked like a woman who had tried to become a bird and—only half succeeding—had found she could not become a woman again.

"You," Cranston said, his gun drifting down. "What are you?"

"I am Della Caine," she replied, singing the vowels.

"They said you had EDAD." His voice was just above a whisper. He didn't know what the feeling was that overcame him, now; he only knew that it rendered all other things irrelevant.

"Yes," Della's hands slid from her head as she walked closer to him. "I got closer to a pocket than anyone in history. I went in and I came out."

"But..." Cranston could not stop looking at her. There was a passion rising in him that wanted to worship her and destroy her at the same time; Venus and Proserpina in a single woman.

"I know." Della stepped in front of one of the windows, reached down and pulled it open. She took a step away. "It's okay." She said, consoling him. "You will doubt yourself, later; but it's not the feathers. I've always had this effect on men."

Just then, a grappling hook came flying through the window. Cranston jumped back as it thumped heavily on the floor, then slid back and up to catch on the sill.

In the strangeness of the moment, Cranston reached out a hand—though he feared touching her—and said: "Wait."

Della Caine's lower lip stretched, raising the half beak in a poor rendition of a smile. "I don't think I will." She lunged forward, hands outstretched, through the window, grabbing the rope as she went and disappeared.

For a moment, Cranston couldn't move. Then, all at once, his faculties returned to him. He ran to the window and saw Della run into the forest with a man by her side. He grabbed the fixed part of the window, pulled up his feet and swung himself out, never minding the rope. Cranston rolled when he hit the ground, then chased after Miss Caine as soon as his feet—protected by nothing more than his socks—were beneath him.

He sprinted through the dark woods, catching only occasional glimpses of the pair through the trees. The detritus of the forest—pebbles, twigs, small bushes—dug through his socks and into the flesh of his feet. His soles were well-callused by the harsh conditions of the war, but the hundred tiny pains succeeded in slowing him down.

Finally, the forest gave way to a grassy beach. A few hundred feet away, Della Caine sat in the passenger seat of a small yacht that her companion was pushing into the river. It was hopeless, but Cranston ran after them as best he could. The man jumped into the boat and started the engine. White water sprayed up behind them and the boat turned sharply away from the shore and out to sea, leaving Cranston on the shore to stare futilely after them.

Epilogue:
Witnesses

September 17th, 1920. Montague PD.

Less than twelve hours after Rosamund Syme was kidnapped, she walked into the Montague police department with her two bodyguards and a pair of vigilantes from Silkhaven. To his own, quiet shame, Lieutenant Roach breathed a sigh of relief that the bodyguards had found the taken woman.

Roach had told his men to ask around town if anyone had seen any odd trucks. No one had, of course, and Roach figured that the truck had stayed on the rural roads. The trouble with the rural roads was that there was no one to ask about them. Plus, their jurisdiction ended not too far from where the roads turned to dirt. There really wasn't much they could do but kick it up to the vigilantes, anyway, authorized as they were to work anywhere on the island.

The little building had never had five witnesses in it before, not all at once. Roach had Sergeant Parish do the paperwork with the vigilantes: copy down their code names, registration numbers, and get statements. Roach himself grabbed whatever chairs he could find so that Miss Syme and her bodyguards could sit at his desk.

In retrospect, Roach would realize that he should have separated them all, but separated them where? He didn't

have an office. The station didn't have offices. The building
had been an Episcopal church back when there was but one
constable for the whole town. They took the steeple off when
they made it a police station. Didn't seem right having one
when it wasn't a house of God. Roach was not an especially
religious man, but he was Christian enough to not want to
claim the kind of authority people ascribed to a steeple.

Officer Rose, who had given up his chair for the inter-
views, brought the trio some coffee. The two bodyguards had
a layer of dirt on them from the road, mixed with some blood
that didn't look like it was theirs. Miss Syme wasn't in any
makeup and had circles under her eyes. They all looked tired.

"Well, folks," Roach said, taking out his notepad. "It looks
like you've had a doozy of a day. But you're here, so go ahead
and tell me what happened."

He was surprised when Miss Syme did the talking, but he
wrote down all she said as best he could, just the same.

Witness Statement of Miss Rosamund Syme
17 September, 1920

*This afternoon, I was at my home where I do counseling
sessions for ladies suffering from exposure to dimensional
pockets. That day, I was seeing a woman named Della
Caine. She had a highly advanced nervous condition and
I had ordered my bodyguards to stay outside the house for
Miss Caine's comfort.*

*At about three o'clock, I was on the second floor, helping
Miss Caine prepare for dinner, when I heard a truck engine
on the road. A few minutes later, the truck crashed through
the hedgerow about the property. Naturally, I went to the
window and saw the truck turn itself around so that the rear
of it was facing my front door.*

Because of the porch roof, I couldn't see anyone get out of the back of the truck, but I did hear someone force their way inside. There was quite a bit of shouting from the first floor. Fearing for Miss Caine's condition, I told her to hide in a wardrobe. Only a few seconds after that, two masked men barged into the room and one laid hold of me.

Miss Caine shrieked from inside the wardrobe and the other man took her out of it by force. In a panic, she fought him and succeeded in taking off his mask. He struck her in the head and she went limp. That man then carried Miss Caine out of the room. I tried to calm the man who was holding me, afraid of what he might do in his excited state. He began taking me down to the truck as well, as I had seen one of their faces.

One of my bodyguards, Mr Walker, attempted to stop him and the two fired on each other. My kidnapper was using me as a shield, which impaired Mr Walker's endeavor. I was taken into the truck where the other kidnapper and Miss Caine were. I heard more gunshots outside the truck as it began to drive away.

I'm afraid I lost track of time in the truck. It seemed only a few minutes before the unmasked man told the driver to stop at a bridge. He got out, carrying Miss Caine. I heard a gunshot and a splash before the man returned to the truck without Miss Caine.

After that, we continued to a house. There, I was kept in an upstairs room. The driver of the truck was a woman who called herself Mary. The men called themselves James and John. I was bound to a chair. Mary looked after me and was mostly civil. She had a gun to prevent me from trying to escape.

None of them spoke to me much. I do not know exactly why they kidnapped me. On Sunday afternoon, I heard someone calling for James and John outside. James went down and shortly thereafter, there was a gun battle. James rushed back upstairs to where I was being kept. He and John were trying to decide what to do.

I gathered that my bodyguards had arrived, though I wasn't sure who they were in the gun battle with. Mary panicked and demanded that they release me. John shouted at her and called her an 'apostate'. Mary drew her gun on him. She shot him, but he took the gun from her. He pushed her into the bathroom and killed her.

Moments later, my bodyguards broke into the adjoining room and opened fire on both James and John, killing them. After that, they affected my rescue and I ordered them to drive me here.

The two bodyguards had little to add. They explained how the Barnaby girl had volunteered to leave after some untoward behavior by her grandfather. That wasn't a surprise. With the things those boys were said to be up to, Roach didn't put much past them in the way of depravity. Nor was it any surprise that the Barnabys had shot first. Nonetheless, Roach would send his officers up to have a look.

On their way out, Roach asked them all to stay in town for a couple days in case there were any more questions. At that, the Walker man removed a business card from his wallet and handed it over. It was for a lawyer in Silkhaven and any further questions were to be addressed to that office. That ruffled Roach's feathers a bit—just seemed unneighborly—but folks had their rights and he didn't really expect there to be anything further to this case.

He did contact the harbormaster to tell him to be on the lookout for the body of Della Caine. It had been a whole day, at that point, and the river current was fast. So, Roach went ahead and filled out the 'presumed dead' papers and sent them to the county clerk before finishing his shift.

The street outside the Syme Lodge had even more cars. Twice as many men were loitering about, a few with cameras slung around their necks. As soon as the Chandler came into view, they rushed towards the car. Cranston had to slow down, lest he run one of them over, but that only seemed to encourage them to get directly in his path.

When the first bulb flashed, Lucien threw himself in front of Rosamund as best he could, the back seat offering him very little room to move. The best they would get were the bloodstains on his gloves. Then, a civil war seemed to break out amongst the reporters with a handful of them wrenching the others away and soon a brawl commenced with men being punched in the face and gut, cameras being thrown on the ground, and a great deal of shouting.

As Cranston pressed slowly through the melee, he saw Vivienne standing in the Lodge's driveway looking pleased with herself. Cranston gave the car a little gas and his sister moved out of the way, so he and the vigilantes' truck could get in. Cranston pulled into the old horse stall. The vigilantes had stopped just inside the driveway and were trying to break up the fight.

They waited in the car for a minute. Neither Cranston nor Lucien entirely sure they wouldn't need to leave immediately. When he felt calmer, Cranston asked: "So, it was all a coincidence? The people who tried to kidnap you once before just happened to target a woman you were counseling and succeed in kidnapping you collaterally?"

Rosamund drew in a long breath through her nose. "No," she said. "It was Della's plan all along. As soon as we were in that truck, she was as calm as could be. She painted a target on herself so they'd come for her. She came to my house to put me in the line of fire and she tore off that mask to make sure they wouldn't leave me behind."

"What did she want?" Lucien asked.

"I don't know." Rosamund shrugged, emotion creeping into her voice. "I thought she really wanted my help. She was so earnest about how her condition made her feel alien, inhuman. I thought she wanted to become herself again."

"So...well, why?" Cranston asked.

"I don't know." Rosamund sniffed again, putting some gravity back into her voice. "But I think I know who might: my Uncle Benjamin. This misdirection—making the CHJ think they were accomplishing one goal, but really doing something else—that's just his kind of magic trick."

"Alright, we're going inside. Around the back." Lucien announced as he helped Rosamund from the car.

"Mmm," was all the reply Cranston could manage.

Lily was on the porch. When she saw Cranston, or rather the blood splattered across his clothes and face, she recoiled for a moment before running to him. He had no words in the moment; neither did she. Instead, she carefully found a clean spot on his arm and laid hold of it, guiding him to the staff house.

She found a laundry basket for him to deposit his gloves and jacket in before helping him disrobe down to his underwear. Then, she took him to the bathroom, drew a sink of hot water and began to wipe the dirt and blood from him. The water had darkened a shade before she spoke.

"When I came home from the war," she said, gently

scrubbing at a scratch he had gotten running through the woods. "My mother was waiting for me with a pair of tickets to America. I never even unpacked my case before we were boarding another ship. My father had protested the conscriptions and the English threw him in gaol for brawling. He caught pneumonia while he was there and died after two months.

"Then came the Easter Rising. My brother, Eamon, fought the English, but he wasn't important enough to be executed. A year later, some soldiers found him and, when he wouldn't say 'God save the king', them beat him to a pulp. Mother said he wasn't the same after. He got angry at the tiniest things and threw horrible fits. In one of these fits, he suddenly went still and died right there in the kitchen.

"What they did," she continued stonily. "It was right. But it was like it says in the gospels: 'Those who live by the sword die by the sword.' I decided a long time ago that I wouldn't take up with men that chose violence.

"Now, I've no idea what future you may have thought we had. But if you're going to stay or ask me to go with you, I'll take it as a promise that you'll never come home to me bloody again. Or we can say our good-byes, here and now."

There were no words in Cranston's mind. He just reached up and took Lily's hand away. Then, he stood and turned on the water, giving his hands one last rinse. She stepped back, pressing against the wall. He turned to look at her, but still couldn't muster any words. After a moment, Lily nodded and began to cry. He reached out to hug her and it turned into a kiss and then he was taking off her dress.

They held their naked bodies close together. There was nothing wild or joyous in it. It was slow. It was quiet. It was good-bye.

September 18th, 1920. Silkhaven.

The sun had set and a cold rain pattered against the long windows of the penthouse. Cranston swirled his third glass of whiskey as he looked at the lights of the city. Even with the liquid courage, it was too difficult to look at Vivienne as he recounted the tale to her.

"She was like a woman who had tried to become a bird," he said to the glass. "Only, when she tried to turn back, she found she couldn't. Her hair had all turned to feathers; bright blue and green feathers. There were long nails on her toes and the skin of her feet was scaly like a bird's."

He sipped his whiskey. "When I heard that she had supposedly gone into a pocket and come out the other side, I didn't put any stock in it. Back in France, soldiers told all sorts of weird tales. They saw spirits and devils. And dimensional pockets were a constant danger. Men told stories of hearing the voice of God from inside them. Or that one had opened just as they were about to be shot and saved their life. Campfire stories.

"But when I saw her," his voice lowered to a whisper. "I knew it was true. There is no earthly explanation for her. It must have been the pocket. It must have." Steeling himself, he turned to face Vivienne. She was sat with her bare feet tucked up underneath her, listening in riveted silence. "Have you seen what the pockets can do to a man?"

"No," Vivienne replied quietly.

Pockets were rare in cities and there were a thousand theories as to why.

"I saw entire wards of men that had been struck dumb, motionless by them. It was like they were prisoners in their own bodies. There were men who would scream or cry until they had used every bit of strength in themselves. They'd fall asleep only to repeat it when they woke. But not her."

Cranston sat across the driftwood table from Vivienne. "Della Caine could walk and talk and scheme. Whatever it was that had destroyed the minds of those boys I saw had left her mind alone and gave her feathers, instead." He took a deep breath. "I want to help those men; the ones that can be helped. Dr Syme is making progress, but imagine what he could learn from Della Caine. If he could study her, he might learn the real secrets of those terrible, white spheres."

"You're not suggesting..." Vivienne searched for the word. "Vivisection?"

"No, but if she were truly caught, perhaps she would say what really happened to her. Maybe there is something in her blood. I don't know. But I need to find her, Vivienne. I need to know what she saw inside the pocket."

They fell into silence. After a moment, Vivienne got up and stepped up onto the driftwood table, then down again. She plopped herself on the sofa beside her brother and rested her head on his shoulder. They shifted a little, as Cranston put an arm around her shoulder. They finished their drinks together.

THE END

YOU REACHED THE END OF THE BOOK! THANK YOU!

Seriously, thank you for giving my weird little novel enough of a chance that you got to the end. Would you mind writing a review for it, somewhere? Amazon, GoodReads, anywhere at all. This is an indie book and needs all the help it can get finding readers. If you're not sure what to say, here's some 3-star review starters for you:

"As novelizations of podcasts that you've never heard of go, this is probably in the top ten."

"Remember in school when you had to read 'The Great Gatsby' and you thought 'what this book needs is superheroes and Cthulhu'? No? Well, this guy clearly did."

"In the 90's, there was this attempt at reviving 1920's adventure movies. We got Brendan Fraser in 'The Mummy', but we also got 'Dick Tracy', 'The Rocketeer', 'The Shadow' and 'Sky Captain and the World of Tomorrow'. Most people forgot about it (apart from 'The Mummy'), but the writer of this book appears to have made it his whole personality."

www.ingramcontent.com/pod-product-compliance
Lightning Source LLC
Chambersburg PA
CBHW060220030726
47499CB00004B/1130